BEING JOSIE

Darcy McInnis

Copyright © 2016 Darcy McInnis
All rights reserved.

This is a work of fiction. Any resemblance to actual persons, living or dead, or actual events, is purely coincidental.

ISBN: 1530920647
ISBN 13: 9781530920648
Library of Congress Control Number: 2016905769
CreateSpace Independent Publishing Platform
North Charleston, South Carolina

1

Josie
July 2015
Seattle, Washington

"Tambra!"

I sat bolt upright in bed, sweat beading my forehead and my heart pounding. I stared into the dark, trying to catch my breath, the scream—"Tambra!"—still reverberating in my head. The dream. Again. As my breathing slowed and my heart began to return to a normal rhythm, I thought about how many times I'd had the dream this month. Twice this week. Three times last week. Once the week before. But that count was just the beginning. I'd been having this dream over and over for nearly a year.

I looked at the clock. 4:04 a.m. It was always 4:04 a.m. when I woke up from this dream. I sighed and heaved myself from the bed, knowing I wouldn't go back to sleep now. I never could after these dreams. I ambled down the hallway to the kitchen and started a pot of coffee, trying to shake the feeling of doom the dream always brought.

"Tambra," I said aloud. "Who or what is Tambra?" My cat, Jezebel, just stared at me, not the least bit interested in my troubles or the fact that I would go to work—again—on four hours of sleep.

Once the coffee was done, I poured a cup and sat down at the kitchen table. I took a sip and mulled over the only details from the dream that I could ever remember: a blood-spattered newspaper with its glaring headline, "Nixon Resigns!," sitting on a fireplace hearth, and the scream, "Tambra!" I had always puzzled over the Nixon reference. I was born in 1981 and had never lived in a world where Nixon was president. Why was the newspaper in the dream? And Tambra? It sounded like a name, but if it was a name, it wasn't one I was familiar with.

I drained my cup and wondered if it was too early to call someone. I thought of Celeste, my closest friend and one of only two people I'd ever told about the dream. I looked at the clock. 4:30 a.m. Celeste would definitely not appreciate getting a phone call at this hour.

My thoughts moved quickly to the only other person who knew about the dream—my mom. She was on the East Coast—Florida to be exact—where it was 7:30 a.m., a more respectable hour for phone calls, but just barely. I picked up my phone and dialed her number.

She answered on the second ring. "Josephine! To what do I owe this honor?" she said in her rich, melodic voice.

I flinched slightly at the use of my given name, which I've never liked. Everyone else called me Josie or Jo, but not my mom. "Josephine was the name I gave you. Why on earth would I call you anything else?" she always said—a logic I found hard to argue with.

"Hi, Mom," I said, a smile in my voice in spite of the early hour and my upset over the dream. "How are you?"

"I'm well," she said. "It's going to be hot today, though, so I'm planning on staying in, where it's air conditioned."

"Yeah, it's been hot here too, but no air conditioning where I'm going. That's Seattle for you." We both laughed.

"Good Lord, I just realized it's four thirty in the morning there," she said. "Why are you calling so early?"

"I woke up early, and I couldn't go back to sleep." Jezebel rubbed against my leg, and I reached down to scratch her head.

"Did you have that dream again?" she asked.

I sighed. "Yeah, I did."

"Oh, honey," she said. "How often are you having it?"

"Two or three times a week," I answered. "Mom, it's really getting to me. I keep thinking it's going to stop, but it hasn't, and it's been almost a year." I was silent for a long moment. "It scares me. It feels ominous, like it's warning me that something awful's going to happen."

"I can understand why it bothers you, sweetie. It would bother me too." She paused. "And isn't there a strange name in the dream?"

"Yes, I hear someone scream, 'Tambra!'"

"That's right. And something about Nixon or..." Her voice trailed off.

"Yeah, there's always a newspaper in the dream with the headline 'Nixon Resigns.'"

"Ah, right," she said. "My goodness, honey, that was decades ago. Before you were born. That would suggest that it's something that's already happened."

I laughed humorlessly. "I'm dreaming of something that happened before I was born? That's such a bizarre thought, Mom."

"Yes, it's definitely bizarre, but it's happening. I think you have some clues you could use to do some research. Tambra's an unusual name. I'm sure you'd find something."

"But, Mom, it terrifies me. There's blood in the dream. I don't think I want to know."

"Josephine, these details aren't random," she said firmly. "The dream is telling you something. I think the way to stop it is to figure it out. Find out what it is and take its power away."

My mom and I had always shared an interest in the metaphysical, for want of a better term. When she was still living in Seattle, we spent many evenings having long, fascinating conversations about the nature of time, life after death, angels, and karma. She was more a student of such things, though. She'd studied astrology, tarot cards, numerology, dream interpretation, meditation, and more that I probably didn't know about. It was one of the many things I loved about her.

"And where would I start?" I asked. "How do I research something that happened so many years ago?"

"Well, why don't you start on the Internet," she said matter-of-factly.

"I suppose." I didn't want to go over the same territory with her again. She was well aware that I'd resisted researching the dream because I was afraid of what I might find.

"Honey, this dream is really troubling you, and it has been for a while now," she said. "Don't you think it's time to find out what it means?"

"I know you're right, Mom. I'll think about it," I said, wanting to change the subject now. "So, have you talked to Gwen lately?" Gwen was my younger sister.

"I talked to Gwendolyn yesterday," she said. "She and Scott are settled in their new house, and she's looking for a job."

Gwen and Scott had been married for two years, and they'd recently moved to Mount Vernon for Scott's work. My sister and I weren't particularly close. We saw each other a few times a year and stayed in touch on Facebook, but we didn't share a lot in common.

"You should call her," she said. "She asked about you. She said I talk to you more than she does, and I'm three thousand miles away."

I laughed. "Yes, that's true." My mom had a hard time understanding that Gwen and I had grown apart as adults. I had told her why—many times—but it fell on deaf ears. I imagined that parents wanted their adult children to be close no matter what, but I knew that wasn't always possible—especially when religion and politics got in the way.

We chatted for a few more minutes about work, weather, and her new beau, Harold, and then we said our good-byes.

Once off the phone, I filled Jezebel's food dish and poured myself a bowl of cereal. I carried my breakfast to the table and sat, staring idly out the window.

I could see the first light of the July morning as it began to illuminate my view of downtown Seattle. I still marveled at finding this house on Beacon Hill with a picture-perfect view of the city from the large picture window just off the kitchen. The house was small—only nine hundred square feet—but it was plenty of space for me: two bedrooms, a utilitarian kitchen, a quaint living room, and one full bath. I had bought it for a song back in 2008, when the bottom fell out of the Seattle housing market, and I hadn't regretted the purchase for a minute.

I did regret the reason I'd bought the house in the first place: a tough breakup. Erica and I had been together for five years, and for the first four years we had been happy. We had moved into a Capitol Hill apartment together after dating for a year and had begun talking about buying a house together and maybe even getting married one day. Then I'd innocently mentioned having kids. I wanted them and assumed Erica did too. I was wrong. She adamantly, passionately did not want to be a parent, and I adamantly, passionately did. What began as a simple conversation about the future became a huge argument. We eventually made up and continued on, but when I broached the subject again six months later, she summarily shut me down. We limped along for another three months, but I think we both knew the relationship was over. I could deal with lots of things—personality quirks, political differences, maybe even infidelity—but I couldn't deal with something as fundamental as her decision not to become a parent. I told Erica on a rainy March morning that it was over, and she accepted that without argument, knowing as I did that we could never overcome this impasse. We split amicably but with heavy hearts. I think we both thought we had found "the one," and it was a rude awakening to realize our relationship was not to be.

We both moved out of our Capitol Hill apartment and went our separate ways. I longed to put down roots, so—even though I was now single—I borrowed money from my mom and bought this little house on Beacon Hill. Erica and I still had a couple of mutual friends, so we saw each other from time to time, and even though I would always love her, I knew we would never again be together.

I pulled my mind into the present and headed to the bathroom to shower and get ready for work. I dreaded going to work on days when the dream had disrupted my sleep, knowing that by midafternoon I'd be dragging. But rising early meant I'd get to work early, and, given my workload, that wasn't a bad thing.

I stepped out of the shower, dried my shoulder-length auburn hair, applied a bit of makeup, and dressed for the day: black trousers, a teal sleeveless blouse, and black sandals. I grabbed my keys and purse and headed out the door.

At a little before seven, I arrived at Harmony Northwest, a nonprofit organization near downtown Seattle. I'd landed the job eleven years ago, not long after getting my BA in English literature at Cascade University. I'll admit, I hadn't given a lot of thought to what I'd do with an English degree, so I felt fortunate to have found this job. I was hired as the office manager, but I quickly moved up the ranks once they discovered my aptitude with the written word and my overly developed sense of responsibility, both of which could be in short supply in nonprofit organizations.

Harmony had mostly used my writing talents for grant writing—the art of crafting proposals to corporations and foundations to ask for money for human service programs. Luckily, I loved the mission at Harmony—bringing music education to at-risk youth in Seattle. The organization served over one thousand kids every year and had won several awards for its programs. Our best story involved a young woman who began our music program in fifth grade and became a well-known recording artist by age nineteen. Most kids didn't have outcomes like that, but our longitudinal research had shown that the majority stayed in school and eventually graduated at a rate much higher than that of their peers.

I found my job immensely satisfying—especially those days when I got a call saying that Harmony had been awarded a large grant for our program—a grant that I had written. Those moments made the agonizing hours I spent crafting my proposals worth it.

I parked and made my way to my office. I logged on to my computer and then sat staring at the screen. Finally I opened Internet Explorer and typed "Tambra" into the search field. My finger hovered over the Enter key as I contemplated whether or not to press it.

I'd typed "Tambra" into the search field many times before, but I'd never had the nerve to actually do the search. As I'd told my mother earlier, something about it terrified me.

My finger hovered, and I was about to press the key when a voice behind me boomed, "Josie! You're here early."

I jerked my hand back as if the key were on fire and quickly exited out of Internet Explorer. I turned around and looked into the face of my boss, Miranda Reaves. "Oh, hi, Miranda," I said. "Yes, I'm here early. So are you."

"Yes, lots to do. I'm sure you're busy too," she said.

I nodded. "Yeah, I have that application to the Adagio Foundation due on Friday. Just trying to get it finished up," I said, shuffling through some papers on my desk to try to look busy.

"Well, you've got work to do, so I won't keep you," she said. "I just wanted to say good morning."

"Thanks. Hope you have a good day." As Miranda left, I turned back to the computer and thought for a moment. Then I shook my head, opened Outlook, and said aloud, "Now on to some real work."

By eleven thirty I was ravenous and headed to the kitchen. I'd brought last night's leftovers for lunch—pasta primavera—and I pulled the plastic container out of the fridge and popped it in the microwave. Then I headed down the hall to see if Celeste was in her office.

Celeste and I had known each other since high school. We hadn't been friends back then—just friendly—but we'd bumped into each other five years ago and had gone out for a drink. Erica and I had split up two months earlier, so I was relieved to have someone neutral to talk to. As the evening progressed, we discovered that we had quite a bit in common, including that we lived only two miles from each other. She was getting over a breakup too, and we spent that first evening commiserating. We began spending a lot of time together, and before long we were close friends. Celeste was as straight as they come, but she was a terrific friend—smart, compassionate, and funny.

Celeste worked as the HR specialist at Harmony, a job I'd told her about when it opened three years ago. Truth be told, I had ulterior motives in encouraging her to apply for the job because I liked the idea of my best friend working in the same building, but I'd had nothing to do with the hiring process. She had gotten the job on her own merits.

I reached her office and rapped softly on her door.

"Come in," she said.

I walked through the door and saw that she was staring intently at her computer screen. Celeste was looking fine this morning. Her long, dark-brown hair was swept into an updo, black eyeliner framed her lovely deep-brown eyes, and she was wearing a gold sleeveless top and white linen trousers.

She glanced at me. "Oh, hi, Jo. What's up?"

"Not much. I was just making my lunch and was wondering if you'd like to join me," I said.

She didn't take her eyes off the computer screen as she answered, "Sure. Give me five minutes though."

"Okay. Come to the break room when you're done."

Five minutes later she joined me in the kitchen and grabbed her lunch bag out of the refrigerator. She unwrapped her sandwich and put it on a plate as I took my food out of the microwave. "Are you okay?" she asked, a hint of concern in her voice.

Celeste had an uncanny way of deciphering my every mood. "Yeah, I'm all right," I said, trying to keep my voice light.

She peered at my face. "Because you look tired. What's wrong?"

I stirred my pasta while I tried to gather my thoughts. I was always a bit hesitant to tell her about the dream yet again because I was always worried that she'd grow tired of hearing about it. She waited patiently, and finally I said, "I had that dream again, so I've been up since four. So yeah, I'm a bit tired."

She frowned. "The same dream? The one about Timbra?"

"Tambra, and yes. That dream."

She picked up her plate and carried it to the table, and I followed. We sat down across from each other.

"Jo, why don't you do some research into that name," she said. "Tambra? I've never even heard that name before. There can't be many people out there with that name."

I nodded. "I know. That's what my mom said too. I called her this morning."

"And isn't there some reference to Nixon or Kennedy or someone like that in the dream?" she asked.

"Nixon," I answered. "There's a newspaper in the dream with the headline 'Nixon Resigns.'"

"Well, why don't you figure out when that happened," she said, shrugging. "That would give you somewhere to start, right?"

I smiled. "My mom said that too. I almost looked up 'Tambra' on the Internet this morning, but I chickened out."

She gave me a quizzical look. "Jo, what's there to chicken out about? Just type it in and see what comes up. No big deal."

"It is a big deal, Celeste. It scares me."

Her face softened. "But it's also disrupting your life, honey," she said gently. "Are you going to live with it forever?" She waved her hand in the air. "Figure it out so it'll go away."

I twirled my fork around in my pasta. "There's blood in the dream. What if it's something that happened to me when I was little? Something I saw?"

She paused for a moment to think. "That doesn't jibe with the Nixon reference. I'm not sure when that was, exactly, but I think it was before you were born."

I took a bite of my lunch. "It *was* before I was born. I don't know exactly when, but before 1981."

"Okay, so I doubt the dream is about something that happened when you were little," she said. "Start by looking up when Nixon resigned and go from there." She paused to take a bite of sandwich. "You're smart, Josie. You do research all the time for your job. You'll put those puzzle pieces together in no time and then—voilà!—the dream will stop."

I frowned. "Well, I doubt it'll be quite that easy, but I think you're right that I need to do some research." I didn't want to talk about the dream anymore, so I asked Celeste about work and whether she'd made any progress with her latest crush—her neighbor, Matthew Devine. We finished our lunch while making small talk, the dream not mentioned again.

When I got back to my office, I sat for a while and mulled over Celeste's suggestion to look up the date that Nixon resigned. Of course I'd thought of doing this many times before, but I'd never actually done it. Maybe my mom and Celeste were right—maybe it was time to dig a little deeper. I had a bad habit of putting off the hard stuff or ignoring it altogether. I'd been like that with Erica too. I'd stayed with her for months, knowing that we had an insurmountable problem, because it was easier to do that than face the truth. But I'd had to face the truth eventually in that situation, and I would have to in this one too. The dream had been disrupting my life for nearly a year, and I was ready for it to stop. Finally, the desire to know what the dream meant was outweighing the fear. I resolved to begin my research when I got home that evening. I didn't know at that moment that I was about to embark on a quest that would change the course of my life.

2

Once home for the day, I fed Jezebel and then made myself some dinner. I disliked cooking for just myself, but I'd gotten used to it. I whipped up some spaghetti with marinara sauce and a salad and then sat at the kitchen table and ate quickly. Now that I had resolved to begin my research, I was eager to get started.

I put my dishes in the dishwasher and then settled myself on the couch with my iPad, feeling determined to find out something about this dream. I opened a browser window and typed "Nixon resigns." The Internet answered immediately with a slew of articles. I reviewed my choices and settled on the *New York Times* link. I clicked into the article and read.

> Washington, Aug. 8—Richard Milhous Nixon, the 37th President of the United States, announced tonight that he had given up his long and arduous fight to remain in office and would resign, effective at noon tomorrow...

August 8, 1974. That was the day before he officially resigned, so the next morning's paper must be the one in my dream. But how old was the paper? It could have been sitting on that hearth for days or even weeks. I decided that was unknowable, but at least August 1974 was somewhere to start. Determined now, I opened a fresh browser window and typed "Tambra August 1974."

Again, I faced a page of results, which I began to sift through. As I scrolled down, one result jumped out at me:

Tambra Lynn Delaney (1946–1974)—Grave Searcher

I felt the hair on the back of my neck stand up. I hesitated, arguing with myself about whether or not I really wanted to click the link. I took several deep breaths and then clicked it.

The page opened to reveal a memorial of sorts. At the top was her name, Tambra Lynn Delaney, and below that her birth and death dates. She was born on June 6, 1946, and died on August 11, 1974. "Only twenty-eight years old," I murmured. Below that it said "inscription," which I guessed referred to the words on her headstone. It read, "Beloved Wife and Mother."

Below that it said "Burial," and as I read what followed, my heart skipped a beat. Tambra Delaney was buried at Evergreen Memorial Cemetery in Tumwater, about sixty-five miles south of Seattle.

I sat quietly for several minutes, trying to digest this information. My mind kept coming back to the fact that Tambra was a real person. A wife and mother. It also had not escaped my notice that she had died in August—the month I had started having the dream.

Intensely curious now, I typed, "Tambra Delaney death August 1974" into the search field, hoping I might find an obituary or death notice. But what popped up in the first position was a website called Infamous Murders through Time.

"Murder?" I said incredulously. I clicked on the link, and a page opened with the title "Infamous Murders." The list was arranged by year, going back centuries. I scrolled down to 1974 and found the entry for Tambra Delaney. It said:

1974, August 11. Tambra Delaney, 28 years old, was murdered in her home in Olympia, Washington. Her neighbor, Vivian Latham, was convicted of her murder in October 1974.

I stared at the screen, stunned. Almost without thinking, I picked up the phone and dialed Celeste's number. When she answered, I dispensed with the pleasantries and said, "Tambra is real."

"What?" Celeste said, confused.

"Tambra. The name I hear in my dream. She was a real person." I held my breath, waiting for her response.

She was quiet for a long moment. "How do you know?" she finally said.

"I searched on the Internet. First Nixon to find the date he resigned—August 9, 1974—and then the name Tambra. I figured the paper might be a day or two old, so I searched for Tambra August 1974." I was speaking excitedly now. "That pulled up information about her grave. She died in August 1974, and I found out her last name—Delaney. Then I searched again with her first and last name and the date, and I found this site called Infamous Murders through Time, and her name was on the list. She was murdered, Celeste. And it was her neighbor who killed her—a woman." I took a deep breath.

"Okay, Jo, slow down," Celeste said calmly. "How do you know this is the same Tambra you're dreaming about?"

I hesitated. "Well, I don't know for sure, but all I can tell you is my gut is telling me she *is* the same person I'm dreaming about."

"Well, it's hard to argue with that," she said. "So her name is Tambra Delaney, and someone murdered her in August 1974."

"Not someone," I said, a tone of annoyance creeping into my voice. "Her neighbor. A woman named Vivian Latham."

"Okay, her neighbor, Vivian Latham."

"Right. And this all happened in August, and my dream started in August of last year. Don't you think that's weird?"

"Creepy's more like it," she said.

I gave a short laugh. "And get this—this all happened in Olympia. Our Olympia, Celeste. The state capital of Washington. Isn't that strange?"

"Yeah, it's all pretty strange," she agreed.

I started to chew on my thumbnail. "What should I do now, Celeste? I want to know more."

"Well, Olympia must have had a newspaper back then," she said. "What about searching for some old newspaper articles?"

"That's a really good idea," I said. "I'll look into that and call you back."

I hung up the phone and picked up my iPad again, resolving to get to the bottom of this. I typed in the relevant search terms and pressed Enter. Immediately I found the name of the Olympia newspaper—the *Olympia Herald*—but came up empty handed when I searched for archived newspapers. Apparently it wasn't that easy to call up decades-old news stories. What I did find was a website offering thousands of US newspapers going back to 1880. It was a paid service, so I pulled out my credit card and set up an account.

Once in the newspaper site, I found the search field, entered the appropriate terms, and pressed Search. After several moments the site returned a number of results in no discernible order. I scrolled down until one jumped out at me: "The *Olympia Herald*, August 12, 1974." I sighed with relief that they had the paper I was looking for.

I clicked the image of the newspaper's front page, and it opened. I scrolled through the page until a headline jumped out at me: "Olympia Woman Found Dead." The story read:

> Olympia, August 12, 1974—An Olympia woman, Tambra Lynn Delaney, 28, of 1705 Walnut Street, was found dead of an apparent head wound at her home in the early morning hours of August 11, 1974. Olympia police arrived on the scene following a distress call made from the home shortly after 4:00 a.m. Present

at the scene were Mrs. Delaney's husband, Thomas Delaney, 28, and a neighbor, Vivian Latham, 32. Mr. Delaney stated that Miss Latham killed his wife in a fit of rage. Miss Latham was arrested and booked into the Olympia jail, pending an investigation.

Mr. and Mrs. Delaney had been married since June 1971, and they had an 11-month-old child.

"I am very sorry about what happened to Tambra," said Agnes Reed, the Delaneys' next-door neighbor. "I knew something was wrong with that woman, Vivian Latham. I'm not surprised to hear that they arrested her."

Police will launch an investigation into the apparent murder.

I read the story a second time, and then a third. My eyes kept returning to the time of the distress call: shortly after 4:00 a.m. I thought of my dream. Invariably, I'd woken from it at 4:04 a.m. That couldn't be a coincidence, could it?

I read over and over the quote from the neighbor, Agnes Reed: "I knew something was wrong with that woman." I wondered about Vivian Latham. What kind of woman killed another woman in a fit of rage? Women murderers were rare. What real or imagined thing had Tambra Delaney done to lead Vivian Latham to kill her? My thoughts began to run wild, picturing the deranged neighbor stalking Tambra for months before breaking in one night and killing her. I envisioned Tambra's husband trying to fight off the intruder but being no match for the woman in her demented state. I thought of the eleven-month-old baby, soon to be motherless.

Tears sprang to my eyes as I imagined the dark months that followed. The husband who replayed the scene over and over in his mind, wondering if he could have done something differently to save his wife. The guilt, the remorse. The widower raising his child alone, sadness consuming him as he tried to be both father and mother, and dread filling his heart as he thought of the day he would have to tell his child that his or her mother had been murdered.

Thinking about the events of that night troubled me, not just because of what had happened back in 1974, but because it made me think of my own father. My dad had died suddenly of a heart attack when I was just fifteen. He'd collapsed on a Saturday afternoon as he and I stood in the kitchen arguing heatedly about my low grades, my lack of focus. Suddenly his face contorted in pain, and he clutched his chest and fell to the floor. I didn't know what to do, and, panicked, I called my mom at work in her real estate office, and she told me to call 911. By the time the medics got there, my dad was gone. Even though an autopsy revealed an undiagnosed heart condition, grief and guilt consumed me for months. I told myself that if I'd thought to call 911 immediately, my dad would still be alive. If we hadn't been fighting, he wouldn't have had the heart attack. If I'd known CPR, I could have saved him. Now, as an adult, I had forgiven myself, but still the feelings lingered.

I shook my head and brought myself back to the present. I wondered if there were any follow-up stories—perhaps a report on the police investigation or the trial. I was very curious about Vivian Latham and her fate. I typed "Vivian Latham Olympia WA 1974" into the search field of the newspaper site and pressed Enter. Three matches appeared, and I searched each for something relevant.

The first hit talked about Vivian's arrest and just rehashed the original story I'd already read. The second article, dated several days after Tambra's death, was about the police investigation.

> Olympia, August 16, 1974—Police have completed their investigation into the murder of Olympia resident Tambra Delaney. Mrs. Delaney died of a head wound in her home on August 11, 1974.
>
> Vivian Latham has been charged with second-degree murder in the death. If convicted, Miss Latham faces a prison sentence of 15 to 20 years.

> Police collected a variety of evidence during the investigation, including Miss Latham's fingerprints on the weapon, blood matching Mrs. Delaney's blood type on Miss Latham's skin and clothing, and statements from Mrs. Delaney's husband, Thomas, who was at the scene when his wife was killed, as well as from neighbors who knew Miss Latham.
>
> From the beginning, Miss Latham, Mrs. Delaney's next-door neighbor, was the primary suspect. According to Mr. Delaney, Miss Latham became enraged and killed Mrs. Delaney.
>
> Miss Latham's trial is set to begin on October 21, 1974.

The next story was about the trial.

> Olympia, October 31, 1974—The trial of Vivian Latham, who was charged with second-degree murder in the death of Tambra Lynn Delaney of Olympia, concluded on October 23. The trial lasted two days.
>
> The jury, which took three hours to deliberate, voted unanimously to convict Miss Latham. Sentencing took place one week later. Miss Latham will serve 20 years in the Women's State Penitentiary in Bakersville, Washington.
>
> Thomas Delaney, the victim's husband, stated, "I'm happy with the verdict and sentence. It can't bring my wife back, but at least justice has been done."

I sat quietly for several minutes, trying to process this information. Something didn't seem quite right about this. A murder trial lasting two days and jurors deliberating three hours to convict someone of murder and sentence her to twenty years in prison? That struck me as odd. Perhaps they had an open-and-shut case—lots of physical evidence that identified Vivian Latham as the perpetrator, or a neighbor who saw something damning. Still, something seemed off. And of course the bigger question remained: why was I dreaming about this?

I called Celeste back and filled her in on everything I'd discovered. "What do you think?" I asked.

"It's very sad, and it does make you wonder why the neighbor killed her," she said. "There's definitely more to the story."

"Yeah, it's sad and mysterious all right. But why the hell am I dreaming about it?"

Celeste hesitated. "I really don't know, Jo. This all seems a little otherworldly to me, and you know that stuff creeps me out. I'd call your mom and see what she thinks."

"Yeah, that's a good idea," I said. "It's too late to call tonight, though. I'll have to call her in the morning."

"Sorry I can't be more help, Jo." She sounded discouraged.

"That's okay." As I hung up, I looked at the clock. Nearly 11:00 p.m. I decided to go to bed and tackle this in the morning.

3

The alarm woke me at 6:30 a.m. As I opened my eyes, my first thought was, "No dream, thank God." I stretched and considered the day ahead. Then everything I'd discovered the night before came flooding back. I needed to call my mom.

I got up, fed Jezebel, and brewed a pot of strong coffee. I carried my steaming mug to the couch, got settled, and dialed my mom's number. She picked up on the third ring.

"Hi, Josephine. What's up?"

"Mom, I did some research into my dream last night," I said.

"Oh, how exciting! What did you find out?"

I relayed everything I'd discovered the night before.

"Wow, honey," she said. "That's pretty amazing. And how are you feeling? Do you think this is the Tambra from your dream?"

I thought for a moment about how to answer that. "I have no evidence to back it up," I said. "But my sixth sense or my gut or whatever you want to call it is telling me yes, this is the Tambra from my dream."

"Trust your gut. That's what I always say," she said.

"Okay, so now what, Mom? Given all that I've learned, what is the dream telling me?"

I heard her take a deep breath. "Josephine, I've thought this for a while, but now I think you're ready to hear it." She paused. "Honey, I think the dream is a past-life memory."

I was quiet for a long moment. I believed in reincarnation as an elegant way of explaining the suffering and seeming unfairness in the world. Why did some people live lives of relative ease while others endured one difficulty after another? Why were some rich and others poor? Why did some people live well into old age while others died young? Why did some enjoy complete health while others faced illnesses or physical challenges? I believed that the universe was intelligent, ordered, and fair, and the only explanation that made sense was that we all lived multiple lifetimes so we could experience many different circumstances and learn a variety of lessons.

I'd toyed with the possibility that I was dreaming about a past life, but that was as far as I'd taken it. Now that I knew Tambra had been an actual person, this all felt very real and very strange. "Tell me what you're thinking, Mom," I said.

"Honey, I think you were…that you're having these dreams because you were…" She was silent for several seconds, and then she said in a rush, "That you were Tambra in your past life. That these memories are yours. That this happened to you."

I took a drink of coffee and contemplated my mom's words for a moment. "Mom, you know I believe in past lives, but it's always seemed kind of abstract. This seems very real." I paused. "What should I do? Why is this happening?"

"All I can guess is there's something about the situation that needs to be resolved. Something left undone," she said.

"And how do I resolve it?" I asked.

"What I'd do is go down to Olympia and investigate," she said. "Maybe go see Tambra's gravesite, or—do you know where she lived?"

I thought for a moment. "Actually, I do. The newspaper article gave her address."

"Well, there you go. See if her house is still there and how it makes you feel. You could talk with a neighbor or even Tambra's husband, if he's still living there. I think this will help you know what the next step is."

I sighed. "Mom, this is all so strange."

"Yes, honey, it is," she said. "It's definitely outside my personal experience, but I've read many accounts like yours."

"Really?" I said doubtfully. "Because I've never heard of anything like this."

"Trust me, honey. You're not the only one."

We talked for a few more minutes, and then my mom said she had to go. As I hung up, I thought about making the trip to Olympia. Suddenly, I realized I wanted to go today. I could call in sick to work. I dialed Miranda's work number. She wasn't there yet, so I left a voice mail, explaining that I wasn't feeling well and wouldn't be in to work. Next I called Celeste and filled her in. Then I set my sights on getting ready for my trip to Olympia.

I pulled out of my driveway at 9:30 a.m. I'd gathered the essentials for my trip: the address of the cemetery where Tambra was buried and the location of the grave, the address of Tambra's house, and the names of her husband, the neighbor quoted in the newspaper story, and, of course, Vivian Latham.

The trip took a little more than an hour, and by 10:45 a.m. I was parking in the cemetery lot. I'd decided to tackle this task first, as it seemed the easiest one. I stopped in at the office to ask how to find the grave and then walked to the site. As I approached the headstone, I stopped in my tracks. A single pink rose had been laid on top of Tambra's marble headstone. A small white card was attached to the rose with a pink ribbon. I stepped closer to the headstone so I could get a better look. The words on the card read, "Mom, I miss you."

My breath caught in my throat. Tambra's child had been here, and given the freshness of the rose, he or she had been here recently. I peeked at the note again. The newspaper article I'd read about the murder hadn't given the child's name or gender, but based on the handwriting on the note and the pink rose, I guessed daughter. She must be at least forty-one by now. I pulled a notebook and pen from my purse and jotted the information down.

I then studied the headstone. I now faced in real life the words I'd read on the Internet:

Beloved Wife and Mother
Tambra Lynn Delaney
June 6, 1946
August 11, 1974

As I stared at Tambra's name, a wave of tremendous sadness swept through me. But it was more than just sadness. I felt a mix of grief, regret, and utter heartbreak. Was this what Tambra had felt as Vivian attacked her? I imagined Vivian bursting through the front door, a weapon of some kind in her hand. I saw Thomas and Tambra, surprised by the intrusion, trying to calm Vivian down. Vivian escalating, yelling, hitting Tambra. Tambra falling. Is that what had happened? What was Thomas and Tambra's relationship to Vivian? Why had Vivian targeted Tambra? What was the whole story?

I stood quietly for several moments and then decided it was time to go. As I turned to leave, I noticed another, smaller headstone next to Tambra's. This one said:

Steven Thomas Delaney
December 30, 1971
Our Baby Angel

I drew in a sharp breath, taking in all that the headstone implied. Given the single date, I guessed the baby was stillborn or had died in childbirth. How awful for Tambra and Thomas. Again, sadness swept over me, and I felt tears sting my eyes. I stood for a few moments in silent contemplation, gazing at the two headstones side by side. Before leaving, I dutifully wrote down the details from Steven's grave.

I returned to my car and sat for a few moments, thinking about what I should do next. My stomach growled, and I realized I needed something to eat. Remembering a café just off the exit I'd taken to get to the cemetery, I retraced my steps, and I arrived at the restaurant a few minutes later. While I ate I looked over my notes. I decided after lunch I would head to the neighborhood where Tambra had lived. I would see about finding the neighbor and possibly even Tambra's husband, Thomas. After I finished eating, I headed out to my car, ready for the next leg of my journey.

I parked at 1705 Walnut Street and got out to survey the house that Tambra had lived in forty-one years ago. It was definitely worse for wear. The gutters dangled from the roofline, and chips of tattered paint littered the front porch. I could see a crack running the length of the picture window beside the front door. The grass in the yard—or weeds, more accurately—came up to my knees. It looked as if no one lived there. I fought the urge to knock on the door and instead settled for taking a photo of the house.

I then continued on my mission: to talk with Agnes Reed, the next-door neighbor who had been quoted in the newspaper article. There were houses on both sides of Tambra's. I had to guess, picking the one that looked as if it had been lived in for at least forty years. Of course, it was just a crapshoot that Agnes Reed still lived there at all. She could be dead or living elsewhere. But I had to give it a try. I strode up the walk at 1707 Walnut Street and knocked confidently.

A minute later the door creaked open and I was greeted by a wrinkled face, probably seventy-five years old or more. She was a good six inches shorter than I was, and she wore an old-fashioned apron and knee-high stockings.

"Yeah?" the woman said gruffly, peering at me through the screen door.

"Hi, ma'am, are you Agnes Reed?" I said.

"Yeah. Who are you?"

I was relieved that I'd picked the right house. "Hi, ma'am—Mrs. Reed. I'm Josie Pace from Seattle." I shifted my notebook nervously to my other arm. "I'm a…" I hesitated, realizing I hadn't come up with a story about why I was there. The truth certainly wouldn't do. "I'm a reporter from Seattle," I improvised. "I'm wondering if you remember Tambra Delaney."

She took a step back. "Tambra Delaney. Good Lord, I haven't heard that name in years. That's the gal that was killed back in the seventies, right?"

"Yes, ma'am, that's right. Do you remember her?"

"She lived right next door. Of course I remember her," she said. "And she was murdered. That kind of thing didn't happen in this neighborhood. In this town. Not back then. It was big news." She continued to peer at me through the screen door, making no invitation for me to come in. "Why do you want to know?"

"I'm a reporter, and I'm doing a story about her death. Would you mind if I come in and talk with you for a few minutes?"

She hesitated for a moment but then opened the screen door wide. "I guess not. But I've only got a couple minutes."

Yes, you seem terribly busy, I thought. "Thank you, ma'am. I really appreciate it."

I entered the foyer and then followed her into the living room. The room looked like a time capsule straight out of the 1970s: a gold velvet couch; heavy, dark furniture; and lace doilies on every surface. I sat down on the gold couch and was greeted by a puff of dust. I stifled my displeasure, opened my notebook, and turned toward Mrs. Reed, who was sitting opposite me in a large armchair.

"So how long did you know Tambra Delaney?" I asked.

She shrugged. "I don't know," she said. "A year or two. They moved in a few months after they were married."

"So would you say you knew Tambra well?"

She shook her head. "No, I didn't know her well. We talked every so often, but we weren't friends or anything. My kids were teenagers and she had a new baby, so we didn't have a lot in common."

I nodded. "Did you know her husband, Thomas?" I asked, my pen poised over my notebook.

"Can't say that I did. I saw him leave for work in the morning, and I saw him come home at night. And I saw him mowing the lawn. That's about it."

"Does he still live there?" I asked.

"Oh, goodness, no. He moved out not long after his wife was killed. I heard he moved to Yelm with his baby. That's all I know."

"Yelm?" I said. I knew I'd heard of Yelm, but I didn't know where it was. "Where's Yelm?"

She thought for a moment. "It's twenty or thirty minutes southeast of here."

"What about Tambra's baby? What do you remember about him or her?" I asked.

"Her," she said, "and no, I don't remember much. She was only a year old or so when her mom was killed."

"Do you remember her name?"

She looked up at the ceiling. "Something short with a hard 'C.' Carol, Carla, something like that." She thought for a few more seconds. "Sorry, I don't remember."

"That's all right," I said, writing down the new information about Tambra's child. I looked up at Mrs. Reed. "Does anyone live in the house now?"

She shook her head. "Someone used to, but they moved out a few years ago, and it's been empty ever since. Someone comes and mows the lawn two or three times a year, but that's about it."

I wrote some notes and looked up at her. "What about Vivian Latham? Did you know her?"

Her eyes narrowed. "What's this for again?"

I gathered myself for a moment. "An article I'm doing. I'm looking into some, uh, some irregularities in the murder investigation."

She tipped her head to the side and glared at me. "Irregularities? What was irregular about it? Vivian Latham killed that woman. She was convicted."

I thought Mrs. Reed's tone sounded defensive. "Did you know Vivian?" I asked evenly.

She pursed her lips as if she'd tasted something sour. "I wouldn't say I knew her, exactly," she said. "I talked to her a time or two. Never thought much of her."

"Can you tell me more about Vivian? I know you didn't know her well, but anything would help."

She thought for a few moments. "She moved here from somewhere in the Midwest. Iowa, Kansas? Something like that. She told me her father had died recently and her mom had passed on when she was a child. She didn't have any other family out there, and she wanted to start over. She moved out here because she had family near Olympia." She paused dramatically. "That's what she said, but the rumor was that the school where she worked had fired her because she was, um, different."

"The school? Was she a teacher?" I made a note of this.

Mrs. Reed made a noise—somewhere between a laugh and a snort. "A gym teacher. Not a real teacher in my book."

I ignored her comment. "What do you mean, she was different?"

She broke eye contact and looked down at her hands. "She was, you know, different."

I was beginning to feel annoyed with this woman. "No, I don't know. Different how?"

"You have to understand, this was decades ago. The world wasn't the same back then. People weren't as tolerant."

I rolled my eyes, my head down so she couldn't see my face. I hated the word "tolerant." To me it was the same as saying, "I don't like you, but I'll put up with you because I'm so quasi-enlightened."

I began to understand what she was getting at, but this conversation was making me feel peevish, and I wanted her to squirm a bit. I met her eyes.

"So Vivian was…what?" I asked in a quizzical voice. "Raised by wolves, able to breathe underwater, born on another planet? How was she different?"

"Don't be ridiculous," she barked. "Not different like that. She was, you know, sexually different."

Sexually different? That was a new one. I gave her my best phony smile. "Oh, I see. Do you mean she was a lesbian?"

She scowled. "That's what they say now, but back then we called them queers or homosexuals." She pronounced it "homa-seck-shulls."

I chose not to dignify that with a response. "So the rumor was that she'd lost her job and moved here. Did she work?"

She shook her head. "Not that I ever saw. She was home a lot. Doris McLellan—she lived across the street—said that Vivian was a writer. She also said Vivian had inherited some money from her father and she was living off that. I don't know. Maybe both things were true." She paused. "Or neither."

I wrote more notes. "Can I talk to Doris McLellan?" I asked.

"Oh, Lord, no," she said. "She's been dead fifteen or twenty years."

"Okay. So what else did you observe about Vivian?" I asked.

She thought for a few moments. "She lived on the other side of Tambra, and when I was out walking my dog, I saw her a couple of times sneaking around Tambra's side door. The one that goes into the kitchen. Once I knew what happened to Tambra, I figured Vivian had been casing the place."

I made a note of that. "Did Vivian seem mentally unbalanced to you?" I asked.

She smirked. "All those people are unbalanced, aren't they?"

This woman was infuriating me, but I wanted to finish my interview. "I don't think that's true," I said mildly. "I'm just wondering why she killed Tambra. The newspaper said she killed her in a fit of rage. What do you think she was so enraged about?"

She shrugged. "Who knows? I know I don't know. No one talked to Vivian after that. They took her away in a police car, and she never came back here. I testified against her at her trial, but she couldn't even look at me. Her head was down the whole time. The jury convicted her of Tambra's murder."

I was taken aback for a moment. I guess I shouldn't be surprised that Mrs. Reed had testified at Vivian's trial, but still it caught me off guard. "You testified against her?" I finally said. "What did you say?"

She raised her chin and met my eyes. "I told them exactly what I told you today."

"Do you know where Vivian is now?" I asked. "She should have finished her sentence in 1994."

Mrs. Reed sat back, her arms folded across her chest. "They sent her to prison. That's all I know."

As I left Mrs. Reed's house, I felt a faint twinge of sympathy for Vivian Latham. Learning that Vivian was a lesbian—or "sexually different," as Mrs. Reed had so inelegantly put it—made me wonder. I knew I still dealt with discrimination in 2015, so I could only imagine how deep the ignorance must have run in 1974. I would be willing to bet that, like Mrs. Reed, many of the neighbors had disliked Vivian simply because of this. Had Tambra known that fact about Vivian? Had that had anything to do with their altercation and ultimately Tambra's death?

I walked to my car and climbed in. I sat, my hands on the steering wheel, and stared at Tambra's old house. I tried to will myself to turn on the car and drive off, but I couldn't. My eyes traveled along the lines of Tambra's house: the front door, the windows, the roofline. I imagined Tambra coming out the door with the baby in her arms. Had that been me, in a past life?

Almost without thinking, I opened the car door and began walking toward Tambra's house. I had to see it up close. I looked around to make sure no one was watching me. I didn't see anyone, so I sprinted up the driveway and toward the back of the house. I passed the side door Mrs. Reed had mentioned. The top half of the door was a window, and I stopped to peek inside. My eyes searched around, but I couldn't make out much—it looked like a kitchen and small dining area. I tried the door. It was locked.

I continued around to the back and saw a cement patio and sliding glass door leading into the house. The slider looked modern. It must have been added long after the house was built. I moved tentatively up to it, looked around again to make sure no one was watching, and tried the door. I was shocked when it gave way. Miraculously, the door was unlocked. I opened it and then slipped inside.

I blinked in the dim light, trying to make out where I was. I tried the overhead light switch, but when it didn't come on, I figured the power had been turned off. I pulled my phone from my purse and opened the flashlight app. I shone the beam around the room and could see that I was in a bedroom. Somehow I knew this had been Tambra's room—the room she'd shared with her husband.

I looked around the room and realized that it felt familiar. I also noticed that I was filled with the same feelings I'd had at the cemetery—regret and sadness—but there was something else too. Fear. Was this where Vivian had attacked Tambra? Was the room imprinted with her fear? I stood quietly for a few more moments and realized that the sadness and fear were giving way to something else—something lighter. My heart lifted as feelings of happiness, joy, and hopefulness spread through me. What did this mean? Were these the happy feelings Tambra had felt for her husband? Those feelings would be imprinted here too, I thought. I shook my head, not sure what to make of any of it.

I left the bedroom to explore the rest of the house. Down the hallway there was another, smaller, bedroom that I assumed had been the baby's room. Between the two bedrooms was a small bathroom. I continued out to the main area of the house. To the left there was a galley-style kitchen with an adjacent dining area.

I turned to the right and inhaled sharply as my eyes took in the white stone fireplace and hearth that took up the entire far wall of the living room. A shiver shot up my spine. That was the fireplace from my dream. I walked forward until I was standing in front of it. The newspaper in my dream had been sitting on that hearth. I reached down to touch the hearth, and as my fingers made contact with the stone, the scream—"Tambra!"—blared in my mind. I shrieked and yanked my hand back, my heart pounding. I closed my eyes and took several deep breaths to try to calm myself. If I'd had any doubt that I was in the wrong place, that doubt had now been dispelled.

I stood in the living room for several more minutes and then realized I should go. I took one last look around and then headed back to the main bedroom. I opened the sliding glass door and slipped out.

Once outside I tried to catch my breath. That had been one of the most bizarre things I had ever experienced. I turned to head back down the driveway to my car, but as I did I caught sight of the house on the other side of Tambra's. That must be where Vivian had lived. I darted across the grass and stood at the edge of the yard to get a better look. I saw a man watering a hanging flower basket on the porch, so I knew someone lived there. There would be no more exploring beyond this point.

I studied the house, taking in the large window and the gray siding. The house was small and square, with a wide covered porch along the front. I closed my eyes and breathed deeply, trying to notice the feelings that came up. Again, the mysterious feelings of sadness mixed with happiness and hopefulness came over me. I puzzled over their meaning.

I thought about Vivian and Tambra. Had they ever been friends? Had Tambra ever crossed this lawn to visit Vivian? Had Vivian ever gone to dinner at Tambra's house? Had she given Tambra a gift when her baby was born? Had she been friendly with Thomas? If so, what had changed? So many unanswered questions.

I took one last look at the house and then headed back to my car. I thought about everything I'd learned today. I was eager to call my mom and tell her about it. But for now I was exhausted and shaken, and it was time to go home.

4

I arrived back home at a little past six o'clock. I opened the door and greeted Jezebel, who was waiting in the foyer. I dropped my keys and purse on the kitchen counter, and then shook dry food into Jezebel's dish. I picked up the phone and dialed my mom's number.

"Hi, sweetheart," she said. "So, what happened?"

I took a deep breath and told her everything, including the mysterious feelings I'd had as I walked through Tambra's old house.

"Sounds like there's an intriguing story there," she said.

"I know," I said. "And that made me very curious about what really happened—especially after I talked to the neighbor. I think there's more to the story than what was reported in the newspaper."

"There's always more to any story, honey," she said. "The people who were there are the only ones who know what really happened."

"Yeah, so I guess it's not possible to know. Vivian went to prison, never to be heard from again. Tambra's husband moved away, and Tambra died." I sighed. "I think I've hit a brick wall, Mom."

"Not necessarily," she said lightly. "There's a way you could find out what happened."

"Really? How?" I asked.

"When I lived in Seattle, I knew a woman named Susan Krause. She's a very talented and experienced hypnotherapist, and she does past-life regressions."

"Oh, Mom, I don't know."

"I still have Susan's number," she said quickly. "Please call her, honey. I think she could help you."

I was dubious. "Have you done this past-life regression thing?"

"No, I never have, but I have friends who have, and they were impressed with Susan's abilities."

"But how would you fact-check someone's abilities when they're telling you about your life as a peasant in 1686? Anyone would seem good, wouldn't they?"

"They don't tell you about the life, sweetie. You tell them," she said. "They use their abilities to take you back, but you're the one doing the telling."

"Oh, I didn't know that."

"Yes, it's quite fascinating," she said. "Let me give you Susan's number."

"All right." I wrote it down.

"That's where I'd go with this next," she said. "Otherwise, you're spinning your wheels and guessing at events from forty-one years ago."

"Yeah, I'm sure you're right," I said. "Well, I've got to go. Thanks for all your help, Mom. I appreciate it."

"You're welcome, honey. I love you."

"I love you too, Mom. Bye."

I hung up the phone and looked at the scrap of paper with Susan's phone number written on it. I folded the paper and tucked it in my purse, putting it out of my mind for the time being.

But the next morning at 4:04 a.m., I was torn from sleep by the dream, my body trembling and my heart pounding. I got up, made a pot of coffee, and sat at the kitchen table. I sipped my coffee and thought about the dream, my trip to Olympia, and the possibility that Susan Krause held the key to figuring this out. I ate breakfast and then took a shower, feeling like I was sleep walking. I drove to work, sat down at my computer, and watched the clock until it was a reasonable time to make the phone call. At nine o'clock I dug Susan's number out of my purse and picked up the phone. I dialed carefully and waited as the phone rang once, twice, three times.

"Hello, this is Susan Krause."

I sat up straight. "Hi, Susan. My name is Josie Pace. I'm Barbara Pace's daughter."

"Why, hello, Josie," Susan said as if she had been expecting my call. "How's your mother?"

"She's good. Still in Florida, working part time at her real estate business and having fun in the sun the rest of the time."

"That's wonderful. I'm happy to hear that," she said. "So what can I do for you?"

"Um, my mom recommended you. I've been having a dream that I think might be, um, a past-life dream, and I, um, wanted your help with that."

"Well, you came to the right place," she said. "Past-life regression is my area of expertise."

"Yeah, that's what my mom said."

"So here's how I work," Susan said in a businesslike voice. "We have a session that lasts sixty to ninety minutes. During the session I lead you back through time in your current life and then into a past life. That could be your immediate past life or any life that you've lived. I ask you questions about what you're seeing, and I record the session so you can listen back to it."

I twirled my hair nervously. "So I think in my case I'd want to go back to the life I lived immediately before this one."

"Okay, we can do that," she said. "I charge one hundred dollars for the session."

"All right," I said. "Will I learn everything about this life?"

"Well, not everything," she said. "You'll be dropped into a day in that life. You'll learn your name, something about what you do for a living or your current circumstances, maybe the name of a spouse or a child."

"Okay, that sounds good."

"When would you like to do this?" she asked. "I have time this Saturday at four."

"That would work great," I said.

We finalized the details and wrapped up our conversation. I hung up the phone and immediately entered the appointment in my calendar. Saturday was only two days away.

5

Saturday dawned sunny and warm. I had spent the earlier part of the day with Celeste, trying to keep my mind occupied. Our outing had been enjoyable, but I could tell she wasn't too enthusiastic about the idea of a past-life regression.

"I'm just not sure about this past-life theory," she said.

"Celeste, it's not exactly a theory. There have been scores of books written on the subject. There are thousands of case studies."

"I know, but..." Celeste's voice trailed off. She paused for several seconds and then said, "It's just so, I don't know, scary, I guess."

I looked at her intently. "But what if this is the way to figure out my dream and get it to stop?"

She nodded. "Yes, I know that's ultimately what you want." She touched my shoulder then. "I care about you, Jo. I want you to figure this out because I know it's upsetting you. So I'm willing to suspend disbelief for you."

I hugged her. "I appreciate your support, Celeste, even if you don't understand it all. I'll call you as soon as the session is over and tell you how it went."

We'd parted ways then, and I'd gone home to try to center myself and temper my anxiety, which had been rising by the second.

In spite of my best efforts, when I arrived at Susan Krause's house in Ballard, my stomach was in knots and my mind was whirling. I sat in the car for a moment, trying to calm myself down. At four o'clock I took a deep breath and climbed out of the car. Susan had told me to go around the side to the lower level. I found the stairs, descended them to the door, and knocked.

A few seconds later, a woman of about fifty opened the door. She was plump, with a round face and an easy smile. Her ash-brown hair was long and flowing, and brown eyeliner rimmed her hazel eyes. She wore an orange peasant blouse and a long green skirt. Her feet were bare. Something about her instantly put me at ease.

"Josie?" she said, smiling.

I nodded. "Yes. You must be Susan."

"Yes, I'm Susan." She shook my hand. "It's wonderful to meet you, Josie. Please, come in."

I entered the room and looked around. The deep-maroon walls were trimmed with dark wood. I saw an eclectic mix of artwork on the walls: angels, a gold ankh, a Star of David, and the yin-yang symbol. A wine-colored area rug covered the rich-brown wood floor. There was a large, comfortable-looking armchair with a small table beside it and a short red couch opposite the chair. This lady likes red, I thought.

"Have a seat," Susan said, motioning to the couch.

I sat down as she took a seat in the chair and picked up a small notebook and pen. She looked at me. "So, Josie, you want to do a past-life regression. Tell me a little bit about what's going on."

Anxiety seized me, and I began picking at a loose thread on the arm of the couch, not making eye contact with her. "About a year ago I started having this dream—a nightmare, really. When it first started happening, I didn't think too much about it. I mean, it was a disturbing dream, yes, but it was a dream." I took a deep breath and looked at her and saw that she was listening intently.

"What was disturbing about it, Josie?" she asked.

I looked away. "There was blood, and I heard someone screaming a name, 'Tambra.'"

"Okay," she said. "Go on."

"Then I started having the dream two or three times a week, and it began to really bother me." I paused for a moment to gather myself and then continued. "After I'd been having the dream for six months or so, I finally told a couple people about it—my mom and later my best friend. They both started bugging me to research the dream—you know, they wanted me to find out if there was something in the dream based in reality. I resisted that for a long time, but recently I finally did some research."

"It was the right time for you to do that," Susan interjected. "You weren't ready before, but now you are. You're ready to hear whatever it is."

I shifted in my seat and looked away. "Yeah, I guess so. So I did some research, and I found out that the name in my dream, the person—Tambra—really existed. She lived in Olympia in the seventies, and she was killed by her neighbor."

Susan's eyes widened. "Oh my goodness," she said. "Okay. Interesting." She wrote something on her pad.

"My mom said it might be a past-life dream, and she recommended you."

She smiled warmly. "That sounds like good advice from your mother, Josie," she said. "It sounds quite likely that it's a past-life dream. So may I ask how old you are?"

I frowned. "I'm thirty-three. I'll be thirty-four in October."

"I'm not being nosy," she said with a wink. "I just need to know that for the first part of the regression." She sat up straight in her chair. "So shall we get started?"

"Okay," I said nervously.

"Here's how this will go," she said briskly. "I'll begin by relaxing you. I'll just talk to you as you stare at a spot on the wall. I like to use the corner of that picture over there." She pointed to the picture of the ankh. "Once you're relaxed, then we'll begin moving back through time—first through this life and then into a past life. Once you're in the past life, then I'll ask you questions and you'll answer." She picked up a small digital recorder from the table beside her.

"And I record your session so you can listen to it later. How does that sound?"

I nodded. "It sounds all right."

"One last question—do you like the beach better or the woods?"

"The beach," I said.

"Okay, good." Susan picked up the recorder and pressed a button. "So just lean back and focus your attention on the corner of the picture over there."

I settled back against the couch cushion and focused on the picture.

"Okay, just continue looking at the corner of the picture," she said in a soft voice. "As you look, I want you to feel the couch supporting your body. Begin to feel the couch like it's an extension of your body. It supports you and cradles you. Just breathe deeply and feel the couch under your body."

I stared at the spot on the picture and sank more deeply into the couch.

"Your eyes are beginning to feel very heavy," she continued, her voice barely more than a whisper. "Keep looking at the picture, but become aware of how heavy your eyelids are. You can barely keep them open. Your breathing is becoming slower, and your eyelids are so heavy. You just want to close your eyes. You can't keep them open another second."

My eyelids flickered and then closed.

"Feel your feet against the floor," she continued. "Your feet are warm and relaxed. Now feel the warmth spreading up your calves, over your knees, and to your thighs. Your legs feel so heavy and relaxed. Your legs feel like they're melting into the couch."

My legs were heavy, and my brain began to feel fuzzy. She kept speaking in a soft voice, relaxing each area of my body until she got to the top of my head. "Your whole body feels so heavy and relaxed," Susan said. "Feel the couch under your body, supporting you. Just breathe and feel how relaxed you are." She paused. "Now I want you to imagine you're standing on a beach. There's no one else around—just you. The waves are crashing into the beach, and the sand is warm under your feet. You kneel on the sand, and then you lie down. You can feel the warm sun on your body and the sand supporting you. You close your eyes and focus on the sound of the waves, lulling you into total relaxation."

My breathing slowed even further, and I could feel the slow thud of my heart.

"Just breathe. Just breathe," she said in a soothing voice.

"Now I want you to imagine yourself at the top of a flight of stairs. Breathe. Now step down, and as you do, feel yourself become even more relaxed. Now step down again and sink even deeper into the couch. As you step down, you are moving back in time. You are thirty-two years old. Now step down again. You are twenty-nine years old."

Susan continued to lead me down the stairs, taking me further back in time and relaxing me more and more. As I stepped onto the last stair, she took me back to being born.

"Just feel what that's like," she said. "You're beginning your new life. You have a great adventure ahead of you. Just sit with that for a moment." She paused for several seconds. "Okay, just ahead you see a door. You know that when you go through that door, you'll be walking into the life you lived immediately before this one."

There was silence in the room as I breathed and imagined the door.

"Now I want you to step forward and put your hand on the doorknob," she said. "Turn the doorknob and open the door."

I imagined the door in my mind and reached out to grasp the doorknob. I turned the knob, and the door opened.

"Step through the door," she said gently.

I imagined myself walking through the door.

"Now just pause and look around and get your bearings." In my mind's eye, I looked right and then left. "Now look down at your feet," she continued. "Tell me what's on your feet."

I looked at my feet. "Brown loafers."

"What are you wearing on your body?"

I surveyed my clothing. "Jeans and a navy T-shirt."

"Are you a woman or a man?"
"I'm a woman," I said.
"How old are you?"
"I'm thirty-two."
"Are you married?" she asked.
"No, I'm single."
"Do you have any children?"
"No."
"Are you inside or outside?" Susan said.
"I'm outside."
"Is it daytime or nighttime?"
"Daytime," I answered.
"What are you doing?"
"I'm moving into a new house. I'm carrying a box," I said.
"Is anyone with you?"
"No, I'm by myself."
"Where are you? What country? What town?" she asked.
"The United States. I'm in Olympia, Washington."
"What year is it?"
"It's 1974. February," I said.
"What's the house that you're moving into like?"
"It's gray and kind of small. There's a long porch along the front of the house. I wanted to rent this house because I liked the porch."
"Will you be happy in this house?" Susan said.
"I don't know yet. I didn't want to move. I felt like I had to move."
"Why did you have to move?"
"My dad died, and then I lost my job. I had nothing there. I wanted a fresh start."
"What's your name?" she asked.

I hesitated. I knew the answer, but even in my hypnotic state, I didn't want to say it.

"What's your name?" she repeated.

Finally I said, "My name is Vivian."

6

Vivian
January 1974
Applewood, Iowa

I opened the front door and stepped into the foyer, relieved that the work day was over. I'd been counting the moments until I could get home to my father. I moved quickly down the hallway to his room and opened the door. The nurse, Rose, turned toward me when she heard the door open.

"Hi, Rose," I said.

"Hello, Miss Vivian," Rose said.

I looked at my father asleep in the bed. "How is he?"

She gave me a sympathetic look and shook her head. "Not good, dear."

I sighed. "Anything new to report?"

"No, not really," she said. "I've been trying to keep him comfortable. He had a little soup at lunchtime, but he hasn't been very hungry. The doctor increased the morphine today, so I don't think his pain has been too bad. And he had a visitor today, but I'll let him tell you about that."

"Okay. You can go home," I said. "I can take it from here."

"All right, dear. I'll see you tomorrow." Rose grabbed her coat and handbag from the chair beside the bed.

I gave her a wan smile. "See you tomorrow. Thank you, Rose."

As she closed the door, I walked softly up to the bed. My father was lying on his back on a mass of pillows, his eyes closed. "Daddy?" I whispered.

His eyes fluttered and then opened. He looked at me blearily. "Daddy?" I said again, touching his shoulder lightly. I saw his eyes move and then focus on my face.

"Viv," he said in a weak voice.

"Hi, Daddy," I said, smiling.

"My sweet girl." He struggled to raise his arm and pat my hand.

I sat down beside him. "How are you feeling?"

"Like shit," he said, and then laughed feebly. The laugh became a deep cough, and he tried to catch his breath.

"Oh, Daddy," I said solemnly.

"I'm okay, sweetheart," he said.

But he wasn't okay. He was dying. He had pancreatic cancer. He'd been diagnosed three months ago and had been given just months to live. I knew he didn't have much time left. He was taking a lot of morphine, and he spent most of every day sleeping.

"Sweetie, my lawyer came by today," he said. "I'm still of sound mind, you know. It's just my body that's gone to hell. The noggin's fine."

"I know, Dad," I said as I smoothed the blankets around him.

He wheezed heavily, trying to find the breath to speak. "I made sure everything was in order in my will," he said in a voice that was barely more than a whisper. "I left you everything, Viv. All my life savings. It should keep you going for a while."

"Daddy, I have a job. I'll be fine," I said.

He coughed again. "Jobs don't last forever, honey. You'll need it someday."

I thought it best not to argue with him. "Okay, Daddy," I said.

He worked to sit up straighter so he could look at me more closely. "You know I've always loved you exactly as you are," he said. "But the rest of the world won't be so kind." He paused, his breath catching in his throat. "You have a hard road ahead of you, Viv. I just want you to be happy, but I'm not sure the world will let you be happy. Maybe the money will give you a little bit of freedom."

"Please don't worry about me. I'll be okay." I was uncomfortable with this conversation. I didn't want to think about these things right now.

"I've always tried to do right by you. After your mother died, I did my best." He coughed again and slumped against the pillows.

"Daddy, just rest. We don't have to talk about this now."

He tried to focus his gaze on me. "But we do, Viv. I don't have much time left."

A tear ran down my cheek, and I quickly wiped it away. I didn't want him to see me cry. I knew I would cry later, alone.

"I've always loved you more than life itself, my dear girl."

"I know," I said. "I've always loved you too."

"You're a good girl, Viv, a smart girl. Promise me you'll put the money away. Save it until you really need it."

"I will, Dad," I said.

Suddenly he sat up straighter and focused his eyes on the corner of the room. "Helen?" he said. He reached out his hand weakly and then let it fall onto the bed.

Startled, I looked into the corner of the room but saw nothing. Helen was my mother—my mother who had died when I was just eight. I knew that if he was talking to Helen, that wasn't a good sign.

"Helen, I'll be there soon," he said in a quiet voice.

Another tear slid down my cheek. I couldn't believe my father was leaving me. "Daddy, please don't go."

He looked at me, his eyes clearly focusing on my face for a moment. "I have to go, my sweet girl. My body won't last much longer."

A sob escaped my lips, and I put my hand up to my mouth, trying to silence myself.

"I'll be watching over you, Viv."

I nodded, not trusting myself to speak.

"I need to rest now, honey. We can talk again later," he said weakly.

"Okay, Daddy. I love you," I said.

"I love you too, sweetheart," he said, closing his eyes and collapsing against the pillows.

But there was no later for my dad. He passed away early the next morning as I slept fitfully in the other bedroom. When I awoke I knew he was gone. I sat up, swung my legs over the side of the bed, and slid my feet into my slippers. Then I stood, pulled on my robe, and opened the bedroom door. My father's door was open, as I'd left it last night, and I crossed the hall and entered his room. The room was dim, but I could make out his form in the bed. I stood beside him and reached down to touch his face. His skin felt cool under my fingers.

"Daddy?" I said, my voice breaking. I felt for a pulse in his neck and could detect nothing. Tears began to stream down my face. I had known this day was coming, but nothing could have prepared me for the reality. My beloved daddy was gone. I sat down beside him, laid my head on his chest, and sobbed.

I sat like that for a long time. Finally I got up and called Rose to give her the news. She was sorrowful but not surprised. Then I called his doctor's office. They murmured their condolences and said they would handle it from there. They made the necessary calls, and thirty minutes later people from the mortuary arrived and took my father's body away. I sat woodenly on the couch, not sure what to do next.

I was an only child. My father's parents were no longer living, and his only sibling—my aunt Dorothy—was nearly two thousand miles away. I'd already been living with the awful reality of my father's illness for several months, and now, with no one to help, I was forced to deal with his funeral and burial completely on my own.

After spending the day of his death in shock, I forced myself to go through the motions. I mechanically wrote his obituary, purchased a casket, planned the funeral service, and arranged for his burial.

His funeral and interment took place four days later, on a snowy Monday morning. My dad had been a highly respected humanities professor at Iowa State University for many years, and the sheer number of people attending the service and then the gathering afterward overwhelmed me.

Finally, after the last person left at seven o'clock, I collapsed on the couch and closed my eyes. Now that silence filled my brain, thoughts of my father flooded in. Tears welled in my eyes and spilled down my cheeks. For the first time, the realization hit me that I was parentless at thirty-two years old. Alone. I sat and sobbed in the dark for a long time.

I had arranged to take the entire week off from my job at Applewood Elementary, where I'd been a physical education teacher for nine years. My job was the brightest spot in my life, but I knew I needed to take time to grieve my father's death.

Without work to give structure to my days, I found myself wallowing in grief. By Saturday morning I felt as if I couldn't stay in the house another minute. I was determined to pull myself out of my funk before I had to return to work on Monday. I needed an outing. I called my only gay friend, Daniel, and asked if he wanted to take a trip to Des Moines to Gemini Rising, the lone underground gay bar within two hundred miles. Of course he was up for it—he always was—and we arranged to leave at six thirty that evening.

We arrived at Gemini Rising just after seven o'clock, and the place was already packed. The music was loud, and smoke hung heavy in the air. We made our way through the throng of people and found a table. I went immediately to the bar and ordered a gin and tonic for myself and a manhattan for Daniel. I carried our drinks carefully back to the table and plunked down next to Daniel.

We both picked up our drinks, and he clinked his glass against mine. "Here's to you letting loose tonight, Viv," he said.

I gave him a sad smile and took a long sip of my drink. "Yeah, I could definitely use a break."

"There's some good-looking women here," he said, nodding toward the bar. "That dark-haired one over there has been checking you out."

I looked over to where he was motioning and saw a slim, wiry woman of about thirty sitting at the bar. Her short, dark hair was thick and curly, and she wore a Levi's jacket, jeans, and a white T-shirt. She wasn't really my type. She caught me looking at her, and my eyes locked with hers for a moment. I quickly lowered my gaze.

"Ooh, I think she's coming over," Daniel said in an excited voice.

I glanced over, and indeed the woman was crossing the floor toward us. She ambled up to our table and leaned down, looking me right in the eye. "Hi there. Can I buy you a drink?"

I took another sip and considered her for a moment. No, she wasn't my type, but did that really matter? I was here to have fun and forget about my sadness for the evening, and one drink wouldn't hurt anything. I shrugged. "Sure."

"What are you drinking?" she asked.

"Gin and tonic," I said.

"Ah, good choice," she said. "I'll be right back."

I watched as she walked over to the bar. A few minutes later, she came back holding my gin and tonic and a tall mug of beer for herself. "Can I sit?" she asked.

"Please do," I said, pulling out the empty chair beside me.

She set my drink on the table and sat down. "So what's your name, beautiful?"

I wasn't used to this kind of attention, and I could feel my cheeks getting warm. "Vivian," I said. I drained my first drink and picked up the fresh one she'd just brought me.

"Nice to meet you, Vivian. I'm Trish. Cheers." She touched her glass to mine.

"Nice to meet you too, Trish," I said, and then took a deep swallow of my gin and tonic. I nodded toward Daniel. "This is my friend, Daniel."

"Hey, Daniel," Trish said, reaching over to shake his hand.

"Hi, Trish," he said, and waggled his eyebrows at me. I frowned at him.

"Want to dance?" she asked, touching my hand.

I looked at her for a long moment. "Okay," I said. I picked up my glass and hurried to finish my drink before I followed her out to the dance floor. She started to move as the opening notes of Elton John's "Crocodile Rock" began. I wasn't much of a dancer, but the alcohol had loosened me up. I began to sway tentatively and then with more confidence.

The song ended, and the first strains of Marvin Gaye's "Let's Get It On" began. I turned and started to walk back to the table, but Trish grabbed my hand and pulled me toward her.

"Let's dance to this one," she whispered in my ear.

I really didn't want to slow dance with Trish, but she didn't seem like someone who would take no for an answer. "All right," I said uncertainly.

She circled her arms around my waist and laid her head on my shoulder. She pressed her body against mine and began turning in a slow circle. I followed along. I felt her lips against the side of my face and then heard her voice in my ear, singing the words to the song in her raspy voice.

Even though I didn't find Trish attractive, I felt the first stirring of desire deep in my belly. I tightened my arms around her and moved with her to the music.

When the song ended, she kissed me lightly on the lips and then nuzzled my cheek. "You're so pretty, Vivian," she said in my ear. "I like feminine women." She drew back to look at me appreciatively. "I love your hair."

I reached up to touch my thick, brown, chin-length hair, which I had always thought was rather ordinary.

"Your big, beautiful brown eyes, those rosebud lips," Trish continued, her eyes riveted by my mouth.

"Thank you," I said. I wasn't used to such effusive praise. I thought I was pretty average looking.

"Let's go back to the table and I'll get us more drinks," she said, taking my hand. We returned to the table, and she went back to the bar.

Daniel looked at me and winked. "How was it?" he asked.

"Nice, I guess," I said with a shrug.

Trish returned with the drinks and sat down beside me. I picked up the glass and drank greedily. I knew I'd already passed my usual two-drink limit, but I was enjoying the buzzing in my head. That's okay, I told myself. This had been a hard week and I needed to relax.

"I'm going to go ask that guy over there to dance," Daniel announced, nodding toward a young, good-looking man at the bar. He sauntered up to the man, and a few seconds later they headed to the dance floor hand in hand. I smiled, threw back my head, and drained my glass.

"Hey, slow down," Trish said.

"Go get me another one, would you?" I gave her what I hoped was a seductive smile.

She frowned. "Are you sure?"

"I'm sure." I giggled. I could hear how drunk I sounded. Trish returned to the bar and came back a few minutes later with my drink. I took a long swallow and announced, "I'm hot!"

"You are hot, baby," she said, trailing her finger down my arm.

"No, I'm really hot," I said loudly. "Let's go outside."

"Okay," she said. "Let's go."

We made our way through the crowd of people and moved to the door. I threw open the door and felt the cold air hit my face. "That's better!" I said.

We walked down the sidewalk side by side. Suddenly Trish pushed me against the brick building and ground her body against mine. She kissed me roughly, trying to part my lips with her tongue. At first

I was shocked, but then I opened my mouth and kissed her back. Desire raced through me, a feeling I hadn't experienced in a very long time. Her mouth moved wetly across my cheek and to my neck.

"Want to go back to my place?" she whispered in my ear. "I live only three blocks from here."

"I can't leave my friend," I said, logic prevailing even in my inebriated state.

"He's a big boy. He can take care of himself." Her mouth moved over my neck, and her hands kneaded my breasts. At that moment I noticed a silver Cadillac driving slowly down the street. A pale face stared out at me through the passenger window. Suddenly I realized how exposed we were.

"No, I don't want to do this," I said, trying to twist away.

Trish grabbed me and kissed the hollow of my throat. "I'd make it worth your while," she said against my skin.

I could feel my cheeks burning. This woman's aggressiveness was embarrassing me, and I was panicked about standing out on the street.

"No!" I said, pushing her away. I knew I could work it out with Daniel, but truthfully the thought of being intimate with this woman I barely knew made me feel sick. I'd been with only two women—my college roommate and a fellow teacher from another school. That relationship had lasted a year, but it had been four years ago, and I hadn't been with anyone since. I was a romantic at heart, and I dreamed of finding my soulmate, not sleeping with a stranger I'd met at a bar.

"I thought you were cool," Trish said in an angry voice.

"I am cool," I said weakly.

"I don't think so," she said, glowering at me. "Forget it then!" She stalked down the sidewalk and back into the bar.

I stood, dumbfounded, for several minutes, not sure what to do. Finally, I went back into the bar, my head down. I didn't want to see Trish again. I found Daniel sitting at our table talking with the man he'd been dancing with.

"Let's go!" I said urgently.

He looked at me with an annoyed expression. "I'm not ready."

I grabbed his arm. "I need to go now!"

"Okay, okay," Daniel said, rolling his eyes. "Can I get your number?" he said to the man.

The man pulled a pen from his shirt pocket and wrote his number on Daniel's palm. "Call me," he said.

"I will," Daniel said, and then he stood.

I took off toward the door with Daniel behind me. I nearly ran the two blocks to Daniel's car and then stood there waiting for him to catch up.

When he arrived he leaned down to unlock the passenger door, and I opened it and climbed in. He went around to the driver's side and got in beside me. He glared at me. "What the hell was that all about?" he said.

I looked down at my lap. "Trish was coming on to me. And then we were out on the street, and she was kissing me, and someone passed by in a Cadillac. They were watching us. I didn't like it. I didn't like any of it. I just want to go home now," I said in a rush.

He snorted. "Didn't like it? Isn't that what you wanted? To find someone to take your mind off your troubles?"

"No!" I nearly shouted. "I just wanted to have a couple drinks, maybe dance, but I didn't want that!"

"Okay, settle down," he said as he started the car.

We drove home in silence. I knew he was angry, and I didn't want to say anything and risk getting in an argument with him. My head was still spinning, and I knew I wouldn't be able to hold my own in an argument.

Thirty minutes later we pulled up in front of my house, and Daniel turned to me. "Thanks for the outing, Vivian. I hope next time we can stay longer," he said.

I looked at him sheepishly. "I'm sorry, Daniel. I'm still upset about my dad, and I think it was too soon, that's all."

His face softened. "I understand. It'll get better, honey."

I nodded. "I'll call you."

"Okay," he said.

I climbed out of the car, and he drove off. I went in the house and closed the door, happy to be home.

7

On Monday morning I returned to work feeling stronger, with a new sense of purpose. I sighed contentedly as I unlocked my office door. I had just put down my purse when the phone rang. I picked it up. "Hello, this is Vivian Latham."

"Morning, Vivian. It's Betty."

"Hi, Betty." Betty was Principal Erickson's secretary. "How are you?"

"Good. I'm awful sorry about your dad, Vivian," she said. "I know how much he meant to you."

"Thank you, Betty. I appreciate that."

"I'm calling because Principal Erickson needs to speak with you," she said. "He wants you to come to his office now."

"Now?" I said. "I have a class starting in twenty minutes."

She hesitated. "I know. He said to tell you that he's called in a substitute and she'll be here in time for your first class."

I frowned. "A substitute? Why would we need a substitute? I'm here all day."

She ignored my question. "He needs you to come to the office."

"All right. I'll be there in a couple minutes," I said. As I began the walk to the principal's office, a feeling of dread came over me. Something was wrong. I entered the office, greeted Betty, and knocked on Principal Erickson's door.

53

"Come in," he said gruffly.

Principal Erickson was sitting at his desk, and as I went in, he looked at me and gave me a tight smile. "Miss Latham, come in."

Miss Latham? He always called me Vivian. What was going on?

"Have a seat," he said, motioning to the chair opposite his large mahogany desk. "And please close the door."

I pushed the door closed, sat in the chair, and looked at him. My stomach was in knots.

"First, please accept my condolences on the loss of your father," he said, adjusting his glasses.

"Thank you, sir," I said, looking down at my lap.

He cleared his throat and looked at me steadily. "Miss Latham, I had a call from a parent this morning." He looked away. "She and her husband were in Des Moines over the weekend." He cleared his throat again. "They said they were driving through Des Moines and they saw you on the street."

The silver Cadillac that had passed by when I was on the sidewalk with Trish flashed in my mind. I tensed, dreading what he was going to say next.

"This parent said she saw you, uh, kissing another, uh, kissing another, uh, woman." He looked at me sternly. "Is this true, Miss Latham?"

My mind raced. Should I deny it? I wasn't one to lie, but in this case maybe that was the best course of action. Then my mind jumped ahead to a battle with the parents, the PTA, the school board. Months of agony. I couldn't put myself through that—not now. I realized I had been holding my breath, and I let out a quick exhalation of air. "Yes, sir, it's true."

He leaned back in his chair, and his eyes flickered away from mine. "You know you've always been a valued member of our faculty, but I'm sure you understand this is not acceptable behavior for one of our teachers." He paused and stared straight at me, his face stony. "I'm sorry, Miss Latham, but your employment here has been terminated. Please gather your things and go."

"What?" I cried. "Sir, please don't do this. This job is all I have left!"

Principal Erickson picked up a stack of papers from his desk and began looking through them. "Well, you should have thought of that before you conducted yourself in this manner," he said without looking at me.

"Please, sir, I can explain what happened. Please, I..." My voice trailed off.

He set down the papers and looked at me with contempt. "I can't imagine any way you could possibly explain this, Miss Latham. And if we don't terminate you, how would I defend that to the school board or the parents?" He paused as if he expected me to answer. "The parents are deeply offended by what they saw and fearful for the safety of their children," he continued. "And they'll tell other parents. We can't have that. I'm sorry." He stood up and opened the door. "We thank you for your service, but it's time for you to go now. We'll mail your last paycheck to your home address." He turned his back, dismissing me.

Tears stung my eyes, but I'd be damned if I'd let him see me cry. I stood up, uncertain on my feet, and walked blindly through the door. I glanced at Betty, who gave me a sympathetic look but said nothing. I continued into the hallway, tears obscuring my vision.

As I walked, my father's prophetic words suddenly entered my mind: "You have a hard road ahead of you, Viv. I just want you to be happy, but I'm not sure the world will let you be happy." I wondered if my father had somehow known. I couldn't imagine how, but why had he said that?

I walked back to my office in a daze. I mechanically gathered my few belongings and slung my purse over my shoulder. I surveyed my office one last time and walked out.

Once I was outside, the tears began to flow. I found my car, climbed in the driver's seat, and sobbed. I rocked back and forth, a keening sound coming from deep in my throat. After a few minutes the tears stopped, and I sat staring out the window until I felt clearheaded enough to drive. I started the engine, took a long last look at the school, and pulled out of the parking lot, headed for home.

As I drove, I said over and over to myself, "What am I going to do? What am I going to do? What am I going to do?" I didn't know what I was going to do, but I knew I couldn't stay here, in this town. Applewood was a small, tight-knit community, and I knew word of this would spread like wildfire. I'd become a pariah in the town where I'd lived my entire life. I had no idea where I would go—I just knew I had to go.

Once home I sat on the couch in shock, staring at nothing. My heart was breaking. First my father and now my job. Why had I done that? Why had I gone to Gemini Rising that night? Why had I gotten so drunk? Why had I gone out on a public street and kissed a stranger, a woman I didn't even care about, a woman I'd never see again? That mistake had cost me the only thing that still mattered to me—my job.

Suddenly the shrill ringing of the phone pierced the silence. Who would be calling me in the middle of the day? As far as anyone knew, I was at work.

I walked into the kitchen and answered the phone. "Hello?"

"Hello, may I speak with Vivian Latham?" It was an unfamiliar man's voice.

"This is she."

"Hello, Miss Latham. This is Peter McBride. I'm your father's attorney."

"Hello, Mr. McBride. What can I do for you?" I said. I was sure he could hear the annoyance in my voice. I really wasn't in the mood for more condolences. Not now.

"Miss Latham, I need to meet with you about your father's will. My firm is handling your father's estate, and as you probably know, you were his sole heir."

My father's will had been the furthest thing from my mind, but now I recalled my conversation with him the night before he died. "Yes, I'm aware of that," I said.

"Would you be able to come to my office tomorrow in Des Moines so we can discuss this?"

I just lost my job. I'm free as a bird tomorrow, I thought wryly. "Yes, I can come to your office tomorrow," I said.

"Would ten o'clock be good for you?" he asked.

"That would be fine."

"Excellent." He gave me directions to his office, which I carefully wrote down, and then we ended the call.

I went back into the living room and sat quietly on the couch, wondering for the first time about the money my father had left me. He hadn't mentioned an amount, but I guessed it was somewhere in the neighborhood of ten thousand dollars. I thought about my plan to leave Applewood and realized that the money could come in handy. Maybe this was one small thing that would go my way. I would know the amount of my inheritance tomorrow, and then I would begin to plan my escape.

The next morning I drove to the attorney's office in Des Moines. I arrived a few minutes early and found my way to Mr. McBride's office. I entered the formal office and immediately felt underdressed in my navy cotton pants and navy and white striped blouse. I wished I'd worn a skirt.

A pretty young woman was sitting behind the reception desk. "Hello, miss," she said. "May I help you?"

"I'm here to see Peter McBride. I'm Vivian Latham."

"Certainly, miss." The young woman picked up the phone, punched some numbers, and then spoke in a low voice to the person on the other end. She hung up the phone and smiled at me. "He said you can go in. It's the second office on the left." She pointed down the hallway.

"Thank you," I said, before making my way to the office. I knocked on the door.

"Come in," Mr. McBride called.

I entered the large, elegantly appointed office. Mr. McBride was sitting behind an enormous desk with elaborate scrollwork across the front.

"Miss Latham, thank you for coming," he said warmly as he stood and came around the desk with his hand outstretched.

"You're welcome," I said as we shook hands. I studied his face. He looked to be about fifty, but his skin was remarkably smooth for someone that age. Only his bald head and the age spots on his hands gave away his years.

He moved back to his desk and sat down. "Please have a seat," he said, motioning to the velvet-covered chair opposite his desk.

As I settled into the chair, he said, "I'm so sorry about your father. Roger was a wonderful man."

"Thank you, sir."

He cleared his throat and leaned forward. "I visited with your father shortly before his death to make sure everything was in order with his will. He was satisfied that his wishes would be honored."

"That's good to know," I said in a tremulous voice. I was nervous.

He opened a file on his desk. I could see a stack of papers, which I guessed was my father's will. "As I mentioned on the telephone, your father wanted all his assets to go to you," Mr. McBride said.

"Yes, I know," I said, my voice almost a whisper.

"I'll read the relevant section in the will," he said, pulling on a pair of reading glasses. "'I leave my entire estate to my daughter, Vivian Marie Latham. If she does not survive me, I leave my entire estate to my sister, Dorothy Anne Perkins.'"

"That seems pretty straightforward," I said. "So he's leaving me his house and belongings and any savings he had, right?"

"Yes, that's correct," he said with a curt nod. "It's a bit more than savings, however. Your father was a shrewd investor, and his portfolio was—shall we say—healthy. He asked me to liquidate his investments when he realized he was terminally ill." He gave me a tight-lipped smile.

I tried to hide my surprise. I'd had no idea my father was an investor. "How much is it?" I asked.

He glanced down at the paper. "After estate taxes, attorney fees, et cetera, you'll be receiving approximately seventy-three thousand dollars."

My eyes widened, and my mouth fell open. "Seventy-three thousand dollars? Really?"

He tipped his head to the side. "Yes, Miss Latham. As I said, your father was a shrewd investor."

I sat back in my chair. I'd had no idea my father had that kind of money. He'd never said anything about it. I thought of his words, "It should keep you going for a while." That was an understatement. If I was careful, it would keep me going for six or seven years.

"So what do I need to do?" I asked.

He shook his head. "You don't need to do anything," he said. "We'll settle everything with his estate, and then the money and property will transfer to you thereafter." He looked down at the calendar on his desk. "Today is January fifteenth. The estate will take three to four weeks to settle, and then we'll transfer the cash and other property to you immediately after." He glanced at the calendar again. "I estimate you'll receive everything about February eleventh or perhaps a day or two earlier."

"That's fast," I said.

He closed the file and looked at me over the top of his glasses. "We have no reason to delay. Your father wanted things settled quickly, and we'll honor his wishes." He stood up and came around the desk. "I'll be in touch soon."

I pushed myself out of the chair. "Thank you, Mr. McBride. I appreciate you taking such good care of everything."

He smiled at me. "It's my pleasure. I thought very highly of your father."

I nodded. "Yes, lots of people did." Tears sprang to my eyes. I wanted to leave before they began to fall.

Mercifully, he moved to the door and opened it for me. "We'll talk soon," he said.

"Thank you," I murmured as I hurried out of the office. When I got out to the elevator, I leaned my back against the wall, and tears began to stream down my face. "Thank you, Daddy," I whispered.

8

I spent the next two weeks going back and forth about what I should do next. I knew I had to leave Applewood, but I had no idea where to go. One day I was convinced I wanted the sunshine and glamor of Southern California, and the next I craved the sophistication and bright lights of New York City. I bought a map of the United States, and I would sit staring at it, one day envisioning myself in the Deep South and the next in Chicago or Maine. Nothing felt right to me. Each day I woke up hoping it would be clear to me where I should go, but each day I became more confused. I wanted to know where I was going so I could stop thinking about it and just plan.

The phone rang one evening in early February as I sat on the couch watching TV. When I answered, I was surprised to hear the voice of my aunt Dorothy.

"Hi, Vivie. It's Aunt Dorothy. How are you, honey?"

"Hi, Aunt Dorothy," I said. "It's great to hear from you. I'm okay. How are you?"

"Not bad. I'm real sorry I couldn't make your dad's funeral. I just couldn't get the money together to get there," she said.

"That's okay," I murmured. "I understand."

Aunt Dorothy had lived out on the West Coast for three decades, and I hadn't seen her for a long time. In fact, I'd seen her only a few times in my life. My dad and I had gone to visit her three times, and she had come to Iowa once, and that was it. She never forgot a birthday or holiday, and she called once a month to check in, but we weren't close.

"I just wanted to make sure you're doing okay, honey," she said. "I know you took the loss of your dad real hard."

"Yeah, it's been tough, but I'm doing okay," I said.

"And you're still enjoying your job?" she asked.

I hesitated. "Well, actually, I lost my job."

"What?" she said in a shocked voice. "Why?"

I wasn't sure what to say. My aunt had no idea I was gay, and I could never tell her the real reason I'd been let go. "Oh, they had to make cuts, and mine was one of the jobs they eliminated," I lied.

"My goodness, how terrible. Well, that was their loss," she said sympathetically.

I wanted to change the subject. "I'm considering a change. Now that Daddy's gone, there's no reason for me to stay here."

"That's true, dear," she said. "Where do you think you'll go?"

"I'm not sure yet. Maybe California or New York City."

"New York City?" she exclaimed. "You'd get lost in New York City, sweetie. You need someplace smaller. Have you thought about Washington State? It's beautiful out here, you know."

"No," I said. "I haven't thought about Washington State." Why hadn't I thought of it? That was the only place where I had family.

"You should consider it, honey," she said. "You'd have family here, and Louise and Linda would love to get to know you." Louise and Linda were Aunt Dorothy's identical twin daughters.

"That's actually a really good idea, Aunt Dorothy," I said. "I'll think about that. Where do you live again?"

"I live in Tumwater," she said. "But Olympia and Lacey are real close. Olympia's the state capital, you know. I think you'd like Olympia." She paused. "Or there's Tacoma—that's a little farther from me. And Seattle, of course. That's a big city, though. I think you'd be more comfortable in a smaller town."

"Hmm, I'll give that some thought," I said. "Thanks, Aunt Dorothy. Maybe I'll see you soon."

"Okay, honey. You take care of yourself and keep me posted."

We said our good-byes, and I hung up the phone. I sat at the kitchen table for a long time thinking about our conversation. Washington State might be the answer. I would be close to my only living family and have a new adventure. That night when I went to bed, I had the feeling that I might have solved my huge dilemma.

The next morning when I woke up, I immediately thought of my call from Aunt Dorothy. I lay in bed and mulled over a move to Olympia. Somehow it seemed right to me. I decided then and there that I would move to Washington State. I was relieved to have made a decision. Now I could begin planning.

I rose from bed and went out to the kitchen to start my coffee. I glanced at the calendar on the wall. February 11 was just three days away, and Peter McBride would be calling any day to tell me that everything had been settled with my father's estate.

As I waited for the coffee to brew, I began to think about what I would do with my father's house. This was the house I'd grown up in and the place I'd moved back to when my father got sick. There were memories in every room. I walked over to the wall by the refrigerator and traced my finger over the pencil marks there. My mother, and later my father, had measured me every few months and made a mark there to show how much I'd grown. I looked at the bottommost mark, dated September 28, 1944. That had been my third birthday.

As I gazed at the marks that climbed up the wall, my eyes filled with tears. I knew at that moment that I couldn't sell this house—at least not now. The money I was getting from my father made this decision less urgent. I'd come back and check on the house every six months or so and probably sell it eventually, but there was no need to sell it now. I sighed with relief and then poured a cup of coffee.

The phone rang just as I was taking my first sip, and I crossed the kitchen floor to answer it. "Hello?"

"Miss Latham? This is Peter McBride."

"Hello, Mr. McBride," I said. "How are you?"

"I'm well, thank you," he said in a businesslike tone. "I'm calling to let you know that your father's estate has been settled and we have a check for you. There are some papers we need you to sign. Could you possibly come to my office today?"

"As a matter of fact, I can," I said.

"Excellent," he said.

We made the arrangements, and I hung up and hurried to get ready for my trip to Des Moines.

The meeting with Mr. McBride didn't take long. He produced a stack of papers for me to sign, which another gentleman then notarized. The documents transferred ownership of my father's house, car, and personal belongings to me. The last item he handed me was a check.

"These are the funds that came from liquidating your father's investments," Mr. McBride said.

I looked at the check and inhaled sharply. $74,191.00. I felt the sting of tears behind my eyes. I quickly signed the last paper, shook Mr. McBride's hand, and rushed out before emotion overtook me. Once back in my car, I pulled the check out of my purse and stared at it. Tears spilled down my cheeks as I whispered my thanks to my father. This check, along with his house and car, represented all his worldly belongings, and he had left them all to me. I knew they were just things, but they were also proof of how much he had loved me.

Once I got home, I began to pack in earnest. I'd already decided that I would drive to Olympia and I would take my dad's Lincoln Continental. I'd load up the trunk and the back seat of the Lincoln with as much as I could fit and then buy whatever else I needed once I got to Olympia.

The distance between Applewood and Olympia was about two thousand miles, and I figured it would take me a week to get there.

I knew it would take less time if I drove straight through, but that didn't appeal to me. I wanted to stop each night, rent a motel room, and get a good night's rest.

I'd called Aunt Dorothy to let her know I was coming, and she was thrilled. She had promised to help me look for a place to rent once I got there.

I planned to leave Applewood on February 12 and arrive in Olympia by February 19. I would stay with Aunt Dorothy for a night or two while I looked for a place to live.

The evening before I was to leave, I called Daniel to say good-bye. He knew I was leaving—the day after I lost my job, I had called and told him I couldn't stay in Applewood. He understood my reasons, but I knew he wasn't happy about my decision. We'd known each other since high school, and our friendship was important to both of us.

Daniel and I had met during sophomore year. His family moved to Applewood in the middle of the school year, so he didn't know a soul. I first set eyes on him in history class when the teacher introduced him to all of us. He looked so uneasy standing at the front of the room staring out at the sea of unfamiliar faces. He was short for a boy, and his dark, unruly hair kept falling into his eyes. As he slid into the empty desk beside me, I flashed him an encouraging smile.

There was something about Daniel that drew me to him, and that first day I sought him out at lunch and asked if I could sit with him. He didn't know anyone, so he quickly agreed. We began talking and realized we had a lot in common: we both loved to read, we were both only children, and we shared a passion for baseball. We quickly became friends.

I'd had several female friends over the years, but I'd never felt close to any of them. I could never admit to myself that I was a little in love with all my friends and that scared me. Daniel understood because he had those same feelings for other boys. I hadn't known that right away, though. We'd been friends for more than a year when he'd told me in a tremulous voice that he felt different from other boys.

"What do you mean?" I asked, looking at him curiously.

"I've never really had a crush on a girl, and I think about kissing boys," he said. I noticed the blush rising in his cheeks. "Or if I see a handsome boy, I get really nervous around him. Do you think there's something wrong with me?"

I looked at him with surprise, and then slowly awareness dawned. "No, I don't think there's anything wrong with you," I said. "I have those same feelings about girls." I'd never shared this with anyone, and it was such a relief to finally tell someone.

"Really?" he asked. "I thought I was the only one."

I laughed. "I thought *I* was the only one."

From that point on Daniel and I had been inseparable. We spent most of our free time together, going to movies in Des Moines, talking late into the night, and reading books. We sought out novels like *The Well of Loneliness*, *The City and the Pillar*, *The Price of Salt*, and *Nightwood*. In these books, we saw proof that there were others out there like us. For the first time in my life, I felt that I'd found a kindred soul in Daniel.

After high school we'd gone our separate ways, but our friendship had endured. I was accepted at the University of Iowa, and Daniel moved to Des Moines and got a job, but we talked on the phone weekly. He was the one I called after my first kiss with my roommate, Margaret, and he drove the two hours to Iowa City to cry on my shoulder after his first boyfriend, Gary, broke his heart.

Later, after I'd graduated and been hired at Applewood Elementary, Daniel and I had spent many weekends together. Sometimes I would go to Des Moines and stay with him in his tiny apartment, and other weekends he would come to Applewood and stay with me. Later, he lost his job in Des Moines and moved back to Applewood, where he took a job at the local post office. And there he remained. He had been my sounding board when I'd gotten involved with fellow teacher Harriet, and I'd been his through a series of men who came and went but never stayed.

So, after our long history together, it was bittersweet for me to call Daniel to say good-bye. We had a nice conversation, but the time came when we had to end our phone call.

"I hope you find what you're looking for, Viv," Daniel said.

"I hope so too," I said. "I'm not sure what I'm looking for, but I guess I'll know it when I see it."

"I'm sure you will," he said in a kind voice.

I promised I would call him from time to time and let him know how I was doing, and he told me he might come out to Washington and visit me. He told me he loved me, and we hung up.

I sighed, realizing that Daniel was my last tie to Iowa. I would start my new adventure in the morning.

9

February 12 dawned bright, clear, and cold. I loaded the last of my belongings into the Lincoln and bid farewell to the house. I wasn't sad. I knew the house was still mine and I'd be back to check on it. The journey I was about to embark on felt like a new beginning. I felt hopeful that the dark days were behind me and that my future was bright.

I started the car, took a long last look at the house, and headed out. I drove north, heading for the state line. Once I got to southern Minnesota, I turned onto westbound I-90, which would take me all the way to Washington. I had painstakingly planned out my route, knowing I would pass through seven states: Iowa, Minnesota, South Dakota, Wyoming, Montana, Idaho, and finally Washington.

I tuned the radio to a station I liked and sang along to "Bad, Bad Leroy Brown" and then "The Night the Lights Went Out in Georgia." After a while the radio station faded to static, and I turned the dial to find something else. I settled on a station playing oldies from the 1940s and 50s. I sang along to Perry Como's "Don't Let the Stars Get in Your Eyes" and then Elvis Presley's "Hound Dog." These were the songs of my childhood and teenage years, and this music always made me happy.

"Hound Dog" ended, and my breath caught in my throat as the first notes of "I'm Looking Over a Four-Leaf Clover" began. An image of my mom bloomed in my mind. This song had been popular the year before she died, and we used to sing along to it while she ironed and I ate my after-school snack. My mom's singing voice had been lovely—a voice I was proud to say I'd inherited.

I had adored my mom. I didn't have many memories of her, but the ones I did have were special. My mom dropping me off for the first day of kindergarten, tears in her eyes as she hugged me good-bye. Me standing on the tops of her feet while we danced around the kitchen to Doris Day's "Sentimental Journey." My mom throwing back her head and laughing at a joke my dad had told. My favorite memory was my mom tucking me into bed each night with a kiss and the words, "I love you, sweet pea." Some nights at bedtime she would sing "You Are My Sunshine" in her lilting soprano, and other nights she'd hold me close and read my favorite story, *The Velveteen Rabbit*.

When I was older, my dad had told me that he and my mom had tried for four years to have another baby, but it had never happened. Instead, they poured all their love into me.

Then, one rainy April morning in 1950 when I was at school and my dad was at work, my mom went grocery shopping as she did every Tuesday. A Peterbilt truck carrying a load of lumber ran a stop sign and broadsided her Chevrolet Fleetmaster on the driver's side, killing her instantly. My dad and I were heartbroken. I was only eight years old, and I had a child's understanding of death. In my heart I couldn't understand how she could have kissed me good-bye that morning and been dead two hours later.

The months that followed were dark, and my dad fell into a deep depression. His love for my mom had been boundless, and he was lost without her. He took an extended leave from the university and spent his days sitting on the couch in his bathrobe, alternating between crying and staring at the wall. I continued going to school, but I felt as if I'd been abandoned by both my parents.

Then one day, about four months after my mom had died, something changed. Maybe my dad finally came to terms with her death, or maybe he knew he needed to be present for me. Whatever had shifted, he suddenly seemed more like himself. He was never quite the same again, but he at least helped me with my homework again, cooked nutritious meals, made sure I had clean clothes, and tucked me in at night. He also hired a part-time housekeeper named Virginia to be there when I came home from school, to clean the kitchen and bathroom, and to buy us groceries every week. Virginia had stayed until I was thirteen and could be home alone after school.

A car passed too close on my left, startling me. I shook my head, pulling my mind back to the present. I realized I had just driven fifty miles, lost in thoughts of my mom. I hunkered down in the seat, knowing I had a long road ahead of me.

I arrived in Olympia on February 18—a day ahead of schedule—dismayed to see it was raining. During our last phone call, Daniel had warned me about the rain in Washington. "Yes, but I heard the winters are milder in Washington," I'd said. "I'm looking forward to getting away from the crazy Iowa winters. Remember the blizzard we had last April?"

He'd grudgingly admitted that yes, he did remember the blizzard, and he'd agreed that the weather was milder in Washington.

"I don't want to shovel snow if I don't have to," I'd said.

The rain was falling lightly as I parked in front of Aunt Dorothy's house at six o'clock. I rang the doorbell, and my aunt threw open the door.

"Vivian!" she said, grabbing me and enclosing me in a tight hug. "I can't believe you're here!"

Aunt Dorothy looked just as I remembered her: short, curly gray hair; brown eyes a shade lighter than mine; a petite, round body; and an easy smile. "Hi, Aunt Dorothy," I said with a grin.

"Come in, come in. I'm finishing up dinner, so you're just in time."

Aunt Dorothy was a widow. Her husband, Frank, had died of a stroke five years earlier. Her daughters, Louise and Linda, were twenty-eight, and both were married with kids of their own.

"How was the drive?" she asked as she led me into the kitchen.

"Long," I said. "I stayed in a lot of cheap motels, so I'm exhausted."

She patted my arm. "Well, I have a lovely guest room with a comfy bed, so you can get a good night's sleep tonight."

"That sounds wonderful," I said, sitting down at the kitchen table. "And whatever you're cooking smells delicious."

"It's beef stew," she said. She bustled over to the stove, ladled stew into two bowls, and then brought them over to the table. She set the bowls down and then sat next to me.

I grabbed one of the bowls and began eating hungrily.

"Guess what?" she said.

"What?" I said, dipping my spoon into the stew again.

"I found the perfect house for you today. I saw the ad in the paper, and I called. It's on Walnut Street. The landlord said it's one bedroom and one bathroom. The rent is one fifty a month, and he pays all the utilities. And get this—it's furnished. Not much—just a couch, a table and chairs, a bed, and a few other things—but it's enough to get you started. What do you think?"

"That sounds great," I said. "Where's Walnut Street?"

"It's in Olympia, on the east side, about twenty minutes from here," she answered.

"Can we go have a look tomorrow?" I asked and then took another bite of stew.

"Sure. I'll call him in the morning and set something up." She paused and gave me a sidelong look. "Sounds like the house is kind of small, though. It won't do once you're married."

I stiffened. I'd been here less than an hour, and already she was bringing up uncomfortable topics. "I don't expect to get married anytime soon," I said, trying to keep my voice light. "This stew is delicious, Auntie."

"Thank you, dear," she said. "Vivie, you need to think about your future. The world is hard and lonely for a single woman."

I thought of my father's similar words. "I'm an independent woman. I can manage," I said.

"Still, you need to think about it. You're not getting any younger, you know."

I elected not to acknowledge that statement and took the last two bites of my stew in silence. I wiped my mouth with a napkin and looked at her. "Will you show me my room?" I said. "I know it's still early, but I'm beat, and I think I'll hit the hay."

She looked at me for a long moment and then sighed. "Okay," she said. "Follow me."

She led me down the hallway to the guest room and told me good night. I closed the door softly, relieved that she hadn't brought up the topic of marriage again.

I woke in the morning feeling energized for the day. I showered and dressed and then went out to the kitchen, where my aunt had bacon, scrambled eggs, and toast waiting for me.

After we finished breakfast, Aunt Dorothy called the man who owned the rental house and made arrangements for us to look at it at ten o'clock that morning.

At ten o'clock we arrived at 1703 Walnut Street. I stood on the sidewalk and surveyed the small gray house. I noticed there was no garage, but there was a driveway and small carport. The landlord, Mr. Bickford, was already there waiting to show us inside. I walked up to him and introduced myself, shook his hand, and thanked him for coming over on short notice.

"Sure," he said. "I want to rent the place. It's been empty for over a month."

I stepped up onto the covered porch and looked around. There was a wooden chair and small table on the porch, and I imagined myself sitting there in the mornings with my coffee. "I love the porch," I said. I looked out at the rain. "Although I'd worry if it rains all the time."

Aunt Dorothy chuckled. "It doesn't rain all the time, honey," she said. "The summers are really nice."

"That's good," I said. "Because I couldn't take the rain three hundred and sixty-five days a year."

"Oh, goodness, no, that doesn't happen," she said, patting my arm. "And even when it does rain, you'll get to the point where you just ignore it. That's what the locals do." She looked at the porch. "And the porch is covered, so you'll be fine, dear."

Mr. Bickford unlocked the front door and ushered us in. The house smelled a bit stale, but what I could see looked nice. The front door opened into a small living room with a shiny wood floor. A short hallway straight ahead led to the bedroom and bathroom, and to the left was a large kitchen with a table and chairs at one end. The living room had a brown couch, a small coffee table, and a bookshelf. I walked back to peek in the bedroom and saw a double bed and a tall dresser. The bedroom was the only room with carpeting. The house was small, but I thought I could make it work.

"So the rent is one fifty a month, and you pay all the utilities, even electricity?" I asked Mr. Bickford.

"Yep," he said. "I don't pay the phone, but I pay everything else."

"How are the neighbors?" I asked.

He thought for a moment. "Well, there's a young couple with a baby next door and another couple in their thirties next to them. They have two teenage kids—a girl and a boy," he said. "And directly across the street there's an older couple. I don't know much about the other neighbors."

I nodded. "I'll take it," I said decisively.

"Great," he said.

I drew a wad of cash from my jeans pocket and paid Mr. Bickford the rent for the rest of February and for March and then signed the agreement he handed me. He gave me the key and told me I could move in right away.

10

I pulled into the carport of my new house that afternoon. I marveled at how easy this had been. I climbed out of the car, hefted a large box from the back seat, and then walked into my new home. I carried the box, labeled "kitchen," to the appropriate room and dropped it on the counter. I went methodically from car to house, bringing in all the boxes and the two large suitcases filled with my clothes. I stood in the middle of the living room with my hands on my hips and looked around. It certainly wasn't glamorous, but it would work.

I was in the kitchen putting away my dishes when I heard a knock on the door. When I answered it, I saw a tall, thin woman of about sixty standing there. Her gray hair was cut into a shoulder-length bob, and her eyes were pale blue. She wore a red wool coat and black pants. She looked at me without speaking. "Hello. Can I help you?" I said.

"Hello, I'm Doris McLellan. I live across the street." She pointed to the two-story yellow house opposite mine. I thought of Mr. Bickford's description of the neighbors. This woman must be one half of the older couple.

I gave her my best smile. "Nice to meet you. I'm Vivian Latham."

"Nice to meet you too, Vivian," she said briskly. "Where did you move from?"

"Iowa, near Des Moines."

"I see." She cocked her head to the side and looked at me curiously. "Why did you leave? You're a long way from home."

I met her eyes for a moment and then looked away. "My father died recently, and I moved here to be near my aunt."

She frowned. "Oh my, I'm sorry to hear that."

"Thank you," I said.

"Where's your husband?" she asked, craning her neck to peer inside the house.

"No husband," I said lightly. "Just me."

"Are you single then?" she asked, scrutinizing me with sudden interest.

"Yes, I'm single."

She leaned against the door frame, smiling widely. "I have a son, Victor. He's about your age, and he's single too. Would you like to meet him?"

I was irritated, but I tried to keep my expression mild. "No, I'm not really interested in dating right now," I said.

She looked at me as if that was the most ridiculous thing she'd ever heard. "Oh, come on, every girl wants to date," she said. "Just let me introduce you. He's a nice boy—thirty-four and sweet natured. And he has a good job."

I smiled indulgently. "He sounds like a great guy, but I have to say no. But it's nice to meet you. Thanks for stopping by." I was anxious for her to leave so I could get back to my unpacking.

She didn't take the hint. "So where are you working?"

"I don't have a job yet," I said patiently.

"Well, you'll have to work," she said. "I know some people around town. I'll ask around and see if anyone's hiring."

I shook my head. "Oh, no, you don't have to do that. I'm fine."

She looked at me for a long beat. "All righty then. Well, I just wanted to meet our new neighbor," she said. "My husband's name is Bud. You'll see him around. He's playing cards with his friends right now."

"Okay, I'll look forward to meeting him," I said. "Thanks for stopping by."

"Okay, bye now."

Mrs. McLellan turned and walked down the stairs, and I closed the door, happy she was gone.

※

I'd just gotten back to my unpacking when I heard another knock on the door. Three raps in quick succession. "Who is it now?" I said under my breath. I opened the door to see a young blond woman holding a baby.

"Hi, I'm Tambra Delaney, your new neighbor," the woman said in a friendly voice. "I just wanted to say welcome to the neighborhood."

"Hello," I said with a smile. "I'm Vivian Latham." I paused. "Tambra? That's an unusual name. I don't think I've heard it before."

"It's a family name," she said. "It was my grandma's name."

"Oh," I said, opening the door wide. "Would you like to come in?"

"Sure." She walked in and stood in the middle of the living room looking around.

I studied Tambra. She was beautiful. Her hair was long and golden blond and parted down the middle. Her eyes were a brilliant blue, and she had a smattering of freckles across her nose. Her skin was fair, and her cheeks and full lips were a rosy color. She was about an inch shorter than I was, and she wore Levi's and a white peasant blouse that she had covered with a navy sweatshirt jacket. She had white Keds on her feet with no socks. She was quite striking in an uncomplicated way.

The baby girl she held looked to be five or six months old. She had quite a lot of hair already, and she was blond like her mother. They shared the same eye color too. I could see that the baby would grow up to look very much like Tambra.

She turned the baby toward me. "This is Claire," she said. "She's six months old today."

I took the baby's tiny hand between my index finger and thumb and shook it gently. "Hello, Claire," I said. Claire stared at me with her big blue eyes.

Tambra scanned the room again. "Looks like you're getting moved in."

I looked at the living room. "Yeah. It came furnished with the essentials—a bed, a couch, a table, and a few other things—but I'm sure I'll need to get more."

She smiled. Her teeth were white and very straight, and she had the most charming lopsided smile. "Seems like you have enough to get by for now," she said.

I nodded. "Yeah, it'll do."

"So where are you from?" she asked, shifting Claire to her other arm.

"Applewood, Iowa. It's a small town not far from Ames, Iowa. That's where Iowa State University is."

"Oh. I've lived in Washington my whole life," she said. "I've never been to Iowa. Oregon's as far as I've gone. Is it nice in Iowa?"

I shrugged. "I never liked it much," I said. "But my father was a professor at the university, so that's where we stayed."

"Wow, a college professor," she said. "I didn't go to college, so I'm always envious of people who did. Did you go to college, Vivian?" she asked.

I nodded. "Yes, I did," I said. "I went to the University of Iowa, though. I really wanted to be on my own. I was about two hours from home, so close enough to visit but far enough away that I could spread my wings a little."

"What did you study?" she asked.

"Education with a concentration on health and fitness," I said. "I was a PE teacher."

"Was?" she said with raised eyebrows.

I shifted uncomfortably. "I left teaching recently."

She tipped her head to the side. "Why?"

I hesitated. I had just met this woman, and I wasn't ready to tell her my life story. "I guess I just got tired of it."

She frowned. "You can't be more than thirty or so. How'd you get tired of teaching so fast?"

Tambra asked a lot of questions. "I'm thirty-two, and yes, there's more to that story, and maybe I'll tell you someday," I said breezily.

"Hmm, sounds like an interesting story," she said. "Are you married?"

"No, I'm not married. Are you?" I asked. Turnabout was fair play.

She nodded. "Yeah, my husband is Tom. We've been married for two and a half years." She shifted the baby again. "Where are you working?"

"I don't have a job yet," I said. "I guess I'll be looking." I didn't want to tell Tambra that with seventy thousand dollars in the bank, I was in no hurry to find work.

"And why did you choose Olympia?" she asked. "You're a long way from Iowa."

I looked away. "My father passed away recently, and I didn't have any family left in Iowa. My aunt Dorothy and my two cousins live in Tumwater, and I wanted to be close to them."

Her mouth dropped open. "Oh, Vivian," she said. "I'm so sorry about your dad."

"Thank you," I murmured.

"At least you're near family now. That's good," she said. "And this is a nice neighborhood. A few of the neighbors are nice."

I caught her eye and grinned. "Like you?"

She laughed—a melodic, tinkling sound. "Yes, like me." She stepped toward the front door. "I guess I should go. Good luck with your unpacking, Vivian, and welcome to the neighborhood. I'm sure I'll see you around."

"I'm sure you will," I said, opening the door for her. "Nice to meet you, Tambra."

"Same here," she said. She stepped out the door, and I closed it softly behind her.

An hour later I was putting away my pots and pans when I heard another knock on the door. As I walked to answer it, I realized I hoped it was Tambra again. Something about her had intrigued me. But when I opened the door, I was greeted by a petite woman with shoulder-length brown hair and dull brown eyes. She looked to be a few years older than I was. She wore a lime-green polyester jumper with a green and white patterned blouse underneath.

"Hello," the woman said. "I'm Agnes Reed. I saw you moving in and thought I'd come by and introduce myself."

"Hello, Mrs. Reed. I'm Vivian Latham."

"Hello, Vivian. Where did you move from?" she asked.

"Applewood, Iowa, not far from Des Moines."

"Oh, I see," she said. "And you moved here with your husband or...?" Her voice trailed off.

I curbed an impulse to roll my eyes. What was it with these people and the questions about husbands? I gave her a tight smile. "No, just me. No husband."

"Hmm," she said, giving me a once-over with her eyes. "And what brought you here from Iowa?"

"My father passed away recently, and I wanted to be near family," I said. I was already weary of telling that story. "My aunt and two cousins live in Tumwater."

"Oh dear, I'm sorry about your father," she said. "What about your mother?"

"My mother passed away when I was eight," I said.

Her hand fluttered at her chest. "Oh, how terrible. I'm sorry."

I gave her a curt nod. "Thank you."

"And do you work since you're alone?" she asked. Her mouth curled into a slight sneer when she said the word "alone." Clearly she found living alone to be distasteful.

"I was a physical education teacher in Iowa, but I left teaching."

"And why did you do that?" she asked brusquely.

I already knew I didn't like Mrs. Reed, and I thought for a moment about ignoring her question. Instead I told the same lie I'd told my aunt. "They were making cuts, and they eliminated my job."

"Hmm," she said with a frown. "Well, I live on the other side of Tambra there." She pointed to the brown house, the corner of which was just visible. "My husband is Art, and we have two teenage kids—Penelope and Arthur, Jr. I'm sure we'll see you around."

"I'm sure you will," I said. "Nice to meet you, Mrs. Reed."

"Likewise," she said, already turning to leave.

I closed the door, realizing that in the space of two hours I had met every neighbor Mr. Bickford had told me about. I then realized that Tambra was the only one who had welcomed me to the neighborhood.

11

The next morning I awoke feeling energized, ready to get my new house in order. I'd gone to the corner store the evening before to buy coffee and a few other necessities, and I went out to the kitchen and set up the percolator I'd brought from Iowa. As I waited for the coffee to brew, I ate a bowl of Corn Flakes and a slice of toast. Once the coffee was done, I poured a cup, carried it outside to the porch, and settled into the chair. I was glad to see it wasn't raining.

I had a lot to do today. My first order of business was to get my phone hooked up, and then I wanted to pick up some things for the house. I was eager to get started. I finished my coffee and hurried to get ready to go.

※

I returned home at a little after noon, marveling at all I'd gotten accomplished. I had ordered a new phone line, which would be hooked up the next day, and then I'd gone to Sears to buy several things for the house, including a brand-new television set that would be delivered tomorrow. I'd ended at the grocery store, buying everything I'd need for the next two weeks.

I parked in the carport and climbed out of the car. I opened the trunk and took stock of all the bags. I'd need to make a few trips. I grabbed two and headed for the front door. As I crossed the front lawn, I heard someone call out to me.

"Hi, Vivian!"

I looked to the sidewalk and smiled when I saw Tambra there, pushing Claire in a stroller. "Hi, Tambra. How are you?" I said, walking across the grass toward her and the baby.

"Good. Just taking Claire for a little walk," she said. "Are you getting moved in?"

"Yeah. I had to go out and buy some stuff for the house," I said, nodding at the bags in my arms.

"Yeah, you always need stuff," she said, flashing me her crooked grin. "Vivian, I was wondering if—Claire takes her nap at two, and I was wondering if you'd take a break from unpacking and maybe come over for a bit?"

She seemed shy about asking, which touched me. "Sure, I'd be happy to. See you at two then?"

"Okay, see you then." She gave me a wave and then continued down the sidewalk.

I unloaded everything from the car. After I put away the groceries, I focused on the house. I'd bought an area rug for the living room, three lamps, two end tables, a kitchen clock, and a nightstand. I put everything where I wanted it and then walked from room to room admiring my handiwork. I was pleased.

I glanced at the new clock in the kitchen. It was two o'clock and time to head over to Tambra's. I crossed the lawn into her yard and then climbed the three stairs to her front door. She had a nice porch too, I noticed.

I knocked softly on the door, not wanting to wake Claire. A few seconds later, Tambra opened the door. When she saw me, her face lit up with a radiant smile. I was taken aback for a moment by her beauty.

"Hi, Vivian. Claire just fell asleep, so perfect timing."

I entered the house and looked around. The kitchen and a small dining area were to the right, and the living room was to the left. Straight ahead a short hallway led to the back of the house. I took in all that in a matter of seconds and then focused on the large fireplace that stretched across one entire wall of the living room. It was made of white stone with a hearth running the length of the fireplace.

"Wow, that's a huge fireplace," I said.

She looked at the fireplace. "Yeah, it's big," she said. "It's fun to decorate at Christmas."

"I'll bet," I said. I put my hands in my jeans pockets and looked at her. For some reason I felt nervous. "How long have you lived here?"

"About a year and a half."

I nodded. "It's a nice house."

She gave me a shy smile. "Thanks."

Something in the corner caught my eye. "What's that? Is that a baseball bat?"

She looked into the corner. "Oh, that. Yeah, it's a bat. It's my husband's. It's signed by one of the players or something," she said.

I walked over to look at it more closely. "Can I pick it up?"

She shrugged. "Sure."

I picked up the bat and turned it around in my hands. "It's signed all right—signed by Rod Carew!" I said, my voice rising with excitement. "He plays for the Minnesota Twins. That's my team." I gripped the bat and swung it a few times. "That's really cool."

She sat down on the couch. "I don't know much about sports," she said. "But it's my husband's prized possession."

"I'm sure it is," I said, setting the bat down carefully and sitting next to her.

She turned toward me. "Can I get you something to drink?"

"No, I'm okay." I was curious about the purpose of this visit. "So was there something specific you wanted to talk about?"

She met my eyes for a long beat and then shook her head. "No, not really. I just wanted to get to know you, I guess."

I turned toward her. "Okay. What did you want to know?"

She thought for a few moments. "Have you always lived in Iowa?"

I nodded. "Yep, born and raised."

"You said your dad passed away recently. So where's your mom?" she asked.

"My mom was killed in a car accident when I was eight," I said in a quiet voice.

She gasped. "Oh my God, Vivian. How awful. So you're an orphan?"

I gave a small laugh. "I guess you could say that even though I'm thirty-two."

She laughed too. "Yeah, I guess you usually say that about kids, but still, it's so sad that both your parents are gone. And losing your mom at eight—that's really rough."

I nodded. "Yeah, it was hard. What about you? Where are your parents?"

"My parents and my sister are in Everett," she said. "That's where I grew up. All my friends are there too." She paused. "I moved here with Tom not long after we were married. He got a job here."

I noticed that her voice was flat as she relayed this information, which I took to mean that she hadn't been happy about the move. "And what does Tom do?" I asked.

"He's the manager of Peterson Lumber and Hardware."

"That seems like a pretty good job," I said.

She shrugged. "Yeah, he does okay. We won't get rich or anything, but it pays the bills."

"And where's Everett?" I asked. "I just moved here, and I have no idea."

"It's about thirty miles north of Seattle," she said. "So ninety miles from here."

"That's not too far." After driving two thousand miles, I thought ninety seemed like nothing.

She looked down at her lap. "Yeah, but we hardly ever see them. Tom doesn't like to go there."

I frowned. "Why not?"

She met my eyes for a moment, and then her gaze flickered away. "He doesn't really get along with his parents, and his brother lives in Bellingham, so he says there's no reason to go to Everett."

"Except your family is there too," I said. Tom sounded selfish, I thought. Tambra didn't say anything, so I moved to my next question. "Where did you and Tom meet?"

"We met at a party at my friend's house when I was twenty-four," she said. "We had a whirlwind courtship, and we got married just after my twenty-fifth birthday."

"And you've been married two years?"

She nodded. "Yeah, it'll be three in June."

I studied her face. She seemed so indifferent as she relayed this information. I wondered if she and Tom were happy.

"What about you, Vivian? How come you're not married?" she asked, looking at me with raised eyebrows.

I hesitated, not sure how to answer that question. "I guess I've never met the right person," I finally said, looking away as I spoke.

"Have you ever been serious with anyone?" she asked.

I shook my head. "No, not really. I don't think I'm destined to be with someone."

"There's still time," she said, smiling and patting my hand.

I wanted to change the subject. "Could I have some water?"

"Sure," she said as she rose and went into the kitchen. She came back, handed me a tall glass of water, and then sat down. "Will you be looking for work, Vivian?"

I contemplated her question, wondering how much to tell her. Somehow, Tambra felt safe. "Actually, my father left me a good amount of money," I said. "I really don't plan to look for work—not now, anyway. It's not enough to live off for the rest of my life, but it'll keep me going for a few years."

Her eyes widened. "Oh! That's wonderful! I mean, I know it doesn't make the loss of your father any easier, but it's nice for you."

I nodded. "Yes, it is nice."

She chewed her bottom lip and gave me a sidelong glance. "And—I know this will sound selfish—but it's good news for me too."

I looked at her curiously. "How so?"

She held my gaze. "Well, it means that maybe I might have, you know, a friend," she said and then looked away. I noticed her cheeks flush with color. She looked back at me with pleading eyes. "I'm just so lonely, Vivian. I don't know anyone here, and most of the neighbors are so—I don't know—cliquish, I guess. All my friends are still in Everett, and I don't, I mean, I can't…" She paused and took a deep breath.

"I know I have Claire, but sometimes I just want to talk to a grown-up." She glanced at me, trying to gauge my response. "I want to talk about books and movies and music and politics with someone. All Tom ever wants to talk about is sports." She rolled her eyes. "I just want to, I just want someone to…to like me. And if you don't have to go to work every day, then maybe we can, you know, spend time together. Maybe…be friends?" She gave me a tentative smile.

I felt a rush of empathy and tenderness for her. "Yes, I think we could be friends. I don't know anyone here either, so I could use a friend."

She sighed with relief. Before she could speak, Claire let out a loud wail from the bedroom, making us both jump. "I guess she's awake," Tambra said. "That was a short nap."

"I should be going anyway," I said, standing and moving toward the front door.

Tambra stood too and touched my shoulder. Her touch sent a shiver down my arm. "Thanks for coming over, Vivian. I hope you'll come and visit again."

"Don't worry, I will," I said as I opened the front door. "Bye."

"Bye," she said and gave me a wave.

As I walked back to my house, I thought about Tambra. Something about her had moved me. It had been a long time since I'd had such an intense response to another person. Daniel was probably the last one, and that had been years ago. I wasn't sure if it was her honest admission of loneliness or her curiosity about the world. Maybe it was both. Whatever it was, I knew I wanted to spend more time with Tambra.

12

Josie
July 2015

Susan skillfully brought me out of my hypnotic state. She smiled as I blinked and looked around, trying to adjust to being back in the real world. I met her eyes and stared at her, uncertain of what had just happened.

"That was a good session," she finally said.

I ignored her comment. "Did I say my name was Vivian?" I asked in an agitated voice.

Susan looked down at her notes. "Yes, Vivian."

"Oh my God!" I said. "Are you sure? I mean, that's what I remember saying, but that can't be!"

She frowned. "That wasn't the outcome you were expecting?"

"No!" I said too loudly. I tried to tone it down. "No, that's not what I was expecting. Is that for certain? Does this mean I was definitely Vivian in my past life?"

"Well, we can never be certain, Josie," she said, looking at me with a serious expression. "This is an inexact practice because often the past life someone recalls can't be confirmed. And even when it can be confirmed, there's usually no way to prove you were that person. You just have to trust in the process and trust your gut."

My mind was spinning a mile a minute. "But my mom said I was Tambra in my past life, not Vivian."

Susan smiled and cocked her head to the side. "And why did your mother think that?"

"Because of the dream," I said urgently. "Because I hear the scream 'Tambra' in the dream. And because I went to see Tambra's old house and it felt familiar."

Susan looked at me steadily. "That was something you heard in the dream, but that doesn't mean you heard it as Tambra," she said patiently. "Our session today suggests that you heard it as Vivian." She paused, thinking. "Did Tambra and Vivian know each other? Perhaps that's why Tambra's house felt familiar to you."

"Yes, they knew each other!" I said angrily. "Vivian murdered Tambra. She went to prison. I'm a murderer!" I was embarrassed to hear my own voice. I needed to calm down. This wasn't Susan's fault, and I was acting as if it was.

She inhaled sharply. "Oh my," she said. "I didn't realize that. So that's why you're so upset."

I sat back against the couch cushion and sighed. "Yes, that's why I'm so upset."

She gave me a compassionate look. "I know this is shocking information, Josie, but do remember that we live many lives and have many experiences, all intended for the growth and evolution of our souls and the souls of others. This was an experience, but it doesn't define who you are at your core." She looked at me silently for a moment. "What do you base this on, anyway? How do you know that Vivian killed Tambra?"

"Because Vivian was convicted of the crime!" I said loudly. I was getting worked up again. I tried to continue more calmly. "I read the article in the newspaper. I talked to one of Tambra's neighbors. It happened. Tambra died and Vivian went to prison. Why would she… I…kill her? What could Tambra possibly have done to Vivian?"

She looked at me closely. "What happened was that Tambra died," she said. "That much we know for sure. What we don't know is what led up to that. Since this is upsetting you, you might want to do some more investigating. It sounds like you've seen Tambra's house. Maybe you should go back with the knowledge you have now."

"Okay, that's a good idea," I said, my voice more calm now.

She leaned toward me, our knees almost touching. "Maybe talk to the neighbor again or even see if you can locate someone who was close to Tambra. You don't have to tell them about any of this. Just make up a story about who you are. And if there was a murder investigation and a trial, then I believe you can still access those records. You can read what happened and see if that leads to any new memories or feelings. If you were Vivian in your past life, then you know what happened, but you can't just call up those memories at will. You're going to have to help the process along a bit."

"Okay," I said softly. What she said made sense, but it was still a lot to wrap my head around. Suddenly an odd thought occurred to me. "I guess this means that Vivian died before I was born, right?"

She nodded. "Yes, you can safely assume that," she said. "When were you born? What year?"

"1981," I said.

"And Vivian went to prison in what year?"

"1974."

Susan rubbed her chin thoughtfully. "So it sounds like she died in prison. If this was a high-profile case, then you could probably find a newspaper article about that."

"I'll look," I said. It sounded like I had my work cut out for me. Now I had to decide if I wanted to just ignore all this or do something about it. I knew myself well enough to know the answer to that question.

"And if it would help," she continued, "we could do another session somewhere along the way. Maybe try to access memories from another time in Vivian's life."

"All right," I said. I felt as if the center was falling out of my world. Why was this happening now? What was I supposed to be learning from this? What was I supposed to do?

As if she could read my mind, Susan said, "And remember, Josie, you're having this dream for a reason. Most people don't have past-life dreams that are this vivid and this insistent. The dream is trying to tell you something. And the fact that you came to me now tells me that it's time for you to figure it out."

※

I arrived home at a little after six and stood in the middle of my kitchen in a fog. Jezebel was crying for dinner, and I mindlessly fed her. I sat down at the kitchen table and stared out the window. The house was hot, but I barely noticed. I just kept replaying the session over and over in my mind—always ending on those damning words: "My name is Vivian."

My phone rang at six thirty, and I knew it was Celeste before I looked at the caller ID. I ignored it. I couldn't talk to her now. What would I say? "Oh yeah, I had the session, and I found out that I'm a murderer." My mom would probably be calling soon too. I didn't know what to say to either one of them. My phone beeped. A text. I looked at the message. It was Celeste, and all it said was, "Call me." I groaned. I couldn't avoid her forever.

I made a grilled cheese sandwich for dinner. I really wasn't hungry, but I knew I needed to eat something. As I was eating, Celeste texted me again, but I ignored it. Thirty minutes later the phone rang. I sighed, picked up the phone, and took a deep breath before I answered. "Hi, Celeste," I said.

"Hey, hi," she said. "Are you avoiding me? I've been calling and texting since six thirty."

"I know. I'm sorry. I've been in shock since my session."

"In shock? Why?" she asked.

I didn't say anything for a long moment. "Well, it didn't go quite as I expected," I said.

"Why? What happened?" she asked. I could hear the concern in her voice.

"I went back to my past life—the life I've been dreaming about," I said. "According to what I said in the session, I wasn't Tambra in my past life."

"Really? Then who were you?" she asked.

I hesitated for a few moments and then said in a tight voice, "Vivian Latham."

Celeste was silent for several seconds. Finally she spoke. "Well, that's weird."

"Yeah, it's definitely weird. And if this is true, then Vivian Latham must be dead."

"Strange," she said. "I guess you didn't know that before?"

"No, I didn't," I said. "I assumed she'd served her twenty years in prison and then got on with her life."

"Do you know how she died?" she asked.

"No idea," I said. "After Susan brought me out of the regression, she could tell I was upset. She said I should do some more research and try to find out what happened. I'm thinking about doing that, and how Vivian died is one of the things I'll try to find out."

"Or you could just ignore it all and get on with your life," Celeste said dryly.

"And have this dream plague me for the rest of my life?" I shot back. "No, thank you."

"Okay, fair enough," she said. "So you're going to do some research and see if you can figure it out."

"Yeah, I think so. I'm not sure I really have a choice. Having this dream two or three times a week almost makes my decision for me."

"So where will you start?" she asked.

"I don't know. I'll look on the Internet first. Beyond that, Susan thought I could access the court records and maybe even the police records. And she said I should go back and see Tambra's house again."

"Are you sure you want to do all that?" she said and then paused. "Doesn't it scare you, Jo?"

I wasn't sure how to answer that. Yes, it did scare me, but it also scared me not to know. "Yeah, it's kind of scary, but it's also scary to wonder about it and never know. And it's scary to keep having this dream."

She sighed. "Well, I guess you have to do what you think is right," she said. "And I can help if you need me to. You know, if you want me to go to Olympia with you or something."

She didn't sound excited about that offer, but I appreciated her for making it. "Thanks, Celeste. I don't know yet what I'll need, but I'll let you know if you can help."

"Okay. I'll talk to you later," she said.

"Okay. Bye, Celeste."

"Bye."

I disconnected the call and sighed. I was relieved that was done. Now I just needed to talk to my mom.

I had been off the phone for fifteen minutes when my mom called. I told her the same story, but, predictably, she had a broader, more philosophical view. Not that I didn't appreciate Celeste's pragmatic way of dealing with things—I did—but in this particular circumstance, my mom's gentle, spiritual approach was more what I was craving.

"Honey, just remember that there's a rhythm and a plan to the universe," she said. "You had this experience in your past life for a reason, and you're having this experience in this life for a reason. Don't beat yourself up about what happened in the past. That would be counterproductive to your growth in this life. There's something about what happened in the past that you're being called on to address now. Don't hide from it—meet it head on. This may be your chance to make amends for what happened in the past and balance that karma."

I felt comforted as I listened to her perspective. She made it all sound so reasonable. "I'm going to do some more investigating like Susan suggested," I said. "Is that what you mean about meeting it head on?"

"Yes, that would be an excellent place to start," she said. "One of our primary tasks in every life is to become more enlightened. If you chain yourself to what happened in your life as Vivian, then you're making it hard for yourself to grow in this life."

"Okay," I said uncertainly.

"You were born into this life, with this set of circumstances, for a reason, Josephine. Figure it out, and that can set you free."

"That sounds very deep, Mom," I said.

She laughed. "It does, doesn't it?"

"Yep," I said. "So the first thing I'm going to do is try and find out how Vivian died. Then I'll see where that takes me."

"I think that's a great place to start," she said. "I'm sure that's a story all on its own."

"I'm sure it is," I said. "Well, thanks, Mom. I should let you go." We ended our conversation with my promise that I would update her in a few days.

I sat down on the couch with my iPad and opened a browser window. I typed in "Vivian Latham death record" and pressed Enter. The first hit was a website that listed death dates for people with a shared name—in this case, Vivian Latham. An overwhelming number of people named Vivian Latham had died over the span of several decades. Then I noticed search fields to narrow the results, one of which was the death year. I wasn't sure what year she had died, but if we really shared a soul, then it had to be between 1974 and 1981. I entered 1974 and pressed Search. Two results popped up, neither of which were in Washington State. I deleted 1974, typed in 1975, and hit Enter. I scanned the three names that came up and yelled, "Bingo!"

The entry said:

> Name: Vivian M. Latham
> Location: Bakersville, Washington, Skamania County
> Born: September 28, 1941
> Died: February 11, 1975
> Age at death: 33

I knew the women's penitentiary was in Bakersville, so this must be her. I realized this was a major find, but Vivian's age was what riveted my attention: thirty-three. Her birthday had been in

September, which meant she had been thirty-two when Tambra died—the same age I had been when I first had the dream. I remembered I had learned Vivian's age when I found the newspaper article about the murder, but that was before my session with Susan. Now this information took on a new—and unnerving—significance. And the dream had started in August—the same month Vivian had killed Tambra. I wished I had recorded the date I'd first had the dream. I'd be willing to bet a million bucks that it had been August eleventh.

My body vibrated, and the hair on my arms stood on end. I closed my eyes for a long moment and tried to center myself. Then, I looked again at the entry, paying attention to the other details. I noticed there was no cause of death, but I thought her death might have made the Olympia newspaper and the article would give more details. I logged on to the newspaper site I'd joined and typed in the relevant search terms. I was rewarded with a tiny article buried in the local section of the *Olympia Herald*.

> Bakersville, WA, February 13, 1975—Prison officials at the Women's Penitentiary in Bakersville have reported the death of prison inmate and former Olympia resident Vivian M. Latham. Miss Latham died of undisclosed reasons on February 11. Miss Latham had been serving a 20-year prison sentence for the murder of Olympia resident Tambra L. Delaney. Miss Latham was convicted of second-degree murder in October 1974. Dorothy Perkins, Miss Latham's next of kin and a Tumwater resident, said that Miss Latham will be buried in Iowa, where she spent the majority of her life.

Damn, I thought. No cause of death. But the article had given me two more kernels of information: Vivian was originally from Iowa, and she had a relative named Dorothy Perkins. I diligently wrote this information in my notebook.

I turned back to my iPad, typed "Dorothy Perkins, Tumwater, WA" into the search field, and pressed Enter. I scanned the results, and one jumped out at me:

> Obituary for Dorothy Anne Perkins
>
> Dorothy Anne Perkins, beloved mother and grandmother, passed away on March 7, 2002. She was 82 years old. Dorothy was born in Applewood, Iowa, on May 9, 1919, and moved to Tumwater with her husband, Frank, in 1943. She was a loving mother to twin daughters Louise and Linda, and a proud grandma to Christopher, Melissa, Jason and Kevin. She was also an avid gardener, cook and seamstress. Dorothy was preceded in death by her husband of 25 years, Frank Perkins; her parents, John and Marie Latham; her brother, Roger Latham; and her niece, Vivian Latham. She is survived by her daughter, Linda Davidson of Charlottesville, Virginia; her daughter, Louise Maguire of Olympia; and her grandchildren, Christopher and Melissa Davidson and Jason and Kevin Maguire. Services will be held at the Tumwater United Methodist Church on March 14, 2002, at 1:00 p.m. Interment to follow at Evergreen Memorial Cemetery in Tumwater.

I stared at the words "Applewood, Iowa." This had to be Vivian's family. More bread crumbs. I picked up my notebook and wrote down the new clues: Vivian had an aunt named Dorothy Perkins; two cousins, Louise Maguire and Linda Davidson; and either an uncle or father named Roger Latham. Then again, I realized, the obituary hadn't said that Dorothy had any other siblings, so Roger must be Vivian's father. Her aunt had been born in Applewood, Iowa, and chances were good that Vivian had lived either there or nearby.

I had another thought and typed "Louise Maguire, Olympia, Washington" in the Google search field. The first result was one of those people-finding services. It said, "View Louise Maguire's phone number, address, and more." I clicked on the link, which opened to an informational page on Louise Maguire. It listed her address, her phone number, and other people associated with her—in this case, Richard Maguire, who I figured was her husband. It also listed her approximate age: sixty-six to seventy. I wrote down her address and phone number.

I glanced at the clock and saw that it was nearly nine. Too late to call tonight. I would call her in the morning, if I got up the nerve and if I could think of a good reason to be nosing around for information about Vivian Latham.

I felt some relief that I'd uncovered quite a bit of information in a short amount of time. I marveled, as I often did, at the wonder of the Internet. How had we ever lived without it? I yawned and realized it had been a long day. I was exhausted. I closed my iPad and decided to call it a night.

The next morning I awoke feeling resolved to call Louise Maguire and find out what she knew about Vivian. I still hadn't come up with a good reason for asking about Vivian some forty years after her death, but I knew I'd think of something.

After I'd finished my breakfast and fortified myself with two cups of strong, black coffee, I picked up my phone and carried it into the living room. I sat on the couch with my notebook open to the page where I'd written Louise Maguire's phone number. I stared at the number, trying to get up the nerve to dial the phone. It's Sunday, I thought. She's probably at church. Maybe I should try later.

"Ugh, I'm just making excuses," I said aloud as I dialed the number. The phone rang four times, and I was about to hang up when I heard someone answer on the other end.

"Hello?" a woman said.

"Hello," I said in a cheerful voice. "May I speak with Louise Maguire?"

"This is Louise," the woman said, a wary tone in her voice.

"Hello, ma'am. My name is, uh, Josephine Pace, and I'm a reporter with, um, *Pacific Northwest Magazine.* I was wondering if you knew Vivian Latham." There was dead silence on the other end of the line. "Hello?" I said. "Are you there, ma'am?"

"Yes, I'm here," Louise Maguire said in a tight voice. "Who are you again?"

"Josephine Pace," I said, a tremor creeping into my voice. My confidence was waning. "I'm a reporter with *Pacific Northwest Magazine.* Did you know Vivian Latham, Mrs. Maguire?"

"Why are you asking?" she asked haughtily.

I licked my lips nervously. "I'm doing a story about women incarcerated in the 1970s, and I was wondering if you knew Vivian Latham." I had asked the same question three times now, and I hoped the third time was the charm.

"Yes, I knew her," she said sharply. "She was my cousin."

"Oh, good!" I said, relieved. "I've had a hard time finding anyone who knew Vivian."

"Why on earth are you interested in Vivian?" she said. "She died years ago. Good Lord, it must be thirty-five or forty years."

"I'm calling because I'm doing a story about women inmates in the 1970s, and I wanted to ask you a few questions about her." This woman wasn't a very good listener, I thought.

She was silent again. "All right," she finally said. "What do you want to know?"

I grabbed my notebook, the pen poised in my hand and the phone tucked under my chin. "Vivian was convicted of killing her neighbor. Did you know anything about the case?"

"No, I really didn't," she said. "I'd never met that woman she killed—I'm sorry, I don't remember her name."

"Tambra Delaney," I said.

"Right, Tambra Delaney. I didn't know her, but Vivian talked about her a time or two. I haven't—"

"What did Vivian say about her?" I interrupted.

"Oh, nothing of much consequence," she said in an offhand way. "Vivian used to come over to my mom's house for Sunday dinner, and one evening she was telling us about her neighbors and how unfriendly they were to her—except Tambra. She seemed to really like Tambra."

I wrote that down in my notebook. "Did she say anything else about Tambra?"

She was quiet for a long moment. "Vivian mentioned that she had a baby. That's all I remember."

"But as far as you know, Vivian liked Tambra?" I asked.

"Yes, that's what it seemed like to me," Louise Maguire said.

"So do you have any idea why Vivian would have killed Tambra?"

"I haven't the slightest idea," she said. "Vivian stopped coming around my mom's house, so I wouldn't know."

"Did Vivian seem like a murderer to you?" I asked.

"No, but I can't say I knew her well. She grew up in Iowa, and we lived here, so I only saw her a handful of times when we were kids. Like I said, she came to my mom's house several times after she moved here, but I can hardly say I knew her."

"Is there anyone else alive who knew her?" I said.

"Not that I know of," she said. "Her dad, Roger, died a year or so before Vivian, and she had no siblings. My mom, Dorothy—Vivian's aunt—died twelve years ago. It's just me and my twin sister, Linda, left now, and Linda didn't know Vivian any better than I did."

"What about Vivian's mom?" I asked. I knew Agnes Reed had told me that Vivian's mom had died when she was a child, but I didn't necessarily trust that information.

Louise Maguire made a clicking sound with her tongue. "Her mom died when Vivian was young. She was hit by a truck."

"Oh my God," I said, shocked. "What was her mom's name?"

"Oh, good heavens, you're testing my memory here," she said. "What was her name?" she whispered to herself. She was silent a few seconds. "Helen!" she finally said. "Her name was Helen."

I wrote the information in my notebook. "And did Vivian ever live in Applewood, Iowa?" I asked.

"Why, yes, she lived there all her life—until she moved here, to Olympia."

"And Vivian was buried in Applewood, is that correct?" I asked.

"Yes, she's buried next to her parents," she said.

"How did your mom react when Vivian was sent to prison?"

"She was very upset," she said. "There were some, uh, things that came out about Vivian at the trial that my mom didn't know."

That piqued my curiosity. "What kinds of things?" I asked.

There was a long pause on the other end of the line. "She found out that Vivian was gay and that she'd been fired from her teaching job in Iowa because of that," she finally said.

I wrote furiously in my notebook. "So did your mom ever visit Vivian in prison?"

"No," she said shortly, offering no explanation.

"Are you sure there wasn't anyone else Vivian was close to?" I asked. "A girlfriend, maybe?"

"No, I don't think so," she said. "She lived alone, and she kept to herself a lot. She was a private person, but then I guess she'd have to be given her...proclivities."

Proclivities? I thought. This was beginning to remind me of my conversation with Agnes Reed. "What about work? Did she have a job?"

"She was a physical education teacher in Iowa, but she was fired for being gay," she said.

Yes, I thought, so you've said. "I mean here—in Olympia."

"No, she didn't work here," she said. "Her dad had left her some money, and she was living off that until she got her feet under her." She paused. "Of course, before that could happen, she was in prison."

"Do you know how Vivian died?" I asked. "Was it a prison fight or an illness or...?" My voice trailed off.

"Well, for heaven's sake, I thought you knew," Louise Maguire said. "Vivian killed herself."

13

The next week I brooded over what Louise Maguire had told me. I went to work every day, did my job, and then went home. I talked to my mom on the phone a few times and spent time with Celeste, but I didn't tell either one of them what I'd learned. Somehow I felt guilty—as if I'd be telling them about my own suicide, and in a way I guess I would be.

Like many people, I'd thought about suicide a time or two when I was younger, but never in a serious way. Truthfully, I couldn't imagine the pain someone would have to be in to take his or her own life, and I felt thankful that I'd never felt that kind of pain. I wondered about Vivian and her state of mind. Why had she killed herself? What pain had she been in? Had she been consumed with guilt over killing Tambra? Had she been mentally ill? How had she done it? Louise Maguire hadn't offered any details, and I hadn't asked. I searched the Internet and learned that hanging was the most common suicide method in prison, and I imagined that was what Vivian had done.

I also couldn't shake the frustration I felt at my inability to remember anything from Vivian's life other than what was in the damned dream. If I was Vivian, why couldn't I remember any details? Susan Krause had told me that I knew what happened, but I didn't. I'd racked my brain trying to remember even the smallest fact—the color of Vivian's eyes or whether she was right or left handed—and

I'd come up empty. If this life had affected me so deeply that I was dreaming about it now, then why couldn't I remember anything?

After a week of obsessing, I couldn't stand it anymore. I had to talk to somebody. When I got to work on Monday, I picked up the phone, dialed resolutely, and prayed that Susan would answer. I heard her pick up the phone, and I sighed with relief.

"This is Susan Krause."

"Susan, hi, this is Josie Pace."

"Hello, Josie," she said warmly. "How are you?"

"Not so good," I said in a gloomy voice. "I was wondering if you might have some time to talk with me this week. Not for another regression," I added quickly. "I just need to talk to you. I'll pay you for your time."

"I'd be happy to," she said. "But you don't have to pay me. Why don't we meet for coffee one day this week and talk—no charge."

"Oh, thank you. That'd be great," I said.

"Would Wednesday evening work for you?" she asked. "Say eight o'clock?"

"Yes, that works," I said, making a note in my calendar. "Where should we meet?"

"What about the Starbucks on the corner of Market and Twenty-Second in Ballard?" Susan suggested.

Ugh, Ballard again, I thought. Don't get me wrong—I grew up in Ballard, and I loved it. It was trendy and quaint at the same time. It was just that Ballard was a long trek from Beacon Hill, and parking was atrocious. But Susan was doing me a favor, so I couldn't complain. "That'd work fine," I said.

"Great," she said. "I'll see you then."

On Wednesday evening I pushed open the door of the Ballard Starbucks and looked around for Susan. I was a few minutes early, and I didn't think she was there yet. I stepped up to the front counter and ordered a decaf Americano.

As I stood waiting for the barista to make my drink, I heard a voice in my ear. "Hello, Josie." I turned to see Susan Krause. Her hair was pulled back in a messy ponytail, and she was wearing a colorful cotton dress and tan huaraches. Her face was completely free of makeup.

"Susan!" I said. "Thanks so much for meeting me."

"No problem," she said, hefting her large straw purse onto her shoulder. "What are you having?"

"A decaf Americano," I answered.

"Sounds good," she said. "I think I'll have that too." The barista called out my drink, and I picked it up off the counter. "I'll go find us a table," I told Susan.

I looked around and saw a table tucked into the corner. I hurried over and claimed it. A few minutes later, Susan joined me.

She looked at me curiously. "So what's going on, Josie? You sounded upset on the phone."

I looked down at my coffee cup, gathering my thoughts. I raised my eyes and met her gaze. "I've done some research on Vivian Latham, and I found out that she committed suicide in prison."

She leaned back in her chair and let out a long breath. "I was afraid of that," she said. "Did you find out any details?"

I shook my head. "No. I tracked down Vivian's cousin. She's the one who told me. She didn't offer any details."

"And this is bothering you, I'm guessing," she said and then took a sip of her coffee.

I frowned. "Yes, it's bothering me. If I was Vivian, then that means I committed suicide." I paused. "I wouldn't do that."

"You probably wouldn't kill someone in this life either, but it seems you did that in your last life too," she said dryly. She saw my grimace and added quickly, "Listen, Josie, you had a particular set of circumstances in that life, and you have a particular set in this life. You learned things in that life, and you're learning things in this life.

But they're not the same life. With each life the soul creates specific conditions and experiences to grow spiritually and to learn different lessons. To become closer to the Source. To balance karma."

"What do you mean by 'balance karma'?" I asked. My mom had said that too, and I thought I knew what they meant, but I wanted to hear Susan's explanation. The transcendental concepts I'd held on to for so many years had become very real and very confusing, and I needed help understanding them.

She looked away for a moment, thinking. "Okay, here's an example. In Vivian's life, let's say your experience was that someone died as a direct result of your actions. In this life you may be an emergency room doctor, working to keep people alive. Or in Vivian's time your experience was that you felt so hopeless that you took your own life. In this life you might work at a suicide prevention center. That's a simple way of explaining it, but I think you understand what I'm getting at."

"But I'm not a doctor, and I don't work at a suicide prevention center," I said logically.

"That's just an example," she said, taking a drink of her coffee. "We don't know yet how you're balancing your karma and growing in this life."

"And how will I figure it out?" I asked.

"I think you're figuring it out now," she said and paused. "And please don't misunderstand me, Josie. We all have many lessons in any given life. What you're experiencing now is one of several lessons. But your attention is fully on this right now."

"You can say that again," I muttered. "So if all this is true, then how does suicide help someone grow spiritually?"

Susan cocked her head to the side. "It doesn't. Suicide is never part of any soul's life plan. We have an outline of the life we'll live and the lessons we'll learn, but we also have free will once we're in the physical body. Suicide would fall into that category."

"So whatever Vivian experienced led her to exercise free will and kill herself?" I asked.

"Well, we don't know yet what Vivian was going through," she said. "But yes, generally speaking, she exercised free will and took her own life."

"I wish I knew why," I said, looking down at the table.

"Like I told you when you came to see me, Josie, if you were Vivian in your past life, then there's some part of you that knows what happened."

I met her eyes. "But I don't know," I said, annoyance creeping into my voice. "I've got nothing. No memories. Nothing. I can't even remember what color Vivian's eyes were."

Susan didn't seem to notice my annoyance, or if she did, she ignored it. "Because those memories aren't stored in your conscious mind," she said patiently. "You can't call them up at will. Those memories are part of your superconscious mind, and they're tenuous. That's why you have the memories when you're asleep. When you're sleeping, the conscious mind isn't active. Your guard is down."

I took a deep breath. "Okay, I get it. But if that's true, then how will I ever figure out what happened?"

She tapped her finger on her temple. "Because you're smart," she said. "You can use your logic and intelligence to investigate. You've had a fair amount of success with your research. It seems that you've found out quite a bit without a lot of time and effort."

I nodded. "Yes, that's true."

"And it seems to me that the big question you're asking yourself is why. Why did Vivian kill that woman, right?"

"Yes," I agreed.

"So if that were me, I'd think of it as a mystery I'm trying to solve," she said. "Like I said before, you could request the transcript from the trial or the documentation from the police investigation. There's bound to be some details there. And you could go back to the neighborhood where Vivian lived. See if there's anyone who remembers her."

I shook my head. "I asked her cousin that. She said there's no one left who remembers Vivian."

Susan's eyebrows shot up. "Do your cousins know everything there is to know about your life?"

I laughed. "Good point. No, they don't. I only have four cousins. We were pretty close when we were kids, but now I see them only two or three times a year."

"Exactly," she said. "I'm sure the same is true of Vivian's cousin. Her cousin knew a small part of who Vivian was, and I'm sure the time they spent together was limited. I seriously doubt she's aware of everyone Vivian touched during her time on earth. I think with a little digging you could find other people who knew her."

"When would I have time to do all that? I work full time," I said. For some reason I wanted to argue with Susan, even though I knew she was making sense and she was trying to help me.

She didn't miss a beat. "Do you get paid vacation time at your job?" she asked.

I nodded. "Yes, I get three weeks a year."

"Then why don't you take a week off and spend it sleuthing?"

Why hadn't I thought of that? "Yeah, I could probably do that. I have a lot of vacation time saved up."

"Well, there you go," she said, slapping her hand lightly on the table. "Take some time off and investigate. I think you'll feel better if you find out more about what happened."

"I'll think about that," I said, swirling what was left of my coffee around in the cup.

Susan glanced at her watch. "And now I'm afraid I have to run." She stood and looked down at me. "Do some searching, and then if you want to talk again, or maybe do another regression, you can call me, okay?"

"Okay," I said. I stood too and touched her shoulder. "Thank you, Susan. I really appreciate you talking to me."

"You're welcome," she said. She hesitated for a moment and then reached out and hugged me. "You'll figure this out, Josie," she said.

We parted ways, and I headed home to mull over our conversation and think about what I would do next.

14

By Friday I'd decided that I would talk to Miranda about taking the next week off. The dream invaded my sleep again at 4:04 on Friday morning, helping me make the decision. This time the dream was different, though. This time a blond woman was running toward a door. I saw a hand reach out, grab her, and throw her across the room. I couldn't see her face—all I could see was her long blond hair and her form from behind. I could feel her terror. In the background I could hear a baby crying.

My eyes flew open, and I gasped for breath. I lay there for a couple of minutes trying to calm myself. As my heartbeat slowed to a more normal rhythm and my mind cleared, I began to puzzle over these new images. Had the blond woman been Tambra? Whose hand had reached out and grabbed her? I'd seen the hand from behind, so I couldn't tell who it belonged to. Had that been Vivian's hand? And the crying baby. Was that Tambra's baby? I lay there for several minutes trying to call up more images, but nothing came. I gave up and rose from the bed, trying to shake off the dream.

When I got in to work, I sat staring out the window until I saw Miranda pull into the parking lot. I didn't want to descend on her the moment she came in the door, so I waited a respectable amount of time and then walked down the hall to her office. Her door was open, and she was peering at her computer screen as she sipped coffee from a Starbucks cup. I knocked on the doorjamb, and she looked up.

"Good morning, Josie," she said, smiling and moving her reading glasses to the top of her head. "What's up?"

I sat down in the chair opposite her desk. "Miranda, I know this is very short notice, but I need to take next week off."

She looked at me with a frown. "Is everything okay?"

I cleared my throat. "There's some weird stuff going on in my family, and I need to take some time off to deal with it," I said, deliberately keeping my explanation vague. She gazed at me, obviously expecting me to say more, but I didn't offer any other details. I didn't like to lie, so the less said the better.

"All right," she finally said. "Are you caught up on work?"

I nodded. "Yes, I just finished the Baker Foundation proposal, and I don't have anything else due until early next month."

"And I know you have enough vacation time in the bank, so I suppose it's okay for you to be gone next week."

"Thank you, Miranda," I said. "I really appreciate it."

She smiled. "I hope you get things figured out."

"Thanks," I said. "I hope so too."

I spent the rest of the morning filing a big stack of proposals, clearing out my e-mail inbox, and straightening my desk. At noon I went down to Celeste's office. She was standing in front of her filing cabinet, and she turned when she heard me come in.

"Hi, Jo. How are you?" she asked. She looked tired and uncharacteristically disheveled.

I shrugged. "All right, I guess. Are you okay? You look tired."

She gave me a coy smile. "I was with Matthew last night."

"Matthew Devine? Your neighbor?" I asked.

She nodded. "We went out to dinner, and then we went back to his place." She gave me a pointed look.

"Did you sleep with him?" I asked. This was big news. Celeste hadn't been serious with anyone for months.

"Maybe," she said.

"Celeste!" I said, pretend shock in my voice. "So? How was it?"

"Divine," she purred. "It was divine." She giggled at her play on words. "I think I'm in love."

"Take it slow, Celeste," I warned. "You barely know this guy."

"Yes, Mommy," she said, smiling and rolling her eyes. "But I will. I'm not interested in a fling—I want something real."

"And you'll be careful, right?" I pressed.

"Yes, and I'll be careful," she said. "What's going on with you?"

I sat down in her chair and spun around. "I just wanted you to know that I'm taking next week off," I said, trying to sound casual.

She frowned. "Why? Is everything okay with your mom?"

I waved my hand in the air. "Oh yeah. It's not about my mom." I hesitated, suddenly feeling uncertain about telling her. I swallowed hard. "I'm going down to Olympia for a few days to investigate. Susan Krause thinks I can access court records and the police report and maybe talk to someone who knew Vivian."

She stared at me for a long moment. "Really? That's where you're going with this?"

There was a hint of disapproval in her voice, and I immediately felt defensive. "This is consuming my life, Celeste," I said. "And I want to figure it out."

She raised her hands in a gesture of surrender. "Okay, I get it, Jo, and I support you. I just don't want you to open a can of worms you can't close."

I shook my head. "I don't think I will." I really wasn't sure of that, but I didn't want her to worry.

"Do you want me to go with you?" she asked.

Her voice sounded tight, and I knew she didn't really want to go with me, but I loved her for making the offer. "No, that's okay. I can handle it on my own," I said. "Can you feed Jezebel for me, though? You know where the extra key is."

"Sure," she said. "I'd be happy to."

"Besides, you can't be gone anyway." I smiled. "I'm sure you want to spend time with Matthew."

She flashed me a grin. "Yes, you're right about that. I'm counting the minutes until I can see him again." She gave me an exaggerated wink, and I laughed. I was glad she was so happy. "What about you, Jo?" she asked. "Anyone you're interested in?"

I frowned at her. Dating was the furthest thing from my mind right now. "No, not even a little bit," I said.

"You haven't been with anyone since Iris, and that went nowhere. You've got to get yourself out there, Jo."

Iris was the accounting assistant at Harmony, and she and I had dated briefly about a year ago—long enough for me to realize that she was mind-numbingly boring and we had nothing in common. I still felt awkward when I passed her in the hallway, and every time I saw her, I reminded myself never to date a coworker again. "Yeah, Iris is pretty, and that's about it. Bor-ing," I sang, and Celeste laughed. "And as for getting myself out there, that's not where my head is right now. Maybe I'll go on a date once I solve this Vivian mystery, but not now."

She looked at me with one eyebrow raised. "Jo, I'm worried about you. I think you're obsessed with this dream."

I felt a surge of irritation. "In case you don't remember, Celeste, you encouraged me to research the dream."

"I know, I know," she said. "But now we're talking about murder. And you're breaking into houses and talking about digging up old records." She shuddered. "I don't know. It creeps me out."

I pressed my lips together and took a deep breath. I really didn't want to have this discussion right now. "I know you don't understand this, Celeste," I said. "But it's important to me, and I need to do this. You don't have to understand it, but you do have to trust that I know what I'm doing."

She sighed deeply. "Okay. I trust you."

"Thank you," I said, standing. "I need to get back to my office and wrap a few things up before I leave. I'll call you in a day or two."

"Okay," she said, and reached out to give me a quick hug. "Be careful."

I agreed and headed back to my office to finish my work so I could get out of there.

15

By eleven o'clock the next morning, I was on the road and heading south. I'd called around before I left and found a hotel—the Capital Inn—that was running a special for ninety-nine dollars a night. I'd read online reviews and thought it sounded like a decent place to stay. I'd reserved four nights. That would give me two weekend days to poke around Vivian's old neighborhood and two weekdays to find out how I could access the court and police records.

As I drove, I began to think about Tambra. I wished I knew what she'd looked like. I thought about the blond woman in my dream and knew in my gut that she was Tambra. So she'd had long blond hair, I thought. I imagined her eyes had been blue. I'd only seen her from behind, but I could tell that she was on the slender side and a bit taller than average. Had she been pretty? Somehow I thought so. Were these real memories, I wondered, or just my imagination? How would I ever know?

My thoughts drifted to what I envisioned to be the brutality of Tambra's death. Had Vivian done that? Had I done that? I couldn't quite believe it. I was the kind of person who carried spiders outside rather than squishing them under my foot. I was mostly a vegetarian because raising animals for the sole purpose of eating them bothered me deeply. Was it possible that I'd murdered another human being? A wife? A mother? That just didn't seem possible. I knew Susan had said that every life was different, but didn't souls stay basically the same at their core? How could someone be a murderer in one life and in the next be a person who couldn't even kill a spider? I thought of Susan's comments about balancing karma. Could that be it? I just wasn't sure.

Whatever had happened, Tambra had died at the age of twenty-eight. A heavy feeling of sadness pressed against my chest and traveled down into my gut. I felt such grief for Tambra, her husband, and her child. Tears welled in my eyes and spilled down my cheeks.

A car roared past me on the left, and I shook my head and brought my attention back to the road. I was just crossing the Nisqually River, and that meant I was almost there. I knew where I was going first. I had to start this journey by trying to make amends with Tambra, and there was only one place I could do that.

I remembered which exit to take off the freeway and the two turns to make to get to the cemetery parking lot. I even remembered where Tambra's grave was, and I walked confidently there. Today was Saturday, and I noticed there were many more people here today than when I'd been here before.

I walked softly up to Tambra's headstone. I noticed that the pink rose that had been fresh and lush when I was here before was now brown and withered. The note was still attached to it, and it fluttered in the light breeze.

I kneeled down on the grass in front of the headstone and stared at her name: Tambra Lynn Delaney. I cleared my throat, knowing I had to say something. I didn't know if she could hear me, but I liked to think so. I closed my eyes and took a deep breath. My heart was pounding. "Tambra," I said quietly, "I'm so sorry for what happened. I don't know why you died—why Vivian killed you—but I'm going to try and find out. I can't bring you back, but I can try and make amends for this. I'm so sorry."

A sudden sound startled me. I whipped my head around to see a woman about my age standing ten feet behind me, watching me curiously. She had long, straight blond hair parted to the side and the most vivid blue eyes I think I'd ever seen. Her rosy lips and cheeks stood out against her light skin. She was tall, and she wore a turquoise T-shirt, denim capris, and tan sandals. In her left hand she held a single pink rose.

Tambra? I thought, bewildered. Was this a vision? I got to my feet, brushing the grass from my knees.

She squinted in the bright sun and shielded her eyes with her hand to see me better. "Hi there," she said. "Who are you?"

My mouth was dry, and it felt as if my tongue was stuck to the roof of my mouth. My lips moved, but no sound came out. Who was this woman? I swallowed hard and finally found my voice. I was too surprised to make up a name. "I'm Josie," I said.

"Hi, I'm Claire Campbell—I mean, Claire Delaney." She laughed. "I got divorced last fall, and I haven't gotten used to using my maiden name again." She moved forward, her hand outstretched.

Claire Delaney? I thought. Could this be Tambra's daughter? I reached out and shook her hand. "Nice to meet you, Claire."

She tucked her hair behind her ear and smiled at me. "Did you know my mom?"

"Was Tambra your mom?" I asked.

She nodded. "Yes, she was my mom. You look too young to have known her…" Her voice trailed off, and I knew she wanted to add, "So who the hell are you?"

My mind raced. What was I going to say? This turn of events was completely unexpected, and I had nothing at the ready—no story, no lie. I just stared at her blankly.

She waited for me to say something, and when I didn't speak, she said, "And what's your connection to my mom?"

I looked away from her gaze, trying to come up with something. An idea came to me. I met her eyes. "My mom and your mom were friends in high school. When my mom heard I'd be in Olympia for a short vacation, she asked if I'd stop by Tambra's gravesite and pay my respects."

Claire frowned, probably wondering why that simple story had been so hard for me to get out. "Oh, and your mom is...?"

I hesitated again. "Barbara," I said. Damn, why had I used my mom's real name? I needed to get better at this. "Barbara Smith," I added. Oh, that was original.

She smiled brightly. "It's great to meet you, Josie. So you live in Everett?"

Everett? I thought. Is that where Tambra had been from? "No, actually I live in Seattle." I hesitated and then added, "My mom's in Everett, though."

She nodded. "Well, I'm glad you stopped by. My mom doesn't get many visitors—just me, really."

"I'm sorry." I wasn't sure what else to say.

"That's okay. She's been gone almost forty-one years," she said, motioning to the headstone. "I didn't really know her. She died a week before my first birthday."

"I'm sorry," I said again. That meant Claire was nearly forty-two. I scanned her face. She looked great for her age. I had guessed her younger when I first saw her. "And you like to come to the cemetery and visit?" I asked.

She gave me a sad smile. "Yeah. I don't know much about her, so it helps me feel closer to her to come here."

I motioned toward the other headstone—the baby named Steven. "And was that your brother?"

She nodded and looked at the headstone. "Yes, he was stillborn."

"Oh, how terrible," I said.

"Yes, I'm sure it was," she said.

"So you said you didn't know your mom, but aren't there people left who knew her who can tell you about her?" I asked. I wondered if Tambra's husband had passed away. Otherwise, wouldn't he enjoy talking about her?

She shrugged. "Well, there's my dad, but he doesn't like to talk about her. It's like pulling teeth to get anything out of him about my mom. The main thing he's told me is how much I look like her." She paused and held up the pink rose in her hand. "And that she liked pink roses."

So Thomas was still alive, and he didn't like to talk about Tambra. How odd. "Do you know why he doesn't like to talk about her?" I asked. I knew I was prying, but I was intensely curious. I expected Claire to tell me to mind my own business, but she was unfazed by my question.

"I don't know," she answered, shaking her head. "It's really strange. He hates to talk about my mom. When I used to bring her up, he'd get all red in the face and tell me he didn't want to talk about it. Eventually I just stopped asking. Most of what I know about my mom I learned from my grandma—my mom's mom."

"So at least you have your grandma to talk to."

"Had," she said in a flat voice. "She and my grandpa died in a car accident when I was sixteen."

I inhaled sharply. "Oh my goodness. I'm so sorry, Claire. You've been through a lot." I thought about her comment that she'd gotten divorced last year. That was a lot of loss for someone her age.

"My grandma told me some stories about my mom, but they were mostly from her childhood. I want to know about her when she was older. Like, how did she feel when I was born? What kind of mom was she? Did she love me? That kind of stuff."

I gave her what I hoped was a gentle smile. "I'm sure she loved you. Overwhelming love for your child is kind of hardwired into parents, isn't it?"

She raised a shoulder in a half shrug. "Not necessarily. I mean, I love my kids like that, but not every parent does."

So Claire was a parent. I was intrigued by her, and I wanted to keep her talking as long as possible. "I'm sure your mom loved you," I said again. She nodded silently. "Tell me about your kids."

Her face lit up. "I have two—a boy and a girl. My son is Nicholas—we call him Nick. He just turned twenty-one. My daughter is Grace, and she'll be twenty in November. They're both at college—Nick's at Central and Grace is at Western."

I was surprised that her kids were grown. She must have had them young.

As if she could read my mind, Claire said, "I was young when I had them. I wasn't quite twenty when Nick was born, and I had Grace the next year. My husband and I—" She paused and rolled her eyes. "I mean my ex-husband and I—got married right out of high school. Not the greatest decision. I'm surprised our marriage lasted as long as it did."

"How long were you married?" I asked.

"Twenty-two years," she said and then gave a low whistle. "A long damn time. Too long. Adam and I started having problems after about fifteen years, but we held it together until Grace left for college. She left in September, and we were divorced in October." She sighed. "The kids took it pretty hard, but I think they both knew it was for the best."

"Still, that's got to be tough on everyone," I said.

"Yeah, it was." She tipped her head to the side and looked at me. "Hey," she said. "I was planning to stop at the café up the street after this and get a bite to eat. I'd love to have some company. Do you want to join me?"

I was quite taken with Claire. Her honesty and openness were unusual and altogether charming, and I was happy she wanted to spend more time with me. And she was an unexpected link to Vivian's time and one of the possible keys to this mystery. "Sure, I know that café. I stopped there when I came to the—" I caught myself just in time. "When I was in Olympia the last time. It's good." I'd almost said, "When I came to the cemetery last time." I needed to be careful.

"Great." She nodded toward her mother's headstone. "Let me have a few minutes here, and then we can go."

"Okay," I said. "I'll meet you in the parking lot." As I walked to my car, I stole a glance back to where Claire stood and watched as she placed the rose on top of her mom's headstone.

We rode together to the café, Claire driving. She had a sweet little Audi that probably cost more than I made in a year. We got out of the car and walked into the café, which was almost deserted. "Sit anywhere you like," the hostess told us as we came in.

We settled into a booth next to the window, and Claire looked at me with a wide smile. "Well, this is unexpected," she said. "I never imagined I'd be having lunch with someone today."

"Me neither," I said.

"One of the things that sucks about divorce is that you lose a lot of your friends," she said as she opened the menu. "My best friend was my husband's sister, and you can guess what happened there. When push came to shove, it was clear that her loyalty was to her brother, not to me."

"I'm sorry," I murmured. I felt bad for Claire. She'd had some tough breaks. She seemed so cheerful, though, which I admired. I had the tendency to ruminate about things endlessly until I got myself worked up into a frenzy. I admired people like Claire who could stay upbeat during tough times.

She looked at me over the top of her menu. "So I'm wondering if your mom told you anything about my mom." She paused and took a deep breath. "I know that probably sounds odd, but I've never met any of my mom's friends, so I'm curious."

I looked at her blankly for a moment, buying time. I'd have to make up something, as I clearly had nothing genuine to say. I gathered myself and then spoke. "Yes, my mom said Tambra was a good friend. My mom wasn't popular, and your mom took her under her wing and was very kind to her. My mom never forgot that. She was very upset when your mom, uh, passed away."

I saw Claire's sad smile and the tears sparkling in her eyes, and I knew I had said the right thing. I felt a pang of guilt at knowing it wasn't true, but at the same time, she knew so little about her mom—was there really any harm in giving her this small comfort?

"Thank you for that, Josie," she said, her voice choked with tears. "I so wish I had known her."

I nodded. "I wish you had known her too."

Claire cleared her throat and smiled. "And what about you? Tell me about yourself." She settled back against the upholstered booth.

I thought about what I should tell her. Should I tell the truth or make up a fictitious life? Given the lie I had just told, I opted for the truth. "Well, I work at a nonprofit organization in Seattle," I said. "I'm a grant writer. I write proposals to foundations to ask for money to support our programs. The organization I work for—it's called Harmony Northwest—has a music program for at-risk kids. I've been there eleven years."

"That sounds like an interesting job," she said.

"Yes, it is. I really like it there."

The server appeared at our table to take our order. We both ordered turkey sandwiches, which pleased me for some reason. As the server walked away, I looked at Claire. "What kind of work do you do?"

She laughed. "I'm a volunteer extraordinaire." I gave her a quizzical look, and she added, "I don't really work. My ex-husband is a defense attorney, and he makes the big bucks. I got a generous divorce settlement, and I don't really have to work. I volunteer at a few organizations in town to fill my time."

Well, that explained the Audi, I thought. "That must be nice," I said. "You get to feel good about what you're doing without all the workplace politics."

She nodded thoughtfully. "Yes, it's nice, but I'll admit I miss working. I worked my butt off while Adam was getting his undergrad degree and then going to law school. I was a working mom with two young kids, and even though it wasn't easy, I loved it. We lived in Seattle then. We had this beautiful little apartment in Wallingford." She sighed. "And then Adam passed the bar exam on the first try, and he got a great job at a law practice here in Olympia. So we moved back here. He was making such good money that I didn't look for another job. I became a stay-at-home mom."

Claire seemed wistful as she relayed this information. I wondered if she'd been happy with the decision to move. I was about to ask that question when the server arrived with our sandwiches. We ate silently, and my mind began to spin. I wanted to bring up the topic of Vivian, and I wasn't sure how to do it. I wanted to know how much Claire knew about the night her mom died. As I took the last bite of the first half of my sandwich, I decided to just dive in. "So, I know this is hard to talk about," I said. "But I was wondering about your mom's death."

She looked at me with raised eyebrows. "What were you wondering?"

"Well, my mom told me that your mom was, uh, murdered. Is that true?"

She looked down at her plate and nodded. "Yes, she was. My grandma told me her next-door neighbor killed her. A woman. Her name was Vivian Latham. That's all I know."

I frowned. "That's all you know? Your dad never told you anything about it?" I knew she'd told me her dad didn't like to talk about Tambra, but I couldn't imagine that he had never told Claire about the night her mom died. Wouldn't most people want to talk about something so traumatic?

Claire shook her head, her eyes still down. "No, he won't talk about it. I asked him about Vivian Latham when I was fifteen, and he got furious. He said—and excuse my language—'Don't talk to me about that fucking bitch.' I told him I wanted to know what happened, and he told me never to mention that name to him again. Then he just walked out of the room."

Thomas Delaney struck me as a strange individual indeed. "Do you still wonder what happened?" I asked gently.

She looked up and met my eyes. "Yes, of course I do. So much about my mom is a mystery. I know so little about her, and I don't even know why she died." I thought I saw the glint of tears in her eyes again. "It was really hard to grow up without a mom," she continued. "I'd at least like to know why she died. Why did that woman kill her? Why did she take my mom from me?"

An immense wave of sadness and remorse swept through me, and I felt the sting of tears in my own eyes. Not only did I know what it was like to lose a parent, but I also had the secret knowledge that, if I really had been Vivian Latham in my past life, I'd been the one to take her mom from her. But, I realized, there was more to it than that. I had just met Claire, and already I felt such tenderness for her. I sensed a deep bond with her that I couldn't quite explain. I assumed that Vivian had known Claire as a baby, but given what had happened between Vivian and Tambra, I couldn't imagine that Vivian had been close to Claire. So why did I feel such a connection with her?

I knew I might be opening a huge can of worms, as Celeste had feared, but I couldn't ignore the fact that Claire had been placed in my path for a reason. Maybe this was my chance to make some small thing right. "I might be able to help," I said, trying to keep my voice light.

She looked at me curiously. "Really? How?"

I picked at the uneaten half of my sandwich, not meeting her eyes. "Well, we could do some investigating. I know it was forty-one years ago, but I'll bet we could still dig up something. Court records, police records—that sort of thing." I looked up at her expectantly.

"Do you really think so?" she asked, her eyes brightening.

I nodded. "Sure. I'm a researcher by trade, and I'm good at it. I could help you."

"What about your vacation? I'm sure this isn't what you had in mind."

"Oh, it's fine," I said with a wave of my hand. "I don't really have any big plans. I just needed a few days away from work. It's okay."

Claire held my gaze for a long moment. "All right," she finally said. "Let's do it."

16

As Claire drove me back to the cemetery to get my car, she asked me where I was staying. I told her I'd made a reservation for four nights at the Capital Inn.

"Absolutely not," she said firmly. "You'll stay with me. We're connected. Our moms were friends. I can't let you stay in a hotel when I have plenty of room."

I was taken aback. I'd just met this woman a couple of hours ago, and she knew next to nothing about me. And much of what she thought she knew was a lie. "No, that's okay," I said. "I don't want to intrude."

"You're not intruding," she said. "I'm rattling around in that huge house all alone, and I'd love the company. And I just redecorated the guest room." She glanced at me. "Please, Josie."

I frowned. "Claire, you hardly know anything about me. It's not a good practice to ask a virtual stranger to stay at your house."

She shook her head. "You're not a stranger. Our moms were friends, and that practically makes you my friend." She paused. "And if we're really going to investigate my mom's death together, it would be a lot easier if you're staying with me, don't you think?"

I shrugged, still not convinced. "Yes, I suppose so."

She took a deep breath and then looked at me. "I know it seems strange, but I feel, I don't know, like you're a connection to my mom,

I guess, and I haven't felt that in a long time. It would mean a lot to me if you'd stay with me."

I felt a wave of empathy toward her, and I touched her arm. "I understand," I said.

She smiled and poked me with her elbow. "And besides all that, I'm an excellent judge of character, and I can tell you're a good person."

I was thoroughly charmed by Claire, in spite of my misgivings and the guilt I felt about lying to her. I thought about her offer. Although staying with someone I scarcely knew wasn't something I would normally do, I couldn't deny this inexplicable affection I felt for her. Somehow that affection alleviated my usual fears. And it would be nice to save the four hundred bucks. "All right, Claire," I finally said. "If you insist."

"I insist, so it's settled," she said as we arrived at the cemetery.

She told me to follow her to her house. I started my car, and we pulled out of the parking lot. We drove for three or four miles, making several turns. Finally she swung into the driveway of a sprawling rambler, and I parked beside her. I surveyed the house. It was nice—a colonial blue color with sharp white trim.

I got out of the car and grabbed my suitcase off the back seat. As I followed Claire up the walk, I scanned the tidy yard, which had several rosebushes in full bloom. I noticed an especially beautiful pink rosebush and wondered if that's where she got the roses she brought to her mother's grave.

We walked together up to the front door, and as Claire put the key in the lock, I heard a dog barking. She opened the door, and a black lab ran up to greet her.

"Hi, Lola," she said, leaning down to nuzzle the dog's head. "How's my beautiful girl?" Lola licked Claire's face in welcome, her tail wagging furiously.

Lola noticed me standing behind Claire. She eyed me curiously, and I offered the back of my hand to her. She sniffed it and then wagged her tail.

"Lola likes you!" Claire said with delight. "Do you have a dog?"

I shook my head. "No, I have a cat. I love dogs, though."

"That's good," she said. "I forgot to tell you about Lola when I asked you to stay."

"No worries," I said.

She showed me to the guest room, which was small but tastefully decorated. There was a queen-sized bed with a nightstand on either side and an adjoining bathroom. "This is nice, Claire," I said. "Thank you so much."

"You're welcome," she said. "I'm happy to have a house guest. I get lonely here all by myself."

"I'm sure you do," I said with a sympathetic smile.

She touched my shoulder. "So I'll leave you to get settled, and then why don't you come out to the kitchen and we'll have a glass of wine."

"That sounds lovely," I said, hefting my suitcase onto the bed. As she left I pulled my phone out of my pocket and called to cancel my hotel reservation. Once that was done, I dialed Celeste's number. She picked up on the third ring.

"Hi, Jo," she said.

"Celeste, the most amazing thing happened," I said in a quiet voice. I didn't want Claire to overhear me.

"What?"

I told her about meeting Claire, my lie about our mothers' friendship, and the invitation to stay at Claire's house.

"Jo, don't you think that's kind of weird?" Celeste asked. "Would you ask a complete stranger to stay with you?"

"Well, no, probably not," I admitted. "But she thinks we're connected through our mothers. And she's lonely. Both her kids are grown, and she and her husband got divorced last fall. She wants the company." I paused. "And I told her I can help her figure out the mystery of her mom's death. When you think about all that stuff together, then it makes sense that she'd want me to stay here."

She sighed. "Okay, I get it, but be careful. Don't forget that you really don't know anything about this woman."

"I know I like her," I said. "And don't worry. I'll be careful." I didn't want to tell Celeste about the connection I felt to Claire. I knew she wouldn't understand. I told her I had to go, and I hung up the phone.

I grabbed my iPad out of my suitcase and wandered out to look for Claire. Part of me was still in a state of disbelief that I had met Tambra's daughter and I was staying in her house. I had enough presence of mind to know that this was an opportunity I couldn't let pass me by. And by meeting Claire I'd learned that figuring out the mystery of Vivian and Tambra would benefit not just me but her too. Now my challenge would be to engage her in the mystery and enlist her help. I wasn't sure if I could do that without telling her the whole story, but I'd try.

Finally I found the kitchen and Claire. She was uncorking the wine, and she turned as she heard me.

"You found me," she said and then pulled the cork from the bottle. Lola was at her side.

"Yeah, this is a big house. It's probably three times bigger than my house," I said as I set my iPad on the counter.

She laughed as she began to pour the wine into two elegant-looking glasses. "I hope you like chardonnay," she said. "This one's a 2010 from the Napa Valley, and it's amazing."

I was a gin-and-tonic girl who knew next to nothing about wine. I rarely bought wine and had never spent more than ten dollars on a bottle. I had a feeling this one had cost much more than that. "Sure," I said. "I'd love to try it."

As she finished pouring the wine, I looked around the huge kitchen. My eyes traveled from the enormous Viking range to the wide stainless-steel refrigerator, and then to the gleaming quartz countertops and rich wood cabinetry. "This is a nice kitchen," I said.

"Thanks," she said. "It was great when the kids were still living at home and Adam and I were together. We did a lot of entertaining, and the kids had friends over. Now it's just me, and it's no fun cooking for one. I end up having frozen dinners a lot."

I grinned. "Yeah, I do that too. Grilled cheese is my best friend."

She chuckled as she handed me a glass of wine. I took a sip and was pleasantly surprised by the smooth, fruity taste.

"I like that," I said.

"It's one of my favorites," she said as she picked up something from the counter. "Let's go out and sit on the deck."

I followed her and Lola through the kitchen and large eating area and out the sliding glass door. The enormous deck had a sweeping view of the beautiful park-like back yard. She must employ a landscaping service to keep up the front and back yards. Somehow I couldn't imagine her pulling weeds and firing up the lawn mower.

Claire walked over to a large glass table topped with a colorful umbrella, and motioned to a chair. "Please sit," she said. I sat down, and she took the seat across from me, Lola at her feet.

"So I was wondering why your kids aren't here," I said. "Aren't they off school for the summer?"

She sat back in her chair and took a sip of wine. "Well, Nick decided to stay in Ellensburg this summer to do an internship, and Grace is in Europe with her father right now. They'll both be back in late August, and then a few weeks later they'll go back to school for fall quarter."

"Oh, I see." I noticed that Claire was holding something in her hand—whatever it was that she'd picked up off the kitchen counter. "What do you have there?" I asked.

She gave me a shy smile and then turned the item around. I could see that it was a photo. "I just wanted to show you this," she said, leaning forward and handing the photo to me. The photo was of a pretty blond woman holding a chubby baby about eight or nine months old. I felt the hair on the back of my neck stand up, and a chill swept through me. Tambra. She looked so much like Claire that it was uncanny. I studied Tambra's face: her radiant smile, her big blue eyes, her long blond hair. I guessed that the baby was Claire. The two of them looked happy.

"That's my mom," she said softly. "And she's holding me."

I nodded silently, mesmerized by the photo. I thought of Vivian then, asking myself yet again what had happened to lead her to kill this beautiful, vibrant, and happy woman. It defied explanation. "Who took this photo?" I asked.

"My dad," she said. "That's the only picture I have of the two of us together. That was taken about three months before she died."

"She's beautiful," I breathed, awestruck. "You look so much like her."

She nodded. "Yeah, I don't see the resemblance like other people do, but so many different people have told me how much I look like her that I've come to believe it."

"You do," I said. "Trust me." I handed the photo back to Claire. I wanted a copy of it, but I thought she'd think that was strange. "What else do you have of hers?" I asked.

She shrugged. "Not much, really. I have the baby book she kept for me, her high-school yearbooks, and a few of her books and toys from when she was a kid." She paused. "Oh, and her writing desk. The desk was her graduation present from her parents. My dad was going to sell it at a yard sale, and I had a fit. It never occurred to him that I might want it."

"Of course you would," I said gently. I wondered again about Thomas Delaney. Why did he want to distance himself from Tambra? Was talking about her just too painful for him, or was he trying to erase her from his life?

"I don't use the desk," Claire said. "It's up in the attic. I just like knowing I have it."

"Was there anything interesting in it?" I asked.

She shook her head. "No, it was empty. Either my dad took everything out or there never was anything there. How would I ever know? I know I didn't want to ask him about it."

"I see," I said. I felt sad for Claire. I couldn't imagine what it had been like to grow up without a mom. My own mom had always been such an important part of my life, and at that moment I realized how fortunate I was. Granted, I knew what it was like to lose a parent, but I didn't know what it was like to lose a parent when I was so young that I didn't have any memories.

"Tell me something more about yourself, Josie," she said, interrupting my thoughts. "All I know about you is your job. I noticed you aren't wearing a wedding ring. Are you single?"

I nodded and looked down at my lap. "Yes, I'm single." I waited anxiously for her next question. I knew I'd have to come out to Claire eventually, but I didn't look forward to that. Coming out was so often looked at as this significant, one-time event, but really it was a never-ending process. I'd come out to more people than I could ever count—family, friends, neighbors, coworkers, doctors, college professors, strangers on the bus. The vast majority of the world assumed everyone was straight, and sooner or later you had to set them straight. Don't get me wrong—I wasn't ashamed of who I was—but there was always the possibility that someone wouldn't respond positively, and that wasn't a good feeling. It didn't happen often, but it did happen. I had a college friend who never spoke to me again after I came out to her, and one of my neighbors—an Evangelical Christian—wouldn't make eye contact with me, let alone speak to me, when I passed him on the sidewalk. And of course there was my own sister, Gwen, who had let it be known that she didn't approve of my "lifestyle," as she called it. As much as I wished the world was 100 percent accepting, I knew that wasn't likely to happen in my lifetime.

Claire sought out my eyes. "And do you have a boyfriend?" She paused. "Or a girlfriend?"

I exhaled in a rush—I hadn't realized I'd been holding my breath—and relief flooded though me. Claire was even cooler than I'd first thought. "For me it would be a girlfriend," I said. "And no, I don't."

"Well, I'm happy to know that when you do find the right one, you can legally marry her. Isn't that awesome?"

"It is awesome," I said.

"Have you ever been serious with anyone?" she asked.

I nodded. "Yeah, I had a serious relationship for five years—her name was Erica—but we broke up. She didn't want kids, and I did. That was a deal breaker for me."

"That's a big thing to disagree about, so I think you were right to end it," Claire said.

"It was hard, though. Erica was perfect for me otherwise. It shocked me that she was so vehemently opposed to having kids."

"Some people just absolutely don't want to be parents," she said. "I can't relate either, but I've had a few friends like that." She took a sip of wine and looked at me curiously. "So you haven't had a serious relationship since then?"

I shook my head. "No, not really. I was seeing a woman at work for a while, and I've had a few dates here and there, but nothing serious."

"Well, I'm sure you'll find someone you want to spend the rest of your life with. I know I just met you, but I can tell you're special."

I smiled. "Thanks."

She took a deep breath. "I should warn you that my dad is coming over tomorrow—his name is Tom—and he's a big-time homophobe. I wouldn't say anything about this while he's here."

"Okay, I won't," I said. I tried to keep my voice light, but my mind was spinning. Thomas—Tom—was coming here? I was going to meet Tambra's husband? That possibility had never crossed my mind. I could feel my heart beginning to race at the thought. "When is he coming over?"

"Early afternoon, I think," she said. "I haven't seen him in a while, and he likes to come over in the summer and drink beer on the deck. He sold his house a few years back and moved into this crappy little trailer, so coming here on a summer afternoon is like a mini vacation for him."

"Yeah, your back yard is like a park," I said, looking around her yard appreciatively. "Did your dad ever remarry?"

"No, never," she said. "I'm not sure why. He doesn't talk about that stuff."

"Hmm," I murmured. I had wanted to get Claire over to Tambra's old neighborhood tomorrow. I hadn't thought through how I'd orchestrate that, and now that I knew Tom was coming over, I was annoyed by the added complication. And I felt nothing but apprehension at the prospect of meeting him. I tried to bring my thoughts back to what Claire had actually said so I could make an appropriate response. "For some people there's only one person for them," I said. "Once your mom died, your dad probably couldn't see himself with anyone else. She was his one true love, and no one else would do."

She frowned. "Yeah, maybe. Since my dad won't talk about her, I honestly don't know how he felt about her." She paused and then looked at me. "And I don't know if you've picked up on it by now, but my dad and I don't get along very well."

I hadn't picked up on it, actually, which surprised me. Usually I was pretty perceptive about such things. "No, I didn't realize that. Why don't you get along with him?"

She shrugged. "I'm not sure," she said. "He's always been, I don't know, distant, I guess. He came to my soccer games and helped me with homework and stuff like that, but there was always a wall up with him." She looked at an imaginary spot over my shoulder, a faraway look in her eyes. "He went through the motions with me, but I don't think his heart was ever in it." She paused to pick up her wineglass and take a sip. "Once I got to my teen years, I felt almost no connection with him. I started skipping school, drinking, getting shitty grades. I even experimented with drugs. We had some bad arguments. He can get so angry, and that scared me." She looked at me with a sad smile. "I don't know—it's hard to explain."

"I think I know what you mean," I said, watching her expression closely. She looked as if she might cry.

"I just wanted a mom so badly, I guess," she continued. "I felt like I'd been abandoned by both my parents. I felt alone. And then I married Adam right out of high school, thinking I'd finally have what I craved—someone who loved me, a family, a place to belong." She gave a harsh laugh. "But then Adam proved to be an asshole who was only interested in what I could do for him."

I looked at her, speechless. From what she'd said so far, I hadn't gotten that Adam was an asshole. Apparently I needed to hone my skill of reading between the lines.

"I worked to put him through law school," she said, and then hesitated. "Well, that is, until we got a surprise windfall and my burden got a lot lighter. But I worked my ass off for five years for him, and do you know he never once said thank you? He acted like what I'd done for him was what I owed him."

Adam did sound like an asshole. "And that's why you got divorced?" I asked.

"Well, it took a while for that to happen," she said. "But eventually I realized he was all about his career. All I was to him was a pretty woman on his arm, and the kids—they were another box to check. That's why I don't feel guilty about any of this." She swept her arm around to take in the house and yard. "I paid my dues with that asshole. I deserve this."

I sat back in my chair, surprised at her brutal honesty. I didn't know how to respond.

"I got two wonderful kids out of the deal, so I'm happy about that," she continued. "But a happy marriage—I've never known that."

I drew in a deep breath. "Claire, I'm not sure what to say."

"You don't have to say anything. I'm just venting, I guess. Things haven't turned out the way I thought they would, and I'm just sad about that."

"I'm sorry," I said helplessly.

"But enough about that," she said with forced cheer. "Tell me your ideas about researching my mom's death." She sat up straight and looked at me expectantly.

Ah, from one happy topic to the next, I thought. "Well, here's what I was thinking," I began. "I have a subscription to this newspaper service—I use it for work—and I'm pretty sure the Olympia paper is available there." Of course, I knew it was, but I had to appear as if I were discovering all this for the first time. "So these newspapers go back decades, and if they have the paper, then I think we could find some news coverage about your mom's, um, murder." I hated using that word, even though I knew it was accurate. It was an ugly word.

"Okay, that sounds promising," Claire said.

"Have you ever read anything about what happened?" I asked.

She shook her head. "No, nothing. Actually, I didn't know I could do that. I mean, it was forty-one years ago, and I've always thought of it as ancient and inaccessible history."

"Ancient, yes. Inaccessible, no," I said. "I'll be right back. Let me go grab my iPad." I hurried into the kitchen, grabbed my iPad off the counter, and returned to Claire. I opened the browser, logged on to the newspaper site, and looked at her. "When did she die?"

"August eleventh, 1974," she answered.

I entered the search terms and found the correct result. "Here it is," I said in a low voice.

"Seriously?" she asked excitedly.

I handed her my iPad and watched as she read the article. I'd found the first one I'd read the night all this started—the one that reported Tambra's death and Vivian's arrest.

Claire finished reading and looked up at me openmouthed. "Holy shit," she said. "I just got goose bumps."

I nodded. "There were two other articles that came up with this one," I said. "Let me find them for you." I took back the iPad, navigated to the search results, and found the article about Vivian being formally charged. Claire read that one, and then I found the last one about Vivian's trial and conviction. She scanned that one and then looked up at me, her eyes wide.

"Josie, I can't believe you found those articles so easily. How come I never thought of that?"

I shrugged. "Plenty of people wouldn't think of looking for something like this online. Like I said, I love to do research, and I'm good at it."

"I guess so," she said, looking down again at the article about Vivian's trial. "She's dead, you know," she murmured.

"Who?" I asked, even though I knew full well who she was talking about.

She raised her eyes to look at me. "Vivian Latham," she said. "She died in prison. Suicide. That's what my grandma told me."

"Really?" I said, feigning surprise.

"Yeah, apparently she killed herself just a few months after she started her prison sentence. She hanged herself with a bed sheet." Claire's gaze flickered away from mine.

So my suspicion had been right—she had hanged herself. "Oh my goodness," I said.

She looked at me, a fierce expression in her eyes. "Yeah, she took the easy way out. She was a fucking coward." I saw the glisten of tears in her eyes.

I didn't know what to say, so I said nothing. I covered Claire's hand with my own and gave her what I hoped was a sympathetic smile. She stared at the article again, shaking her head.

"What about that house?" I asked. "Walnut Avenue, where you lived. Have you ever seen it?"

Claire wiped the corner of her eye with her fingertip. "No, I didn't even know where it was until now. My dad never talked about it."

"Would you like to see it?" I asked, trying to sound casual.

"Yes, I would," she said. "Will you go with me?"

I nodded. "Of course I will. That could be the first step in our investigation."

She grinned in spite of her upset. "This is beginning to sound like an adventure."

I shrugged. "Well, it kind of is, isn't it?"

"Yeah, I guess it is," she said. "So tomorrow morning we'll go to the old neighborhood and poke around, okay?" She looked at me expectantly.

"Yep, sounds like a plan," I said with resolve.

17

I awoke with a start on Sunday morning. I stared around the room wide-eyed, not sure where I was. Then the events of the day before came flooding back, and I remembered that I was at Claire's house. I had met Tambra's daughter yesterday. As I lay there trying to wake up, the wisp of a dream suddenly floated through my mind. In the dream I'd been walking beside a blond woman who was pushing a stroller. She had been looking at me and laughing. Had it been Claire? I replayed the scene again in my mind, and my gut told me it had been Tambra.

My eyes darted to the alarm clock. Was it 4:04 a.m.? But no, the clock said 7:39 a.m., and I noticed now that bright sunlight was streaming through the blinds and there was a chorus of birdsong outside. That was odd, I thought. I'd had a dream of Tambra that didn't involve blood and screaming. She'd been laughing, and I'd been walking beside her, and I had felt happy. Was that Vivian she'd been walking beside? Had that been Claire in the stroller? Again, my gut told me yes. Was this proof that Vivian and Tambra had liked each other—at least at some point? My mind repeated the sound of Tambra's happy laugh, and I decided they had.

I closed my eyes and lay for several more minutes, trying to conjure up more of the dream, but nothing came. Finally I gave up, rose from the bed, and slipped on my robe. I wandered down the hallway, through the maze of rooms, and into the kitchen. Claire was sitting at the kitchen table drinking a cup of coffee, Lola lying at her feet.

"Good morning," she said brightly.

"Hey, hi, good morning," I said in a gravelly voice. "You got more coffee? I'm worthless without my morning coffee."

She laughed and pointed to the coffee maker on the counter. "Help yourself," she said. "The mugs are in the cabinet above."

"Thanks." I shuffled over to the coffee maker and pulled a purple mug from the cabinet. I filled it and took a sip.

"There's creamer in the fridge," she said.

"No thanks," I answered. "I'm a purist. I like mine strong and black."

Claire laughed again. "Come and sit," she said, patting the chair beside her. I moved over to the table and sat down. Lola raised her head and sniffed at my ankle before lying back down. I reached down to scratch her head, and she let out a heavy sigh.

"Did you sleep well?" Claire asked.

"Actually, yes," I said, nodding. "I'm not always the best sleeper, but I did sleep well. It's so quiet here."

"Yeah, it is quiet. Sometimes it's spooky being in this huge house all alone, though."

"I understand," I said. "I sometimes get scared in my little nine-hundred-square-foot house, so I can only imagine what it would be like in a huge house like this."

"Yeah, I liked it better when I wasn't here alone." Her eyes had a faraway look, and then she shook her head as if to clear her mind. "But enough about that. What can I get you for breakfast?"

I glanced at the spoon, empty bowl, and half gallon of milk on the table and figured she'd had cereal. I didn't want to be a bother, and cereal seemed safe. "Cereal?" I said.

"Sure. I have Honey Nut Cheerios, shredded wheat, and raisin bran," she said.

"Honey Nut Cheerios are good for me," I answered.

Claire stood, walked into the kitchen, and came back a minute later with a box of cereal, a spoon, and a bowl, which she set in front of me. "Here you go," she said, sitting down beside me.

"Thanks," I said. I poured the cereal in the bowl, added a splash of milk, and began eating.

"So, Josie, do you have any siblings?" she asked.

I nodded, my mouth full. I swallowed and looked at her. "Yeah, I have a younger sister named Gwendolyn. We call her Gwen." I paused. "Well, I call her Gwen. My mom doesn't. She calls her Gwendolyn, just like she calls me Josephine even though everyone else calls me Josie."

She laughed. "Gwendolyn and Josephine. How regal."

I smirked. "Yeah, I think that was the idea."

"Are you and your sister close?"

I shook my head. "No, not really. She's, well, shall we say, ultra conservative, and we don't see eye to eye on things. We see each other at family gatherings, and we stay in touch on Facebook, but I wouldn't say we're close."

She nodded. "Oh. That's too bad."

I raised a shoulder in a half shrug. "Yeah, I've gotten used to it. C'est la vie, as they say."

"And your father? Where's he?" she asked.

I lowered my eyes to look at my bowl. "My dad passed away when I was fifteen. A heart attack."

Claire covered her mouth with her hand. "Oh my goodness, Josie, I'm so sorry."

"Thanks," I said softly. "That was a hard loss. I still miss him."

She made a sympathetic noise. "Did your mom remarry?"

I shook my head. "No, she's had a lot of boyfriends, but she's never married any of them. She moved to Florida five years ago, and she's just enjoying the sun and dating different men."

She frowned. "Florida? I thought your mom lived in Everett."

Oh shit, I thought. Major screw up. How would I get out of this one? "She's a, she's a—what do you call those people?" I hesitated, trying to remember the term. "A snowbird, that's it. She's a snowbird. She goes to Florida in October and then comes back here in May."

I noticed the frown hadn't left Claire's face, but she nodded. "Okay, yeah, I know some people who do that. Around here people usually go to Arizona or California, though."

I shrugged, trying to seem casual. "She's a real estate agent. She found a great deal on a condo in Florida."

Claire nodded again, but I was afraid she doubted my story. I absolutely needed to be more careful. I really liked Claire and had become comfortable around her, but I couldn't forget that I wouldn't be telling her the whole truth—at least not yet. I needed to be on my guard.

By ten we were belted into the Audi and on our way to Walnut Street. Claire had punched the address into her GPS, and the mechanical voice played through her car speakers, telling her which turns to make.

Fifteen minutes later we pulled up in front of the house. It looked the same as it had a few weeks ago when I was here. Suddenly I remembered my awkward visit with Mrs. Reed, and my stomach tightened. I prayed she wouldn't be around. If she was, I'd have to make sure she didn't see me. I didn't want another screwup like the one I'd made at breakfast. I quickly scanned the street but didn't see a soul. Maybe I was in luck.

Claire turned off the ignition and looked at me over the top of her sunglasses. "Here we are," she said.

"Yep, here we are," I said.

She peered at the house through the car window. "It's smaller than I was expecting."

I shrugged. "Well, this looks like an older neighborhood. Houses were smaller back in those days."

She nodded. "Yeah, I guess so." She moved her sunglasses to the top of her head and looked at me with raised eyebrows. "Shall we?"

"Let's go," I said, and we both opened our doors and climbed out.

Claire began walking slowly toward the house, her eyes taking in the large front window and then the overgrown yard. "Do you think someone lives here?" she asked. "It looks pretty run down."

Of course I knew the answer to that question, but I needed to seem like I was seeing it for the first time. I surveyed the house and then shook my head. "I doubt it. It looks empty to me."

"I'll go check." She took off for the front door before I could respond. She knocked on the door and waited. After several seconds she knocked again and then turned back to look at me. I raised my hands and shrugged, hoping she would give up. Instead she moved to the front window and peered inside. I knew the window was bare and she'd be able to see inside and discover that it was empty.

She looked back at me, where I was still standing on the sidewalk. "It looks empty," she shouted.

I nearly shushed her but caught myself just in time. I didn't want to draw attention to us—especially not from Mrs. Reed—but I also didn't want Claire to wonder why I was so anxious. I motioned her back with my hand, and a few seconds later she was standing beside me on the sidewalk. "What now?" she asked.

"We could go around back and see if there are other windows to peek through," I suggested. I was hoping the slider was still unlocked and we could get in that way.

"Do you think we should?" she asked with furrowed brows.

I looked up and down the street, seeing no one. "I don't know why not. There's no one around."

"That's true," she said distractedly, and I noticed her eyes were on Mrs. Reed's house. "Do you think that's where Vivian Latham lived?" she asked, nodding toward the house.

I looked at Mrs. Reed's house. "I doubt it," I said. "That house is pretty big, and Vivian Latham was a single woman. She wouldn't need a house that big."

Claire stared at me, a confused look in her eyes. "How do you know she was a single woman?"

Oh crap, not again, I thought. I looked at her dumbly, trying to come up with a response. "I don't know," I finally said. "I just assumed that, I guess, because the newspaper article didn't say she was married."

She looked at me for a long moment, and I struggled to hold eye contact with her. This time she chose to ignore my explanation and said, "C'mon, let's go around back." I was relieved she hadn't pressed the issue.

We started up the driveway without speaking. As we came to the windowed door off the kitchen, Claire bounded up to it and looked inside. "Looks like a kitchen and dining area," she said.

"Oh," was all I said. I didn't trust myself to say more right now.

We continued up the driveway and around the back of the house, and Claire looked in the bedroom windows. I pointed at the slider. "There's a sliding glass door back here. Do you want to try it?"

She frowned. "That's breaking and entering."

"There's no one around," I said. "It'll be fine."

"I'm sure it's locked anyway," she said, and then her mouth dropped open as I pulled the door handle and it slid open. "Well, I'll be damned."

We walked quietly into the house, entering the room that I was sure had been Tambra and Tom's. I went through the motions of trying the light switch, knowing it wouldn't come on. I opened my phone's flashlight app and shone the light around the room.

"Looks like a bedroom," she said, her eyes traveling along the walls.

"Yeah, that's what I was thinking too."

"Do you think this was my parents' room?" she asked.

"Probably," I said. "But I think we'll have to look around some more before we know for sure."

She nodded as she walked slowly from the room. She turned right and continued down the hallway to the other bedroom. I followed closely behind. As she entered the second bedroom, she turned back toward me. "Yeah, that must have been my parents' bedroom. This one's much smaller." I lit up the room with my phone as she looked around. "This was my room," she said in a shaky voice.

I felt her emotion, and I put my hand on her shoulder. "Claire, we don't have to do this," I said.

"I want to," she said, her voice barely more than a whisper.

We stood side by side, neither of us speaking. Her eyes darted around the room, trying to commit it to memory, I guessed. "Want to see the rest of the house?" I finally asked.

"Sure," she said as she turned and followed me out to the main area of the house. We stood between the kitchen and living room and surveyed the space. She took a few steps to the left and looked at the kitchen. "Small kitchen," she said.

"Yeah, it is," I agreed.

She walked into the living room, where she stood gazing at the large fireplace. "Wow, that thing is huge," she said. She turned around and looked at me. "Josie, I know this sounds crazy, but I think I remember that fireplace."

I shrugged. "I suppose that's possible. I mean, it's not impossible, right?"

"Right," she said. She motioned toward the hearth. "That's where my mom died, you know."

Actually, I hadn't known. I had suspected that from my dream, but I hadn't known for sure. "Did your grandma tell you that?" I asked.

She nodded. "Yeah. She didn't tell me a lot of details about that night—she didn't want to upset me—but she did tell me that." She walked over and leaned down to run her hand across the hearth.

I stood silently in the living room, trying to quell my own feelings. As soon as I'd seen the front door, images from the dream I'd had early Friday morning had filled my mind. In my mind's eye, I saw Tambra running toward the door—trying to get away, I guessed—and the hand coming out and grabbing her. I stared at the front door now, realizing that had very likely really happened, and I shuddered, imagining Tambra's terror.

"Josie!" Claire said loudly.

My head whipped around to look at her, suddenly aware that she'd been trying to get my attention and I'd been lost in thought. "Sorry, Claire, I was daydreaming."

"Are you ready to go?" she asked, a hint of annoyance in her voice.

"Sure, I'm ready if you are."

She looked around one last time and nodded. "Yeah, I'm ready."

We slipped out the back door and then walked to her car. We both got in, and Claire started the Audi. As she drove slowly down the street, we passed the house I believed had been Vivian's. She braked and then pointed at the house. "I'll bet that's it. Vivian Latham's house."

"You're probably right," I said, leaning forward to see the house better out the front windshield.

"It's so nondescript," she said.

I looked at the house. It was small—probably no more than five hundred square feet—and painted a flat gray color. I suddenly had a vision of the inside of the house and realized I knew exactly what it looked like: living room just inside the front door, kitchen to the left, bathroom and bedroom straight back. My heart sank. I hadn't wanted to admit to myself that I'd been harboring a secret hope that something here would convince me that I had been wrong—that there was another explanation for the outcome of my session with Susan. Instead, what I'd learned so far had only made me more certain that Vivian and I shared the same soul.

I glanced at Claire, who was still studying the house. I felt guilty that I'd deceived her, but at the same time I couldn't imagine telling her my real interest in her mother and Vivian. Yet I knew at some point I would have to. I wished that day was far off, but in my heart I knew it wasn't. How would she respond? Would she believe my strange tale, or would she think I was a complete wacko? I really liked Claire, and there was no denying the indescribable draw I felt to her. I desperately wanted her to believe me, but she struck me as a pragmatic type, and I couldn't quite imagine it. More likely she would respond with anger, contempt, or fear—or all three. And that meant she wouldn't want to see me again. I sighed deeply.

"What's wrong?" she asked, looking at me with concern.

I shook my head. "Nothing. I'm fine."

She glanced at her watch. "We'd better go. My dad will be at my house soon." She put the car in gear and continued down the street.

Anxiety gripped me as I thought of meeting Tom Delaney. Would he recognize me? That was an odd thing to wonder about—even for me—but didn't someone's essence remain the same from life to life? Something about me might seem familiar to him, and not in a good way. I'd killed his wife, after all.

"He'll probably be there for a few hours, so brace yourself," Claire said and then paused. She looked at me with pleading eyes. "Josie, please don't say anything to him about my mom or about what we did today. He won't respond well, and he doesn't need to know."

I touched her arm. "Don't worry. I won't." I hesitated. "Who are you going to say I am, though?"

She shrugged. "I don't know. An old friend from high school? I know you're younger than I am, but do you think he'd buy that?"

I laughed. "Well, I guessed you to be about my age when I first saw you, so we look more like former classmates than you might think."

She glanced at me and grinned. "Really? That's pretty good. I'll take it." We both laughed. "Okay, I'll just say you're an old friend and you're in town for the weekend. Sound good?"

"Sounds good," I said.

We drove in silence the rest of the way. As we turned down her street, I saw a battered old pickup in her driveway.

"Oh shit," she said. "He's already there."

She turned into the driveway and shut off the engine, and we both got out. A large, beefy man was sitting in her porch swing, and he stood as we headed up the sidewalk. As I got nearer to him and began to make out his features, something inside me recoiled violently. I stopped in my tracks, feeling as if I'd just been punched in the gut. My body vibrated, and my heart raced. I felt as if every nerve was standing at attention.

"Claire!" Tom Delaney said in a booming voice. "How's my girl?"

Claire climbed the steps to the porch and gave her dad a hug. "Hi, Dad. You're early."

He chuckled. "Yeah, I know. I was in the area, and I didn't think you'd mind."

He glanced at me curiously, but I hung back, apprehensive about getting any closer to him. Claire reached for my arm and pulled me up the stairs. "Dad, this is Josie."

He moved toward me and extended his hand. I reluctantly shook it, flinching at his touch and his viselike grip. I fought the impulse to yank my hand back.

He gave me a broad smile. "Tom Delaney," he said loudly. His cold, pale blue eyes locked with mine, and I noticed a shadow cross his face. His smile faded, and he looked at Claire. "Who is she?" he asked bluntly.

She touched my shoulder. "Dad, Josie's an old friend of mine. She's in town for the weekend."

"I don't remember you having a friend named Josie," he said in a gruff voice.

She laughed nervously. "Well, you didn't know all my friends."

He made a guttural sound and said, "Yeah, I guess not. Nice to meet you, Josie."

He nodded toward me, but I noticed he wouldn't look at me now. Something was definitely going on, even if he wasn't consciously aware of it. He'd recognized something in my eyes—I was sure of it. But my own reaction to Tom was what surprised me. As soon as I'd seen him, I'd had a visceral response, making me wonder about Vivian's history with Tom. I scanned my feelings, trying to find something to grab on to, but nothing came. I just knew I'd taken an instant dislike to him, and I was already counting the minutes until he'd leave.

Claire shepherded us into the house and then to the kitchen. She opened the refrigerator, handed her dad a beer, and then poured two tall glasses of wine. She handed one to me and then grabbed the other one, and we all moved out to the deck. I was happy to see Lola come bounding toward us. She'd been cooped up in the back yard while we'd been on our outing. I scratched her back, relieved to have something else to focus on for the moment.

"Pretty, as usual, Claire," Tom said, surveying the yard with appreciation.

"Thanks, Dad. Ted does it all, so I can hardly take credit."

So she did have a gardener, as I'd suspected. Tom sat down, and Claire and I followed. He looked at me, a frown on his face. "So where do you live, Josie?" he asked.

"In Seattle," I said. I remembered the lie Claire had told about me being an old friend, and I quickly added, "I moved there to go to college, and I just stayed."

"And what do you do for work?"

I noticed he was looking near me but not at me. His eyes seemed to be focused on the top of my head. "I work at a nonprofit," I answered. "I'm a grant writer."

He nodded, saying nothing. "And what's new with you, girlie?" he asked, grinning and reaching over to slap Claire on the leg.

She gave me a look and then turned toward her dad. "Not much, really. Still volunteering and enjoying spending my ex-husband's money."

He laughed and took a swig of beer. "Yeah, he turned out to be a real son of a bitch, didn't he?"

"Yep," she said dryly, raising her glass to take a sip of wine. "And what have you been up to, Dad?"

He shrugged. "Not much. Same ol', same ol'."

He continued talking to Claire, but I stopped listening. I was aware of the low murmur of his voice followed by the lighter tones of Claire's, but my attention was on the physicality of Tom Delaney. It was painful for me to look at him, but I couldn't help myself. I already knew he was around seventy years old, and the deep lines around his eyes and mouth seemed in keeping with someone that age. His skin was pale, but his cheeks had the florid look of someone who drank too much. His hair was gray and close-cropped. Given his light skin and pale blue eyes, I guessed he'd been blond in his younger days. He was tall—over six feet—and hefty. His round belly hung over the waistband of his jeans. I guessed he'd been somewhat handsome in his youth, although not in a classic way.

His looks weren't the only thing I didn't care for; his personality also rubbed me the wrong way. He was the kind of person I normally avoided—loud, crass, and pushy. I thought of the photo I'd seen of Tambra. That beautiful, vibrant woman had been married to this man? That seemed almost inconceivable. What had she possibly seen in him?

"Josie?" Claire said loudly.

I shook my head, bringing my attention back to the present. "What? Sorry."

"I asked if you want another glass of wine," she said.

I looked at her. "Oh, no, thank you. I'm fine." My gaze fell on Tom Delaney then, and I was unnerved to see his cold blue eyes boring into mine. "I know who you are," his stare said. I shuddered and looked away.

The rest of the afternoon passed uneventfully, although I noticed that Tom drank a lot. He'd had four beers. He didn't show the effects of the alcohol, and I assumed he was used to drinking that much.

Mercifully, at four o'clock he stood and announced he had to go. Claire stood too and said she'd walk him out. He walked heavily across the deck and then pulled open the sliding glass door. I thought he was going to leave without saying another word to me, but then he glanced back over his shoulder and said in a low voice, "Nice to meet you, Josie."

"Likewise," I said, although nothing could be further from the truth. I'd be perfectly happy if I never saw Tom Delaney again.

18

Vivian
February-March 1974

During the first three weeks in my new house, it didn't take long for me to fall into a routine. I woke like clockwork at seven thirty each morning, shuffled out to the kitchen to start my coffee, and ate breakfast while I waited for it to brew. When the coffee was done, I poured a cup and went out to the porch, rain or shine.

The porch was my favorite thing about the house, and I enjoyed sitting there and watching the neighborhood come to life. I knew that Mr. Reed left for work precisely at eight thirty every morning and that the school bus stopped at the corner to pick up the neighborhood children at eight forty. I had also caught a glimpse of Tambra's husband, Tom, leaving for work at eight twenty. He never looked my way, but I could see that he was a tall, brawny man with dirty blond hair.

On mornings that it wasn't raining, Tambra would emerge from her house at nine o'clock with Claire in her arms. She'd slide Claire into the stroller she kept on the porch and push the stroller out to the sidewalk. She'd always stop in front of my house and call out, "Good morning, Vivian. Want to walk with us?" I always said yes, and we'd walk up and down the quiet streets of our shared neighborhood and chat about politics or music or last night's TV shows. I hadn't made a new friend in a long time, and I looked forward to my walks with Tambra and Claire.

One Friday morning, after I'd returned from my walk with Tambra, I was sitting on my porch enjoying my third cup of coffee when I looked up to see Mrs. McLellan standing before me. She wore the red wool coat again, her hands buried deep in the pockets. She stepped up onto the porch and gave me a tight smile.

"Good morning, Vivian. I saw you outside and thought I'd stop by. I've been wanting to talk to you again."

"Hello, Mrs. McLellan," I said. "How are you on this beautiful morning?"

She peered out at the gray sky and said, "I don't know how beautiful it is, but I'm doing fine."

"I think every day is beautiful in its own way," I said cheerfully.

"Yes, I suppose," she said, giving me an odd look.

"What did you want to talk to me about, Mrs. McLellan?" I asked.

"First, I wanted to tell you that there's an opening for a full-time clerk at Ralph's Thriftway." She paused, waiting for a response from me, I imagined, but I was silent. She cleared her throat and continued. "It's close—only ten minutes away or so. And they pay well—three dollars an hour to start. I know the manager there, and I could put in a good word for you."

I gave her a thin smile. "That's very kind of you, Mrs. McLellan, but I'm not really looking for work right now."

She frowned. "Every girl has to work when she hasn't got a husband."

I sighed. "I'm sure most do, but I don't." When she looked at me with one eyebrow raised, I knew she expected an explanation. "I, um, I do a little writing here and there, and I also have a bit of an inheritance, so I don't need to work right now." I wasn't really a writer, and my inheritance was more than a bit, but I didn't trust Mrs. McLellan with the whole truth.

She cocked her head to one side. "An inheritance from your father?"

I nodded. "Yes, from my father."

She pursed her lips. "Well, your money will run out someday, and when you need a job, let me know, because I know a lot of people in town."

"Okay, I will. Thanks for stopping by." I smiled. I was ready for her to go, but she stood her ground.

"The other thing is, I told Victor, my son, about you," she said. "He wants to meet you and take you out to dinner."

I was certain she could see me recoil. I looked at her, my amiable smile gone. "I'm sorry, but I can't do that."

Her eyes narrowed. "Why?" she demanded. "What do you have against my son?"

I took a deep breath before answering. "I have nothing against your son, ma'am, but I'm not interested in dating." *I'm not interested in dating men, anyway,* I thought wryly.

She drew herself up to her full height. "Victor has a business degree from the University of Washington, and he makes seventeen thousand dollars a year," she said indignantly.

I felt a surge of anger and tried to calm myself before speaking. "I have no doubt that your son is a fine man, but I'm not interested in going on a date with him."

"Why not? You want to get married, don't you?" she snapped. "You're no spring chicken. If you don't get married soon, you'll be alone for the rest of your life."

I was offended by her presumptuousness. "Don't worry about me," I said in a tight voice. "I'll be fine."

She raised her eyebrows. "How will you be fine when you're all alone? Every girl needs a man."

"I'm not interested in men, okay?" I said, my tone more sharp than I intended. I immediately regretted my words.

She took a step back. "What do you mean, you're not interested in men?" She stared at me for a long moment. "Are you one of those women's libbers?"

I heard the accusatory tone in her voice. "No, not exactly," I said.

"Then what is it? What are you trying to say?" She folded her arms across her chest and stared at me.

"Like I said, I'm not interested in men," I said, carefully enunciating each word.

She looked at me openmouthed, and I watched as her brain churned away. I saw the expression on her face change the moment realization finally dawned. "Oh, oh my, oh my," she sputtered. "For heaven's sake. I had no idea."

"I'm sure you didn't," I said shortly as I stood and moved toward the front door. "Now, I'm sorry, but I have things to do. Thank you for stopping by." I turned on my heel, opened the door, and walked into the house. I closed the door firmly behind me, not looking at her again. I leaned against the door and drew in a deep breath. As I exhaled slowly, I whispered, "What the hell have I done?"

By Saturday afternoon the shift in the neighborhood was already evident: a curt nod in answer to my cheerful call of "hello," a neighbor passing me on the sidewalk but pretending not to see me, a back abruptly turned as I came out to get my mail. I didn't need anyone to tell me that Mrs. McLellan had shared her discovery with anyone who would listen.

As I contemplated this turn of events, I told myself that it really didn't matter. I could coexist quite happily with these people without needing any close connections. I'd just keep to myself and live my life. But then my thoughts turned to Tambra. I liked her—a lot. I thought of her shyly asking if I would be her friend. I thought of our morning walks. Remorse washed through me. I was letting her down. But then I reminded myself that, like everyone else in the neighborhood, she had already heard Mrs. McLellan's story and our friendship was, in effect, over anyway. I'd done it to myself. I needed to learn to keep my mouth shut.

When I saw Tambra come outside on Monday morning, I darted inside before she caught sight of me. I wasn't sure how else to handle it. I didn't want to put either one of us in an awkward position, so avoiding her seemed to be the best solution.

That strategy worked until Thursday morning rolled around. I was sitting on the couch reading and was startled by a knock on the door. I opened it to see Tambra standing there holding Claire in her arms. "Hi, Tambra," I said. As always, she looked beautiful. Her blond hair was pulled back into a low ponytail, and the aqua-colored T-shirt she wore made her eyes look an almost impossible shade of blue.

"Vivian, what's the deal?" she said, a hint of anger in her voice.

I knew what she was getting at, but I decided to play dumb. "I'm sorry, I'm not sure what you mean."

She cocked her head to the side and fixed me with a questioning gaze. "I thought we were becoming friends, but now you seem to be avoiding me. Did I do something wrong?"

I wasn't sure how to respond. I'd assumed that Tambra had talked to Mrs. McLellan, but maybe she hadn't. Or maybe she had, and she didn't care. Either way, I'd apparently jumped to a conclusion that wasn't true, and I'd hurt her feelings in the process. After several moments had passed, I finally spoke. "No, you didn't do anything wrong. I just thought you'd heard…that you talked to Mrs. McLellan."

She frowned. "Mrs. McLellan? Why the hell would I talk to that old battle-ax? She doesn't like me, and I don't like her."

I'm not sure I'd ever felt such relief. I let out a long breath. "Yeah, she's kind of a bitch, isn't she?" I said.

"Kind of? She's all bitch." She laughed and then looked at me curiously. "Why did you think I talked to her?"

"Oh, no reason," I said, trying to sound casual. "It's not important. I'm sorry I've been absent. It's nothing you did, so don't worry about that." I opened the door wide. "Want to come in?"

She looked at me for a long beat. "Yes, I do." She stepped into the living room and plopped down on the couch, arranging Claire in her lap. She glanced at the book I had set down on the coffee table. "What are you reading?"

"*The First Deadly Sin*," I said, sitting down next to her. "It's a murder mystery. It's really good but kind of twisted."

"That sounds interesting. I used to read books a lot before I got married, but Tom doesn't like me to read. I read the newspaper when he's around, but that's about it."

I looked at her, aghast. "What do you mean, he doesn't like you to read? What does that mean?" I was beginning to form an opinion of Tom, and it wasn't a good one.

"He thinks reading is a waste of time," she said, shifting Claire in her lap. "He'll proudly tell you he's never read an entire book in his whole life."

I snorted. "That's hardly something to be proud of."

"I know. I agree," she said with a nod. "But he makes the rules, and I just try and follow them."

My eyebrows shot up. "He makes the rules? Doesn't that bother you?"

She sighed. "Yes, it bothers me, but Tom has a temper, and I don't like to cross him."

I took a deep breath and looked at her for a long moment. I wanted to ask about her relationship with Tom, and I didn't quite know how to pose the question. "Tambra," I began. "You and Tom have been together for a while. Tell me something that's really special about your relationship with him."

She chewed on her bottom lip as she considered my question. "Well, he adores Claire."

I fought the urge to roll my eyes. I wanted Tambra to tell me that Tom was devoted to her, that he was grateful for her love, that he couldn't imagine his life without her. That's what I believed she deserved. "Okay, but does he adore *you*?" I asked.

She giggled. "I don't know, maybe. He brings me flowers once in a while, and sometimes he tells me I look pretty."

I wasn't sure what to say. Did telling your wife she looks pretty or bringing her flowers constitute a real, loving relationship? I wasn't well versed in romantic relationships, but I thought the answer to that was no. "I just hope there's something positive about your relationship with Tom other than that he adores Claire and he brings you flowers sometimes," I said. "You deserve someone who'll love you for who you are—reading and all."

Her eyes softened. "Thank you, Vivian. That's nice. And Tom does have other good qualities. He can just sometimes be, I don't know, challenging, I guess."

"Yes, I hear that," I said. "Anyway, about the reading, isn't Tom gone all day? Couldn't you read then?"

She nodded. "Yeah, I read sometimes when Claire's napping. I have this little desk that my parents gave me when I graduated from high school, and I keep it in our bedroom. There's a secret compartment under the bottom drawer, and I hide a book in there." She paused. "It's a skinny secret compartment, and I can only fit skinny books there, so I read a lot of Harlequin romances." She giggled again. "Tom doesn't even know the secret compartment exists."

I found it ridiculous that Tambra had to hide books, but at least she'd found a way around Tom's absurd rules. "Well, that's good, I guess," I said. "Doesn't seem like you should have to hide books, but I'm glad you have a place."

She moved Claire to her other arm, and I noticed the baby was sound asleep.

"Yeah, so enough about that," she said. "Tell me what you've been doing this week."

"I've gone to the library a couple times. I love the Olympia library," I said. "It's much bigger than the one in Applewood. And I discovered this park—Priest Point Park. Do you know it?"

She smiled and nodded. "Sure. We like to go there too."

"It's a beautiful park," I said. "I took a long walk there on Tuesday. And yesterday I visited my aunt and two cousins and their kids."

"That sounds fun," she said wistfully.

"What have you been doing?" I asked. "Other than reading in secret, that is."

She laughed. "Besides reading in secret, I've been taking care of Claire, cleaning the house, doing laundry. That kind of stuff."

There had to be more than that, I thought. "What else?" I pressed.

Claire woke suddenly and began to fuss. Tambra moved her to her shoulder and began to pat her back. "That's it, really," she said. "I have plenty to keep me busy, though."

"I'm sure you do," I said. She sounded a little defensive, and I thought it was time to change the subject. "Well, where are my manners? Can I get you something to drink? A Coke or water or…?"

"Sure, I'd take some Coke," she said, brightening.

"Coming right up!" I went into the kitchen, pulled a glass out of the cupboard, and then grabbed a bottle of Coke out of the refrigerator. As I poured the drink, I thought about Tambra. She seemed so vulnerable. She put on a cheerful face, but under the surface I could sense the sadness. At the same time, she was refreshingly frank and altogether charming, a combination that I found disconcerting and alluring at the same time. In another place and time, Tambra was the kind of woman I could fall for. I thought suddenly of Trish and her small features and wiry body. Tambra and Trish were like night and day.

I wondered again about Tom and his regard—or disregard—for Tambra. I'd never seen the two of them together, so maybe there was something tender and sweet between them that I wasn't aware of. I hoped so. I felt protective of Tambra, and the thought of Tom treating her with anything but loving kindness troubled me.

I carried the glass out to Tambra. "Here you go," I said, handing it to her and sitting down beside her.

"Thanks," she said and then took a long sip.

"So tell me about your family—your parents and your sister, right?" I said.

"Yes, I have a sister," she answered. "Her name is Kathryn, and she's two years younger than I am. She's married to a great guy named Chip, and they're expecting a baby in September."

"How nice. You're going to be an aunt."

She smiled. "Yes, it is nice. My parents are Mary and George. They've been married for thirty years, and they're still going strong. I don't get to see them enough, but I talk to them on the phone every Sunday."

"That's good," I said. "What was your maiden name, anyway?"

"Sorenson."

"Tambra Sorenson," I said. "That has a nice ring to it."

"Yeah, it was a good name," she said. "I was sorry to let it go."

"I've always thought it would be hard to change your name after so many years with the name you were born with," I said.

"It is hard, but you get used to it," she said. "I'm sure you'll find out soon when you find a guy to marry." She gave me a sidelong glance. "You do want to get married, don't you?"

I dropped my eyes and shifted uncomfortably. "I have no plans to get married, no. I'm happy on my own."

To my surprise, Tambra said, "Yeah, I can understand that."

I looked at her with raised eyebrows. "You can?"

"Sure," she said with a shrug. "I'd love not to have anyone to answer to. To go where I want, when I want. There's a lot to be said for freedom." She licked her lips. "But in our society everyone thinks a woman needs a man. That she's not a real person until she gets married. Really, it's kind of silly."

I looked at her, astonished. "Wow, you're the first woman who's ever said something like that to me."

She smiled shyly. "I read *The Feminine Mystique* before Tom and I got married. I learned a lot from that book."

"And still you married him," I said, puzzled. "Why?"

She bowed her head. "I was pregnant," she said in a low voice. "That's why we got married."

"Pregnant? With Claire?" I was confused. Something about that timing didn't seem right.

She shook her head. "No, not Claire. Another baby. A boy. We named him Steven. He didn't make it. He was stillborn."

I gasped. "Oh my God, Tambra, I'm so sorry. I had no idea."

She touched my hand. "No, of course not. How would you know?"

"What happened?" I asked, my voice almost a whisper.

Her chin dipped down to her chest. "I was only three weeks from my due date when I noticed the baby wasn't moving. I was scared, so I went to see the doctor, and he told me the baby had died." She raised her eyes to mine, and I saw they were filled with tears.

"Oh, Tambra, I'm so sorry," I said. "When did this happen?"

"That was at the end of 1971, right after Christmas. My due date was January seventeenth." A tear rolled down her cheek. I wasn't sure what to do, so I patted her shoulder. "It was a sad time," she said. "It took a long time for me to feel normal again. But then a year later we found out we were expecting Claire. I was scared every moment of my pregnancy, but everything was fine. She was healthy and perfect." She reached down and tenderly kissed the top of Claire's head and wrapped her arms more closely around her.

"Thank goodness for that," I said.

"I know," she said, giving me a strained smile. "So what about you?" she said in a bright voice, lightly slapping my knee. "Tell me about your family."

"Well, you know a lot already," I said. "My dad, Roger, passed away in January. My mom, Helen, died when I was eight. I don't have any sisters or brothers. I have an aunt here. Her name is Dorothy, and she lives in Tumwater. And two cousins, Louise and Linda, Dorothy's twin daughters. My mom was an only child, so I don't have any aunts or uncles on that side."

"Wow, kind of a small family," she said. Claire was fussing again, and Tambra bounced her gently on her knee.

"Yeah, it is small. That's why I moved here," I said. "I had one close friend from high school in Iowa—Daniel—but that was it. All my family's here now."

"And have you ever had a serious boyfriend?" she asked.

I thought for a few moments about how to answer that question. I wasn't ready to be fully honest with Tambra. Not yet. "I've had a couple of casual relationships but nothing lasting. Like I said, I don't think I'm destined to be with someone."

"Well, you never know. You're a great girl, and any guy would be lucky to have you," she said, touching my knee again. She suddenly looked at me with wild eyes and sat up straight. "Oh my God, what time is it?"

I glanced at my watch. "It's ten minutes to eleven. Why?"

She stood up and wrapped Claire in her blanket. "I have to go. Tom calls every morning at eleven, and I have to be there."

"Why?" I asked, bewildered by the sudden turn of events.

"If I'm not there, he'll be angry. Sorry, Vivian, but I have to go." Tambra rushed to the door, and three seconds later she was gone.

I stared at the door, wondering what had just happened.

The next day it was raining, so Tambra and I didn't take our walk as usual. She called me in the morning and asked if I wanted to come over that afternoon while Claire was napping. "Sure, I guess so," I said, still perplexed by her abrupt departure the day before.

"Great, I'll see you at two o'clock," she said. "Bye."

"Bye," I said and hung up the phone.

At two o'clock I walked across the grass to Tambra's house and knocked. She opened the door and smiled. "Hi, Vivian. Come on in. Claire's finally asleep. She's been fussy today."

I walked into the living room and sat down on the couch. Tambra had set a bowl of potato chips and two tall glasses of lemonade on the coffee table.

"I hope you like lemonade," she said as she sat down beside me.

"I do," I said and then took a drink. "It's good. Not too sour and not too sweet."

"I'm glad you like it," she said, picking up her glass.

I turned and looked at her. "So what happened yesterday?"

"What do you mean?" she asked, looking at me over the top of her glass.

"Why did you leave so suddenly?"

She shrugged. "I had to be here for Tom's call. Sometimes he calls a few minutes before eleven, so I wanted to make sure I was here. I made it, so it was okay."

I frowned. "Yeah, I understand that part, but why does he call you every day?"

"He calls at eleven and three thirty to make sure I'm home," she said, as if that were the most natural thing in the world.

"I know—well, actually I didn't know he calls you twice a day—but what I mean is, why does he care if you're home or not?"

She smiled indulgently. "I know you haven't had a serious relationship, Vivian, but men are funny. They're jealous. He wants to make sure I'm home and not out flitting about."

I raised my eyebrows. "Flitting about? Does he think you'd be flitting about with a baby?"

Tambra made a face. "Yeah, I know it's silly, but he's a man. That's how men are."

I gave her a questioning look. "No, I don't think that's how men are. My dad never did that. I don't think Tom should be checking up on you. You're an adult."

She met my eyes, and then her gaze flickered away. "Like I said yesterday, Tom makes the rules, and I just follow them."

I tried to hold eye contact with her. "That's not what a woman who's read *The Feminine Mystique* would say," I said lightly.

"I know, I know." She laughed. "I wouldn't make Betty Friedan very happy, would I?"

I grinned in spite of my irritation at Tom and his rules. "No, you wouldn't."

She shrugged. "I just feel like I can never please Tom, so I try to do whatever I can to at least get close," she said. "So if I'm home when he calls and that makes him happy, then I'm happy."

I leaned toward her, my knees almost touching hers. "Why do you say you never please him?"

She threw up her hands. "I don't know. I just don't. The dinner's late, the bathroom isn't clean enough, or I didn't get the stain out of his shirt. Whatever it is, I never measure up."

I thought I saw tears in her eyes. "Honey," I said, covering her hand with mine, "he's holding you to impossible standards. No one's perfect. And I happen to think you're pretty special. Tom should be grateful for every day he has with you."

She smiled sadly, the tears now evident. "Thank you, Vivian. I wish Tom felt that way."

I thought Tom sounded like an ass. I didn't understand why women put up with men like Tom, but I knew many did. But I also knew there were lots of wonderful men out there—men like my dad. I wished Tambra had found that kind of man. "Have you and Tom ever been happy?" I asked.

She looked away. "Yeah, for the first four or five months we were. We were excited about the baby, and we liked spending time together."

"And then what happened?" I asked, my hand still on hers.

She shrugged. "I don't know. We moved here, and he started to change. He started picking on me and complaining about my cooking and cleaning. He got mad when one of his shirts wasn't clean when he wanted to wear it or if I spent too much money on groceries." She paused. "And then, when the baby died, things got bad. It was hard on both of us."

"What about now? How is he now?"

"Just kind of distant," she said. "Or angry. He's hardly ever nice to me."

"Do you think he loves you?" I asked.

She shook her head. "Honestly, no, I don't think he loves me. I think he loves the idea of me, but I don't think he loves *me*."

"And your parents? What do they say about all this?"

She gave a derisive laugh. "They think Tom's great. They think I'm lucky to have him. But I never pleased my parents either."

"What do you mean?" I asked.

Tambra looked down at her lap and tucked her hair behind her ear. "They were hard on me when I was young. My grades were never good enough, for one thing. My mom used to say, 'It's a good thing you're pretty because you aren't very bright.' And my dad wanted me to be good at sports, and I wasn't. He made me play softball and basketball, and I was awful. He'd yell at me after every game and tell me everything I'd done wrong." She sighed deeply. "They wanted me to be perfect, and I wasn't."

I shook my head. "That's terrible," I said. "Were they hard on your sister like that?"

She snorted. "Hell no. Kathryn was perfect. She got straight A's, and she was a great athlete." She paused. "And she didn't get pregnant out of wedlock."

"Yeah, I was wondering what they thought about that," I said.

"Oh God, they were furious! My dad called me a slut," she said bitterly. "They made me marry Tom. I wanted to raise the baby on my own, but they wouldn't hear of it. I never wanted to marry Tom. They forced me to."

"You never wanted to marry Tom?" I asked, confused. This was new—and surprising—information.

She gave a fierce shake of her head. "No, I didn't. He wasn't my type."

And still you slept with him, I thought. To my surprise, Tambra said, "I know what you're thinking. If he wasn't my type, then why did I screw him?"

I could feel my cheeks getting hot. This wasn't a topic I normally talked with other people about, and that wasn't a word I was used to hearing—especially from a woman. "Well, yes, I guess I was wondering about that," I said.

She raised one shoulder in a half shrug. "I was lonely, and I wanted someone to want me. After our first date, Tom drove me up to this make-out spot, and we started kissing, and one thing led to another, and…you know. It happened."

I marveled at how matter-of-fact she was about it all. "Okay, I get it," I said.

"Anyway, I didn't really like Tom, and I wasn't even going to see him again, and then…" Her voice faltered, and she took a deep breath. "And then I found out I was pregnant. I felt so stupid. I told my parents and said I was going to raise the baby on my own and not even tell Tom. But they forbade it. They said if I didn't tell him, they would. They forced me to marry him."

I leaned back against the couch cushion and sighed. "Oh, Tambra. I'm sorry all that happened."

She gave me a wan smile. "It's okay. It's in the past now. I tried to make the best of it, and I did learn to love Tom. But now things have changed. I just can't make him happy no matter what I do. I don't know—I think he's angry at how things worked out. I think he feels like I trapped him into marrying me by getting pregnant, but I didn't!" She looked at me, her eyes blazing. "I didn't even want to see him again after that first date!"

I felt the sting of tears behind my eyes. I felt terrible for Tambra. She was such a kind, gentle person, and it troubled me that Tom didn't love her the way she deserved to be loved. He didn't know how good he had it. He was going to drive away this amazing woman because of his sheer stupidity.

"Well, all I can tell you is what I see in you," I said, putting my arm lightly around her shoulders. "I see a person who's smart, funny, beautiful, honest, kind, and a great mother. I think Tom is the luckiest man in the world. He should be thanking God every day that he has you."

She looked at me with wide eyes. "Do you really think that?"

I nodded. "I absolutely do."

She gave me a grateful smile. "Thank you, Vivian. I needed to hear that."

"I'd really like to meet Tom," I said. "I've heard a lot about him, and all I've ever seen is the back of his head when he gets in the car in the morning."

She laughed, and then her eyes lit up. "Hey, maybe you could come over for dinner."

"Really? Do you think he'd be okay with that? Does he know we're friends?" Based on what I knew about him, I didn't think he'd be too keen on the idea.

She shrugged. "I think he'd be okay with it. I told him we've been spending some time together. He wasn't thrilled about it, but he wasn't mad either."

"Well, that's good, I guess, and yes, I'd love to come for dinner," I said.

She nodded. "Okay, I'll ask him tonight, and I'll let you know."

I noticed Tambra's mood had lifted, and I hoped Tom would agree to me coming for dinner. "Sounds good. And now I should get going." I squeezed her hand. "Thank you for sharing all this with me. I'm sure it wasn't easy to talk about."

She reached over and gave me a hug. "I'm just happy I have you to talk to, Vivian. It's been a long time since I've had a new friend."

"Me too," I said and then stood up. "Bye, Tambra."

She stood too. "Bye, Vivian. I'll call you tomorrow."

As I walked home, I thought about our conversation. Every time I saw Tambra, she revealed something more about herself, adding another color to what was becoming a troubling picture. To me the solution was simple—take Claire and leave the bastard—but she wasn't ready to hear that yet. Until she was, I'd have to bite my tongue.

As I reached my front door and entered the house, I admitted to myself that my feelings for Tambra were becoming more than friendly. She was the kind of woman I'd been looking for all my life. I had no illusions that Tambra would ever return those feelings. I knew quite well the pain of unrequited love—I'd had romantic feelings toward more friends than I cared to remember. I had pretended with them, and I could pretend with Tambra too. I would be her friend and confidante, and she would never know the depth of my feelings for her.

19

Tambra called me the next morning to tell me that Tom had given his approval for me to come to dinner. "He wants you to come over tomorrow night at six," she said.

"So soon?" I said with surprise. I was expecting next week or the following one but not tomorrow. Reluctantly, I agreed.

By Sunday afternoon, I was a bundle of nerves. I'd never been one to fuss over my clothes, but I found myself trying on one outfit after another, not pleased with any of them. I finally settled on black slacks paired with a gray and lavender paisley blouse.

I then faced my freshly washed hair in the bathroom mirror, combing it first this way and then that. My hair was thick and wavy, and it had always been challenging. I kept it short to minimize my struggle with it. Tonight I wanted to look put together. I rummaged around in the bathroom drawer looking for something to help. I found a wide tortoise-shell barrette, parted my hair to the side, and then secured it with the barrette. I had seen a tube of mascara in the drawer, and I grabbed it and carefully applied it to my lashes. I examined myself in the mirror. I looked pretty good.

At six o'clock I left my house and crossed the lawn to Tambra's front door. I felt my stomach tighten. I took a deep breath and then knocked. Several seconds later Tambra opened the door.

"Hi, Vivian," she said in a soft voice.

I swept my eyes over her. She was wearing wide-legged black pants and a shiny silver blouse with loose sleeves that came just above her elbows. There were three silver bangles on her wrist and large silver hoops in her ears. She had pulled her hair back in a loose chignon, and wisps of hair fell around her face. My stomach did a flip. She looked achingly lovely. I met her eyes and then frowned. She looked as if she'd been crying. "Is everything okay?" I whispered.

She gave a barely noticeable shake of her head and opened the door wider. "Vivian, come in!" she said in a loud voice.

I stepped into the house and looked around. Claire was in her baby seat next to the couch, gurgling happily to herself, but Tom was nowhere to be seen.

"Tom will be out in a bit," she said, giving me a weak smile.

"Okay." I walked over to Claire. "Hi, sweet pea," I said, and reached down to touch her hand.

"Vivian, hello!" a deep voice boomed.

I turned and saw a tall, muscular man with dark blond hair parted to the side. His icy blue eyes looked small in his wide face. He was vaguely handsome in an unrefined way. He wore jeans and a blue short-sleeved shirt. I moved toward him, my hand outstretched. "Hello, you must be Tom," I said, giving him my most charming smile. "It's nice to meet you." He grabbed my hand and shook it firmly, pressing my fingers together painfully. I tried not to wince.

"Nice to meet you too, Vivian," he said. "Tambra's told me all about you."

I doubt that, I thought wryly. "That's great. I've enjoyed getting to know your wife."

Tambra came to stand next to Tom, and he put his arm around her, pulling her into his side. She was tall for a woman, but the top of her head barely came up to his chin. "Yeah, she's a fun gal to be around, isn't she?" he said.

"Yes, she is," I said. "Something smells wonderful, Tambra."

"We're having spaghetti," she said. "I hope you like it."

I gave her an encouraging smile. "I love spaghetti."

Tom tightened his arm around Tambra, and she squirmed. "I thought Tambra was making a homemade sauce," he said, "but she went and bought that crap in a can."

I smiled. "Oh, I like spaghetti sauce in a can just fine." Jeez, you asshole, I thought. Cut the woman some slack. So far my impression of Tom wasn't positive.

"Well, that's good because that's all we got," Tom said. "Can I get you a beer, Vivian? I've got Olympia Beer. Got to support the local brewery, you know." He barked out a short laugh, and I thought he already seemed a little drunk.

"Or we have Blue Nun," Tambra added.

I wanted a beer, but I wanted to support Tambra more. "I'll have some wine," I said.

"And bring me another beer, honey," Tom said.

Tambra ducked into the kitchen and came out a few minutes later with two wineglasses balanced in one hand and a can of beer in the other. "Here you go," she said, handing a wineglass to me and the beer to Tom.

"Thanks." I took a sip. "That's good." It really wasn't—I wasn't a wine lover—but I wasn't about to say anything negative tonight.

"Shall we sit?" She motioned toward the living room.

"Sure," I said as I walked to the couch and sat down. Tambra sat beside me, and Tom took the armchair. She set her glass on the coffee table and then reached over to lift Claire out of her baby seat, settling her in the crook of her arm. She picked up her wineglass and took a long sip. She caught my eye in the process and gave me a sly wink, as if to say, "You're doing great."

"So, Vivian," Tom said in his booming voice, "Tambra tells me you live alone. What line of work are you in?"

"Oh, I'm kind of taking a break from work right now," I said. "I just moved here from Iowa last month, and I'm trying to get the lay of the land before I look for a job."

He leaned forward, his elbows on his knees. "Well, I know a few people in town, so check with me when you start looking, and I'll see what I can do," he said.

"Thank you, Tom. That's very kind," I said.

He took a swig from his beer can. "So what do you do with your time then?"

I leaned back against the couch cushion. "I've been getting my house put together and exploring Olympia a bit. I really like your parks here, and downtown Olympia is nice."

Tom nodded. "Yeah, it's a nice little town. We like it here."

Tambra drained her wineglass, stood up, and handed the baby to Tom. "I've got to finish up dinner."

I panicked. The thought of sitting here alone with Tom filled me with dread. "Let me help you," I said quickly, grabbing my wineglass and following her into the kitchen.

I watched as she stirred the loathsome canned spaghetti sauce, which was bubbling on the stove. Next to that, a large silver pot filled with water was boiling furiously. "I need to start the spaghetti," she said. She picked up a package of spaghetti from the counter, tore it open, and dumped it into the boiling water.

"Babe!" Tom yelled from the other room. "Bring me another beer."

Tambra sighed heavily. "I'll do it," I said, setting my wineglass on the counter. I opened the refrigerator and grabbed a beer.

"Thank you," she said, her voice almost a whisper.

I brought the beer to Tom and then returned to Tambra's side. "What can I do?" I asked.

"The garlic bread's over there," she said, pointing to a silver bag on the counter. "You can put that in the oven. It's hot."

I picked up the silver bag and read the directions. "So the whole thing goes in the oven?" I asked.

"Yep," she said.

I popped the silver bag into the oven and then sidled up to her. "What's wrong?" I said under my breath.

"Nothing," she said in a terse voice. "Everything's fine."

I stared at her for a long moment. She wouldn't look at me but pretended to concentrate on stirring the spaghetti. I gave up. "Now what can I do?" I asked, picking up my wineglass and taking a sip.

"There's a salad in the refrigerator. You can get that out."

I opened the refrigerator, took out the salad bowl, and set it on the counter. "What about dressing?" I asked.

"Oh shit!" she said. "I forgot to mix up the Good Seasons."

"Everything okay in there, girls?" Tom shouted from the other room.

"Everything's fine, honey," Tambra shouted back, rolling her eyes at me. She picked up the Good Seasons packet off the counter. "Can you mix this up?" she asked, handing the packet to me. "Oh crap. I have to find the cruet first." She opened the cupboard door next to the refrigerator. "Shit. It's way up there," she said.

She stood on her tiptoes and began feeling around on the top shelf. As she did, the sleeve of her blouse slipped down, and a flash of purple caught my eye. "What is *that*?" I whispered.

"What?" she said in an irritated voice, still fishing around in the cupboard.

"That," I said, pointing to the angry purple bruise on her upper arm.

She looked where I was pointing and quickly pulled her sleeve down. "It's nothing. I just walked into Claire's crib in the middle of the night. No big deal."

I drew back her sleeve. The bruise was about four inches wide and appeared to go around most of her upper arm. "You did *not* get that from walking into a crib. Did *he* do that?" I said in a tense voice.

Tambra met my eyes for a second, and then her gaze slid away. "No, I told you, I walked into the crib," she said, pulling her sleeve down again.

I stared at her, but she wouldn't meet my eyes. "Tambra, if he's hurting you…" My voice trailed off.

She gave me a tight smile. "Everything's fine, Vivian. Don't worry about it. You're a little taller than I am. Can you reach the cruet?"

I sought out her eyes, and again she held eye contact for a moment and then looked away. I thought about saying something more, but instead I moved to the cupboard. I stood on my tiptoes, raised my arm, and caught the edge of the cruet in one smooth movement. I handed it to her. "There you go."

"Thanks. Now mix up the dressing," she said, handing the cruet back to me.

I found the oil, measured it into the cruet, and then ran tap water up to the appropriate line. I poured the powder in, snapped on the lid, and began to shake the container. As I mixed the dressing, I thought about the bruise on Tambra's arm. Given the way she'd responded, I was almost certain Tom had given her the bruise. I thought about the force that would be needed to leave a bruise that large and purple. He would have had to grab her with a lot of intensity. When had that happened? This morning? Yesterday? The color of the bruise suggested hours or possibly even days ago. I remembered that Tambra had looked as if she'd been crying when I'd arrived. Had they been arguing? Tom had been unreasonably angry about canned spaghetti sauce. If he got that angry about something so inconsequential, how must he be with big things like parenting, money, sex, or another man flirting with his wife?

"Vivian!" Tambra said loudly.

I started. "What?"

She shot me an annoyed look. "Where's your head? I told you three times that you can stop shaking the dressing now."

"Oh, sorry."

"It's time to eat," she said. "Get the bread out of the oven. I'm going to drain the spaghetti."

We worked silently to put the finishing touches on the meal and then carried everything to the round table off the kitchen. "It's time to eat," Tambra called with forced cheer. "Bring Claire, would you,

Tom? I have some baby food for her, and I want her to eat in her highchair."

"Sure, sweetie," he said. Tom came to the table carrying Claire. He dragged the highchair over to the table with one hand and slid Claire into it. He pulled the strap across her legs and fastened a bib around her neck. Tambra took the chair next to Claire and set a jar of baby food on the table. She scooped up something green in a tiny spoon and popped it into Claire's mouth. Claire ate the spoonful of food with great relish.

I watched, feeling a bit awkward about being part of their family dinner ritual. "Everything looks delicious, Tambra," I said nervously.

"Well, thanks for your help," she said, handing me the bowl of spaghetti.

We filled our plates and began eating. As I ate, I stole glances at Tom. I'd noticed he was having another beer with dinner. Was that his third? Tambra had never mentioned him having a drinking problem, but I wondered about it now. Had he been drunk when he grabbed her arm? I saw that he was shoveling spaghetti in his mouth. He seemed to be enjoying the food, and I was relieved he hadn't made a comment about the sauce. Just as I had that thought, he piped up.

"The sauce tastes tinny," he said in a gruff voice.

"I think it tastes good," Tambra said, not looking at him.

"I do too," I said, and took a bite of spaghetti to prove my point.

"Hmm," he grumbled. "I think it tastes like a tin can."

I wanted to change the subject and get Tom talking about something more pleasant. I thought of the bat in the corner—his prized possession. "Tom, Tambra tells me you have a signed baseball bat," I said. I didn't want to tell him that I'd picked it up and swung it. I knew he wouldn't like that.

"Yes, I do," he said, his eyes lighting up. "Do you like baseball?"

"I love baseball," I said. "My team is the Minnesota Twins."

He beamed. "My bat is signed by Rod Carew!"

He sounded excited, and I was glad I'd brought it up. "One of the greatest baseball players of all time!" I said, trying to match his tone. "Definitely one of the best to play for the Twins."

"You said it!" he nearly shouted.

"Where'd you get the bat?" I asked.

"My uncle got it for me," he said. "He bought it from a collector when he was in Minneapolis on business a couple of years ago."

"That's great. I'm sure you're very proud of it," I said.

"I sure am." His eyes swiveled to Tambra, and his expression darkened. "Tambra doesn't like baseball. She can't understand why I'm excited about owning a bat." He shook his head and glowered at her.

I was dismayed that he'd found a way to criticize Tambra again. Were there no safe topics? "Well, not everyone likes sports," I said.

He looked at me. "Don't you think if I like baseball that she should too? Isn't that what any good wife would do?"

I didn't have the slightest idea how to answer that question. Agreeing would mean being disloyal to Tambra, and disagreeing would certainly anger Tom. Rather than giving an answer, I simply said, "Oh, I don't know." Tom said nothing and focused on eating, mercifully quiet for the rest of the meal.

After dinner, I helped Tambra with the dishes as Tom sat with Claire in the living room. She washed as I rinsed and dried. I felt awkward with her. We'd always had so much to talk about, but tonight she didn't seem like herself. "That was a good dinner," I said tentatively as I dried a plate.

"Thanks," she said.

I tried again. "I liked the garlic bread. I've never had it in the silver bag. I'll be buying that from now on."

"Yeah, it's good," she said as she concentrated on washing the silver pot.

"Tambra, what's wrong? You seem…different," I said.

She looked at me, her eyes sad. "I'm just tired, that's all."

I opened my mouth to ask a question about the bruise but then thought better of it. We finished the dishes in silence.

After the dishes were done, we went back into the living room. Tom was sitting on the floor, his back against the couch, with Claire on his lap. I noticed he had another beer next to him. I made a mental note to ask Tambra about the drinking.

"Would you like another glass of wine, Vivian?" Tambra asked.

"No, thank you. I really should be going," I said. I glanced at the clock on the wall: nearly eight thirty. I was surprised; it felt like it was ten o'clock. This had been a trying and awkward evening, and whatever was going on between Tom and Tambra was wearing on me.

"Really?" she said. "It's still early."

"Oh, I'm sure you need to get Claire to bed soon, and I really should get home," I said. "Thanks for dinner, though. It was nice."

Tom struggled to his feet. He stood with Claire under his arm and held out his hand to me. "It was great to meet you, Vivian," he said, shaking my hand again with that viselike grip. "Thanks for coming over."

I gave Tom a phony smile. I'd come here with a negative impression of him, and now that I'd met him, and seen the bruise on my friend's arm, I could say without hesitation that I disliked him intensely. "Sure, Tom," I said. "I'm glad to finally meet you." I moved toward the door, and Tambra followed.

"I hope I'll see you tomorrow," she said quietly.

"I'll be around," I answered, just as quietly.

"Okay. See you later." She opened the door for me.

"Bye, and thank you," I said as I walked out.

I crossed Tambra's lawn into my own yard, and the mildness of the evening surprised me. It was just barely spring, but the temperature seemed almost warm. Once I got to my front door, I looked at the porch. It would be nice to sit out here for a while. I sat down in the wooden chair and sighed deeply. This had been a rough evening. The bruised arm aside, something was really off between Tom and Tambra. For one, he was so critical of her. For another, he seemed to annoy her to no end. The best thing they had going together was Claire. They both clearly adored her.

I thought of my own parents. I remembered them being so sweet to each other. My mom had always kissed my dad good-bye when he left in the morning and hello when he came home at night, and my dad often brought small gifts for my mom. Sometimes in the evenings my mom would turn on the radio, and my parents would dance in the middle of the living room. I'd sit on the couch and watch them as I hummed along to the song. When the song ended, my dad would kiss my mom on the mouth and say, "I love you, Helen," and she would answer, "I love you too, Roger." I thought about Tom and Tambra. They hadn't even touched each other tenderly, let alone kissed. I wondered if they had a sex life to speak of. Somehow, I couldn't imagine it.

My eye caught movement under the streetlight. A person with a white dog. I could just make out the face of Mrs. Reed.

She realized I'd seen her, and she began walking quickly away.

"Hello, Mrs. Reed!" I called.

She froze for a moment and then looked back over her shoulder. "Hello," she said in a terse voice and then hurried away. Once again I was rudely reminded that, with the exception of Tambra, the neighbors wanted nothing to do with me.

I thought it was time to go in. I was just about to open the front door when I heard shouting. I stopped and listened, trying to determine where the noise was coming from. I finally decided it was coming from Tom and Tambra's. I strained to hear. I could definitely make out the distinctive tone of Tambra's voice followed by the deep bellow of Tom's. They were clearly arguing. I tried to make out the words, but I couldn't understand what they were saying.

The bruise on Tambra's arm came into my mind again, and I felt afraid for my friend. I wondered if I should go over and intervene but then immediately rejected the idea. Somehow I felt that would make matters worse. I listened for a few more moments, said a prayer that Tambra and Claire would be safe, and then went inside. I would definitely ask Tambra about it tomorrow.

20

Tambra was knocking on my door at 8:25 the next morning. I had woken late and was just pouring my first cup of coffee and scanning the newspaper. I opened the door a crack and peered out. Tambra stood there with Claire in her arms.

"Morning, Tambra. Come in," I said, opening the door wide.

She bustled in and took a seat on the couch with Claire in her lap.

"Can I get you some coffee?" I asked.

She nodded. "Sure, I'd love some. Cream, no sugar."

"Is milk okay?" I asked. "I don't have any cream. I like my coffee black, so I hardly ever buy cream."

She shrugged. "Sure."

I went into the kitchen and busied myself getting out a cup, pouring the coffee, and then adding a splash of milk. I carried the cup out and handed it to her. "Careful, it's hot," I said.

"Thanks." She blew on the coffee, took a tentative sip, and then turned toward me. "Thanks for coming over last night."

I nodded. "Sure, it was nice."

"What did you think of Tom?" she asked.

"He was…interesting."

"Yeah, he's definitely interesting." She gave a short laugh.

I took a deep breath. "I wanted to ask you about that bruise on your arm."

Her face darkened, and her smile vanished. "I told you, I walked into Claire's crib."

I frowned. "Tambra, I wasn't born yesterday. Nobody gets a bruise that big from walking into a crib. Did Tom do that?"

She looked down at the top of Claire's head. She didn't speak for a long time. Finally she raised her eyes to mine. "It's not a big deal."

"What happened?" I asked gently but firmly.

She hesitated. "Tom and I were arguing, and things got a little heated, and he grabbed my arm. That's all."

"That's all?" I said. "He must have grabbed you with a lot of force to cause a bruise like that. What were you arguing about?"

She shifted uncomfortably. "You know, couple stuff."

"Couple stuff? What does that mean?" I asked.

She looked at me. "We went out to dinner on Saturday night, and he got angry because he thought the waiter was flirting with me and he thought I was flirting back."

I rolled my eyes. "Oh, for heaven's sake. Is he really that insecure?"

"Yes, actually, he is," she said. "And the funny thing is—I don't think the waiter was flirting with me, and I know I wasn't flirting with him."

I shook my head with disgust. "Does he know he gave you a bruise like that?"

"I made sure he saw it. And he did apologize later," she said.

I ignored the comment about the apology. Who cared if he was sorry? He never should have grabbed her in the first place. I leaned toward her. "Has he ever done something like this before?"

Again, she squirmed, clearly uneasy. "Not really, no," she finally said, her eyes down.

I looked at her for a long moment. I didn't think she was being truthful, but I didn't feel comfortable prying more deeply. I decided to drop the subject for now. "Okay," I said. "And what about the drinking? I noticed Tom had a lot to drink. Is that just a weekend thing?"

Tambra sighed. "He drinks pretty much every night."

"How much?"

She looked up at the ceiling. "He brings home a six-pack every day or two."

I gave a low whistle. "Wow, that's a lot," I said. "Doesn't that worry you?"

She leaned her head back against the couch cushion. "Yeah, it worries me. When he drinks too much, he acts like a jerk. I try and stay out of his way."

I thought about the argument I'd heard the night before and the four beers I'd seen Tom drink. "Is it okay with you that you're like a guest in your own home?" I asked. "Always walking on eggshells, always managing Tom's moods?"

She turned toward me, her face angry. "No, it's not okay with me, Vivian, but what the hell am I going to do about it?"

I flinched. I'd obviously struck a nerve. "There are things you can do, you know," I said. "To get out, I mean."

"What, like divorce?" she said bitterly. "What the hell would I do, a twenty-seven-year-old woman with a baby and no job skills? How would I support myself?"

I could see she was upset, and I tried to keep my voice calm. "I didn't say it would be easy. I just said it was possible."

"Do you think I haven't thought of that?" she said, her tone sharp. "I think about divorcing Tom at least once a week, but I'm stuck. I won't be one of those women on welfare and food stamps and no way to get out of that cycle. No thank you!" Claire could sense her mother's distress, and she started to cry. Tambra put the baby on her shoulder and began to rub her back, cooing softly in her ear.

"If you really wanted to leave, I might be able to, you know, help you with the money part," I said. "Not long term, but I could help you get on your feet until you can get a job."

She gave me a tight smile. "That's very nice of you, Vivian, but no thanks. Number one, the only job I've ever had was at Fotomat, and I don't know what kind of real job I could possibly get with that experience, and number two, I don't want to be on my own."

"Okay," I said, knowing it was time to drop the subject. "Just know the offer's out there if you ever want to take me up on it."

"Thanks. I appreciate that," she said in a curt voice and then stood up. "I really should be going now. I need to feed Claire, and then I have some housework to do."

I tried to hide my surprise. "Are you sure? You haven't been here very long." And I haven't had a chance to ask you about the argument I heard, I thought.

"I know, but I have things to do," she said, not looking at me as she shifted Claire to her shoulder and moved toward the door.

"Okay, well, I'll see you soon. Thanks for stopping by," I said.

She opened the door. "Okay, see you later." She walked out and closed the door behind her.

I looked at the closed door and wondered what had happened. I'd apparently either offended her or gotten too close for comfort—or both. I knew the topics I'd discussed with her were difficult, but I wouldn't have felt right not saying something. I just hoped that in my eagerness to help her I hadn't done irreparable harm to our friendship.

I didn't talk to Tambra the rest of that week. She waved at me each morning as she left for her walk, but she didn't stop. I wasn't sure what to make of it. Did I owe her an apology? I wasn't sure, but she'd evidently taken offense to something I'd said. I wanted to talk it over with someone, but there was no one here I felt comfortable talking with about something so personal.

On Saturday morning it dawned on me that I could call Daniel and ask his advice. I hadn't talked to him yet since I'd arrived in Olympia, and this would be a good reason to call and catch up. I picked up the phone and dialed his number. I imagined his kitchen phone ringing two thousand miles away.

"Hello?" Daniel said.

I closed my eyes for a moment and let the familiar, comforting sound of his voice wash over me. I hadn't realized how much I'd missed him. "Hi, Daniel. It's Vivian."

"Vivian! My God, I was just thinking about you this morning. How are you?" he said.

"I'm good. I've been here about a month and a half, and so far I like it. They have nice parks here and a great library—much bigger than the one in Applewood."

"That's good. I know how you love books. And the people? Are the neighbors friendly? Have you made any new friends?" he asked.

"The neighbors are a bit chilly," I said.

"How come?" I could hear the concern in his voice.

"Well, I accidentally came out to one of them," I said. "Now everyone knows, and they're giving me the cold shoulder." It felt good to finally tell someone this.

"Oh shit," he said. "So now you're an outcast in your own neighborhood?"

"Something like that," I said. "So that part's not so great."

"So no new friends, I guess?" he asked.

"Actually, there's this woman—a neighbor—that I'm friendly with. I get the feeling she's a bit of an outcast herself. In fact, she didn't hear the gossip about me because the neighbors don't talk to her much."

"Well, that's good, I guess," he said. "Although I don't like to hear about people being blackballed—especially you."

"Yeah, I know," I said. "I've enjoyed getting to know this woman, though. Her name is Tambra."

"And...?" he said.

"And what?"

"Do you think she could be more than a friend?" he asked.

I laughed. "She's married and straight as an arrow, so no."

"You might be surprised. Arrows can bend," he said in a suggestive voice.

"She's married, Daniel, and she has a baby," I said flatly, amused and irritated at the same time.

"I know, but do you like her?"

"What does it matter?"

"Vivian?" he pressed.

I sighed. "Let's just say, if things were different, then yes, she's someone I'd be interested in. She's very charming and very sweet and very beautiful." I didn't want to tell him that I'd already fallen in love with her a little. What would be the point?

"Ooh, she sounds alluring," he said.

This conversation had taken an unexpected turn, and I wanted to get it back on track. "But that's not why I called. I need your advice, and actually this is about Tambra."

"Okay, tell me more," he said.

I told Daniel about my burgeoning friendship with Tambra, what I'd learned about her and Tom, and my awkward interaction with her on Monday. I ended by telling him that I thought Tambra was angry with me and I wasn't sure why. "What do you think?" I asked.

"I think you pissed her off, first and foremost," he said matter-of-factly. "You were acting like you have her life all figured out and you know her better than she knows herself. Nobody likes that."

"But I can't not say something," I said. "Her husband hurt her and has very likely hurt her before. How could I ignore that?"

"I didn't say you should ignore it," he said patiently. "You can—and should—say something, but she has the right to her own reaction, which in this case is anger and irritation. That doesn't mean you didn't make sense to her."

"So what should I do?"

"I think you should apologize," he said. "You clearly care about her, and you—"

"I do care about her," I interrupted.

"And you want to make things right with her," he continued.

"I do."

"So you should just say something like, 'Tambra, I'm sorry if I offended you. That wasn't my intention. I said what I said because I care about you. I want you to be happy, and I want you to be safe.'" He paused. "How does that sound?"

"That sounds good, actually," I said. "I think she'll be able to hear that." I paused for a moment. "She's an interesting person. I think she's the most genuine and uncomplicated person I've ever known. I think that's why this has thrown me so much. She's been so open with me up to this point that I started to think I could say anything to her and she'd be okay with it."

"So now you know she has limits," he said.

"Yes, now I know. But I still do want to help her. I want to help her get away from her husband."

"And I think you'll get there eventually, but it might not happen as quickly as you want," Daniel said.

"Probably not, but I can keep trying."

"You can keep trying, but keep trying respectfully and gently," he said. "Don't pressure her, or you're going to push her away."

"I know. You're right. I'll try and temper myself."

"So Tambra doesn't know about you?" he asked.

"Not yet," I replied. "I'll tell her, though. Eventually."

"Probably should be sooner rather than later, before she hears it from someone else."

"Yeah, I hadn't thought about that, but you're right," I said. "I don't want to make matters worse because she thinks I've deliberately kept something from her."

"No, you don't."

"But enough about that," I said. "Tell me what you've been up to." We chatted for another fifteen minutes about Daniel's work, the weather in Iowa and Washington, politics, and his love life, and then he said he had to go.

"Please call again, Viv. I miss you," he said.

"I miss you too. And I will call again."

"Okay. Bye. Take care."

"You too. Bye," I said. I hung up the phone and thought about Daniel's advice. I knew he was right—I'd offended Tambra, and I needed to make things right. But it was Saturday, and I knew the weekend was her time with Tom. I resolved to go see her and apologize on Monday after Tom left for work.

21

On Monday morning I awoke and went to the kitchen to start my coffee. I looked out the window and was happy to see a beautiful azure sky. As I poured my first cup of coffee, I glanced at the calendar and realized it was April first. "April Fools' Day," I said aloud.

After I saw Tom leave for work, I crossed the lawn to Tambra's front door. I knocked and waited for her to answer. A few moments later the door opened, and she peered out. "Oh, hi, Vivian," she said.

Was it my imagination, or did she seem a bit cool? "Hi, Tambra. I hope I'm not interrupting anything." I noticed she was holding a baby spoon in her hand.

"Nope, just feeding Claire her breakfast. Come in." She opened the door wider, and I stepped inside. I looked over and saw Claire sitting in her highchair. She was waving her hands frantically, probably wondering where her mom had gone with the food.

I walked over and kissed the top of her head. "Hi, Claire."

Tambra sat down at the table, and I took the chair beside her. She glanced at me. "What's up?" she asked as she filled the spoon with cereal and fed it to Claire.

I took a deep breath. "I just wanted to apologize to you, Tambra. The last time you came over and we were talking about Tom, I think I offended you, and I just wanted you to know that I'm sorry." I paused to gauge her response. Her face was expressionless as she looked at me. "It's just that the things you've told me about Tom make me feel scared for you. I want you to be happy and safe, and that's where I was coming from. I care about you. That's why I said those things. But I overstepped my bounds, and I'm sorry." I exhaled slowly, relieved that part was over.

She held my gaze for a long moment before she spoke. "Thank you, Vivian. That means a lot to me." She paused to feed Claire more cereal. "You did kind of offend me, I guess. I felt like you were judging me, and I didn't like that."

"I'm sorry," I said. "I wasn't judging you. I just want you to be happy. You deserve to be happy."

"I know," she said. "I want that too, but it's a difficult situation."

I nodded. "I know it's complicated and there are no easy answers. I just want you to know that I'm here to help if you need me." I touched her hand.

She smiled. "Thank you. I really appreciate that." Claire let out a little yelp, and Tambra fed her another spoonful of cereal. "So, Vivian, I wanted to ask you about something," she said, looking at me out of the corner of her eye.

"Okay, sure."

"Last week I was in the front yard doing some weeding, and Mrs. Reed walked by with her dog." She paused and looked at me for a long moment. "She stopped to chat for a minute, and your name came up."

I went rigid, fearful of what she would say next. "Really?" was the only word I could manage.

Tambra wiped Claire's face and unbuckled her from the highchair. "Yeah. She asked me if I'd heard the news about you."

I laughed nervously. "Heard the news about me? Whatever that means."

She pulled Claire out of the highchair and sat her on her lap. "I told her I didn't know what she meant, and she told me that you're... that you...that you're a...a homosexual." She gave me a confused look. "Vivian, is that true?"

I sat in stunned silence for several moments, unsure of how to respond. I thought about Daniel's advice to tell Tambra before she heard it from someone else. Well, it was too late for that. I'd screwed up again. Finally I said, "Tambra, I'm sorry, but I—"

She leaned toward me and looked me straight in the eye. "Vivian, is it true?"

I slumped back in my chair. "Yes, it's true."

She covered my hand with hers. "Why didn't you tell me?"

I met her gaze. "When would I have told you? That's not something that just naturally comes up."

She raised her eyebrows. "I asked you a couple times about you getting married someday. That would have been the perfect time."

I sighed deeply. "I didn't tell you because I was really enjoying our friendship and I didn't want to ruin it," I said, not looking at her.

She frowned. "Vivian, a friendship is based on honesty, and keeping something that big from me isn't what a friend would do."

I was astonished by the simple profundity of that statement, and I didn't know what to say. After a long moment, I spoke. "Yes, you're right. But in my experience, once someone knows that about me, the friendship is over."

Her frown deepened. "Is that what you think I'd do? End our friendship? You don't know me better than that by now?"

I was at a loss for words again, and I stared down at my hands, which were working nervously in my lap. Tambra waited for my response, and when I didn't speak, she said, "I wouldn't do that, Vivian."

"I'm just saying that every other person who's found out has had a problem with it," I said. "People I thought might be cool about it. But I was wrong every time."

"Do you mean your parents?" She looked at me with concern.

I shook my head. "No, not my parents. Well, my mom died before I...came out, but my dad knew, and he accepted me."

"So not everyone," she said.

I smiled in spite of my upset. "No, not literally everyone," I said. "But my dad loved me in a way that no one ever has, so he was a little different." I paused. "I mean friends and coworkers. I lost my teaching job in Iowa because the school found out about me."

"Oh, I see," she murmured. "How awful."

"Yeah, so that's not something I go around telling people," I said. "And I was going to tell you when the time was right. I wanted to be the one to decide when that time was, not Mrs. Reed. Right now I'm just really pissed about that."

She gave me a sympathetic smile. "I know. I'm pissed on your behalf, believe me. But now I know, so let's move on, okay?"

I nodded. "Yeah, okay."

She looked at me for a long moment. "So I was wondering—have you ever had a serious relationship with a woman?"

I thought about how to answer that. My first relationship, if you could call it that, had been with my college roommate, Margaret, during my sophomore year. Margaret and I had lived in the same dorm room for three months without so much as hugging each other. Then one Saturday night we'd gotten our hands on a bottle of whiskey and had sat on Margaret's bed drinking and laughing into the wee hours. At some point—I could never remember exactly how it happened—Margaret was in my lap, and we were kissing.

That had been the beginning of a furtive and intense relationship that had lasted the rest of that school year. I had fallen head over heels in love with her, but my feelings hadn't been returned. She loved to curl up against my naked body and stroke my skin. She got lost in my lips ("kissing you is like eating a peach," she would say). Many nights we would stay up late talking, which was always followed by passionate lovemaking. But when it came to real feelings, Margaret was like a brick wall. After we made love, I would always whisper, "I love you, Margaret," and she would just smile, never saying anything in return.

At the end of sophomore year, we'd gone our separate ways for the summer—I went back to Applewood, and Margaret went to her parents' house in Dubuque. I'd called her in late July to ask about her plans for the coming school year and to find out if we could room together again. She hadn't been happy to hear from me, and she'd told me bluntly that she wasn't going back to college.

"What do you mean?" I asked.

"I'm getting married," she said in a tight voice.

"Married?" I cried. "Married to whom?"

"Bobby, my high-school sweetheart."

I was confused and heartbroken. "But you like girls," I said.

She barked out an icy laugh and said, "Just because you and I did things doesn't mean I'm like that. It was fun while it lasted, but it didn't mean anything."

I was crushed. "Seemed like you were like that to me," I said bitterly.

Margaret sighed loudly. "This is a man's world, Vivian, and the sooner you learn that, the better. Do yourself a favor and find a man to marry. You'll be much happier."

"I'll never do that," I answered fiercely.

"Suit yourself," she said. "But you'll have a lonely life. Now I have to go. Good-bye."

I'd hung up the phone with tears blurring my vision, the echo of Margaret's cruel words filling my head. I'd felt very foolish to think that I'd had something real with her, and I'd vowed never to make that mistake again. I had never seen her again.

I hadn't ventured into another relationship until several years later, when I was a teacher at Applewood Elementary. I'd met Harriet, an English teacher at the high school, at a district-wide meeting, and we'd hit it off immediately. Harriet lived alone, and we spent many evenings at her apartment drinking beer, listening to records from the forties and fifties, and talking late into the night.

One night Harriet asked me point-blank if I was looking for a boyfriend. I cautiously said no, I wasn't interested in having a boyfriend.

"Why not?" she asked, her eyes searching my face.

I shrugged and said, "It's just not my thing."

"Are you...do you...do you like to be...with women?" she asked haltingly.

I looked at her, stunned. How had she known? I wasn't sure what to say, so I told the truth. "Yes, actually, I do."

She sighed with relief. "Me too!"

We laughed and hugged then, both overjoyed that we'd found a kindred soul. Before that evening was over, we had shared our first kiss.

Harriet and I began a tentative relationship. We spent time together in the evenings and on weekends, but we had to be careful about being seen out together too often. Applewood was a small, tight-knit community, and people noticed the comings and goings of others. We knew that if our relationship was discovered, it would be the end of both our careers. After nearly a year of sneaking around, we were both tired and irritable. I knew that, as much as I liked spending time with Harriet, she wasn't my soulmate. I was convinced there was someone out there for me and it wasn't her, and I suspected she felt the same. We made the mutual decision to end our relationship. We had remained friends, going to the movies or out to dinner once in a while, but we had left it at that.

I pushed these memories out of my mind and forced myself to look Tambra in the eye. "I had a brief relationship—six months or so—with my college roommate," I said. "And then a few years later, I dated a teacher in Applewood for about a year. That didn't go anywhere. I haven't been with anyone since. So no, I've never had a serious relationship—not someone I'd risk everything for."

Tambra cocked her head to the side. "Is that what you want? Someone you'd risk everything for?"

I thought for a moment and then nodded. "Yes, I think I do. I want to be so in love that I'd risk everything to be with her."

She raised her eyes to meet mine and held my gaze for a long time—so long that I had to look away. "Well, I hope you find her, Vivian," she said. "You deserve to be happy." Claire began to fuss, and Tambra glanced at the clock. "Claire's getting tired. I should go put her down for a nap."

"It's time for me to go anyway," I said, and then I rose and moved toward the door.

She set Claire in her baby seat and then followed me to the door. She turned toward me, and before I could speak, she enclosed me in a hug. I felt the warmth and softness of her body pressed against me and smelled the sweetness of her breath on my cheek. My head began to spin a little.

She pulled back, her hands still on my arms, and looked at me for a long moment. There was an expression in her eyes that I couldn't read, but it made my stomach flutter.

"Thank you for sharing this with me, Vivian," she said. "I'm sure it wasn't easy."

I hesitated, not sure what was happening. "I'm just glad you know now," I finally said. "It's a relief to have it out in the open."

She smiled. "I'm sure it is. And thank you for the apology." She opened the door. "See you later."

"See you later." I walked out, and she closed the door behind me.

As I walked home, I let relief wash through me. Tambra had accepted my apology, and she now knew every major thing about me, and she still wanted to be my friend. But beyond that, I had the feeling that something else had happened between us that I didn't quite understand. I couldn't put a name to it—all I knew was that it had made me feel unsure on my feet. Had I imagined it? I replayed the scene over and over in my mind, and by the time I reached my front door, I had convinced myself that nothing had happened between us—it was all wishful thinking on my part. Tambra was a straight, married woman, and even though she wasn't happy with Tom, she had absolutely no interest in me beyond friendship. Whatever I thought had just happened had been completely concocted inside my own head.

22

Josie
July 2015

I was up early the next morning. By the time Claire shuffled into the kitchen, I'd been sitting at the kitchen table for nearly an hour. "Good morning," I said brightly as she came into the room.

"Morning," she mumbled.

"I made some coffee. I hope that's okay," I said.

She laughed. "More than okay. That's great," she said as she pulled a mug from the cabinet. "It's been a long time since anyone's made me coffee." She filled her mug and then opened the fridge to grab the creamer. She added a splash to her coffee, moved over to the table, and took the seat beside me. "You're up early."

"Yeah, I couldn't sleep. I'm excited about our adventure today." Claire and I had decided the evening before that we'd go to the Thurston County Clerk's Office and find out how we could request a transcript from Vivian's trial. Claire hoped that the transcript would explain why Vivian had killed her mother. I had a similar hope, even though my underlying motivation was different. "I've already looked online and found the case number and the location of the clerk's office, where the old court documents are stored," I said.

She gave me an odd look. "You're awfully interested in this," she said. "Almost as much as I am."

I could feel my cheeks getting warm. Maybe I needed to curb my enthusiasm a bit. I certainly wasn't ready to tell Claire the whole story. "I just know this is important to you, and I get excited about research and mysteries," I said. "It's very satisfying to me to solve them."

She looked at me, an amused expression on her face. "Okay, I get it. You're a frustrated PI."

I laughed. "Yeah, something like that."

We ate breakfast together, and then parted ways to go to our respective bathrooms and get ready for the day. By nine thirty we were both showered, dressed, and ready to head out the door. I looked at Claire appreciatively. She was a beautiful woman with a lot of style. She wore navy capris and a silky navy and white tank top that showed off her toned and tanned arms. In her ears were large silver hoops, and she'd gathered her hair up into a loose updo. Her eyes were rimmed in navy eyeliner that made her eyes look lovely. "You look fantastic," I said.

"Why, thank you," she said. I noticed her cheeks pinken and hoped that meant she'd appreciated the compliment.

We headed out to the Audi and got in. Claire started the car, pulled on her sunglasses, and then backed out of the driveway. She'd looked up the directions earlier and said she knew exactly where the clerk's office was. She drove there confidently, singing in an off-key voice to every song that came on the radio. I watched her appreciatively. I found Claire intriguing, and there was no denying that she was gorgeous. I sat back, content to be in the company of a woman who was both beautiful and a kindred spirit.

Fifteen minutes later we parked at the clerk's office and got out. We made our way up to the building, both of us feeling apprehensive about what we'd find. Claire pushed open the door, and I followed. She walked up to the counter and flashed a smile at the receptionist.

"Hello," Claire said, moving her sunglasses to the top of her head.

"Hi," the woman said in a bored voice. She was young—no more than twenty-three or twenty-four—and she had purple hair and a small silver ring in her nose. She was chewing gum furiously. "How can I help you?" She looked at Claire, snapping her gum.

Claire tipped her head to the side. "We need to find out how to access records from a criminal trial that happened forty-one years ago."

The woman nodded her head toward the corner of the room. "Over there," she said. "We have computer terminals, and you can look up the information there and then print it out." She paused. "It costs money, though. Fifty cents per page."

"That's fine," Claire said.

The woman gave us instructions on how to log on to the computer, and we walked over to one of the terminals and sat down. Claire touched the mouse, and the computer came to life. "So what's the case number?" she asked.

I pulled the paper out of my pocket and looked at the note I'd made earlier. I read the case number to her, and she typed it in and pressed Enter. The computer churned away for several seconds, and then the document opened on the computer.

"Yep, this is it," she said.

I looked over her shoulder and read the words, "The People of the State of Washington vs. Vivian Marie Latham." I felt a chill sweep through me. Was I about to find out what had really happened?

"Shall we print it and go somewhere to read it?" she asked.

I shrugged. "Sure. That sounds good."

She pressed the Print button, and we waited as the printer at the end of the table began spitting out page after page. By the time it was done, it looked like a stack of fifty pages. Claire gathered the pages and then marched back up to the desk. I watched as the purple-haired woman carefully counted every page and then told Claire her total. "Twenty-six fifty," she announced. Claire dug around in her handbag and found her checkbook. She hurriedly wrote a check and then motioned for me to follow her.

We walked to the car silently and climbed in. "Where to?" Claire asked.

"We passed a Starbucks about five minutes from here," I said. "Why don't we go there?"

"Sounds good," she said, starting the car and backing out of the parking space.

As we drove I eyed the pages Claire had set on the center console. It was all I could do not to snatch them and start reading.

We pulled into the Starbucks parking lot, and Claire turned off the car and grabbed the stack of papers. "Ready for this?" she asked.

I nodded. "Yes, I'm ready." I opened my door and got out.

At the Starbucks counter, we each ordered a coffee and then stood waiting for them. The store wasn't busy, and I already had my eye on two comfy-looking chairs in the corner. As soon as my coffee came up, I plucked it off the counter and headed over to the chairs. Claire followed at a more leisurely pace, stopping to add cream to her coffee. She sat down in the chair beside me and set the pages on the table between us. She blew on her coffee and then took a tentative sip. "Why don't you have a look," she said, nodding toward the papers. "I can tell you're champing at the bit to read it."

She didn't have to tell me twice. I picked up the pages from the table and began scanning them eagerly. I remembered I wanted to make notes, and I took my notebook and pen from my purse. "I want to write down some key points," I said, feeling a bit sheepish.

"Of course," she said, taking a sip of her coffee and looking at me over the top of the cup.

I pored over the first few pages, reading through the two attorneys' opening statements. I made a note of their names: Douglas Armstrong, the prosecutor, and Fergus Atkinson, Vivian's attorney. I wondered if either one was still practicing. This was forty-one years ago, I reminded myself, and that was unlikely. I couldn't tell how old they had been from their words, but I guessed they had been in their forties or fifties when Vivian was on trial. That would mean they'd be in their eighties or nineties now. I doubted they were still alive, much less practicing law.

I returned my attention to the court document. I was surprised to see that the prosecution's first two witnesses had been Vivian's neighbors, Agnes Reed and Doris McLellan. I knew that Mrs. Reed had told me she'd testified, but still it was a shock to see it in black and white. I read their words. Vivian was odd. She kept to herself. Neither woman claimed to be able to confirm that Vivian and Tambra had been friends.

I read further down and came to the testimony of the detective who had conducted the investigation. I made a note of his name: Sean O'Neil. I skipped ahead to his accounting of what he had found at the crime scene. He talked about the blood, Tambra's wounds, and then the murder weapon: a baseball bat. My breath caught in my throat.

"What?" Claire asked with alarm.

I looked at her. "Did you know your mom was killed with a baseball bat?"

She moaned and then covered her eyes with her hand. "No," she said. "I didn't know that." She uncovered her eyes and looked at me. "What else have you found out?"

"Nothing else major yet," I said, returning to the document. The next section covered Fergus Atkinson's cross-examination of Sean O'Neil. Mr. Atkinson first asked if Vivian had ever confessed to killing Tambra. Detective O'Neil said no. Fergus Atkinson then said, "In fact, didn't she adamantly express her innocence?" Detective O'Neil confirmed that she had. Something lightened in me then. I know it probably didn't mean much, but still it made me feel better. I returned to reading Detective O'Neil's testimony.

"What the hell?" I said, almost in a whisper. I looked at Claire with wide eyes.

"What?" she asked.

I couldn't speak the words I had just read, and I handed the papers to her. "Right there," I said, pointing to the section.

She read the words and then met my eyes, a look of disgust on her face. "Seriously? Did Vivian Latham really think anyone would believe that she and my mom were romantically involved and my dad killed her out of jealousy?" She snorted. "That's utterly ridiculous." She handed the pages back to me.

I picked up my cup and took a sip of coffee. It was lukewarm, but I drank it anyway. I thought about Claire's comment. Was it ridiculous? There was no denying that Vivian Latham had been convicted of Tambra's murder, which meant that the police and the prosecuting attorney had presented enough evidence to convince a jury of her guilt. Had Vivian been mentally ill and imagined that she and Tambra were lovers? Had she concocted this story to save her own skin? Had Vivian and Tambra been lovers; had Tambra ended it and Vivian flown into a murderous rage? Or, as Vivian contended, had they been lovers, and had Tom found out about the affair and murdered his wife? Which version was the truth? My mind spun with the possibilities. And of course my underlying question always was, why was I dreaming about this night over and over?

Claire interrupted my thoughts. "Don't you think that's ridiculous, Josie?"

I glanced at her, not trusting myself to look her in the eyes. "I don't know," I said meekly. "I certainly don't know what your mom's relationship was with Vivian Latham."

She stared at me as if I were crazy. "She had no relationship with Vivian Latham. Vivian Latham killed her. My mom was married to my dad. They had a baby—they had me. She was happy. She wouldn't cheat on him."

I shrugged. "I'm sure you're right, Claire," I said. "Vivian was probably mentally ill, and she convinced herself that your mom was in love with her."

"Vivian?" she said in a shrill voice. "Are you on a first-name basis with her now?" She sounded angry.

I laughed nervously. "No, of course not. It's just easier than saying Vivian Latham every time." I was about to say more and then thought better of it. Something had definitely pushed Claire's buttons. I considered that for a moment and decided I could understand her reaction. I wouldn't be too pleased either if there was a suggestion that my dad had murdered my mom in a jealous rage because she was having an affair with the next-door neighbor.

Claire looked at me but said nothing. Finally she looked away, and I went back to reading the transcript. Fergus Atkinson had brought up other interesting points in his cross-examination of Detective O'Neil: that Vivian's fingerprints were on the bat because she'd been trying to protect Tambra with it, that the cops were biased against Vivian because she was a lesbian, that Detective O'Neil was inexperienced and had mishandled the case, and that the neighbors might have given false statements because they didn't want Vivian in their neighborhood. I thought of Mrs. Reed and her comment that Vivian had been different. I could definitely imagine her wanting Vivian out of the neighborhood.

I made note of Detective O'Neil's statement that he'd been on the police force for six years. Assuming he had been in his early to mid twenties when he joined the force, then he'd be sixty-five or seventy now. He probably wasn't still working, but he was likely still alive. I wanted to talk to him.

I settled back in the chair and began to read Tom Delaney's testimony. He maintained that Vivian had been obsessed with Tambra and that when Tambra spurned her advances, Vivian had broken into their house and killed her. He even contended that Vivian had put a note in Tambra's mailbox that said, "You're going to be sorry you ever met me." The prosecutor ended by asking Tom Delaney if he had ever laid a hand on Tambra in anger. "Never," he had said.

Claire stood up. "I'm going to get more coffee," she said. "Do you want anything?"

The interruption startled me, but then I handed her my cup. "Could you get me a refill of drip coffee?" I asked.

She nodded and headed toward the front counter. I sat back in the chair and began to read Fergus Atkinson's cross-examination of

Tom. I thought he had done a good job of revealing some discrepancies in Tom's testimony, including wondering how Tom, a large man, had been unable to restrain Vivian when she broke into their house. Tom gave a far-fetched response, claiming that Vivian had "superhuman strength," which I found laughable. Fergus Atkinson even suggested that he had some doubts about Tom's truthfulness, and I smiled at that. "You go, Fergus," I said under my breath.

Claire returned with my coffee, and I took it from her wordlessly, captivated by what I was reading. I continued with the document, scanning the testimony from Vivian's friend, Daniel Frazier, and then Vivian's aunt, Dorothy Perkins. I made a careful note of the name Daniel Frazier, wondering if he was still alive. Daniel reported that Vivian had told him about her love affair with Tambra, and I wondered again—could it be true? I glanced at Claire, worried she could read my thoughts.

"What?" she asked.

"Nothing," I said. "Just making sure you're okay."

"I'm fine," she said shortly, picking up a newspaper from the table beside her and snapping it open. "Are you almost done?"

"Yeah, almost," I said. I scanned down the page, reading Douglas Armstrong's swift annihilation of both Daniel Frazier and Dorothy Perkins. He successfully made Vivian look like a complete nutcase, painting her as a woman who was both delusional and deceptive. I sighed, feeling sad for Vivian. I looked at Claire, worried she'd respond to my sigh, but she seemed to be engrossed in an article.

I read on, finally getting to the section I wanted to read: Vivian's testimony. She recounted her friendship with Tambra and explained how it had deepened over time. She said Tambra had told her that Tom was abusing her. Vivian said she'd seen the cuts and bruises on Tambra's face and arms. Fergus Atkinson asked if Vivian had advised Tambra, and Vivian said yes, she'd advised Tambra to leave Tom, but Tambra had said it wasn't the right time. Vivian then testified that she and Tambra had become lovers in early May.

Fergus then asked Vivian about what had happened the night Tambra died. She said Tom had gone to Bellingham to stay with his brother for the weekend, and she and Tambra had planned to escape to California while he was gone. Tom had surprised them by coming home in the middle of the night, enraged that Tambra was in bed with her lover, and he became violent with Tambra. Vivian's next words made me freeze: "We ran out to the living room to try and get out the front door. I tripped and fell, but Tambra made it to the door. Tom came running out of the bedroom and grabbed her before she could get the door open." I thought immediately of my dream—the blond woman running toward a door and a hand coming out and grabbing her. The words were there in black and white. That had actually happened. I swallowed hard, becoming more convinced by the second that Vivian's accounting of events described what had really happened.

I read on, coming next to Vivian's description of Tom beating Tambra with the bat. I felt sick to my stomach. I looked away from the ugly words, trying to calm my stomach and my nerves.

After a few moments of deep breathing, I returned to the page, reading Vivian's account of how Tom had killed Tambra and then called the police to tell them that Vivian had murdered his wife. Fergus Atkinson asked her point-blank if she had killed Tambra, and Vivian said she loved Tambra and she would never hurt her. Tears welled in my eyes as I felt Vivian's desperation and grief. She'd been about to escape to a new life with Tambra. Then, in the blink of an eye, her lover was dead, and she was on trial for her murder. A tear rolled down my cheek, and I wiped it away quickly before Claire could see. I knew her opinion on this matter—an opinion I no longer shared. I was convinced that was what had really happened—Tom had killed Tambra in a jealous rage and then framed Vivian for it. Now I just needed to prove it.

23

We headed back to Claire's house, the court transcript clutched in my hands. As we waited at a stoplight, I turned toward her. "I think you should read this, Claire."

She looked at me and raised an eyebrow. "I don't need to read it if that's the kind of shit she says." She turned her eyes back to the road as the light turned green, her hands gripping the steering wheel. "I thought that court document would explain why Vivian Latham killed my mother, not spread a bunch of lies about her." She paused. "And lies about my father, too, for that matter."

"Just read it," I said.

"I don't need to read it!" she said, her voice rising. "It's nothing but lies!"

I sighed. "Then ask your dad about it."

She looked at me as if I were crazy. "I'm not asking my dad about this! He'll think I'm insane!"

I looked at her with pleading eyes. "Claire, it explains a lot, like why your dad won't talk about your mom." I paused. "Just read it and then form your opinion."

She surprised me by pulling the car to the shoulder. She turned to look at me, and I saw the fierce anger in her eyes. "Why are you so sympathetic toward Vivian Latham, Josie?" she yelled.

"I wouldn't call it sympathy, exactly," I said. "I'm a researcher and this docu—"

"Enough with the 'I'm a researcher' bullshit!" she shouted. "Why are you on Vivian Latham's side?"

I ignored her question. "What if it's true?" I asked softly. "What if your mom really was in love with Vivian and that was more than your dad could handle?" I picked up the pages. "Vivian said your dad was abusing your mom—that he beat her so badly in late July that she had to go to the emergency room. That was when they devised this plan to run off together."

Claire's cheeks were bright red, and her eyes looked wild. "You are fucking insane! My dad never laid a hand on my mom. That's complete and utter bullshit!"

"How do you know that?" I asked, trying to keep my voice calm. "You were a baby, Claire."

"I know because he's my dad and he wouldn't do that!" she yelled. "Vivian Latham was just trying to come up with a story to get out of prison time. She's a Goddamn liar!"

I knew I should stop, but I couldn't. Claire hadn't read the testimony, and I had. "You yourself told me how angry your dad can get," I said. "Do you think he was any different with your mom?"

"Being angry isn't the same as being a wife beater!" she roared. "Or a murderer, for that matter!"

I took a deep breath, trying to keep myself calm. "And Vivian said your dad was supposed to be staying with his brother in Bellingham that weekend and he came home in the middle of the night to ambush them. Can't you call your uncle and ask him if that's true?"

"No!" Claire shouted. "I'm not wasting one more second of my time on this bullshit!" She looked straight ahead, her jaw set angrily, and then pulled back into traffic. "Don't say another word to me about it!"

I leaned back in my seat, ready to be quiet. There would be no convincing her. I knew that now.

We drove wordlessly the rest of the way to her house. When we arrived, Claire turned off the car and stalked up the sidewalk and into the house without saying a word to me. She marched down the hallway to her bedroom and slammed the door. I went to the guest room and pushed the door closed. I stretched out on the bed and stared up at the ceiling, wondering what I was going to do now.

I must have dozed off, because some time later I was startled awake when I heard a knock on the door. I glanced at the clock. An hour had passed since I'd first lain down on the bed. I stood up, smoothed my hair down, and then said, "Come in."

Claire opened the door and stepped inside. Her face looked grim. I saw that she was holding a book, which she opened and thrust into my face. "I looked at all my mom's old yearbooks," she said loudly. "She never went to school with anyone named Barbara Smith." She threw the book onto the bed and then glared at me. "Do you mind telling me who the fuck you are, Josie?"

Oh shit, I thought. Barbara Smith. My imaginary mom. "My mom was probably sick on picture day," I said weakly.

"Every year for four years? Please," she scoffed. "Don't insult my intelligence." She looked at me, her eyes blazing. "Who the fuck are you, and why are you so interested in my mother?"

I sat down on the bed and looked at her. "I don't think that's something I should tell you right now, Claire," I said.

"Are you Vivian Latham's daughter or her niece or something?" she asked, an accusatory tone in her voice.

I shook my head. "No, no. Nothing like that."

"Then who the fuck are you?" Her voice was becoming shrill again, and at that instant I wanted nothing more than to run from the room. I stood my ground, though, and thought of my options. I could tell her my true and bizarre story, or I could come up with another lie. I'd been doing a lot of lying lately, and frankly, I was tired of it. Lying required so much creativity and energy—creativity and energy I really didn't have at my disposal at that moment. I sighed deeply and looked her in the eye.

"All right, Claire. I'll tell you everything." I patted the bed beside me. "Why don't you sit down."

She looked at me for a long moment, rolled her eyes, and then sat next to me. I turned to look at her, took a deep breath, and began.

※

I finished my strange tale and looked at Claire. I desperately wanted her to believe everything I had just told her, but I really didn't expect that she would. She was frowning intensely, and her mouth was set in a hard line.

"I hope you know how utterly ridiculous that story sounds," she finally said.

I nodded. "Yes, of course I do, but it's the truth."

"You seriously expect me to believe all this? That you were Vivian Latham in a past life? That you're dreaming about the night my mom was murdered?" She shook her head. "You must think I'm pretty gullible."

Now I was getting angry. Why would I lie about this? It was such a ridiculous story that it had to be true. "If I was going to lie about my connection to Vivian Latham, why the hell would I tell you that story?" I said. "Doesn't the sheer absurdity of it all tell you that it's true?" When she didn't say anything, I continued. "Up until a year ago I'd never heard of the name Tambra, and until a month ago I'd never heard of Vivian Latham. Now their story has taken over my life. Do you think this is what I want? To be living this?" Claire just stared at me. "Do you?"

"I want you out of here," she said, looking at me coldly. "You were right—I never should have asked you to stay here. But in my defense, I didn't know you were a psycho."

"Nice, real nice," I said. "You sure didn't turn out to be the person I thought you were either." I stood and grabbed my suitcase off the floor, threw it on the bed, and started tossing my clothes inside. Claire just sat on the bed, her arms crossed over her chest, watching me. I stormed into the bathroom and snatched my toiletries off the counter. I stuffed them inside my suitcase, zipped it up, and then looked at her.

"I'm out of here," I said angrily. I nodded toward the nightstand. "There's the court transcript. I hope you'll read it once you pull your head out of your ass." I paused. "I wrote my phone number on there. Call me when you want to apologize." I picked up my suitcase off the bed, grabbed my purse and iPad, and stomped out of the bedroom. Then I made my way to the front door, opened it, and left her house.

24

Vivian
April–August 1974

Tambra and I became almost inseparable over the next few weeks. Tambra and Claire would come over to my house after Tom left for work, and we'd sit on the porch drinking coffee, talking, and laughing. Then she'd strap Claire into her stroller, and we'd take our walk through the neighborhood.

When the weather got warmer, we'd pack a picnic lunch and go to the park. We'd spread a blanket on the grass, lie there looking up at the sky, and talk about everything under the sun. Tambra had an insightful mind, and her knowledge about current events impressed me. I guessed that came from reading the newspaper from front to back every day.

We'd come back around two o'clock so Claire could take her nap. While she slept, Tambra and I would play cards—crazy eights was her favorite—or we'd just talk. We always made sure Tambra was near her phone at eleven and three thirty so she could answer Tom's call. I still thought that was ridiculous, but I kept my mouth shut. I laughed inwardly because I was sure Tom had no idea that the rest of the time Tambra was "flitting about" with me.

I'd reluctantly head home at four o'clock—right after Claire got up from her nap—so I was long gone by the time Tom came home at five.

As the time we spent together grew, so did my feelings for Tambra. By the time May first rolled around, I was hopelessly in love with her. I knew those feelings would never be returned, so I kept them to myself. I was satisfied to be in her company, to talk and laugh with her, and to gaze upon her beautiful face. She had ruined me for any other woman; I couldn't imagine ever loving anyone as much as I loved Tambra.

On a Tuesday morning in early May, I rose as usual, got dressed, and started the coffee. As it brewed I stood on the porch waiting for Tom to leave. At 8:20 a.m. I watched him roar away in his Ford Galaxie and then went back inside to pour Tambra's coffee and wait for her arrival.

By nine o'clock she wasn't there, and I began to worry that something was wrong. Ten minutes later she still hadn't appeared, and I knew I had to go check on her. I crossed my yard to her house and knocked on the front door.

The door creaked open, and Tambra stared out at me with one eye. "Hi, Vivian," she said in a monotone voice. She looked terrible. Her hair was disheveled, and the eye I could see was bloodshot. She was still wearing her bathrobe.

She opened the door wider, and I gasped as I saw the purple bruise rimming her right eye. "Tambra, what the hell happened?"

Tears filled her eyes. "Tom did it last night," she said in a hoarse voice.

"What? Why? What happened?"

She looked down at the floor. "I burned the dinner, and he got angry."

I led Tambra over to the couch, and we sat down. I noticed that Claire was in her baby seat playing with a rattle, blissfully unaware of her mother's distress. "Tell me what happened," I said gently.

Haltingly and with hiccuping sobs, Tambra told me the story. Tom had come home already angry about something that had happened at work. Tambra had been making pork chops for dinner and had left them cooking in the pan so she could run and change Claire's diaper. When she got back, one side of the meat had been charred.

About that time Tom came home, ranting about his coworker, Jerry, who had stolen a huge lumber sale from him. Tambra listened to him as she frantically searched the refrigerator and then the freezer for something else to make for dinner, finding nothing. She said she'd debated with herself about whether to be honest about the burned meat or serve the pork chops and take her chances that he wouldn't notice. She chose the latter, reasoning that he was preoccupied by his work troubles and he wouldn't pay any attention to overdone pork chops. They sat down to dinner, Tom still carrying on about his lost sale.

Tambra watched him cut the meat, bring it to his mouth, and chew as he continued to fume about Jerry. He took another bite of pork and didn't say anything. As he brought a third bite to his mouth, Tambra sighed, thinking she was in the clear.

"What the hell?" Tom finally said. "This pork tastes burned."

"I think it's good," Tambra said, her eyes fixed on her plate.

"It's burned," he growled. "I can taste it."

She looked at him meekly, watching as he picked up the chop with his fork and flipped it over. "Jesus Christ, Tambra, this pork is black. What the hell did you do?"

Her eyes flickered toward his and then away. "Claire needed her diaper changed, and I left it in the pan for a few minutes too long. It's just a little overdone. It's fine."

"It's not fine—it's black!" he roared. "It belongs in the trash!" Then he stood up, marched into the kitchen, and dumped his pork chop in the garbage can. "Now make me something else to eat!" he barked.

Tambra lowered her head, not looking at him. "We don't have anything else. I'm going to the grocery store tomorrow."

Tom's face went beet red, and his nostrils flared. He stood up, grabbed her ponytail, and yanked her head back. "Are you telling me you don't have anything to make your husband for dinner? The husband who works his fingers to the bone so you can stay home and have your nice life?"

Her hand went instinctively to her head to protect herself. "Tom, stop. You're hurting me."

"'Tom, stop. You're hurting me,'" he said in a mocking tone and then slapped her hand away.

Tambra looked at Claire then. Claire's big blue eyes were wide and full of confusion. "Tom, stop. Claire is watching," she said.

"I don't care," he snarled. "She should know what a loser her mommy is." Then he picked Tambra up by her hair and pulled her face toward his, his nose almost touching hers. "Now go in the kitchen and make your husband something to eat!"

"I told you, I don't have anything else," she said in a wooden voice. "You don't give me enough money to buy extra stuff. I can only afford enough for our meals." As soon as the words were out of her mouth, she regretted them. She could see his rage grow.

"Are you saying I don't provide for my family?" he roared.

"No, of course not. I do fine with the money you give me. I just don't have anything else to make right now." She gave him a tentative smile. "We have cereal. I could fix you a bowl of cereal."

"Cereal?" Tom scoffed. "You think after a hard day's work I want cereal? What the fuck is the matter with you, woman?" he shouted, pulling her head back again.

"Ow!" she said, trying to twist away from him.

He then grabbed the back of her neck and pushed her roughly over to the refrigerator and opened it. "Find something!"

Tambra looked in the refrigerator, but she knew what was there, as she'd just checked it minutes before: milk, a partial loaf of bread, pickles, ketchup, and a half dozen eggs. "Eggs! I can make you eggs," she said.

"Eggs?" he shouted. "Eggs? I. Don't. Want. Fucking. Eggs." As he said each word, he pounded the side of her head against the edge of the refrigerator. The pain bloomed sharply down her face and behind her eye, and she knew she was going to have a terrible bruise.

"Tom, please stop! Claire is watching you!" Tambra shouted. He looked at Claire then, who indeed was watching him with fear in her eyes.

He had pushed Tambra away then, picked up his jacket and keys, and yelled, "I'm going to the tavern to get something to eat because my Goddamn wife is so fucking stupid!" He had looked at Tambra with disgust as she sobbed and held her face. "Get yourself together, woman!" Then he had stormed out.

I was horrified and infuriated. "What happened then? When did he come home?"

She wiped her nose with the back of her hand. "He came home at one in the morning. He was drunk. He got into bed next to me and put his hand on my shoulder. He said in his drunk voice, 'I'm sorry, baby. Can you forgive me?' I just pretended I was asleep. Finally he rolled over and went to sleep."

"And this morning?" I asked.

She gave a derisive laugh. "He acted like nothing had happened. Just ate his breakfast—eggs and cereal, if you can believe it—and left for work."

I covered her hand with mine. "Is this the first time he's hurt you this badly?"

Tambra looked away for a long beat, as if she was debating with herself, and then looked back at me. "He's hurt me before. He's given me a black eye a few times, and last year he broke two of my fingers. And you saw the bruise on my arm. And I've had other bruises when he's grabbed me and pushed me around. Other times he just yells at me and calls me ugly names."

I was outraged. "I want to talk to that son of a bitch myself and tell him to leave you alone," I said.

She shook her head. "No, no, no, you can't do that, Vivian. Please don't," she said. "It'll just make matters worse."

"Then you have to leave. You can't let him treat you like that," I said fiercely.

"We've already gone over that, Vivian. I can't leave—not now."

"Then when?" I asked. "I don't want that bastard to hurt you again."

She let out a long breath. "I don't know. I'll figure something out."

I grabbed both her hands in mine and stared into her eyes. "Tambra, I can help you with the money. I'll help you if you'll let me." I could hear the desperation in my voice.

She smiled sadly. "I'm sure you can, but I don't think so. I don't know when I could ever pay you back for one thing, and I wouldn't feel right using your inheritance for that. Your dad wanted that money to go to you, not me."

I held her hands more tightly. "I know, honey, but he'd understand."

"I'm sure he would, but no, I can't do that."

"Then what are you going to do?" I asked, holding her gaze.

She squeezed her eyes shut as tears flowed again. She lowered her head and began to sob. I reached out and wrapped my arms around her, and she collapsed against me. I could feel the warmth emanating from her body through the thin cotton of her bathrobe. She pressed her face into my neck and wept. I rubbed her back in slow circles and murmured, "It's okay," over and over.

"Why doesn't Tom love me?" she said against my skin. "Why doesn't anyone love me?"

My heart skipped a beat. I couldn't let that statement pass. "I love you, Tambra," I said in her ear, my voice cracking.

She drew back and looked at me, her nose just an inch from mine. "You do?"

I nodded. "Of course I do. How could I not? You're the most amazing woman I've ever known."

She looked at me with wide eyes. She held my gaze for what seemed like an eternity. I felt the soft weight of her in my arms, and I breathed in the alluring fragrance of her hair and skin. The closeness of her was intoxicating. My head was spinning. Something came over me then, and, before I could stop myself, I leaned forward and kissed her. I felt the velvety softness of her lips and tasted the sweetness of her mouth. Desire raced through me, and I surrendered myself to that delicious feeling for one singular, blissful moment.

Then good sense took over, and I jerked back, mortified. "Oh my God, Tambra, I'm so sorry. I don't know why I did that. I didn't—" But my words were stopped by her mouth. She pressed her lips against mine urgently, her arms reaching out to pull me against her. For a brief moment, I was frozen with shock, but the warmth of her mouth and the suppleness of her body rendered me senseless, and my lips began to move with hers. She pushed me back against the arm of the couch and pressed her body to mine, kissing me deeply, passionately. I wrapped my arms around her, losing myself in her luscious lips and silky tongue.

Just as my lips left hers to begin traveling down her neck, Claire let out a sharp cry. Startled, we pulled apart. Tambra sighed, pushed herself off me, and then moved to pick up Claire.

I sat stunned for a moment before I could speak. "Tambra, I'm... I'm so...I'm so sorry," I stammered. "I don't know what happened."

She sat down beside me and gave me a bemused smile. "I think you know what happened, Vivian. We kissed," she said. "And I wanted to. I've wanted to for a while. But I'll admit I never thought about kissing you in my bathrobe."

I'm sure my eyes were filled with confusion. "But I'm a woman."

She laughed. "Yes, I've noticed."

I frowned. "But you like men."

She looked at me, her brows drawn together in thoughtful contemplation. "Is that really the most important thing, whether you're a man or a woman?" I sensed that the question was rhetorical and said nothing. "What's more important to me is being with the person who makes me happy," she continued. "The person who loves me the way I am. The person I'm connected with. The person I feel like I've known forever. That's you, Vivian." She paused to take a deep breath. "I made a stupid mistake and got stuck marrying Tom, and I've paid for that mistake for almost three years. It's my turn now to be with the person who makes me happy."

I was flabbergasted, and I just looked at her, openmouthed. "I'm not sure what to say," I finally said.

"You don't have to say anything," she said. "Just know that this is something I've thought about—a lot." She looked at me with the most earnest expression. "Vivian, I want to be your lover. Do you want to be my lover?"

I couldn't believe she was asking me this question. Being Tambra's lover was something I'd only dreamed of. But again, good sense reared its ugly head, and I frowned. "Tambra, you're married."

She pointed to the bruise around her eye. "Married to a man who'd do this to me because I burned the pork chops."

I nodded. "Yes, I agree that's unforgivable, but still, you took wedding vows, and you..." My voice trailed off.

Tambra snorted. "Tom broke our wedding vows the minute he put his hands on me in anger."

I couldn't argue with that logic. "That's true, but..." I was out of arguments, and I looked at her helplessly.

She took my hand in hers. "Vivian, we're connected," she said softly. "The connection I have with you is greater than anything I've ever felt with anyone."

I squeezed her hand. "I know. I feel the connection too. But it can just be a friend connection. It doesn't have to be more."

She gave me her crooked smile, a flirtatious look in her eyes. "Vivian, are you saying you're not attracted to me?"

I shook my head. "God no, that's not what I'm saying at all. You're the most captivating woman I've ever known. I'm saying I can live with that and just be your friend."

She leaned forward and kissed me once, gently, on the lips. "Or we can see where this takes us."

I looked into her beautiful blue eyes, and I knew I was a goner. There was no way I could ever say no to this woman. "Okay," I said, my voice barely more than a whisper.

She sighed with relief. "So I have to go get some groceries and do a few other things, but will you come back at two when Claire's napping?" She looked at me, watching my expression.

I hesitated for a moment. "Yes," I said. "I will."

"Good." she said. "I'll see you at two."

At two o'clock I rapped on Tambra's door. The door swung open, and she stood there looking resplendent. She wore a sea-green sleeveless blouse, wide-legged white pants, and gold low-heeled sandals. Her hair was loose and flowing, and her skin glowed. She had artfully concealed the angry bruise on her face with makeup. Black eyeliner rimmed her eyes, and her lips were rosy. I caught a scent in the air—lily of the valley. Tambra's perfume.

"My God, you're beautiful," I breathed.

Her cheeks flushed with pleasure, and she reached out and took my hand. "Thanks, Vivian. Come in. Claire's asleep."

I stepped through the door, and Tambra shut it behind me. I looked at her, and all it took was a small upturn of her lips for me to be in her arms kissing her. She moaned and pressed her body against me, her mouth moving against mine with an urgency that took my breath away.

She broke the kiss, and I felt her breath in my ear. "Let's go to the bedroom," she whispered. She took my hand and led me across the room and down the short hallway to the bedroom she shared with Tom. I stopped just outside the door.

"I'm not sure about this," I said. "It's your private space with Tom."

"Believe me, not much goes on between me and Tom in this room," she said as she pulled me forward. "And I really couldn't care less about him right now. At this moment all I care about is you." I hesitated another moment and then moved forward, and Tambra closed the door behind us.

We lay next to each other, our limbs entangled. I breathed in Tambra's scent. I smelled the intoxicating fragrance of sunshine mixed with lily of the valley mixed with sex. Her hair was fanned out on the pillow, and her cheeks were flushed. "My God, Tambra, you're so beautiful," I said, trailing my finger down her arm.

"So are you," she said, and she raised her head and kissed my bare shoulder. She rolled over onto her stomach and propped herself up on her elbows. "Vivian, that was so amazing. There aren't words for it."

I rolled onto my side and draped my arm across her back. "Yeah, it was amazing for me too," I said.

"Was it?" she asked shyly. "I wasn't really sure what I was doing."

I could feel my cheeks getting warm. "Trust me, you were a natural," I said.

She laughed. "Whew, that's a relief." She rolled onto her side and faced me. "Vivian, thank you for…for leading me back to myself. I'd gotten lost somewhere along the way, and I feel more…more like myself again, I guess. Not just because of this…today…but all of it. Because of you." She shrugged. "I don't know how to explain it."

I smiled. "I think I know what you mean. And thank you too. I haven't felt like myself since my dad died—since he got sick, really. You've brought hope back into my life. I know that probably sounds corny, but it's true."

Tambra gazed at me. "It doesn't sound corny at all. It sounds wonderful. It makes me happy." She kissed me.

The shrill ringing of the phone interrupted our reverie. She rolled her eyes. "Shit, that'll be Tom. I've got to answer it." She rose naked from the bed and rushed out to the living room to answer the phone. I strained to hear, but all I could make out was Tambra's muffled voice. She returned a few minutes later and lay down beside me.

"That was Tom checking up on me. I told him not to worry—I'm safe in bed with my lover." She laughed.

"Very funny," I said. "But seriously, Tambra, you can't let on about this with Tom. Not a word. Not even a tiny hint."

She nodded. "Don't worry—I know," she said. "I won't say anything. Not a peep. I can keep a secret."

An alarm bell went off in my head suddenly. I realized I'd never asked Tambra if Tom had heard the neighborhood rumors about me. "Does Tom know about me?" I asked.

She shook her head. "No, I didn't tell him, and he doesn't talk to the neighbors, so I don't know how he'd find out. I wouldn't worry about that."

"I do worry. I worry about you," I said, kissing the tip of her nose.

"It'll be okay," she said. "Tom's not too bright. He won't figure it out. This wouldn't even enter his mind, believe me."

She was probably right. In my experience most people had very little imagination. They saw the world through their own lens, and they explained away or simply did not see anything that didn't fit with their reality. "Yeah, you're probably right," I said. "To him I'm just the harmless neighbor."

"Exactly. So don't worry," she said. At that moment Claire let out a cry from her bedroom. "Guess who's awake?" Tambra said as she rose from the bed and slipped on her bathrobe. Seeing the bathrobe made me remember that she had been crying and upset just hours before, and now we were in bed together. This was all very surreal.

As I waited for her to return with Claire, I thought about what had happened between us. Where was this going? Tambra was married, and she'd made it clear that she wasn't interested in leaving Tom. Would I be her secret lover, sneaking around to find time alone with her? What would we do when Claire got older and could talk? Would she unwittingly out us to Tom? I knew I was getting ahead of myself, but I couldn't help it. My other relationships had ended badly, and I didn't want this one to be another in a line of failures. I loved Tambra so much, and I wanted it to work out. "I'll figure it out," I said aloud.

"Figure what out?" Tambra said as she came back into the bedroom with Claire in her arms.

"Oh, nothing, just talking to myself," I said.

"Oh. Sorry I was gone so long. Claire needed a diaper change," she said.

"That's okay. I should be going anyway. Tom will probably be home soon."

"Oh, yeah, in an hour or so," she said. "I guess I need to start dinner pretty soon. He gets irate if dinner's not on the table when he walks in the door."

"Hmm," I grumbled. I swung my legs over the side of the bed and stood. I reached for my clothes and pulled them on quickly. I caressed Tambra's cheek and kissed her lingeringly. "Thank you. That was really amazing."

"Yes, it was, and don't worry—we'll do it again," she said, and gave me a wink. I felt my cheeks getting warm again. "How cute. You're blushing," she said, and stroked my cheek, which made me blush even harder and made her laugh.

She walked with me to the door. "I think I should go out the side door," I said. "You know, in case anyone's watching. I know how these old biddies love to gossip, and I don't want to give them fuel for the fire."

She shrugged. "Sure, if you want to." She walked over to the kitchen door and opened it. "Bye, Viv," she said, kissing my cheek. "I'll see you tomorrow."

"See you tomorrow," I said as I slipped out the door, and Tambra closed it behind me.

25

We did do it again. And again and again and again. I was drunk on love. Tambra was my dream woman in the flesh, and she wanted to be with me. I couldn't believe my good fortune.

During the week we spent every morning together. We drank coffee; talked at length about books, movies, art, and music; played with Claire; and laughed. We'd part ways around noon, and later, when Claire was napping, I'd cross the lawn into Tambra's back yard and knock softly on the side door. She would pull me inside, kiss me hungrily, and then lead me into the bedroom. By the time we celebrated her twenty-eighth birthday together on June 6, we'd become so closely entwined that I couldn't imagine my life without her.

One afternoon in early July, we lay sprawled out on the bed, my arm around her shoulders and hers draped over my belly.

"Viv?" she said in a small voice.

"Yes, my love," I answered.

She raised her head to look at me. "I really love you. I love you more than I've ever loved anyone."

Tears sprang to my eyes. This wasn't the first time she had expressed her love, but it was the first time she'd spoken with such emotion. "I love you too, Tambra," I said in a thick voice. "More than I've ever loved any woman. More than I'll ever love anyone again. You're my heart and soul."

She stroked my cheek. "No one has ever loved me like you do. You really see me. You accept me for who I am. I didn't think I'd ever have that with someone."

I kissed the top of her head. "I didn't think I'd ever have that with someone either." I sat up and looked at her shyly. "I wrote you something," I said.

"What?" she asked curiously.

I reached for my pants and pulled a folded envelope out of the pocket. "A letter. A love letter, I guess you'd say." I handed the envelope to her.

She smiled. "Wow, thanks, Viv. Nobody's ever written me a love letter before."

"Don't read it now," I said. "Wait until Tom goes to work tomorrow morning."

"Okay, I can wait," she said. She reached over, opened the drawer of her bedside table, and slipped the letter inside.

"Be careful with it," I cautioned. "Don't let Tom find it."

"He won't find it," she said as she lay down beside me again. "Don't worry."

I put my arm around her shoulders. "How are things with Tom, anyway?"

She shrugged. "Okay, I guess. He hasn't hit me lately, if that's what you mean. He's gotten angry and called me names and pushed me around. But he hasn't hit me."

I sighed deeply. "I won't say good, but I'm happy he hasn't hit you."

"He can't hurt me, because I'm in love," she said gaily, reaching up to kiss me.

"I wish that were true," I said in a serious tone. "Have you thought any more about leaving him?"

I felt her stiffen. "No, I haven't. I mean, I have, but it's not the right time. I will—eventually."

"I want to be with you, Tambra. I want to live with you," I said. "I want to wake up next to you every morning. And most of all I want you to be safe."

"It'll happen, Viv. Just be patient." She glanced at the clock on the bedside table. "And now, I hate to say it, but Claire will be awake any minute, and then Tom will be home. I think we should say good-bye for today."

"Yeah, I guess you're right." I rose from the bed and began to dress. We kissed good-bye, and I walked out to the kitchen and slipped out the side door. As I crossed Tambra's driveway, I glanced behind me and noticed I hadn't quite closed the door, so I went back to push it shut. As I did, I caught movement out of the corner of my eye. Mrs. Reed was standing on the sidewalk with her dog, watching me.

"Hi, Mrs. Reed," I said shortly, none too pleased to see her.

"Hello," she barked and then scurried off.

"Bitch," I said under my breath and headed home.

As I reached my front door, I suddenly thought of Daniel. I hadn't talked to him since late March, and here it was July already. I wanted to tell him about Tambra.

Once inside the house, I made a beeline for the phone. I glanced at the kitchen clock. It was four fifteen here, so it was six fifteen in Iowa. He should be home from work. I dialed his number and waited for him to pick up.

"Hello?" Daniel said.

I smiled when I heard his voice. "Daniel, hi. It's Vivian."

"Vivian!" he said jovially. "To what do I owe this honor? It's been a while."

"I know. I'm sorry. Things have just been crazy."

"Really? What's going on?" he asked.

"Well, you remember the woman I told you about? My neighbor, Tambra?"

"Sure, I remember."

"Well, she and I have gotten, uh, involved."

I heard him gasp. "Vivian, are you sleeping with the woman who's straight as an arrow?" he said with pretend shock.

I chuckled. He always made me laugh. "Yeah, I am, so I guess she's not so straight."

"Apparently not," he said dryly. "That's fabulous, Viv! I'm happy for you. And the husband? Is he out of the picture now?"

I sighed. "No, he's not. She keeps telling me she's going to leave him soon, but nothing's happened yet."

"Well, it's not that easy to leave someone, especially when there's a kid involved. You did say she had a baby, right?"

"Yeah, a little girl."

"So, it's complicated. My advice is to just hang in there, and I'm sure it'll happen."

"He beats on her, Daniel," I said in a low voice. "He gave her a black eye a couple months ago because she burned the pork chops."

"Good God, he sounds like a savage. She needs to leave him."

"I know. I keep telling her," I said.

"Do you love her?" he asked in a serious tone.

"I love her so much, Daniel. I've never loved anyone the way I love her."

"And does she love you?"

"Yes, she loves me too," I said. "I can't believe how lucky I am." My voice sounded giddy, even to myself.

"That's great, Viv," he said. "I'm so happy for you. You deserve this. And it'll work out. Just be patient."

"Thanks, Daniel. I hope so. So tell me what you've been up to."

He told me about his recent promotion at the post office, a new man named Henry that he was head over heels in love with, and the changes that were going on in Applewood. "I miss you," he said.

"I know. I miss you too," I said. "Why don't you come out to Washington and visit?"

"That sounds wonderful," he said. "Maybe I'll come and visit this fall."

"I'd love that," I said wistfully.

We ended our conversation, and I hung up the phone feeling happy and relieved that I'd finally told someone about Tambra.

26

Our affair continued through the rest of July. I urged Tambra to leave Tom at least once a week, and she always put me off with her promises of "Soon," or "Be patient." I became resigned to our situation, knowing that at some point it would reach a critical mass and Tambra would be ready to leave. But when that critical mass finally came at the end of July, I wasn't prepared.

We'd made plans to meet at my house that morning after Tom left for work. I sat on my porch waiting for him to leave. When he hadn't left at his usual time, I began to wonder. Finally, at a few minutes after nine, he came out of the house and stalked to his car. He started the car and backed out of the driveway. He seemed angry. I expected Tambra to be there soon after, but when she still hadn't arrived by ten o'clock, I became concerned and decided to walk over and check on her.

As I was about to knock on the side door, I glanced to the sidewalk. I groaned as I saw Mrs. Reed watching me. "Oh shit, not again," I whispered to myself. Why was this woman so damned nosy?

"Can I help you with something?" she said in an icy voice.

Who the hell did this woman think she was, the neighborhood police? "Unless you live here, then no," I said, my voice equally icy. "I'm stopping to say hi to my friend, so your help isn't required." Mrs. Reed huffed and hurried off.

I rolled my eyes and knocked on the door. There was no answer, and I knocked again more loudly. Tambra still didn't answer, and I began to get worried. I glanced out to the sidewalk to make sure Mrs. Reed wasn't still around. I saw Doris McLellan across the street watering her rose garden, but Mrs. Reed had moved on. I turned the doorknob, and it opened. I walked into the kitchen and looked around. Tambra was nowhere to be seen.

"Tambra?" I called. I froze as I heard muffled cries coming from the back of the house. I raced back to her bedroom, but she wasn't there. I looked in the bathroom, but she wasn't there either. She must be in Claire's room. I hurried down the hall and saw that the door was ajar. I pushed it open and found Tambra sitting in the rocking chair with Claire in her arms. Her head was down, and she was sobbing.

I rushed to her side. "Tambra, what's the matter?" She kept her head down and just rocked back and forth, crying. I kneeled in front of the rocking chair and touched her arm. "Tambra, honey, look at me. What is it?" She began making an eerie moaning sound low in her throat and just kept rocking, rocking. Fear seized my heart. "Tambra, please look at me!" I said loudly.

Finally she raised her head and met my eyes. I inhaled sharply as I saw her face. "Oh my God! Tambra, honey, what the hell did he do to you?" I cried.

She just looked at me, expressionless. Her left eye was badly bruised and swollen shut. There was a deep gash across her cheekbone, and her nose was bloody, bruised, and possibly broken.

I began to cry. "Oh my God, Tambra, what did he do?" I wailed.

She stared at me, tears flowing down her face. "He...he beat me...he beat me up," she said, her voice choked by tears.

"Why? What happened? I thought things had been better."

"He knows I'm having an affair," she said woodenly.

"What? How? How did he find out?" This was bad. Very bad. If Tom knew about us, I didn't know what would happen.

"Because I'm happy," she said as tears flooded her eyes again. "He could tell because I've been so happy."

"Tell me what happened," I said.

She took a deep breath. "The alarm didn't go off this morning, and we overslept. He woke up ranting about being late for work. He blamed me for the alarm, and he was yelling and calling me names. Then he started saying that I've been acting different. 'Why are you so Goddamn happy lately?' he said. I said I didn't know what he was talking about." She paused as a sob caught in her throat. "Then he pushed me up against the wall and said, 'What have you been doing while I'm at work?' I said I haven't been doing anything. The same as always. He called me a liar. He said, 'You're fucking some other guy, aren't you?' I said, 'No, of course not.'"

She wiped a tear from her good eye, and I could see that her hand was trembling. "He just kept at me. He got right in my face and screamed at me, 'You're fucking another guy, aren't you? You slut.' I kept saying no over and over, and he kept screaming 'Liar! Liar!' Then he grabbed me around the neck and slammed my head against the wall. I tried to get away, and he slapped me across the face." She pointed to her swollen eye. "That's how I got this. Then he slammed my face into the wall over and over. He kept saying, 'No one will want you now, you ugly bitch.'" As she repeated Tom's hateful words, she put her head down, and her shoulders heaved.

Claire started to cry, and I pried her from Tambra's arms and held her close. "It's okay. It's okay," I murmured in Claire's ear. I put my hand on Tambra's shoulder, not sure what to say. I knew what I was thinking, though—Tambra needed to leave Tom now—but I also knew this wasn't the time to bring that up. "I think we need to take you to the doctor," I finally said. "It looks like your cheek needs stitches and your nose might be broken. And you could have a concussion." She just stared at me vacantly.

Tambra was in no condition to think clearly, and I knew I had to act. She was still wearing her nightgown, and I brought her some clothes and helped her get dressed. Then I ran back to my house to get my car. I pulled up in front of her house and dashed in to get her and Claire. I helped Tambra out to the car and eased her inside.

Then I settled Claire in her arms and fastened the seat belt across Tambra's lap. Not a perfect setup, but it would have to do.

She didn't want to go to her regular doctor because she didn't want to explain to him what had happened. I decided it was best to take her to the emergency room. I raced to the hospital, looking at her every couple of minutes. I noticed that her cheek had stopped bleeding profusely, but I could see it was still oozing blood.

Once we reached the emergency room, they ushered Tambra back quickly as I sat in the waiting room with Claire. She came out an hour later with a white bandage on her cheek and papers in her hand. She found us and sat in the chair beside me. "They put stitches in my cheek," she said in a dull voice. "Seven of them. The doctor said I'll probably have a scar."

"And your nose? Is it broken?" I asked.

"No, he didn't think so. Just badly bruised. Same with my eye. He said they just have to heal on their own." She waved one of the papers. "He gave me a prescription for painkillers."

"What about a concussion? Did they talk about that?"

"He said I wasn't showing signs of a concussion," she said. "But I should watch for symptoms like nausea, sleepiness, a bad headache—stuff like that."

"Did they ask you what happened?"

She nodded. "Yeah, they asked me. I told them I fell."

"Why didn't you tell them the truth?" I asked, my voice rising.

"What good would it do?" she said. "'What happened, doctor, is that my husband beat me up.' And he'd say, 'Sorry you're married to an asshole, but there's nothing we can do.'"

"What about leaving the son of a bitch?" I said fiercely. "That's what you can do."

"Not here, Vivian," she said, standing. "Let's go. We'll talk about it later."

We drove to the pharmacy so Tambra could get her prescription filled, and then she said she was hungry, so we stopped at Big Tom's for deluxe cheeseburgers and soft-serve ice cream for Claire. By two o'clock we were back at Tambra's house, and it was time for Claire's nap. I told Tambra to rest on the couch and I'd put Claire down for her nap. By now I loved Claire as if she were my own daughter, and Claire adored me. When she saw me each morning, she would cry out with delight and clap her hands together. "Good morning, sweet pea," I'd always say, scooping her up in my arms and kissing her cheek, making her squeal with delight. She was eleven months old now and already babbling and starting to take her first tentative steps.

I changed her diaper and then rocked her gently in the rocking chair. I sang softly to her until her eyes fluttered and then closed. I laid her down in her crib and then tiptoed out.

I went back out to the living room and sat on the edge of the couch where Tambra was resting. She was dozing, but she stirred when she felt me sit beside her.

"Hi," she said in a weak voice.

"Hi. How are you feeling?"

"Okay, I guess. My cheek is throbbing, but it doesn't hurt. They gave me lidocaine. They said it would wear off in a few hours."

"Any nausea or headache?" I asked.

She pushed herself up to a sitting position and shook her head. "No, no nausea or headache."

"That's good." I looked at her grimly. "So now I want to know when you're going to leave that bastard."

To my surprise, Tambra said, "I have a plan."

I'd expected more excuses or hand wringing, but I hadn't expected a plan. "Really? What's your plan?"

She looked away, gathering her thoughts. She looked back at me, took a deep breath, and began. "Okay, in two weeks Tom's going to his brother's in Bellingham for the weekend. They do this fishing weekend every August, and it's a big deal to him. He's leaving on Saturday morning, and he won't be back until Sunday evening."

I frowned. "Aren't you going?"

She smiled conspiratorially. "I was going to go, but unfortunately I'm going to get sick the day before he leaves. You know, throwing up, diarrhea, the whole shebang." She paused. "The other thing is that my wounds won't be healed by then, and he won't want me to go anyway. Can you imagine him trying to explain that to his brother? He'll be relieved I'm not going."

"Do you really think he'll still go if you're not going?" I asked dubiously.

She snorted. "He's been talking about this stupid fishing trip for months. He couldn't go last year because I was just a few days from my due date, so he's really looking forward to it. I don't think he'd miss it for the second year in a row."

"Even if he thinks you're having an affair?" I was still skeptical.

She patted my arm. "Oh, ye of little faith, I know my husband. He'll go."

"Okay, you know your husband," I conceded. "Then what?"

"We spend Saturday packing, and on Sunday morning we take off into the sunset." She gave me her crooked smile. "Or the sunrise. Either way, it's adios, asshole."

"And where are we going?" I asked.

She shrugged. "I don't know. Somewhere where it's warm in the winter. California or Arizona maybe. I don't care—just away from here. We'll get in your car and just drive."

I furrowed my brow. The plan had too many variables for me. What if Tom refused to go without her? What if he didn't believe she was sick? What if he got angry again and beat her? "I don't know, Tambra…" I said.

"Viv, I've told you before, Tom's not very smart. He'll buy it hook, line, and sinker. Trust me."

"And what about the days between now and then?" I said. I wanted to make sure Tambra had thought of everything. "How are you going to live with him after he did this to you?"

She smirked. "You'd be surprised. He's a master at pretending like nothing's happened. He'll bring me flowers tonight and be extra sweet. Tomorrow he'll act like nothing happened."

I quelled my impulse to let out a deep sigh. Why did her thoughts go first to how Tom would respond? "But I asked about you, Tambra. How are you going to live with him?"

She stroked my cheek. "You forget that I've done this before. I just do it. I go through the motions. It'll be fine—especially if I know I'm getting out."

I gave her a stony look. "But he thinks you're having an affair. He won't let that go."

She raised a shoulder in a half shrug. "Who knows if he really thinks that? He says shit all the time that I don't think he really believes. He's just trying to get a rise out of me, that's all."

I raised my eyebrows. "I think you're underestimating him, Tambra."

"I don't think so," she answered. "He's as dumb as a door."

"I don't think he's as dumb as you think," I insisted.

She glared at me with her one good eye, and I saw her lips flatten into a hard line. She was getting frustrated, and I knew her well enough to know that it was time to drop the subject. Tambra thought she knew her husband, and really, how could I argue with that? I just knew I couldn't shake this feeling of foreboding.

27

The next two weeks passed at a snail's pace. Tambra's injuries were healing, and she had somehow found a delicate balance with Tom, but I couldn't shake my apprehension. I woke every morning thinking about our escape plan, and it was the last thing on my mind as I fell asleep each night.

Saturday dawned sunny and warm. I awoke and realized it was August tenth—the day Tom would leave for Bellingham and Tambra and I would begin our escape. I rose from bed, got dressed, and then went out to the kitchen to make my coffee. Once the coffee was done, I carried my cup outside to the porch, as I did every morning. As I stared out at the neighborhood, a feeling of sadness came over me; this was the last time I'd do this, in this house, in this town. Tambra wanted me to spend the night with her at her house—"My final fuck-you to Tom," she had said—and I had reluctantly agreed. Something still bothered me about the plan, but I'd convinced myself that it was just general apprehension and I would feel this way no matter what the plan was.

At ten o'clock I saw Tom emerge from his house carrying a duffel bag and a fishing pole. He walked to his car and threw the bag and pole in the back seat. He looked angry, but his movements were purposeful. He climbed in the driver's seat, started the car, backed out of the driveway, and then roared away. A few minutes later I saw

Tambra's side door open, and she stepped out with Claire in her arms. She saw me and gestured for me to come over.

I pushed myself out of the chair and walked over to her. She ushered me inside and shut the door. I looked at her face. Her left eye was open now, and the bruises had faded to a greenish-yellow color. The doctor had removed the stitches from her cheek four days ago, and the laceration was healing nicely. She kissed me and flashed me her lopsided grin.

"Good morning, darling. Are you ready to hightail it out of here?"

"Does that mean Tom bought your story?" I asked, smiling in spite of my worry.

She wrapped her arm around her belly and moaned. "I've been so sick all night. In and out of the bathroom, throwing up and all that." She giggled. "That's what Tom thought, anyway. I should get some kind of acting award."

I laughed. "And how did he take it? Was he okay with you not going?"

She rolled her eyes. "Oh, he was pissed. He kept telling me I could go, that I'd be okay, but then I said, 'First of all, Tom, I'm sick. Do you want me puking in your Galaxie?'" She laughed. "Then for extra insurance I said, 'And do you really want your brother asking me why I have bruises on my face and a gash on my cheek?' Well, that really shut him up. He threw his clothes in a bag, grabbed his fishing pole, and stormed out. He didn't even kiss me good-bye. Good riddance, asshole—that's what I say."

I put one arm around her waist, placed the other around her shoulder, and wrapped her and Claire in a hug. "I love you two," I said.

"And we love you," Tambra said. "Okay, let's get to work. I have some stuff I want to take with us. Not a lot, but I do need some essentials." She gave me a sheepish look. "I really want to take my little desk. Do you think it'll fit in your car?"

I thought about the space in the Lincoln. The trunk was cavernous. "Yeah, I think it'll fit."

"Thank you," she said. "I've had it a long time, and I don't want to leave it behind." She buckled Claire into her baby seat, marched into the bedroom, and came out a few minutes later carrying the desk.

"Here, let me help you," I said. I picked up the desk and carried it outside.

We packed for the next few hours. I put the desk in the trunk and then fit everything around it. What I couldn't fit in the trunk I stacked in the back seat, leaving just enough room for Claire's car seat. The car was packed to the gills, but I got it all to fit.

By midafternoon Claire was sleepy, and Tambra put her down for a nap. As she slept, we sat at the kitchen table with a map and sketched out our route. We'd decided that California was the best destination—at least for now. Tambra liked the thought of Santa Barbara, so we planned our route to end up there. By the time Claire woke up from her nap, it was nearly dinnertime, and Tambra made us a delicious meal of steak, potatoes, and salad.

By ten o'clock we were exhausted, and we decided it was time to turn in for the night. Tambra wanted to leave at dawn on Sunday so we'd be hundreds of miles away by the time Tom got home on Sunday evening. We climbed into bed and carefully set the alarm clock for 4:30 a.m. "By the time he realizes what happened, we'll be long gone," she said. We kissed good night and both fell into a deep sleep, dreaming of California and freedom.

A loud noise jolted me from sleep. My eyes flew open, but I couldn't see a thing in the dark. Seconds later, the blanket was yanked off the bed, and then the overhead light came on, blinding me. I sat up, squinting in the bright light and trying to understand what was happening. I looked beside me and saw that Tambra was also awake, sitting up and struggling to see.

"Get up!" a deep voice thundered. "Get up, you fucking bitches!"

My eyes adjusted to the light, and I saw Tom Delaney standing at the foot of the bed, his face contorted with rage. Oh my God, no, I thought. Tambra's mouth fell open, and her face filled with terror.

"Tom, what are you—" she said.

"Shut the fuck up, you bitch!" he yelled. He moved quickly to her, grabbed a handful of her hair, and jerked her head up. "This is what you're doing when I'm not here? You're fucking this bitch? Are you a fucking dyke now?" His eyes bulged, and his face was flaming red.

I rose quickly to my knees and gripped Tambra by the arms. "Get your hands off her, you bastard!" I yelled.

His head snapped toward me. "Who the fuck do you think you are?" he shouted, reaching over and covering my face with his huge palm. "You don't tell me what to do, bitch!" He pushed me back against the headboard, and I hit it sharply, seeing stars.

Tambra spun around toward me, and then leaned down to cup my cheek in her warm hand. She looked concerned. "Are you okay, Viv?"

I was dazed, but I managed to nod. "Yeah, I think so."

She turned back to Tom, a forced smile on her face. "Tom, honey, I can explain." Her voice was surprisingly calm.

"You can't explain this, you fucking bitch!" he yelled, and then slapped her hard across the face. The blow threw her back onto the bed, and she cried out as the gash on her cheek opened up again. She sat up quickly, and I saw the fierce anger rise in her eyes.

"I'm leaving you, you bastard!" she screamed. "I don't love you! I never loved you! I love Vivian, and we're leaving and taking Claire with us! You'll never see us again, you asshole!"

"You aren't going anywhere, you fucking bitch!" he roared, as he reached down to grab her by the arms. He probably outweighed her by eighty pounds, and he picked her up as if she were a feather. He pushed her up against the wall, toppling the lamp on the bedside table, which shattered against the wood floor.

He pinned her against the wall, and she struggled in his grip. "I hate you!" she yelled. "I'm leaving you, you bastard!"

I jumped to my feet and tried to pull back his arms. "Tom, stop!" I screamed. "You don't have to do this! Please don't hurt her!"

Tom whipped around to face me. "Stay the fuck out of this, you dyke bitch!" he shouted, and then punched me square on the cheekbone. This time I fell to the floor, against the foot of the bed.

"Tom, no!" Tambra shouted. "Don't hurt her!"

"Shut the fuck up!" he growled, as he slapped her face a second time. She screamed out as blood began to gush from her wound. He drew back his hand again, and punched the side of her head. "You ugly, fucking bitch. You think you can disrespect me? You'll pay for this!"

Suddenly I remembered the baseball bat out in the living room. I scrambled to my feet and ran out to get it. I was back in seconds, and I stood in front of him, the bat in my hands.

"Let her go, Tom!" I yelled at the top of my lungs. "We just want to leave. Nobody needs to get hurt. Just let her go!"

He was drawing back his fist to punch Tambra again, and he stopped, swiveled, and then fixed me with his icy stare. A twisted grin spread across his face. "Ooh, you're a tough dyke, are you? Do you think I'm scared of you, you stupid bitch?" he barked.

At that moment, my eye caught Tambra's and our gazes locked. The love and gratitude in her eyes was almost palpable. I knew I would do anything to protect her. I raised the bat higher, ready to swing it. "I said, let her go. We're leaving!"

"You aren't going anywhere!" he yelled, as his hand darted out to try and grab the bat from me. I was too fast for him, and I pulled it back. I could see his anger grow.

"You fucking bitch!" he roared.

"Tom, you need to calm down!" Tambra shouted. "Stop it, now!"

Tom ignored her. He moved closer to me, and his hand shot out again to try to claim the bat. This time his aim was true. He wrapped his giant hand around the wood and tried to wrestle it from my grip. I held on with all my might, but I was no match for his strength. He twisted it this way and that, and finally pulled it from my grasp.

He gave a mirthless laugh, and then swung the bat wildly, connecting hard with my left hip. The pain raced down my leg. He swung the bat again, this time striking my left shoulder.

"Hah! You're a fucking pussy!" he taunted.

"Stop!" Tambra yelled, and then ran toward us. She jumped between me and Tom and spread her arms wide. "Don't hurt her!"

Tom raised the bat in both hands. His nostrils flared and his face flamed red. "You're protecting this dyke bitch?"

"Yes!" she shouted. "I told you, I love her! We're leaving! Don't you get it, you stupid idiot? I'm leaving you!"

Sheer rage flooded his face. "Over my dead body!" he roared, and then swung the bat at her stomach. She hopped back against me, the bat barely grazing her.

Tambra made an unearthly screeching sound and surged forward, digging her fingernails into his cheeks, drawing blood. "I hate you!" she screamed. "I wish I'd never met you!"

"Fuck you, you bitch!" he yelled. "You aren't leaving me for this dyke!" He reached out his arm and wrapped it around her neck, locking her in a chokehold. She struggled against him for a moment, and then lowered her head and sank her teeth in his arm.

He howled and loosened his hold on her. "You bitch!"

With Tom's attention on his pain for a moment, Tambra saw our chance. "C'mon!" she said, and pushed me out of the room. We ran into the living room, and toward the front door. I tripped against the foot of the armchair and fell, but Tambra kept going. Tom came thundering out of the bedroom, bellowing like a bull, just as Tambra reached the front door. She desperately tried to open the door, but he reached her before she could get it open.

"You aren't leaving me for some dyke, you bitch," he shouted, as he grabbed the back of her cotton nightgown and threw her across the room. She tumbled onto the floor, landing against the fireplace hearth.

I was suddenly aware of Claire crying—screaming, really—in her bedroom, and part of me wanted to deny this was happening and go to her. I knew I couldn't, though, and I forced myself to ignore her cries. I turned to see Tambra, dazed and struggling to sit up.

Tom stalked over to her, the bat still gripped in his hands. The rage in his face was unlike anything I'd ever seen. I saw him raise the bat, and I knew what he was going to do. "No!" I shouted, getting to my feet and running toward him. I jumped on his back and tried to reach the bat and couldn't. I scratched at his neck and cheeks and pulled his hair, trying to keep him from lowering the bat.

"Get off me, you filthy dyke!" he shouted, and then pushed me away with all his strength, sending me sprawling onto the floor. Then he returned his attention to Tambra. "You don't love me anymore, you bitch?" he yelled, as he brought the bat down on her ribs. "Well, this is what you get!"

"Tom, no!" she screamed, putting up her hands in self-defense and trying to roll away. "No, please don't!" He brought the bat down on her ribs again, and she shrieked in pain.

I pushed myself to my feet and again ran at Tom. He turned toward me, raised the bat, and shoved it against my chest, and I stumbled backward and then fell. "Stay out of this! This doesn't concern you!" he yelled at me, and then spun around to face Tambra. "You want to go with this dyke bitch and leave me? I don't think so!" he shouted at her. He lifted the bat again, and this time he brought it down on her face. She made a horrific noise as blood bloomed against her pale skin, and she collapsed onto the fireplace hearth.

"No, stop!" I shouted as I got to my feet and ran at Tom again, trying to wrestle the bat from him. I dug my fingernails into his arms, drawing blood.

"Get away from me, you bitch!" he roared, pulling me up by the collar of my nightgown and tossing me against the couch. He again raised the bat, and I watched in horror as he brought it down on Tambra's skull. I heard a sickening crack as her skull opened up.

"Tambra!" I screamed.

"You fucking bitch," he said as he again brought the bat down on her skull with all his power. "You said you'd love me till death do us part. You're a liar!" He raised the bat again, and it connected once more with her skull. "If I can't have you, nobody will!"

I was frozen in horror as I saw her ruined face, her crushed skull. Her beautiful blond hair was covered with blood. She rolled onto the floor, and I dropped to my knees and crawled toward her, not caring what Tom did to me.

I reached her, gathered her in my arms, and began rocking her. "Tambra, Tambra, Tambra," I cried, my voice choked with sobs. The newspaper lying on the hearth caught my eye, and I saw that it was spattered with her blood. I read the headline mindlessly: "Nixon Resigns!" I thought how surreal it felt to be reminded at this moment that there was a world outside this room. I looked at her, tears blurring my vision. Blood was pouring from her destroyed skull. Her breathing was shallow, and she was trembling violently. I knew she couldn't come back from this. She was dying. "Tambra, honey, I love you," I said in an urgent voice. "I love you more than I've ever loved anyone. You're the one I'd risk everything for."

I watched her eyes, and I saw them flutter. Her lips moved ever so slightly, and I leaned down as close to her as I could. I couldn't be sure, but I thought I heard her whisper, "I love you too." She made a gurgling sound, and then she expelled one long, rasping breath. Seconds later, her body went limp in my arms. She was gone. I squeezed my eyes shut and held her tightly in my arms, rocking her and sobbing, "Tambra, I love you," over and over.

I turned to Tom, who was panting like an animal, his eyes wild. He still gripped the bat in his hands—the bat that was covered in Tambra's blood. "You killed her, you bastard!" I cried.

He covered his mouth with his hand and stared at Tambra's body for a long moment, a look of bewilderment in his eyes. He dropped the bat and then moved over to the armchair and sat down heavily, his head in his hands.

I sobbed quietly, my arms still around Tambra, not sure what was happening. I closed my eyes and rocked back and forth, a keening sound coming from deep in my throat. I was trying to comfort myself, and trying to block out the sound of Claire's cries, which were becoming louder and more frantic. I thought of her—now a motherless child—and my heart broke for her.

After several moments, Tom bolted to his feet, startling me. "This is your fault!" he shouted. "If you hadn't gone in there with that bat, this never would have happened!"

I wiped tears and snot from my face and looked at him as if he were mad. "I was trying to protect her! You're the one who used it against her! You did this! You killed her!"

He moved close to me, and leaned down until his nose was almost touching mine. "No, it's your fault!" he yelled. "You moved into this neighborhood, you seduced my wife, you turned her into a dyke, you turned her against me! If you'd just left her alone, this never would have happened!"

I shook my head fiercely. "I didn't turn her against you! You did that yourself!" I screamed. "And you're crazy—you killed her! Don't blame this on me!"

He stood up and stared at me. "Like I said, if you'd just left her alone, this never would have happened!"

I lowered my head and began to sob. "Stop saying that!" I said through my tears. "Tambra loved me. You heard what she said!"

He took a step back and then snorted. "Nobody's going to believe that! Nobody's going to believe my wife was in love with the dyke neighbor!"

I looked away, tears streaming down my face. "That's the truth," I said, my voice breaking. "We loved each other, whether you like it or not. We were running away to get away from you."

He fell silent, and his eyes narrowed as he considered me. Finally he spoke. "Nobody's going to believe my wife was in love with you," he said slowly. "Not one person."

A shiver went up my spine. "What are you talking about?"

He stood over me, his hands on his hips. "In fact, what really happened is that you were in love with Tambra. She despised you, but you wouldn't leave her alone. She told you to stop bothering her, and you wouldn't. You couldn't stand the fact that she didn't want anything to do with you, so you broke into our house and you killed her with the bat."

My insides went cold. "That's not what happened, Tom."

He continued as if I hadn't spoken. "And you were so accommodating to pick up that bat, so now your fingerprints are all over it."

The room began to spin. "Nobody will believe that story," I said in a shaky voice. "You killed her. You're going to prison."

An evil smile spread across his face, and he laughed. "You're wrong. Everyone will believe it. And you're the one who's going to prison."

My eyes followed him as he moved to the telephone beside the couch. First he opened the phone book and looked up a number. Then he raised the receiver and dialed a phone number. He looked at me unwaveringly, his eyes icy and full of hate, as he spoke into the phone. "Hello, yes, please send the police. My wife is dead. Our psycho dyke neighbor just killed her."

28

Josie
July 2015

I tore out of Claire's driveway, my tires screeching. I wasn't sure where I was going—I just knew I wanted away from there. I drove a mile or so and then pulled off to the side of the road. I tried to calm myself by doing some deep breathing: in through my nose, out through my mouth, over and over. I could feel my heart slowing down a little, and the tension in my shoulders eased a bit. I continued breathing, trying not to replay that scene in my mind.

What was I going to do now? I took my phone out of my purse and dialed Celeste's number, praying she'd answer.

"Hi, Jo," I heard her say.

I sighed with relief. "Hi, Celeste."

"What's up?"

"Claire kicked me out," I said in a monotone voice.

"What? Why?"

"It's a long story, but suffice it to say that she found out I lied about our moms going to school together," I said. "And she thinks I'm being too sympathetic toward Vivian Latham."

She was quiet for a long moment. "I told you it wasn't a good idea to stay with her, Jo," she finally said.

"I know, I know," I answered. "Anyway, I'm not sure what to do now."

"Come back home," she said, a tone of urgency in her voice. "Just be done with this now."

I considered her words and realized I wasn't ready to go home. I still had things I wanted to do here. I knew Celeste meant well, but she wasn't living this and I was. I needed to get to the bottom of this, and the only way to do that was to stay and keep digging. "I hear what you're saying, Celeste, but I can't give up," I said. "I have to figure this out. I'm so close."

"Really, Jo? Why? Why do you care so much?"

"I care because I know somebody else did this murder, and I have to prove it. I can't let him get away with it." I paused. "And I want this damn dream to stop. I know that's what the dream is about now. Tom Delaney needs to pay for his crime."

I heard her sigh. "All right. I know you're stubborn. Figure it out and then come home. I miss you."

"I miss you too," I said. "And I *will* figure it out," I said. We said good-bye, and I hung up.

I found the number for the Capital Inn and called them and booked a room for the night. I wasn't sure how long I'd be staying, but one night would be a start. I looked up the directions, got my bearings, and reentered traffic.

Fifteen minutes later I was turning into the hotel parking lot. I checked in and then pulled my suitcase down the hallway to my room. I scanned the key card and pushed the door open. The room smelled stale, but it was nice enough: a queen-sized bed flanked by nightstands, a desk and chair, and a flat-screen TV. The bathroom was tiny but clean. I walked over to the large window and drew the heavy drapes to the side. I saw that it was actually a sliding glass door and a small balcony with a view of Capitol Lake and the state capitol dome. The midafternoon sun sparkled on the surface of the lake, and it looked beautiful.

I sighed and closed the drapes. I settled into the desk chair and opened my iPad. I went to the Internet, typed "Daniel Frazier, Applewood, Iowa" in the search field, and pressed Enter. The same people-finding site I'd used to find Vivian's cousin popped up. I clicked on the link and read the words on the screen: Daniel Alan Frazier, approximate age seventy to seventy-four, 3345 Euclid Road, Applewood, Iowa, and then his phone number. I picked up my phone, entered the number, and listened as the call connected. A few seconds later I heard someone answer.

"Hello?" It was a male voice.

"Hello, may I speak with Daniel Frazier?" I said.

"This is Daniel," the man said. "May I ask who's calling?"

"Hello, Mr. Frazier. My name is Josie Pace." I was nervous, and I paused to catch my breath. "I live in Seattle. I'm calling because I'm wondering if you're the same Daniel Frazier who knew Vivian Latham."

There was silence on the other end, and I began to think that I had the wrong Daniel Frazier, but finally he spoke. "Yes, I knew Vivian," he said in a quiet voice. "Why are you asking?"

I cleared my throat. "Mr. Frazier, I'm—"

"Please call me Daniel," he said.

"Okay, Daniel." I hesitated. "I'm doing some research into Vivian Latham's trial, and I just wanted to ask you some questions."

"What kind of research?" he asked.

I took a deep breath. "It's kind of complicated, but let's just say that I became aware of Vivian's case recently and it made me curious. I read the transcript from her trial—that's how I found your name—and I'm beginning to think she was framed for the murder of Tambra Delaney."

"Oh, thank God," he said.

"Excuse me?"

"Sorry," he said quickly. "I know that's an odd response, but I've been waiting forty-one years to hear those words."

I sat back in my chair as a feeling of affection for Daniel Frazier swept over me. But it was more than just affection. The rich tone of his voice and the rhythm of his speech were so familiar to me. Unbidden, an image bloomed in my mind: a slight teenage boy with dark hair and eyes stood awkwardly at the front of a classroom. I gazed at him from where I sat, flooded with feelings of empathy. I blinked hard several times, unsure of what was happening. Was I imagining Daniel as a teenager? Was this how he'd looked when Vivian knew him?

"Hello? Are you there?" I heard Daniel say.

I shook my head to clear it. "Yes, I'm sorry. I was distracted for a moment. You were saying that you've been waiting forty-one years to hear those words. Tell me more about that." I tried to push the image of what I guessed was the young Daniel out of my mind so I could focus on Daniel in the here and now.

"I've always known Vivian was innocent," he said. "I knew her for eighteen years. She was my best friend. She couldn't kill someone. It simply wasn't in her nature." He paused. "And she loved that woman—Tambra—with all her heart. She would have done anything for her. She never would have hurt her."

"How do you know she loved her so much?" I asked.

He didn't speak for a long beat. "Well, that's a sore subject. The man prosecuting Vivian asked me a similar question, and—"

"Yes, I know. I read your testimony," I interrupted.

"He made me look like a fool," he said angrily. "I think I ended up hurting Vivian more than I helped her." He paused. "That's always haunted me."

"You can't blame yourself," I said. "Attorneys are masterful at that—discrediting someone by pointing out holes in their testimony."

"I know, but still, it troubles me," he said. "Vivian called me and told me about Tambra. She told me how in love she was. I was so happy for her. Vivian hadn't been lucky in love, and I was thrilled that she'd found someone who loved her the way she deserved to be loved. So why didn't I ask to talk to Tambra on the phone? Why didn't I ask

Vivian to send me a photo of the two of them together?" He sighed heavily.

"Please don't beat yourself up about it," I said gently. "That's not something most people would think of doing. Why would you? You had no idea Tambra would end up dead."

"You're right," he said heavily. "Henry tells me that too."

"Who's Henry?" I asked.

"Henry's my husband," Daniel said. "We've been together for nearly forty-one years, but we were finally able to marry in 2009 here in Iowa."

"Congratulations," I said. "That's wonderful."

"Yes, and now with the Supreme Court decision, same-sex marriage is the law of the land. I can't believe so much of the world is finally coming around," he said, a tone of wonder in his voice. "Things have changed so much since Vivian left us. She would have loved all this."

We were both silent for a long moment as we felt the weight of his last statement.

I cleared my throat, preparing myself for my next question—one I'd been curious about but felt awkward asking. I decided to be direct. "So, Daniel, were you and Vivian ever, uh, girlfriend and boyfriend?"

He laughed. "Oh, heavens, no. Vivian had no question about who she was—she was captivated by women. She loved women. No question."

Something we had in common. "Good to know," I said. "What else can you tell me about Vivian? What kind of person was she?"

"Hmm, what kind of person was she?" he repeated. "She was kind and very smart. She graduated cum laude from the University of Iowa. She was a great teacher—the kids loved her, and she loved them. She was loyal and someone you could really count on." He paused. "She was a great friend."

"Sounds like she was a wonderful person," I said.

"She was," he said wistfully.

"Well, thank you, Daniel," I said. "You've been most helpful."

"What are you going to do with your research?" he asked. "Are you hoping to clear Vivian's name?"

I hesitated, not sure what to say. "Yes, actually, I do hope to clear her name," I finally said. "I think Tambra's husband was actually the one who killed her, and if I can prove that, then I hope to get him convicted."

"I think you're on the right track with that," Daniel said. "Vivian didn't like Tambra's husband—she said he physically and verbally abused Tambra. And I'd feel so much better if Vivian's name was cleared." He paused, and I thought I heard him stifle a sob. "I know it can't bring her back, but still, it would mean a lot to me."

"I'll do my best," I said. "Thank you so much for talking to me, Daniel. It's been a pleasure."

"Likewise," he said. "Thank you for calling me, Josie. It's been nice to talk about Vivian. And if I can help in any other way, please let me know."

"I will," I said.

As I hung up and tucked my phone back into my purse, I decided I'd done enough investigating for the day. My argument with Claire and our abrupt and contentious parting had left me shaken. I'd packed a swimming suit just in case, and I changed into it. I wrapped a towel around me, walked down the hallway to the hotel swimming pool, and slipped into the water. I loved being in the water and had since I was very young. I wasn't a great swimmer, but what I lacked in skill, I made up for in enthusiasm. The pool was empty, and I began swimming laps, concentrating on nothing but my strokes and turns. I climbed out of the pool twenty minutes later, my body and mind rejuvenated.

I toweled off and returned to my room. I got dressed, walked down the block to a small diner, and ate an early dinner. Then I went back to my room and called my mom to update her on everything that had happened. I got ready for bed and slipped under the sheets. They felt deliciously cool and crisp against my skin. I read e-mail and then flipped through Facebook to get caught up on the latest. At ten o'clock I switched off the light, exhausted to my bones. As I lay in the dark, I thought about the next day. I'd do some digging into what had become of Fergus Atkinson and also Detective Sean O'Neil. I closed my eyes, and minutes later I was asleep.

❧

I woke early the next morning and looked at the alarm clock on the bedside table: 6:30 a.m. I was happy I hadn't had the dream again. I thought about that for a moment and realized I'd been having the dream much less often since I'd started investigating. I'd had other dreams that I thought were about Vivian and Tambra but not the dream that had started all this.

I rose from the bed and went to peek out the sliding glass door. I could see it was going to be another beautiful day. I let the drape fall and then got dressed so I could go down to the hotel's breakfast buffet.

Fifteen minutes later, I was back in my room with a cup of fresh coffee and a plate piled high with toast, scrambled eggs, and fruit, which I set on the balcony table. I went back for my trusty iPad and brought it outside with me.

Even though I suspected that Fergus Atkinson, Vivian's defense attorney, was deceased, I figured there was no harm in searching for him. I opened an Internet browser window and typed in his name. It didn't take long to find numerous articles about him, and I was surprised to discover that the most recent one had been written earlier that year. I was wrong—he *was* still alive. I read the article, which talked about an award he'd received for his volunteer work at a legal aid organization. The article said he had retired from his law practice, but he gave generously of his time by volunteering to help people who had found themselves on the wrong side of the law. He volunteered for the Thurston County Legal Aid Society. I looked up their website and wrote down the phone number. The website said they opened at eight, and I'd call them then.

Next I searched for Detective Sean O'Neil, the police detective who'd been the lead investigator on Vivian's case. There were several hits for him, some going back many years, but the top result referred to his retirement several years earlier. The article, written in 2003, reported that he was retiring after thirty-five years with the Olympia Police Department. I made a note of this and then thought that he most likely still had friends who worked in the department and probably knew how to get in touch with him. I wrote down the number; I'd call there too.

I finished my breakfast and then sat with my feet up on the railing, gazing out at the lake. I thought about my conversation the day before with Daniel Frazier. He was the only person I'd talked with so far who had truly known Vivian, and he adamantly believed in her innocence. That held a lot of weight with me. I wished I could tell Claire about it, but I knew that was out of the question. I wondered if I'd ever see her again.

I sighed, pushed myself out of the chair, and went inside to shower and get ready for the day. As I blow-dried my hair, I glanced at my phone and saw that it was a few minutes before eight. I finished my hair, picked up the phone, and dialed the number of the organization where Fergus Atkinson volunteered.

"Good morning. Thurston County Legal Aid Society. How can I help you?" a woman said.

"Hello. I'm trying to reach one of your volunteers—Fergus Atkinson."

"Sure, I know Fergus," the woman said in a friendly voice. "He's not here today, though. Can I leave him a message?"

"I really need to talk to him today," I said. "It's urgent. Can you give me his phone number?"

"I'm sorry, ma'am. We can't give out personal phone numbers for our staff and volunteers," she said. "I can relay a message to him, though. Do you need legal help?"

"No, nothing like that," I answered. "This is about one of his cases from years ago."

"Oh, okay," she said. "What's your name and number?"

I gave her my information and then said, "Please tell him it's about Vivian Latham."

"Vivian Latham," she repeated. "Got it. I'll call him and let him know."

"Thank you," I said and hung up. I picked up the paper where I'd written the number for the Olympia Police Department but then set it down. I really needed some more coffee first. I grabbed my cup off the table and hurried back to the dining room.

Once back in my room, I picked up my phone and was about to enter the number for the Olympia Police Department when it rang. The caller ID showed a 360 number I didn't recognize. I pressed Answer and said, "Hello, this is Josie."

"Hello, this is Fergus Atkinson. I got a message from my office that you're trying to reach me."

Wow, that was fast. "Yes, Mr. Atkinson. Thank you for calling me so quickly," I said. "I was wondering if you remember Vivian Latham."

"Yes, of course I remember her," he said. "How could I forget? But why are you asking about Vivian, all these years later?"

I took a deep breath. "I recently became aware of her case, and I'm investigating the fairness of how the investigation and trial were handled—not by you," I added quickly. "By the police and the prosecution. I wanted to talk to you about your observations."

"Certainly, I'd be happy to talk with you," he said briskly. "Can you come by my house today? I don't enjoy talking on the phone. I'd really like to talk in person."

"Sure," I answered. "I don't mind talking in person." He gave me his address, and we agreed to meet at nine. As I disconnected, I thought about my planned call to the Olympia Police Department. It was 8:20 a.m. now, and I thought that would have to wait until later. I then realized that I'd have to stay here another night, and I called down to the front desk to make sure they could accommodate me. The woman at the front desk said it was no problem, and she extended my stay for one more night.

At 9:00 a.m. sharp I stood at Fergus Atkinson's door, taking in what I could see of his palatial estate. Clearly lawyering had treated him well. I pressed the doorbell and waited. When no one answered, I rang the bell again. Several seconds later a young woman in a tank top and shorts pulled the door open. I noticed she had colorful tattoos covering her left arm from shoulder to wrist, a ring in her eyebrow, and a disheveled mop of blue hair. The sight took me aback for a moment. She certainly wasn't the person I'd expected to answer the door. I smiled.

"Hello, I'm here to meet with Fergus Atkinson," I said. I peeked behind her and saw a wide entryway and an elegant staircase leading up to the second floor.

The young woman turned her head and yelled, "Grandpa!" Then she glanced back at me. "He'll be right here." She flashed me a smile and then began moving toward the staircase.

An older man with a shock of gray hair was coming down the stairs, and as he passed her he gave her a stern look. "Where are your manners, Alice?" She shrugged and continued up the stairs.

Fergus Atkinson came toward me, his hand outstretched. As I shook his hand and looked into his eyes, a sudden impulse to hug him consumed me. I felt as if I was greeting an old friend I hadn't seen in a very long time. I thought of my similar response to Daniel Frazier. Another deep memory from Vivian's time, no doubt.

"Fergus Atkinson," he said. "It's wonderful to meet you, Miss…I'm sorry. I don't think I know your last name."

I smiled. "It's Pace, but you can call me Josie."

"Josie," he said. "And you can call me Fergus. It's very nice to meet you." He glanced up the stairs. "I apologize for my granddaughter. Young people today seem to have forgotten their manners." He paused and then added dryly, "Or perhaps they never had them."

"That's okay," I said as I studied him. He was tall—probably six feet two inches—and lanky. When I'd first seen him on the stairs, I'd noticed his hair, and up close I could see it was abundant and a beautiful silver color. Long lashes framed his dark eyes. He was quite striking for an older gentleman. Again my mind shifted, and for a moment a picture of a young Fergus flashed behind my eyes: his unruly mop of dark hair, his gangly frame, his commanding presence in the courtroom.

"Let's go outside and sit on the deck," he said. "It's a lovely morning."

"Yes, it is," I agreed. He guided me through the entryway and then into a family room with an adjoining kitchen. As we passed through the kitchen, he offered me coffee, which I gratefully accepted. We then went out through a French door and finally to the deck. I was surprised to see a swimming pool in the back yard. Not many people around here had them, because the weather was nice enough for a pool only four or five months out of the year. Today was going to be hot, and I looked at it longingly, thinking of my swim the day before.

"The pool is indulgent, I know," Fergus said as he sat down at a circular glass-topped table. "But I love to swim. When the weather cooperates, I come out here early in the morning and swim laps."

I nodded as I sat down next to him and set my mug on the table. "I understand," I said. "I like to swim too."

He leaned forward and looked me straight in the eyes. "So you want to talk to me about Vivian Latham."

His candor flustered me a bit, but I managed to nod. "Yes, I'm doing research into women who were convicted of murder in the seventies, and I came across Vivian's case." I swallowed hard. "I read the transcript from her trial, and I wanted to ask you some questions."

He looked at me, a rueful smile on his face. "Every defense lawyer has at least one case that haunts them." His gaze flickered away, and a distant look entered his eyes. "Vivian's was mine."

"Tell me about that," I said gently.

He folded his hands on top of the table. "I failed her, Josie, plain and simple. I committed the ultimate crime for a defense attorney:

I didn't believe in her innocence. She told me over and over that she was innocent, and I didn't believe her." He sat back and ran his hand through his hair. "It wasn't until I saw that man testify—Tambra Delaney's husband—that I realized she'd been telling me the truth all along." He looked at me with doleful eyes.

"Tom Delaney," I said in a flat voice.

He snorted. "Yes. Tom Delaney." He closed his eyes, lost for a moment in his memory of the trial, I guessed. He opened his eyes and fixed his gaze on me. "When he testified, I knew. I knew he'd killed his wife and framed Vivian." He sighed deeply. "I think that was one of the worst moments of my life. I know it was the worst moment of my professional life."

I looked at him sympathetically. "How could you have known, Fergus? You probably hadn't even met Tom Delaney before the trial."

"No, but I should have believed Vivian. She told me what happened, and I ignored her." He laughed humorlessly. "I still remember what I said to her: 'Why would a happy man kill his wife?'"

I nodded, not sure what to say. I looked at Fergus. I could see the glint of tears in his eyes.

"Had I believed her, I might have tried harder to defend her," he said. "She might have been acquitted."

I shook my head. "No, I don't think so. The prosecution had it in for her," I said. "Tom Delaney, the police, the neighbors—they were all against her."

"Did you know Vivian was gay?" Fergus asked.

I nodded. "Yes, I know."

"That's why they were all against her. It was a witch hunt," he said bitterly. "That was forty-one years ago, and people were ignorant, myself included. People like Vivian scared them, and they didn't want them in their neighborhood, in their community." He leaned forward and rested his elbows on the table. "So their solution was to send her to prison." He paused, closed his eyes for a moment, and then looked at me. "She killed herself, you know."

"Yes, I know," I said softly.

"She had nothing to live for," he said in a thick voice. "Tambra was dead. Her parents were both gone. She was staring at a twenty-year prison sentence. Who could blame her?"

"Yes, who could blame her," I said. I felt it best to keep my responses short. Fergus clearly still had a great deal of remorse about Vivian, and I thought I should just let him talk. I took a drink of coffee and watched him.

"I saw her the day before she died," he continued. "She'd called me out to the prison to get my help with a—" He hesitated. "With a business matter. I had no idea she was planning to kill herself." He held his head in his hands. "Why didn't I see the signs?"

I reached out and touched his hand. "Fergus, please don't blame yourself. All this is clear in hindsight, but I don't know how you could have known any of it when it was happening."

He looked up at me and smiled sadly. "You sound like Marjorie, my wife. She told me much the same thing."

"She's right," I said. "We don't always understand why things happen the way they do, but I know it's not healthy to punish yourself for what you think you should have done."

He nodded, saying nothing.

I leaned toward Fergus and looked him in the eye. "One thing I haven't been able to explain to myself is why Tambra didn't get help before it got to this point." I paused to take a sip of coffee. "Vivian testified that Tom was abusing Tambra. Why didn't Tambra turn him in? Get him arrested?"

Fergus gave me an odd look, and then a small smile played at the corners of his mouth. "Ah, you're a young woman, aren't you? What are you, thirty, thirty-one?"

I sat up straight, not sure what he was getting at. "I'm thirty-three," I said.

He nodded. "I'm sure to your thirty-three-year-old sensibilities it seems obvious that she should have called the cops and turned him in. But this happened forty-one years ago. The world was very different back then, my dear."

"Yes, of course," I said, feeling a bit foolish. Clearly I hadn't done my homework.

He folded his hands on top of the table and looked at me thoughtfully. "Back then the police viewed domestic violence as a family problem rather than a criminal matter, and they were extremely reluctant to get involved in what they saw as a personal matter between husband and wife," he said. "It wasn't until 1979 that the Washington State Legislature passed the Domestic Violence Prevention Act. So you see, there really was no recourse for Tambra in 1974."

"Wow, 1979," I murmured. "That was two years before I was born." I found myself both aghast and angry that such a seemingly simple and important thing had taken so ridiculously long to become law.

"Change happens slowly," Fergus said. "But change does happen."

I nodded, thinking of Tambra and her impossible situation. She and Vivian had devised the best plan possible, given the times. I sighed. I thought a change of topic was in order, so I took a drink of coffee and then sat back in my chair. "Tell me about your family, Fergus."

His eyes brightened. "Marjorie and I have three kids—two girls and a boy. Our eldest daughter is Karen, and then there's Rebecca, and our youngest is Bradley. They're all grown now with kids of their own. You met my granddaughter Alice, and then there are six more grandkids: Jesse, Samantha, Zach, Derek, Belinda, and Logan. They're all great kids."

"That's wonderful," I said.

"What about you, Josie? Do you have kids?" he asked.

I shook my head. "Not yet, but I hope to someday."

He nodded and smiled. "Being a parent is the best job you could ever have."

"That's what I've heard," I said.

He looked at me curiously. "I'm wondering what you're planning to do with the information you're gathering about Vivian. Are you writing an article or…" His voice trailed off.

I thought for a moment about how much to tell him. I really didn't want to go into the details about Claire, and I certainly didn't want to tell him about the dream, so I decided to tell a half-truth. "Yes, I'm planning on writing an article, but really, after learning Vivian's story, I want to do more. I've become quite intrigued by her case, and I'm hoping to clear her name."

"Really?" he said with surprise.

"Yes. I plan to talk to the police next. Sean O'Neil was the detective on the case, and I hope to meet with him."

He smiled. "I know Sean. He worked a lot of the cases I was involved in. He's a good guy. He's retired now, though. I hope you can still find him."

I nodded. "Yeah, I hope so too."

Fergus stood, signaling that it was time for me to go. I drained my coffee cup and stood too. "Thank you for sharing all this with me, Fergus. I appreciate it."

He took my hands in his and looked at me closely. "And thank you for what you're doing, Josie. I truly hope you do clear Vivian's name. And please keep me posted on what's happening and let me know if I can help in any way. You can always reach me through the legal aid society."

"I will," I said.

"Let me show you out," he said.

He led me back through the kitchen and family room and then to the wide entryway. I would have loved to see the rest of the house, but I knew that wasn't going to happen. He opened the front door and looked at me. "Good luck, Josie."

"Thank you, Fergus." I stepped out the door, and he closed it behind me.

I sat in my car and thought about my next move. I glanced at the clock on the dashboard: 9:45 a.m. There was plenty of time to contact the Olympia Police Department and possibly even talk with Detective O'Neil today. I looked up the number on my phone, entered it, and pressed the Call button. After two rings I heard someone pick up.

"Olympia Police Department. How may I help you?" a woman said.

"Hello. My name is Josie Pace," I began. "I'm looking for someone who used to work in your department—Detective Sean O'Neil. Do you know him?"

"I don't know him, but I've heard of him," she said. "His former partner still works in the department. Would you like to talk to him?"

"Yes, please, I would," I said.

"Hold on," the woman said. "I'll connect you."

I heard a series of clicks and then silence, and a few seconds later a man's deep voice was on the line. "Detective Willard."

"Detective Willard, hello. My name is Josie Pace. I'm trying to track down your former partner—Sean O'Neil. I was wondering if you know how I could get in touch with him."

"What's this regarding?" he asked in a tight voice.

I cleared my throat. "I'm doing some research into an old case of his, and I wanted to talk to him about it."

"Which case?" he asked gruffly.

"A murder case back in the seventies. Vivian Latham was charged with the murder."

"Okay, yeah," he said. "I wasn't with the department back then, but O'Neil mentioned that one to me a time or two."

"He did? Wonderful. So he remembers it," I said.

"Yeah, I'm sure he does." He paused. "He's retired now, but I can relay a message to him and ask him to get in touch with you."

"That'd be great," I said. "Do you know if he still lives in the area?"

"Yeah, he's still around. Give me your number, and I'll let him know."

I gave him my information, and then we ended the call. I figured it would be a while until he called, so I considered what I should do while I was waiting. My stomach growled, and I realized I was hungry. I thought I should get something to eat and go back to my hotel room for a while.

First I would swing by the clerk's office, though. I'd given Claire the only copy of the trial transcript, and I wanted my own. I looked up the directions, started the car, and pulled away from the curb.

I was standing in the clerk's office twenty minutes later. The same purple-haired woman was behind the desk, but this time I didn't need her help. I went directly to the computer terminal, found the transcript, printed it, and then paid her. I was back in my car fifteen minutes later. I knew my way back to the hotel from there, and I headed in that direction. On the way I passed a quaint-looking German deli, and I stopped to buy a sandwich.

When I got back to my hotel room, I went out to the balcony and sat down at the table. I laid my phone beside me, hoping that Sean O'Neil would call any minute. I unwrapped my sandwich and took a bite. As I ate I glanced at my phone every few seconds. I began to worry that he wasn't going to call at all. Once he heard what I wanted to talk to him about, he had probably concluded that I was a nut. Who called about a murder investigation from forty-one years ago? I tried to talk myself down, reasoning that he might be out of town or simply not near a phone right now. He was an older man, and he might not have a cell phone, which meant all his calls went to a landline. If he wasn't near his landline, then I might not hear from him for hours—maybe days.

"Stop it, Josie," I said aloud. I had a bad habit of letting my thoughts spin out of control, imagining outcomes that had little basis in reality. My dire predictions rarely, if ever, came true.

My phone rang as I swallowed my last bite of sandwich, startling me. I looked at the caller ID: another unknown 360 number. I hoped it was Sean O'Neil. "Hello, this is Josie Pace."

"Miss Pace," a man's voice said. "This is Sean O'Neil. I got a message that you're trying to reach me."

I let out a long breath. "Yes, thank you for calling me, Mr. O'Neil."

"What can I do for you?" he asked in a stiff voice.

"I'm doing research on women convicted of murder in the 1970s, and I came across the Vivian Latham case," I said. "I found the court record and saw that you were the lead investigator. I'm wondering if you'd have some time this week to talk to me about the case."

He was silent. "What's this research for?" he finally said.

I cleared my throat, worrying that I would once again be forced to lie. "I work for a magazine in Seattle, and I'm writing an article about female murderers from the seventies. I'd like to include some information about the Vivian Latham case if I can talk to you."

I heard him sigh. "Well, I'm retired now, but I guess I can talk to you," he said reluctantly.

"Thank you, sir," I said. "I really appreciate it. When would you be available?"

"I could talk this afternoon," he said. "There's a pie shop on the west side that I sometimes go to in the afternoons. We could meet there."

"That sounds perfect," I said with relief. "What time?"

"Say two o'clock today. Does that work for you?"

"Yes, that works great for me," I said.

He gave me the name of the pie shop, and we hung up. I looked up the place on my phone and made a note of the address. I glanced at the time: nearly noon. In two hours I'd be meeting with Sean O'Neil.

29

I arrived at Pie in the Sky at two o'clock sharp. I walked through the front door and heard the tinkle of a bell announcing my arrival. A woman behind the counter greeted me and told me to sit anywhere I liked. I glanced around. There was only one other person there—a man sitting in a booth by the window. When I walked up to the man, I flashed him my best smile. "Hello, are you Sean O'Neil?"

"Yep, that's me," he said. He looked to be about seventy and was almost completely bald. His eyes were a piercing blue.

"Hi, I'm Josie Pace," I said as I slid into the booth across from him. He nodded at me but made no move to shake my hand. "Thanks for meeting with me on such short notice."

"Sure," he said. "You should try some pie. Best pie I've ever had—especially the cherry."

I noticed that he had a cup of coffee and a large slice of cherry pie in front of him. The pie did look delicious. The woman who'd greeted me was at our table seconds later, and I gave her my order: cherry pie and an iced coffee.

Sean O'Neil cupped his hands around his coffee mug and looked at me. "So how can I help you, Miss Pace?"

I looked down at the table for a moment, gathering my thoughts. Mr. O'Neil struck me as a tough nut to crack, and I wasn't sure he was going to tell me what I wanted to know. I could feel him staring at me, and I looked up at him with more confidence than I felt.

"As I mentioned on the phone, I'm writing an article about women murderers in the 1970s. I came across Vivian Latham's case, and I had some questions about it."

"Yeah," he said. "What kind of questions?"

I decided to dive right in. "Do you think she was guilty?"

He looked down at his coffee cup and started fiddling with the handle. "She was convicted."

"Yes, I know," I said. "But do *you* think she was guilty?"

He met my eyes, his gaze steady. "We conducted a clean investigation, and the trial was cut and dried."

This was going to be harder than I'd envisioned. The server appeared at that moment with my pie and coffee and set them in front of me. I tried a bite of pie, grateful for the brief break, and then took a deep breath. "I'm not questioning police procedure or the trial or anything like that," I said, even though in my own mind I was. I needed to put him at ease so he wouldn't stay on the defensive. "What I'm wondering is if you, over the past forty-one years, have ever wondered if she was really guilty."

He leaned back against the booth and folded his arms over his chest. "What does that have to do with anything?" he asked, his voice gruff.

I gave him a thin smile. "Let me be honest here, Mr. O'Neil. I spoke with Fergus Atkinson, the lawyer who defended Vivian Latham, and he's of the opinion that she was framed."

He snorted. "He was her lawyer. What else would you expect him to say?"

I nodded. "True, but what if I told you that, prior to the trial, he thought Vivian was guilty? It wasn't until Tambra Delaney's husband testified that he began to suspect that Tom Delaney had actually killed his wife and framed Vivian."

Sean O'Neil's gaze slid away, and he didn't say anything for a long time. Finally he sighed deeply and spoke. "I had an encounter with Mr. Delaney after the trial that's always bothered me."

My eyebrows shot up. "What happened?"

He cleared his throat and then looked at me. "He came into the police department the day after the trial was over to thank us for our good police work," he said. "As he was leaving, he laughed, clapped me on the shoulder, and said, 'We got her, O'Neil. That Goddamn dyke got what she deserved.'"

I frowned but didn't say anything.

He shook his head, a look of confusion on his face. "He didn't talk about his grief over losing his wife or the fact that his baby would grow up without a mother. It was all about Vivian Latham getting what she deserved." He paused, looked away for a few seconds, and then looked back at me. "I don't know. Something about that has never sat right with me."

"I can see why," I said. "So let me ask you again, Mr. O'Neil. Have you ever wondered if Vivian Latham was falsely convicted?"

He rubbed his forehead with the tips of his fingers and then nodded. "Yeah, it's crossed my mind a time or two."

Based on what he'd just told me, I guessed it had crossed his mind more than a time or two. "Did you mention this to anyone?" I asked.

He shook his head. "No, I didn't have any proof—just a hunch. The evidence all pointed to Vivian Latham back then. Now we have DNA evidence, and it would have been a lot clearer. But back then it was all about blood type, fingerprints, and motive, and they were all damning for her." He paused and took a drink of coffee. I noticed that he hadn't touched his pie since we'd started talking. "And then Vivian Latham died—she killed herself—and it all seemed irrelevant. She was dead, so what would have been the point in getting it flared up again?"

I felt a surge of anger, which I tried to temper before I spoke. "Except the real murderer got away with it."

"Possibly. We don't know that for sure," he said in a deadpan voice.

But I knew in my heart who was responsible for this crime, and my mind was becoming more certain of it by the minute. "Do you still have the police report from the case?" I asked.

He nodded. "Yeah. All that's been digitized, so it's just a matter of punching the case number into the computer and calling up the report."

"And what about the physical evidence?" I asked. "Do you have that?"

"Of course," he said matter-of-factly. "In murder cases we keep the evidence until everyone involved is dead and gone."

I tipped my head to the side and looked at him. "So in theory the evidence could still be tested for DNA."

He frowned. "Yeah, I suppose so." He paused. "It does degrade over time, but we have a top-notch forensics lab. I'm sure they'd find something."

"Could I see a copy of the police report?" I asked.

He shrugged. "It's a public record. You can put in a request to see it."

"And how long does that take?" I asked.

He shook his head. "I don't know. A week or two."

"I don't have that long," I said bluntly. He shrugged again and took a bite of pie, and I knew I had to play hardball. "You've lived for forty-one years with the suspicion that Tom Delaney was really the one who killed his wife and then framed an innocent woman. Don't you want the bastard to pay?"

He scrutinized me for several seconds before speaking. "What's your real interest in this case, Miss Pace?"

I sat up straighter and met his eyes. "I think it's never too late for justice to be done."

He shoveled the last bite of pie into his mouth and chewed it slowly before speaking. "So you started out writing an article about women murderers, and now you want to play cop? Is that it?"

"There's more to it than that, but that's not something I want to go into right now," I said, a tone of defensiveness creeping into my voice. "Let's just say I want the right person to pay for the crime."

"Fair enough," he said. He studied me silently. I saw his expression change ever so slightly the moment he made his decision. "I still have some friends in the department." He paused to take his last drink of coffee. "I'm sure I could pull some strings and let you see the police report without doing an official request."

"Thank you," I said. "And what about the evidence?"

He leaned back against the booth and gave me an amused smile. "Let's start with the report and see how that goes."

"So when can I see the report?" I asked. I'd made significant progress with Sean O'Neil, and I wasn't about to let this wait and risk losing him.

"The main precinct is only ten minutes away," he said. "We could go over there now."

"Lead the way," I said.

Sean O'Neil and I walked into the Olympia Police Department, and he led me back to a large room that was buzzing with activity. There were desks everywhere, and police officers were speaking on the phone, talking to people, and huddling in small groups.

"There's Ramirez," Sean O'Neil said, nodding toward the back of the room. "She can help you." He motioned for me to follow him, and we walked across the room to the desk of a woman police officer. She looked up and smiled broadly when she saw Sean.

"O'Neil!" she said. "How the hell are you?" She stood and punched him lightly on the arm.

"I'm good, Ramirez," he said. "It's great to see you."

"You too." She looked at him curiously. "What's up?"

Sean looked at me. "This is Josie Pace. Miss Pace, this is Detective Laura Ramirez." He touched my shoulder. "Miss Pace needs to see the police report from an old case of mine." He paused and gave her a meaningful look. "This is a favor for me, Ramirez, so find the report and give her a copy." He paused. "If you find something you need my help with, you can let me know."

Laura nodded and then looked at me. "Hi, Josie," she said.

I took a step back, momentarily unable to speak. I was completely taken by Laura. She was beautiful. Her skin was a rich tawny color, and thick black lashes framed her large dark eyes. Her lips were full and rosy. She was maybe an inch taller than I was, and she was pleasantly curvy. Her silky dark-brown hair was straight, and it came to just below her shoulders. I guessed her to be somewhere between thirty and thirty-five. She was the most alluring woman I'd seen in a very long time.

"Nice to meet you," I was finally able to say, reaching out to shake her hand. I looked in her eyes and felt drawn in. There was something so familiar about her. The touch of her hand sent pleasant tingles up my arm.

She held my hand for two beats too long as her eyes locked with mine. She felt the connection too—I could tell. I noticed her lips curve into a lopsided smile that seemed a bit flirtatious to me.

"I'll leave you in Laura's capable hands," Sean said, completely unaware of what was going on between Laura and me. "Good luck," he said to me. "And contact me through the department if you have any questions about the report."

"Thank you, sir. I really appreciate your help," I said.

He nodded curtly and turned and walked away.

I sat down next to Laura Ramirez and gave her the pertinent case information. She opened her database, pressed a few keys, and then hit Search. The results popped up on the screen, and she clicked into the actual report.

"I think this is it," she said, glancing at me. She motioned me to come closer, and I scooted my chair over next to her. I was so close to her that my thigh was nearly touching hers, and I could feel the heat from her body. I caught an intoxicating scent in the air and realized it was her perfume. I inhaled deeply, smelling a beguiling mix of amber and rose.

"Is this what you're looking for?" she asked.

I turned my attention to the computer screen, feeling a bit disoriented by the closeness of her. I scanned the words on the screen, catching some of the details: Tambra Delaney, Vivian Latham, August 11, 1974. "Yes, that's it," I said.

"Shall I print it for you?" she asked.

"Yes, please," I answered.

Laura pressed the Print button, and I heard the printer next to her come to life. When it was done, she stapled the pages together and then handed them to me. "Here you go," she said.

As I took the pages from her, her fingers grazed mine. My eyes flew to hers, and she gave me her lopsided smile again. I could feel my cheeks getting warm, and I looked down quickly at the papers in my hand. My eyes moved over the top page, pretending to read it, as I tried to gather myself. "What about the evidence collected at the scene?" I asked, looking at her.

She nodded toward the papers in my hand. "There should be a section in there about the evidence they collected."

I shook my head. "No, I mean the actual evidence. The physical evidence. Where's that?"

"We have a storage locker for evidence." She paused, looking at me. "Did O'Neil say you could see the actual evidence?"

For a second I thought about lying, but I rejected the idea. I already knew I liked Laura, and I didn't want to get her in trouble. "No, but we did talk about it. He said I should look at the police report first and then we could talk about seeing evidence."

"So let's go with that for now," she said. She reached over to her desk and grabbed a card from a plastic holder. "Here's my card. Call me if you need more help."

I took the card from her. "Thank you, Laura," I said. "I appreciate it."

"Anytime," she said and then gave me a wink. "See you, Josie."

I could feel the blush starting on my cheeks again, and I turned quickly to go.

I took the police report back to my hotel room and began poring over it. The report was broken down into sections: a description of the scene, the evidence collected, the murder weapon, the witnesses, and the suspects, Vivian Latham and Tom Delaney. The language used made it clear that Vivian was the primary suspect and Tom had been thrown in simply because he was the only other person at the scene. It seemed to me that they'd never considered him a serious suspect.

Next came a section detailing Vivian's arrest; the police questioning; the statements of Tom Delaney, Vivian's neighbors, and Tom's brother; and then the official charge of second-degree murder. I read Tom Delaney's statement with a sneer on my face.

"Vivian Latham was in love with my wife, Tambra Delaney, and the feelings weren't returned. When my wife rejected Vivian Latham, she went crazy and attacked and killed my wife." The report continued with his recounting of his version of the events of August 11, 1974: Vivian broke into their house in the middle of the night. He tried to restrain her and wasn't able to. Vivian killed his wife with a collectible baseball bat he kept in the living room. Utter bullshit, I now believed.

Vivian's neighbors—Agnes Reed and Doris McLellan—had made statements describing Vivian as "odd" and "unfriendly." Both said they'd seen no proof that Tambra and Vivian were friends, much less lovers. I mulled this over in my mind. Both neighbors came off as nosy in their statements, and I remembered that Agnes Reed had struck me that way when I'd visited her. If what I now believed was true—that Vivian and Tambra had been friends and later lovers—then nosy neighbors Doris McLellan and Agnes Reed most certainly would have noticed their closeness, and that meant they had lied under oath. I knew Doris McLellan was dead, but Agnes Reed was alive and well. I toyed with the idea of paying her a visit again and pressuring her to tell me the real story.

I returned my attention to the report. Michael Delaney, Tom's brother, had made a statement that Tom had not visited him in

Bellingham that weekend, as Vivian had contended. He claimed he hadn't seen his brother in several months. I recalled that Vivian had suggested in her testimony that Tom's brother had been covering for him. I was almost certain that was what had happened, in spite of what Claire thought.

I then focused on the police questioning of Vivian. I read the words over and over: "The suspect denied repeatedly that she murdered Mrs. Delaney. She stated that she and Mrs. Delaney were romantically involved and Thomas Delaney found out about their relationship and murdered Tambra Delaney in a fit of jealousy and rage."

Next I read the section on the evidence collected. The items were listed with a short description after each. The bloody bat, Tambra's nightgown, Vivian's nightgown, Tom's clothing, the sheets from the bed, and a section of the carpet that had been under Tambra's body. The report mentioned photos of the crime scene, which I guessed were housed with the actual physical evidence. It also listed biological materials collected, including blood and scrapings from under Tambra's, Tom's, and Vivian's fingernails.

Lastly the report detailed fingerprints lifted from the scene—from the bat in particular. Vivian's fingerprints had been lifted from the bat. Tom Delaney's fingerprints had also been on the bat, but, as was noted in the report, the bat belonged to him, and those fingerprints were not considered relevant. "Like hell they're not," I said aloud.

Forty-one years ago, there had been no such thing as DNA evidence, so they had focused on blood type to include or exclude someone as a person of interest. Tom and Tambra shared the same blood type—A positive—and Vivian's blood type was O positive.

A positive blood had been found under both Tambra's and Vivian's fingernails. There had been A positive blood under Tom's fingernails, but because he and Tambra shared the same blood type, there had been no way to include or exclude him. The report noted that Tom's face had been bleeding when the police arrived at the scene, and they had concluded that Tom had touched his own blood. I was certain that had not been the case and that DNA analysis would prove that Tambra's blood had been under his fingernails and his blood under hers. There was no mention of Vivian's blood type—O positive—being on either Tom or Tambra. The report did mention a deep bite mark on Tom's arm; Tom had claimed that Vivian was responsible for it. Police had swabbed the bite for good measure, but the blood found in the wound was—not surprisingly—A positive. The wound would also have contained saliva, and I was sure that modern-day DNA analysis would show that the saliva was Tambra's, not Vivian's.

I sighed and thought of what Fergus had said: that the murder investigation and trial had been a witch hunt. I knew he was right. I set the scene in my mind. A woman, quiet by nature, moves into a small, tight-knit neighborhood in 1974. The neighbors view her as odd and unfriendly. Somehow, they find out that the woman is a lesbian, and the witch hunt is on. Tambra Delaney ends up dead, and every finger points at Vivian Latham. The husband contends that Vivian is in love with his wife and that when Tambra spurns her advances, Vivian goes crazy and murders his wife with a bat. No one will dare confirm that Vivian and Tambra are friends, because everyone wants Vivian out of the neighborhood. The police themselves are prejudiced, as are the attorneys, as Fergus readily admitted.

That's what Tom had been counting on—that everyone's homophobia would take over and Vivian would be found guilty. I knew this would never happen today, but in 1974 it had been common. The Stonewall Riots had happened only five years before in New York City, the biggest and most diverse city in the nation. In small-town America, gay and lesbian people had been viewed with distaste and suspicion, especially by the older generations. Tom had set Vivian up, knowing exactly how people would respond.

I thought of Claire. I longed to talk to her and tell her what I'd found, but I didn't have her phone number, and I wasn't about to go to her house and get the door slammed in my face. I knew it wouldn't go anywhere even if I could call her. She had her own reasons for not wanting to believe her dad had murdered her mom. If he went to prison, then she'd be truly alone. And she'd be left with the knowledge that she had no mom, not because of the crazy neighbor, as she'd always thought, but because of her own father. She had a lot to lose and very little to gain.

I set the report aside and realized it was time to go out and find some dinner. I thought about the next day—I wanted the physical evidence tested for DNA, and I wasn't sure how I'd make that happen. I decided I'd call Sean O'Neil in the morning and appeal to his sense of justice. If a murderer was walking around free, shouldn't he be made to pay for his crime? I hoped he'd agree.

The next morning I called the Olympia police department at eight o'clock sharp. I spoke to Detective Willard once more and explained to him that I needed to speak to Sean O'Neil again. He sounded slightly less helpful than he had the day before, but he took my information and said he'd relay it to Sean.

I waited for him to call me back, trolling Facebook, checking e-mail, and reading the police report over and over. I called down to the hotel's front desk to make sure I could stay another night (I could) and then took a shower. As I dried my hair, I thought about calling Celeste or my mom, but I didn't feel like rehashing everything. I'd call them later when I had the new information from Sean.

I was about to head outside to take a walk when my phone rang. I answered quickly. "This is Josie Pace."

"Miss Pace, Sean O'Neil here. I heard you were trying to reach me." His voice sounded tense.

"Hello, Mr. O'Neil," I said. "I got the police report from Laura Ramirez." Saying her name gave me a little tickle in my stomach. I swallowed hard and continued. "I saw there were biologicals collected at the scene, and I wanted to find out how we can get those tested for DNA."

He laughed. "I can't just call up and demand a DNA analysis. It's not that simple."

"What do I need to do then?" I asked, annoyance evident in my voice.

"Listen," he began. "I get that you're hot to prove that Vivian Latham wasn't the guilty party here but from the police perspective, the case has been solved. There's no reason to do a DNA analysis."

"Sir, you said yourself that you had doubts about Tom Delaney," I said. "If he was the one who really killed his wife, don't you want him to pay for his crime?"

"Of course I do," he said. "But as of right now, all we have is a hunch. Find me some real evidence, and we'll talk."

"What?" I said in disbelief. "Where am I supposed to find evidence in a forty-one-year-old crime? That's practically impossible." Tom Delaney had covered his tracks for forty-one years. The trail was stone cold, and I couldn't imagine where I'd find evidence that would point to his guilt.

"The department has real crimes to solve—current-day crimes," he said. "They can't use their limited resources to analyze DNA from a case that's four decades old."

"Even if a murderer's gone free?" I asked.

"Even if," he said. "Like I said, find some real evidence, and we'll talk."

"All right," I said. I was highly annoyed. "Can I at least have the help of one of the officers? Maybe Laura Ramirez?" I wanted to see Laura again, and I wasn't sure how else to make that happen.

"I think you know the answer to that, Miss Pace," he said patiently. "The department wouldn't be able to devote any resources to this until you have some real evidence."

"Fine," I said shortly. "I'll work on it myself. Do I have your approval to call you directly when I find something?"

"Sure," he said, a tone of amusement in his voice. I could tell he thought I'd strike out.

"I'll find something," I said, my voice sounding more confident than I felt. "And when I do, you'll be the first to know."

30

Vivian
August 1974–January 1975

I heard a knock on the door, and I glanced at the clock: 4:15 a.m. The police had gotten here in mere minutes. After Tom ushered the two officers inside, everything happened in a blur. They asked him what had happened, and I heard him say that I'd broken into their house and attacked Tambra with the bat. He showed them the bat, covered with her blood. "Vivian's a dyke," I heard him say. "She's mentally unbalanced. She was in love with my wife, but Tambra despised her. Vivian couldn't handle the rejection so she broke into our house, went crazy, and killed my wife."

The police officers turned to me. "What happened, Miss Latham?" the younger one asked.

I had moved to the couch, and I was sitting there, sobbing. After several deep breaths, I was finally able to speak. "He did this. Tom did this," I said. "Tambra and I were in love. We were leaving for California in the morning to get away from Tom. He killed Tambra because he was crazed with jealousy and he didn't want her to go."

I saw Tom exchange glances with the two police officers, and I heard Tom say, "See, she's cuckoo."

I stood up and ran toward them. "No!" I yelled. "He's framing me! He did this! Please listen to me!"

The younger one reached out and grabbed my arms. He was strong. "Whoa, stop right there, ma'am."

He held me tight as I struggled against him. "Listen to me! Tom did this! Tom killed Tambra!" I screamed.

"That's enough, Miss Latham," the young officer said firmly.

The older police officer turned to Tom, talking to him in a low voice. The younger officer held me back, no doubt thinking I was insane. Tom had seen to that. I stood, quiet now, staring at Tambra's body, tears streaming down my face.

The older police officer came over to me and turned me around. I felt him pull my arms behind my back and lock the handcuffs around my wrists.

"No, please don't do this!" I cried. "You have it all wrong!"

The officer ignored me. "You have the right to remain silent," he said. "Anything you say can and will be used against you in a court of law…" I stopped listening. I couldn't understand what he was saying. The two officers led me to the door, and I turned to look back at Tambra lying on the floor.

"Tambra," I said, my voice almost a whisper. "I can't leave Tambra."

The younger one put his hand on my shoulder. "It's okay, Miss Latham. We'll take good care of her," he said in a surprisingly kind voice.

I took a long last look at Tambra and then stumbled out the door, down the walk, and into the police car. I saw Agnes Reed and Doris McLellan and their husbands standing out on the sidewalk, watching. I stared vacantly out the car window as the police officer started the engine and then drove away.

Once at the police precinct, I went into a state of shock. They told me to remove my bloody nightgown, and a police officer sealed it in a plastic bag. He gave me an olive green jumpsuit and paper shoes to put on, and I pulled them on mechanically. He photographed me from various angles and took my fingerprints and a blood sample. Then he used small wooden sticks and carefully scraped under each of my fingernails.

Once that was over, he led me down a hallway to a small room, sat me down at a table, and left. A few minutes later, another police officer came in. I didn't recognize him. He asked me over and over to tell him what had happened, but I couldn't think straight. The sight of Tambra's battered and bloody body lying on the floor was the only thing that filled my brain.

"Tell me what happened, Miss Latham," he said again.

I stared at him blankly as tears filled my eyes and began to run down my cheeks. "We were leaving together, to California," I said. "We were leaving in the morning."

"But what happened? How did Mrs. Delaney end up dead?"

"We were leaving in the morning," I answered, my eyes staring ahead, looking at nothing.

The officer finally gave up and locked me in a cell. "Get some rest, and we'll talk again in the morning," he said.

I stretched out on the hard cot and almost immediately fell into a deep, dreamless sleep. I awoke four hours later with a start. I couldn't remember where I was, but I knew something terrible had happened. Tambra, I remembered. Oh my God, Tambra was dead, and they thought I'd killed her. A sob caught in my throat. I had to tell them what had really happened.

I bolted off the cot. "Hey!" I yelled. "Hey!" A few minutes later, a young man in a police uniform appeared.

"Yeah?" he said, clearly disinterested.

"I need to talk to someone about what happened," I said urgently. "I don't belong in here."

"Detective O'Neil will be back at noon," the young officer said. "He'll talk to you then." He walked away.

I sat down on the cot and replayed everything that had happened. The vision of Tambra's ruined face and skull, the last flutter of her eyes, her final shuddering breath, played over and over in my mind. I wept, whispering "Tambra," over and over. How had this happened? Why had Tom done this? I had known he was violent, but I had never dreamed he would kill her. I knew Detective O'Neil would be back any minute, and I needed to clear my head so I could tell him what had really happened. I couldn't let Tom get away with this.

At noon the young officer came back and led me to a stark room with a table and three chairs. A few minutes later, two police officers came in. I recognized them as the two officers who had come to Tambra's house. One was tall, handsome, and clean cut, with piercing blue eyes. He looked to be around thirty. The other one was older and shorter, with a round belly. The younger one threw a file on the table and then sat down across from me. The older one sat down next to him and smiled tightly at me.

"I'm Detective Ronald Spencer, and this is Detective Sean O'Neil." He nodded toward the younger man.

"You want to tell us what happened?" Detective O'Neil said.

I took a deep breath and then launched into the story of my friendship and then my love affair with Tambra. I told them about Tom's abuse of Tambra and the plan we had devised to run off together. I began to sob and couldn't continue. One of the officers handed me a tissue, and they waited patiently for me to go on. Once I found my voice again, I told them that Tom was supposed to be staying with his brother in Bellingham but that he had come home in the middle of the night and gone crazy.

"Call his brother and ask him!" I said loudly. "He'll tell you that Tom was there and he left in the middle of the night—left to come home and kill Tambra!"

Detective O'Neil pulled a notepad out of his breast pocket and wrote something down. "We'll check that out," he said.

I then told them how I had gone out to the living room to get the bat to try and protect Tambra, but Tom had grabbed it from me. "He swung it at me a couple times, but then he used it on Tambra," I said, trying to fight back tears. "He beat her with it until she died."

"You do know that Mr. Delaney tells a very different story," Detective Spencer said grimly. He reached for the file, opened it, and scanned the top page. "He said you were obsessed with Mrs. Delaney and you were harassing her. He said Mrs. Delaney told you to leave her alone, but you wouldn't listen. He said you—"

"No!" I cried. "That's not what happened!"

Detective Spencer glared at me, not happy to be interrupted. "He said you broke into their house and attacked Mrs. Delaney with the bat."

"Tom was the one who attacked Tambra with the bat, not me!" I yelled. I tried to tone it down. "We were in love," I continued in a softer voice. "We were leaving for California to get away from Tom. He's been abusing Tambra. Didn't you see the bruises on her face and the gash on her cheek?"

Detective Spencer snorted. "Her face wasn't even recognizable. We wouldn't be able to see any bruises or a gash."

I let out a long breath and closed my eyes, thinking about Tambra's ruined face. I could feel the tears building behind my eyes again, and I fought hard to compose myself. I sat up straighter and looked at him. "Well, they're there, and Tom did that," I said. "Check with the hospital. I took her to the emergency room. She needed stitches."

Detective O'Neil made a note on his pad. "I'll look into it," he said airily.

I pointed to my cheek. That side of my face hurt like hell, so I knew it had to be bruised and swollen. "He did this to me. He hit me because I was trying to protect Tambra. And Tambra scratched him and bit his arm. Didn't you see the scratches on him or the bite on his arm?"

Detective Spencer smirked. "He told us you scratched him and bit his arm. We'll test the scrapings they took from your fingernails and see if they contain blood and if it matches his blood type. And we swabbed the bite on his arm, and we'll see if there's any blood there." He paused and looked down at the file again. "And Mr. Delaney admitted to hitting you, but he said he was trying to stop you from harming his wife."

"That's not what happened!" I shouted. "Tom did this. He killed Tambra!" Tears flooded my eyes again. Why wouldn't they listen to me?

Detective O'Neil raised his eyebrows. "And he says you did it. Seems like we have a classic case of he said/she said here." He reached for the file. "And I have to say the tiebreaker has been your neighbors."

My shoulders slumped, and I lowered my head. "What did they say about me?"

"Well, you haven't made a lot of friends, let's say that," Detective O'Neil said, looking through the papers in the file. He pulled out a single sheet and scanned it. "A Doris McLellan said that she tried to be friendly with you on two occasions, but you were rude to her. She said you slammed the door in her face. She also said she saw you trying Mrs. Delaney's door about two weeks ago and..." He glanced at the paper in front of him. "And I quote, 'Looking around furtively.' She said she saw you enter Mrs. Delaney's house without being invited in."

"What? I never—" I said, and then I remembered the morning I'd gone to Tambra's—the morning Tom had beaten her so badly—and Doris McLellan had been out watering her flowers. I didn't think she had seen me, but apparently I was wrong. "That was the morning Tom beat Tambra. The day I had to take her to the hospital. I was trying to help her. We were friends. She needed help, and I let myself into her house."

The two detectives looked at each other. "And a neighbor named Agnes Reed said you've acted strangely since you moved into the neighborhood," Detective O'Neil said. "She stated that you keep to yourself and you haven't been friendly. She's also seen you—and again I quote—'skulking around Mrs. Delaney's house.' She said she's seen you doing this on at least two occasions."

"I wasn't skulking around!" I said, almost shouting. "Tambra was my friend. I was visiting her like any friend would."

Detective O'Neil stared at me. "No one in the neighborhood could corroborate that you and Mrs. Delaney were friends," he said evenly.

"Well, we were," I said in a flat voice.

The door opened, and a short man came in, handed an envelope to Detective Spencer, and then walked out. Detective Spencer gave me a pointed look and opened the envelope. He scanned the pages inside and then raised his eyes to meet mine. "The lab has tested the blood on your nightgown. The blood is a match for Mrs. Delaney's blood type, A positive."

I rolled my eyes. "Of course I had her blood on me. I was holding her as she died. Tom had crushed her skull with that bat. She was dying. I loved her. I was comforting her."

Detective Spencer raised an eyebrow. "And the lab has confirmed that the blood on the bat is Mrs. Delaney's, and they've matched your fingerprints with the fingerprints on the bat."

"Well, of course my fingerprints are on the bat!" I shouted. "I've already told you, I was trying to protect Tambra with it!" I paused. "And Tom's fingerprints are on the bat too because he used it to kill Tambra!"

"Miss Latham, the bat belonged to Mr. Delaney," Detective O'Neil said slowly, as if he were talking to a child. "Of course his fingerprints are on it."

I began to cry. The two detectives waited patiently as I wiped my eyes and nose with the tissue and tried to pull myself together.

Detective Spencer cleared his throat. "Mr. Delaney and the two neighbors also said that you're a…a homosexual. Is that correct?" he asked.

"What does that have to do with anything?" I yelled.

Detective Spencer looked hard at me. "That's what we call motive, Miss Latham. A homosexual woman in love with her female neighbor who didn't return those feelings. A homosexual woman obsessed with her neighbor and harassing her repeatedly."

"That's not what happened!" I said loudly. "Tambra was my lover. I was the first person who'd ever really loved her. That's what she told me."

The two officers exchanged glances. "So you're confirming that you're homosexual?" Detective O'Neil said.

I glared at him. "Yes, I'm confirming it!" I snapped. "Are you happy now?"

Detective O'Neil didn't say anything as he made notes on a form.

"Why won't you listen to me? Tambra loved me!" I insisted. "We were in love. We were running off together to get away from Tom!"

Detective O'Neil leaned toward me and looked me dead in the eye. "There is absolutely no evidence to support that claim, Miss Latham."

I closed my eyes and tried to think. "My car!" I said. "My Lincoln is in Tambra's driveway, and it's packed with our stuff—mine, Tambra's, and Claire's—because we were leaving for California. That proves it!"

Detective O'Neil stood up. "I'll send an officer over there to check it out. In the meantime we're sending you back to your cell. We'll let you know when we have something to report." He opened the door and called out, and a few moments later, the young officer came and led me back to my cell.

I sat down on the cot, my head in my hands. This could not be happening. How had everything gone so wrong? Why hadn't we told someone of our plan? Tambra's sister? Daniel? Someone? We'd been so cavalier, and we'd both underestimated Tom.

Two hours later the young officer came back to get me, and he took me to the same room. Detective O'Neil was already there, but Detective Spencer was nowhere to be seen. "Miss Latham," he said. "Have a seat."

I sat down and looked at him. "Did you find my car?"

He nodded. "We found your car. It was sitting in your carport. It was completely empty." He paused. "Well, that's not entirely true. We found a pair of women's underwear in the front seat. Mr. Delaney has confirmed that they belonged to his wife."

"What?" I shouted. "That can't be. The car was loaded down—I packed it myself!" I caught sight of myself in the two-way mirror and was shocked to see how crazy I looked. My eyes looked wild and were red from crying. An almost-black bruise covered my swollen cheekbone. My hair was disheveled, and my skin was blotchy. I couldn't stop shaking.

"Ma'am, the car was empty," Detective O'Neil said. "The keys were in the ignition, but the car was empty." He cleared his throat. "Except for the underwear."

Tom had done this. I'd left my keys on Tambra's kitchen counter. Why wouldn't I? I hadn't thought there was anything to fear. Tom had found the keys, unlocked my car, and unloaded it. He had put everything back—except for one pair of Tambra's underwear. But how had he returned my things? I thought for a moment and then groaned. My house key was on the key ring. He'd simply found the right key, unlocked my door, and put my belongings inside. I shuddered at the thought of Tom Delaney in my house.

"Tom put that stuff back!" I yelled. "I left my keys on Tambra's kitchen counter and he took them! The stuff was in the car when we went to bed, I swear!"

Detective O'Neil looked at me and raised an eyebrow, but he didn't say a word. I knew he didn't believe me. He sighed and then continued. "We've also spoken with a Mr. Michael Delaney—Thomas Delaney's brother—and he denied that Thomas Delaney was staying with him. In fact, he said he hasn't seen his brother in several months."

"That's a lie!" I yelled. "Tom was there. His brother's lying." I stopped myself, realizing I had no idea where Tom had been. That's where he had said he was going, but he could have been anywhere.

Detective O'Neil glared at me. After several seconds he went on. "We also checked with the hospital. Mrs. Delaney did indeed visit the emergency room recently, and she did get stitches in her cheek, but the injury was due to a fall down her front porch stairs, not a beating."

"That's not what happened!" I shouted. "That's what she told them, but she went there because Tom beat her."

He shook his head. "No, Miss Latham, the hospital record shows that the visit was due to a fall."

I squeezed my eyes shut. Why had Tambra lied to the doctor? The feeling of hopelessness that came over me then nearly overwhelmed me. There was not one shred of evidence to prove what had really happened.

"We also got the results from the fingernail scrapings," he continued. "The scrapings from under your nails contained blood. A positive blood. The scrapings from under Mrs. Delaney's fingernails also contained A positive blood. Mr. and Mrs. Delaney had the same blood type—A positive—so those results are inconclusive. And Mrs. Delaney was bleeding profusely and distraught, so she likely got her own blood under her fingernails," he explained.

I stared at him. "That's a fucking lie! That's Tom's blood! The blood was under her fingernails because she scratched him when he was attacking her!"

He gave me a stern look. "Miss Latham, please watch your language," he cautioned.

I took a deep breath. "That's a lie," I said more calmly. "There was blood under her fingernails because she scratched him."

He smiled indulgently. "There's no way to prove that, Miss Latham, so the fingernail scrapings taken from Mrs. Delaney are inconclusive."

"Was my blood on anything?" I asked.

"Your blood type is O positive, and no, your blood was not found on either victim."

"Victim?" I shouted. "Tom is *not* a victim! He was the perpetrator!"

Detective O'Neil smirked. "Miss Latham, once again, there is absolutely no evidence to support that claim."

Tears welled in my eyes. I didn't know what else to say. They were hell-bent on finding me guilty, and nothing I said would sway them.

He leaned toward me so his face was only inches from mine. "If I were you, Miss Latham, I'd confess at this point," he said. "A confession may get you some leniency with the judge. You can say it was a crime of passion. You'll serve ten years, tops. Maybe five."

I looked at him as if he were insane. "I'm not confessing to something I didn't do! I loved Tambra. I'd never hurt her."

He regarded me somberly. "If you don't confess, then we have no choice but to charge you with second-degree murder. You'll be looking at fifteen to twenty years. Considering the malice that preceded the murder, it'll probably be twenty."

"Malice?" I said with a frown. "What do you mean by that?"

He cleared his throat. "The obsessive nature of the crime. The fact that Mrs. Delaney told you to leave her alone and you didn't. The brutality of the murder."

Oh my God, how had this all gone so wrong? I met his eyes. "I want a lawyer."

I searched the yellow pages for a lawyer. I had money to pay a lawyer—that wasn't the problem. I called lawyers from Centralia to Tacoma and everywhere in between, and they all were either too busy or too daunted by my case, thinking it was a losing proposition. While I was calling lawyers, the Olympia Police Department formally charged me with second-degree murder.

Finally, after what seemed like hours on the phone, I found someone—Fergus Atkinson—who was willing to take my case. I met with him the next day. When I first set eyes on him, I groaned inwardly. He looked like a kid. He was tall and skinny and had an unruly mop of almost-black hair and eyes the color of strong coffee. He wore a cheap, ill-fitting navy suit and shiny brown shoes. He seemed friendly enough, but I didn't think he looked like a serious lawyer. Once I began to talk to him, though, I realized he was more savvy than I first thought; he had already defended three other people accused of murder, two of whom had been acquitted. He was also older than he looked—thirty-one—and was a husband and father. He was happily married to a woman named Marjorie, and they had three young kids.

I sat across from him and painstakingly told him my story, but it quickly became clear that he didn't believe me. He told me several times that I could plead guilty, he'd present Tambra's death to the judge as a crime of passion, and I'd get less prison time. "Everyone can relate to a story of unrequited love," Fergus said. "Even though you're, uh, different, he'd still understand."

I sighed loudly. "But I'm not guilty," I said for the third time. "There was no crime of passion because there was no crime. There was no unrequited love. We were lovers. Tambra loved me. I loved her. Her husband killed her in a fit of jealous rage. Aren't you listening to me?"

Fergus stared at me as if I were crazy. "Vivian, I've seen the police work," he said, exasperated. "The neighbors have all corroborated Tom Delaney's statement that he and his wife were happy. Nobody heard fighting or saw bruises on Mrs. Delaney or anything of the kind. And Tom Delaney said he and his wife were happy and you disturbed their happiness. Why would a happy man kill his wife?" He waited for a response from me, but I sat in stony silence. "And why would a happily married woman with a husband and a baby take up with her homosexual neighbor? Do you really think a jury will buy that?"

"I don't care what a jury will buy. That's the truth!" I said, making no effort to hide my anger. "And Tambra wasn't happily married. Far from it. Her husband was beating her! He killed her, for God's sake. Have you paid any attention to what I've been telling you?"

He looked at me sternly and shook his finger just inches from my face. "You'd better care what a jury will buy, Vivian. They hold your fate in their hands." He paused. "I don't think you understand the kind of trouble you're in here. You have no defense other than your claim that Mrs. Delaney was in love with you—a claim no one can confirm. You're looking at prison time, Vivian, plain and simple. My advice to you is to plead guilty and ask for a reduced charge of voluntary manslaughter."

I sat back, folded my arms across my chest, and glared at him. I could feel the sting of tears behind my eyes. "I loved Tambra. I'd never hurt her, and I am *not* entering any plea except not guilty, so stop talking to me about it."

"Suit yourself," he said, gathering his papers and standing. "I'll do my best to defend you, but the odds are stacked against you."

On Thursday morning I appeared in court, and the charges against me were read.

"How do you plead, Miss Latham?" the judge asked.

I raised my chin and looked him in the eye. "Not guilty, Your Honor."

"Duly noted," the judge said. He announced that I'd be held without bail and my trial would begin on October 21, 1974. Then he banged his gavel and walked out.

※

I bided my time in the city jail, writing copious notes about my relationship with Tambra and sharing them with Fergus. He read them and filed them away, but I could tell he didn't believe a word I said. My thirty-third birthday came and went on September twenty-eighth, and I scarcely noticed.

Right after my birthday, Fergus began strategizing for my trial, which was set to begin in three weeks. He asked if I knew anyone who could testify on my behalf as a character witness. "I don't have much of a defense," he said. "So we can use all the help we can get."

"What's a character witness?" I asked.

He waved his hands in the air. "You know, someone who tells the jury how great you are and how you'd never hurt a fly."

I immediately thought of Daniel but wondered if he'd be able to make the trip from Iowa. I hesitated. "Yes, my oldest friend, Daniel Frazier, lives in Iowa. I've known him since high school. I don't know if he'd be able to make the trip out here, but maybe if you call him and tell him what happened, he could work it out."

"Okay," Fergus said. "Anyone else?"

I thought for a few moments. "Well, there's my aunt Dorothy. She's come to see me in jail a couple of times, but she doesn't know the, um, the details of the case."

"She knows a woman is dead, doesn't she, and you're accused of killing her?" he asked in a stern voice.

"Yes, she knows that. She just doesn't know about…me," I said quietly.

He gave me a hard look. "You mean she doesn't know you're a homosexual?"

"Right," I said, looking away.

Fergus smirked. "Right now, Vivian, you can use all the help you can get. That should be the least of your worries. Give me her number." He handed me his yellow legal pad and a pen. I hesitated a moment and then carefully wrote down Daniel's and Aunt Dorothy's phone numbers. I said a silent prayer that they would be able to help me.

31

The trial began on October twenty-first. As the bailiff led me into the courtroom, my heart skipped a beat when I saw Tom sitting in the front row. He turned as I entered, and his cold, beady eyes followed me as I walked toward him. I noticed that an older couple was sitting next to him. As I walked past, I realized they must be George and Mary Sorenson, Tambra's parents. I looked at Tambra's father. He was about fifty-five and quite handsome. His eyes locked with mine, and my breath caught in my throat when I saw they were the same vivid blue as Tambra's. Her mother was a bit younger and pretty. She had the same golden-blond hair that Tambra had been so proud of. As I walked by, her mother lowered her head and brought a handkerchief to her mouth.

I was led to a table and seated next to Fergus. I looked around the courtroom, and my eyes rested on the jury. I studied their faces. Would they believe what had really happened? I'd already told Fergus that I wanted to testify in my own defense. He hadn't agreed with that decision, but I knew it was my right and the only chance I'd have of convincing the jury of my innocence.

I tried to focus on what was happening in the courtroom, but I was having a hard time. As if in a dream, I heard the two attorneys making their opening statements. Their words floated around me, but I couldn't quite make sense of them. Seeing Tom again had shaken me to the core. I knew he was behind me, and I could feel his eyes boring into my back. It was everything I could do not to turn around and look at him. It was everything I could do not to jump over the railing, put my hands around his thick neck, and choke him until he fell dead onto the courtroom floor.

The images from the night Tambra had been killed came crowding into my mind, and I wondered for the millionth time if I could have done something differently. Why hadn't we left once the packing was done? Why hadn't we stayed at my house? Why hadn't I thought to call the police when I was out in the living room getting the bat? Why hadn't I gone into the bedroom with the bat and hit him in the back of the head with it? If any of those things had happened, Tambra would still be alive.

"Vivian, pay attention!" Fergus said in an urgent whisper.

I shook my head and tried to focus on the trial. I was surprised to see that the prosecution had already begun calling witnesses. I scowled as I saw Agnes Reed on the stand.

"Vivian, neutral expression, please," Fergus said quietly. "The jury is watching."

My gaze swiveled to the jury, and indeed three of them were looking at me. I wiped the scowl from my face and tried to focus on what Mrs. Reed was saying.

"I found Vivian to be odd," she said. "She kept to herself, and I wouldn't call her friendly. I went over to welcome her to the neighborhood, and she was very cool toward me."

The prosecutor, Douglas Armstrong, murmured something to Mrs. Reed that I couldn't understand, but I heard her response just fine. "I found out that Vivian was a…a…a homosexual, and I was immediately concerned."

"Why were you concerned, madam?" Mr. Armstrong asked.

"Well, we have lots of children in the neighborhood, and, well… it made me nervous," she said, shifting uncomfortably. "And there weren't any of, uh, her kind in the neighborhood. I just didn't think she fit in."

"Did you ever see Miss Latham interacting with Tambra Delaney?" Mr. Armstrong asked.

Mrs. Reed's chin dipped down to her chest. "No, I never did."

"So you never observed that the two women were friends?"

Her eyes slid away from the prosecutor, and she fidgeted in her chair. "No, I saw no indication that they were friends."

"Did you ever see Vivian Latham near Mrs. Delaney's house?"

Mrs. Reed nodded. "Yes, I saw her sneaking around Tambra's driveway and her side door on at least two occasions. Now that I know what happened, I think she was working up a plan to break into their house."

I scowled again. That was a lie. I'd never sneaked around Tambra's house. Mrs. Reed had seen what she wanted to see, not what was true.

"Objection, Your Honor!" Fergus barked, startling me. "The question has already been answered by the witness. She's giving an answer that goes beyond the question posed."

"Sustained," the judge said. "Please restrict your responses to the question that's asked, Mrs. Reed." He glanced at the jurors. "And the jury shall disregard that last statement."

She nodded stiffly. "I saw Vivian Latham by Mrs. Delaney's door on two occasions."

"Thank you, Mrs. Reed. Your witness," Mr. Armstrong said, gesturing toward Fergus.

Fergus stood and gave Agnes Reed a steely look. "Mrs. Reed, do you know for a fact that Tambra Delaney and Vivian Latham were not friends?"

She frowned. "Well, no, I can't say for sure that they weren't friends, but I never—"

"Thank you, ma'am," Fergus said. "And did you ever see Miss Latham talking to any children in your neighborhood?"

Mrs. Reed gathered herself up, her mouth in a hard line. "No, I never saw her talking to any children."

"Did you ever see or hear fighting or violence between Tambra Delaney and her husband, Tom Delaney?" he asked, looking at her intently.

She pressed her lips together and looked at the floor. "No."

"Are you certain of that?" Fergus said. "Let me remind you that you're under oath."

Mrs. Reed sat up straighter. "Yes, I'm certain!" she spat.

Fergus slipped his hands inside his pants pockets and regarded her silently for a few moments. "And what about at the time of the murder? Do you recall hearing a disturbance at the Delaney household?"

She shook her head. "No, I didn't hear anything."

Fergus stood for several seconds looking at her, but she wouldn't meet his eyes. "Thank you, Mrs. Reed," he finally said. "No further questions." He returned to the table and sat down beside me.

My attention was wavering again. My brain felt foggy, and I was having a hard time paying attention. I tried to focus and saw that Doris McLellan was on the stand now, telling a tale similar to Agnes Reed's. I was unfriendly and rude. She told the story of her visit to my house when I'd slammed the door in her face.

"There was a little more to it than that," I grumbled under my breath.

She recounted seeing me let myself into Tambra's house, uninvited. Fergus looked at me and raised one eyebrow. Apparently I'd forgotten to tell him that story.

Then Fergus stood and cross-examined Mrs. McLellan. He asked similar questions to those he had posed to Mrs. Reed. A few moments later, he was sitting next to me again.

I lowered my head and closed my eyes as images of Tambra filled my head. Tambra lying naked on the bed. Tambra laughing as she beat me at crazy eights again. Tambra feeding Claire her lunch. Tambra clinking her wineglass against mine. Tambra kissing me the first time. Tears stung my eyes. How had everything gone to hell?

Fergus prodded me with his elbow, and I struggled to bring my attention back to the proceedings again. I saw that Detective O'Neil was on the stand now. He was describing the murder scene to the jury. He talked about Tambra's wounds, the blood, the bat, the broken lamp. He talked about the blood evidence. He said that blood matching Mrs. Delaney's was present on my nightgown and the bat. The blood under my fingernails was A positive, a match to either Mr. or Mrs. Delaney's. The bloody bat was shown to the jurors and then admitted into evidence. My eyes were riveted on the bat as I remembered my terror at seeing Tom swing it at Tambra's head.

Finally Mr. Armstrong's questions were over, and Fergus took his turn. He stood and looked at Detective O'Neil. "Did Vivian Latham ever confess to killing Tambra Delaney?" he asked.

"No," Detective O'Neil said.

"In fact, didn't she adamantly express her innocence?"

"Yes, she did," he said.

"What did Miss Latham tell you happened?" Fergus asked.

Detective O'Neil cleared his throat. "She told us she and Mrs. Delaney were, um, romantically involved and they were going to run away together. She said Mr. Delaney was supposed to be away for the weekend, but he came home unexpectedly. Mrs. Delaney and Miss Latham were, uh, together in the Delaney's bed, and Mr. Delaney went into a jealous rage and killed Tambra Delaney with the bat."

Fergus looked at the detective thoughtfully. "Do you have definitive evidence that proves beyond a shadow of a doubt that Tom Delaney did not kill his wife?" he asked.

"No, we do not," he said in a clipped voice.

"And do you have definitive evidence that proves that Miss Latham and Mrs. Delaney were not romantically involved?"

Detective O'Neil was silent for a long beat. "No, we do not."

Fergus walked over to the table where I sat, and tapped the file. "I've reviewed the evidence collected at the crime scene, and I have to say that it's largely circumstantial. Wouldn't you agree?"

Detective O'Neil raised his chin and met Fergus's eyes. "Fingerprints, blood evidence, and a murder weapon aren't circumstantial."

"Yes, we know," Fergus said. "Miss Latham's fingerprints were on the bat. But isn't it possible, as Miss Latham contends, that her fingerprints were on the bat because she was using it to try and stop Mr. Delaney from harming Mrs. Delaney?"

The detective shrugged. "Yes, it's possible."

"And isn't it possible, as Miss Latham contends, that Mrs. Delaney's blood was on Vivian Latham's nightgown because she was holding Mrs. Delaney in her arms as she died, because they loved each other?"

The detective shifted in his chair. "Yes, it's possible."

Fergus looked closely at Detective O'Neil. "Were you looking at any other suspects, or did you focus your investigation on Miss Latham?"

Detective O'Neil shook his head. "No, we weren't looking at any other suspects. The evidence pointed us to Vivian Latham."

Fergus gave a tight smile. "Did you focus your investigation on Vivian Latham because she's a homosexual and wasn't well liked by her neighbors because of that?"

Detective O'Neil paused and looked at the jury. "We focused on Vivian Latham because she was at the scene wearing clothing covered with Mrs. Delaney's blood and her fingerprints were on the murder weapon. We coupled that with a witness statement from Tom Delaney and statements from Miss Latham's neighbors."

"So the fact that she's a homosexual never entered your minds at all?" Fergus asked, fixing the detective with a piercing gaze. "You were purely looking at evidence?"

"Objection!" Mr. Armstrong said. "Asked and answered, Your Honor."

"Overruled," the judge said. "Please answer the question, Detective."

Detective O'Neil took a deep breath and met Fergus's eye. "We considered Miss Latham's homosexuality as it pertained to Tom Delaney's claim that Miss Latham was, um, romantically obsessed with Mrs. Delaney."

Fergus tipped his head to the side. "Did you consider the possibility that Miss Latham and Mrs. Delaney were indeed romantically involved?"

The detective looked steadily at Fergus. "There was no evidence to support that claim."

"So you only considered the possibility that Miss Latham was obsessed with Mrs. Delaney. Does that mean that in your mind any homosexual person is murderous if the object of their affections doesn't return their romantic feelings?"

"Objection!" Mr. Armstrong roared. "He's badgering the witness, Your Honor!"

"Overruled," the judge said. "Please answer the question, sir."

Detective O'Neil fidgeted in the chair. "No, we don't make that assumption. We looked at this case in isolation."

"Do you know any homosexual people, Detective?" Fergus asked, rocking on his heels. "Besides Miss Latham, of course."

"No, I do not," the detective answered.

"Do you consider yourself to be fair and impartial?"

Detective O'Neil raised his eyebrows. "Yes, I do."

"So you treated Vivian Latham the same way you would have treated a heterosexual suspect?"

The detective did not meet Fergus's eyes. "Yes, we did."

"Hmm," Fergus said, nodding. "Did you investigate Miss Latham's claim that it was actually Tom Delaney who killed his wife?"

"We looked at it, but it wasn't credible," the detective said. "We interviewed the neighbors, and not one confirmed that Mr. Delaney was violent."

"And do you think the neighbors would know something like that about Mr. Delaney?"

The detective raised a shoulder in a half shrug. "It's a quiet neighborhood. I think they would have heard something."

Fergus paused. "Did you investigate the possibility that the neighbors gave false statements about what happened because they didn't want Miss Latham in their neighborhood?"

Detective O'Neil frowned. "No, we didn't consider that. I trusted the information the neighbors gave us."

"Hmm," Fergus said, rubbing his chin. "How long have you been on the police force, Detective?" he asked.

"About six years," he answered.

"And in that time, you've handled how many murder cases?"

Detective O'Neil looked Fergus in the eye. "Four, including this one. Thankfully, Olympia doesn't have a lot of murders."

"So you could hardly be called an expert on murder investigations, could you?" Fergus said.

"Objection!" Mr. Armstrong said. "The detective isn't on trial here."

"Sustained," the judge said. "Watch it, Counselor."

"I'll rephrase," Fergus said, smiling. "Do you consider yourself an expert on murder investigations, Detective?"

Detective O'Neil smiled tightly. "No, but I do consider myself an expert on human nature and motive, and both point to Vivian Latham as the murderer."

I saw Fergus hesitate, clearly shaken by this response. "Thank you, Detective. No further questions, Your Honor," Fergus said.

The judge banged his gavel and said we would break for lunch until two o'clock. Fergus returned to the table and gave me a sheepish smile.

"Why did you end on that note?" I demanded. "That wasn't good for me."

He shrugged and shook his head. "I'm sorry. He caught me off guard. I didn't know what else to say."

The bailiff came over, grabbed my arm, and began leading me away. This was not going well so far. I was escorted back to my cell and given a roast beef sandwich and a glass of milk. I ate quickly and then sat waiting impatiently for someone to come and get me.

At 1:45 p.m. I was led back into the courtroom, where I took my seat next to Fergus. "What's going to happen now?" I asked.

"I think they'll be calling Tom Delaney to the stand," he said.

I gasped. "What? Tom is going to testify?"

"Of course he is," Fergus said, looking at me as if I were mad. "He's the only other person besides you who was there."

I sat back in my chair, shocked, as the jury began filing back into the courtroom. It hadn't even occurred to me that Tom would testify. Why hadn't Fergus warned me? I glanced up as the judge slipped in and took his seat. Court was called into session.

"The prosecution calls Thomas Delaney to the stand," Mr. Armstrong said.

I heard Tom lumber out of his seat and then shuffle up to the witness box. I looked daggers at his back, hoping he felt it just as I'd felt his eyes on me. Tom took the oath and then sat heavily in the chair. I scowled. He wasn't going to tell the truth. He was going to lie through his teeth.

"Mr. Delaney, when did you first meet Vivian Latham?" the prosecutor asked.

Tom thought for a moment. "I first met her when she came to our house for dinner. That was in March."

Douglas Armstrong flashed a phony smile. "Why did she come to dinner at your house, given that she was harassing your wife?"

"That was before the obsession got really bad," Tom said. "I think my wife felt sorry for her, so she asked her over for dinner."

"She didn't feel sorry for me," I said to Fergus under my breath. "That's a lie." Fergus's eyes slid toward me and then away, but he didn't speak.

"What was your impression of Miss Latham?" the prosecutor asked.

Tom shrugged. "I thought she was harmless. She seemed a little odd, but I didn't think too much of it."

"And when did you realize she wasn't harmless?"

"Objection!" Fergus roared. "Leading the witness."

"Sustained," the judge said. "Watch yourself, Mr. Armstrong."

Douglas Armstrong gave the judge a thin smile. "I'll rephrase, Your Honor." He cleared his throat. "When did your wife report to you that Miss Latham was behaving obsessively?"

Tom leaned back in his chair. "Early June. Around her birthday. Tambra told me that Vivian was coming over uninvited and bringing her small gifts. And Tambra reported to me that on a few occasions she'd seen Vivian sitting on her porch and watching her with binoculars."

"That never happened," I whispered to Fergus. "He's lying." Fergus glanced at me but was silent.

"And what did your wife think about this?" Douglas Armstrong asked.

"Objection!" Fergus said. "Speculative. He can't know what his wife was thinking."

"I'll rephrase," Mr. Armstrong said quickly. "Did your wife tell you her thoughts on this matter?"

Tom wiped his mouth with the back of his hand and nodded. "Yeah, she told me it scared her."

I seethed inside. Tom was such a liar, and the jury seemed to be buying it lock, stock, and barrel. I looked at their faces. They were hanging on his every word. Every few seconds one of them would glance at me, judging me, I was sure.

Douglas Armstrong jammed his hands in his pockets and began pacing back and forth in front of Tom. "Mr. Delaney, did you ask Miss Latham to leave your wife alone?"

He wiped his hands on his pants and nodded. "Yeah, in June I went over to Vivian's house and told her to stop bothering Tambra or I'd report it to the police."

"And did she stop?" the prosecutor asked.

Tom shook his head and looked down at his hands. "No, she didn't stop. In fact, it got worse. Vivian was disturbing Tambra every day through most of July."

"Were you ever fearful for your wife's safety?" Mr. Armstrong asked.

Tom looked up, his eyes brimming with tears. "Yes, sir, I was."

How could the bastard call up tears on demand? I'd seen him display no remorse whatsoever as Tambra lay dying on their living room floor. Tom was twisting the truth so completely, and there was no evidence or testimony coming that would reveal his lies. There was still my testimony, but I was becoming more fearful by the moment that the jury wasn't going to believe me. Tom was hell-bent on sending me to prison—the punishment he thought I deserved for loving Tambra.

"Did Miss Latham ever make threats against your wife?" Mr. Armstrong asked.

Tom scratched his nose. "Oh, yes. After I went over and told her to leave Tambra alone, she put a note in our mailbox addressed to Tambra that said, 'You're going to be sorry you ever met me.' I found the note—Tambra never saw it. I didn't want to scare her."

I couldn't let that one pass. I jumped to my feet and yelled, "That's a lie! They're all lies!"

The judge glared at me and banged his gavel. "Mr. Atkinson, please control your client," he said. "And please strike that outburst from the court record."

Fergus pulled me back down into my chair and spoke softly but firmly in my ear. "That's enough, Vivian."

"But he's lying, Fergus," I whispered urgently. "He can't get away with that."

"That's enough."

Tom shot me a look of disgust and turned his attention back to the prosecutor. I glanced at the jury, and they were all looking at me, openmouthed. Why had I said that? Now I looked even crazier. I needed to pull myself together. I pasted a neutral look on my face and turned back to the proceedings.

The prosecutor smiled stiffly. "So Miss Latham put a note in your mailbox, addressed to your wife, that said, 'You're going to be sorry you ever met me'?"

"Yes," Tom said.

Mr. Armstrong nodded somberly. "Mr. Delaney, tell us what happened in the early morning hours of August eleventh."

Tom shifted uncomfortably in his chair and rubbed the back of his neck. "Tambra and I were asleep, and all of a sudden a loud noise woke us up. Vivian Latham was standing at the foot of our bed with the bat in her hands."

"And then what happened?" Douglas Armstrong asked.

Tom cleared his throat. "Tambra tried reasoning with Vivian, but she was deranged. She started swinging the bat around, and Tambra got scared and ran out to the living room." He paused and took a deep breath. "Vivian followed her, and I ran after her. I tried to grab the bat and restrain her, but she was crazy. She just started beating Tambra with the bat. She hit her in the head two or three times and crushed her skull, and she died soon after."

I felt my throat constrict, and tears burned my eyes. I squeezed my eyes shut and lowered my head. It was all I could do to stop myself from bursting into tears or vomiting on the courtroom floor. I had never felt so heartbroken and so hopeless—not when my parents died and not when I lost my job. Never. The love I'd had with Tambra had been tender and true. Tom was twisting that love into something ugly and brutal. He was erasing it from existence—as if it had never happened. A tear slid down my cheek, and I quickly wiped it away before anyone could see. Then I swallowed hard and forced myself to look up.

"What happened after your wife, uh, died, Mr. Delaney?" Mr. Armstrong asked.

Tom paused and licked his lips. "Vivian was panting like an animal. I called the police right after and held her down until they got there."

"What happened when the police got there?" Mr. Armstrong asked.

Tom shrugged. "They asked what happened, and I told them. Vivian told some crazy lies about what had happened. Then they arrested her and took her away."

Douglas Armstrong looked closely at Tom. "Mr. Delaney, did you ever lay a hand on your wife, Tambra Delaney, in anger?"

Tom raised his chin and looked at the prosecutor. "Never."

"Thank you, Mr. Delaney. Your witness," he said to Fergus.

Fergus stood and silently considered Tom Delaney for a few moments. "Mr. Delaney," he finally said, "you testified that you went over to Miss Latham's house in June and told her to leave your wife alone. Is that correct?"

Tom met Fergus's eyes and then looked away. "Yes, I did."

"And how did Miss Latham respond?"

Tom shrugged. "I don't know. She was angry."

"She was angry," Fergus repeated. "But what did she say?"

Tom moved his mouth, but no words came out. "I, um, I don't really remember," he finally said.

Fergus frowned. "So you were upset enough to go over to Miss Latham's house and confront her, but you don't remember what she said. Is that your testimony, sir?"

"Yes," Tom said stiffly.

Fergus fixed Tom with a steady gaze. "And you claim that Miss Latham put a note in your mailbox, addressed to your wife, that said, 'You're going to be sorry you ever met me.' Is that correct?"

Tom gave a curt nod. "Yes, that's right."

"Of course, you called the police when you received this note. Isn't that correct?"

Tom squirmed in his seat as his cheeks turned crimson. "No, I never called the police."

Fergus stared at Tom for several seconds. "A woman threatens your wife, and you don't report it to the police? How is that possible, sir?"

"I...I...it didn't...I never...I didn't think of doing that."

"You didn't think of doing that," Fergus repeated. "According to your testimony, you threatened to report her behavior to the police when you allegedly went to warn her to stay away from your wife. Yet when you received this alleged note, it didn't occur to you to call the police. Is that your testimony, Mr. Delaney?" Fergus gave Tom a hard look.

Tom stared at Fergus, his mouth hanging open. "I...I just...I didn't think of it."

"A simple yes or no will suffice."

Tom cleared his throat. "Yes, that's my testimony."

Fergus folded his arms across his chest. "And where is this note, sir? It should be admitted into evidence."

Tom let out a huff of air and sat back in the chair. "I don't have it anymore. I threw it away."

Fergus looked at Tom as if he were insane. "And why on earth would you do that? If you were so fearful for your wife's safety, wouldn't you think it was important to keep the note?"

"I just didn't...I never...it didn't occur to me," Tom said.

Fergus smirked. "Or perhaps it's because the note never existed."

"Objection!" Douglas Armstrong yelled.

"Withdrawn," Fergus said smoothly. He stared at Tom for a long moment and then began to pace back and forth, rubbing his chin. Finally he stopped and looked at Tom. "I have to ask, Mr. Delaney. You're probably six or seven inches taller than Miss Latham, and you look to outweigh her by fifty or sixty pounds. When she allegedly broke into your house on August eleventh, how is it, sir, that you were unable to restrain her?"

Tom seemed taken aback by the question. He scratched his face and blinked hard several times. "I don't know. She was crazed. She was like a wild animal. I don't know how to explain it—superhuman strength, I guess."

"Superhuman strength," Fergus said, slowly enunciating each word. "So due to Miss Latham's supposed superhuman strength, you, a large man, were unable to restrain her, a one-hundred-and-sixty-five-pound, five-foot-seven-inch woman, is that correct?"

"Objection, Your Honor!" Mr. Armstrong barked. "Asked and answered."

"Overruled," the judge said. "I'd like to hear Mr. Delaney's response."

Tom looked nervously at the judge and then back at Fergus. "She was crazed. I couldn't hold her."

"Hmm," Fergus said, tapping his finger against his chin as he scrutinized Tom. "So she was crazed, and you couldn't restrain her, yet after you called the police, you, and I quote, 'held her down until they got there.' How is it, Mr. Delaney, that you were suddenly able to restrain this crazed woman when, just minutes earlier, you supposedly couldn't stop her from killing your wife?"

Tom ran his hand through his hair, and his face reddened again. "I don't know. She was exhausted after killing my wife, I guess. She settled down once she did what she came there to do."

Fergus stood as close to Tom as was possible and stared at him. "Mr. Delaney, did you murder your wife?"

Tom sat up straight and looked at Fergus. "No!" he yelled.

Fergus frowned. "Something doesn't add up, Mr. Delaney, and I have some doubts about your truthfulness today."

"Objection!" Douglas Armstrong shouted.

"Sustained," the judge said. "Mr. Atkinson, please limit your cross-examination to the case before us."

Fergus flashed the judge a smile. "I apologize, Your Honor," he said. "No further questions." Fergus pivoted on his heel and returned to the table.

Tom heaved himself out of the witness chair and headed back to his seat. I looked at his face, and for the first time I saw fear in his eyes. I felt a wave of gratitude toward Fergus. I leaned toward him. "Thank you, Fergus," I whispered. He gave me a thin smile and nodded.

"Mr. Armstrong," the judge said, "call your next witness."

Mr. Armstrong stood and faced the judge. "The prosecution rests, Your Honor."

"Very well," the judge said. "We'll resume at ten o'clock tomorrow morning, and you'll be up, Mr. Atkinson. Court dismissed." The judge banged his gavel, and everyone stood as he exited the courtroom. Immediately, the bailiff was at my side with the handcuffs open, ready to snap them around my wrists.

Fergus stopped him with a hand on his shoulder. "I need to talk with my client," he said. "Please bring her to the meeting room, and I'll be there shortly."

As the bailiff led me from the courtroom, I wondered what Fergus wanted to talk about. I was deposited in the meeting room, and Fergus slipped in a few minutes later. We sat across from each other, and I searched his face. "What's wrong, Fergus?"

He leaned his elbows on the table. "I'm beginning to think that Tom Delaney is a liar," he said matter-of-factly.

I let out a long breath. "What made you change your mind?"

He looked at me thoughtfully. "When Tom was on the stand, I noticed him making several gestures and mannerisms that I've observed in others as dishonesty."

"What do you mean?" I asked.

"He often looked down or away when answering questions, and he touched his face, head, and neck a lot. Those are mannerisms I've observed in other people who aren't telling the truth."

I nodded. "Okay. What else?"

"He claims you made a threat against his wife's life—this note he says you left—but he didn't report it to the police or keep the note. I find that highly unlikely." He paused and rubbed his chin thoughtfully. "If Tom really was fearful for his wife's safety, of course he would have called the police."

"He didn't call the police because there was no note."

"Indeed," Fergus said, nodding. "He also stated that he couldn't restrain you when you attacked Tambra, and I find that very hard to believe. He must weigh two ten or two twenty, and he's tall. A man that size would have had no trouble restraining you." Fergus paused and sighed deeply. "But sadly I don't know that any of this is going to help your case, Vivian."

"What?" I cried. I'd begun to feel a sliver of hope, and now he was telling me it wouldn't make a difference.

He looked at me helplessly. "The testimony of your neighbors, the police officer, and Tom, coupled with your fingerprints on the bat and Tambra's blood on your nightgown, are all going to be hard for the jury to ignore. And I hate to say it, Vivian, but your homosexuality will make matters worse. None of the jurors would admit to being prejudiced, but we know they are. You're different from them in one key way, and they don't understand it. Right now the best we can do is put you on the stand and let you tell your story. And the character witnesses we've lined up—your aunt and your friend—may help."

"So Daniel is coming?" I asked excitedly.

"He is." Fergus nodded. "I talked with him yesterday, and he should be landing at Sea-Tac in about an hour. I'll put him on the stand in the morning."

I closed my eyes and sighed deeply. "Oh, thank God."

"We'll do the best we can with what we have—and I hate to say this—but if they convict you, then I can look at filing an appeal."

"An appeal? What's that?" I felt completely out of my element with the legal process. I'd never gone through anything even remotely like this in my life.

He steepled his fingers and gave me an earnest look. "That's where we ask a higher court to review your case for legal errors. It's a long shot, but I'll go through everything with a fine-toothed comb and see if I can find any irregularities. That's the best I can do."

"So are you saying you believe me, Fergus?"

He was silent for a long moment before answering. "What I'm saying is I am now of the opinion that your version of events is more accurate."

I sighed. "I can't tell you what a relief it is to hear you say that," I said. "Thanks, Fergus."

He gave me a sad smile. "I'm really sorry about all this, Vivian."

"I know," I said with a nod. "I am too."

Fergus gathered his papers and stood. "Get some rest, Vivian, and tomorrow we'll do our best to put a kernel of reasonable doubt in the minds of those jurors."

32

The next morning I was seated in the courtroom at ten o'clock sharp with Fergus by my side. The judge entered, and court was called into session.

"Mr. Atkinson, call your first witness," the judge said gruffly.

Fergus stood. "Thank you, Your Honor," he said. "The defense calls Daniel Alan Frazier to the stand."

As I turned and watched Daniel come through the double doors, a sob caught in my throat; I hadn't realized until that moment how much I had missed him. He held my gaze and gave me a small smile as he walked past. He took the oath and then sat down in the witness chair.

"Mr. Frazier, thank you for coming today," Fergus said. "I know Washington State is a long way from Iowa."

"Anything for Vivian," Daniel said.

"So, Mr. Frazier, tell us how long you've known Vivian Latham."

Daniel looked up at the ceiling for a long moment and then back at Fergus. "I met Vivian when I was fifteen, so eighteen years."

"And where did you meet her?" Fergus asked.

"We met in high school during sophomore year."

"So would you say you know her well?"

Daniel nodded. "Yes, Vivian and I spent a lot of time together. We were inseparable during high school. After graduation we remained friends. We saw each other regularly until she moved out here. So yes, I know her well."

"What are your impressions of Vivian? What kind of person would you say she is?" Fergus asked.

Daniel smiled. "She's probably the kindest person I've ever known. I've never heard her say a harsh word to anyone. And she's very generous—she'd give you the shirt off her back if you asked her to. She's honest, straightforward, and caring."

"She sounds like a special person," Fergus said with a smile. "Did Vivian tell you about her friendship and her love affair with Tambra Delaney?"

"Yes, she did," Daniel said. "She called me in March and told me she and Tambra had become friends, and then in July she called again and said she and Tambra were in love. During that phone call, she also told me that Tambra's husband was abusing her and she'd been pressuring Tambra to leave him."

"Did she tell you about any specific plan they had to get away from Tom Delaney?"

Daniel shook his head. "No, they didn't have a plan at that time. Vivian said they were just talking about it."

Fergus looked closely at Daniel. "And what did you think when you heard that Vivian Latham had been charged with the murder of Tambra Delaney?"

"I thought it was absurd," Daniel huffed. "First of all, Vivian isn't capable of murder. And second of all, she loved Tambra. She told me she'd never loved anyone as much as she loved Tambra. Vivian never would have hurt Tambra."

I closed my eyes and said a silent thank you to Daniel. I was relieved that he was telling the jury, Fergus, everyone, that I loved Tambra and I would never hurt her.

"Thank you, Mr. Frazier. Nothing further." Fergus looked at Douglas Armstrong. "Your witness."

Douglas Armstrong rose and approached Daniel. "Mr. Frazier, did you ever meet Tambra Delaney?"

Daniel shook his head. "No, I never met her."

"So you never saw Vivian Latham and Tambra Delaney together. Is that correct?"

"No, I never saw them together, but I—"

"Thank you, Mr. Frazier," Mr. Armstrong interrupted. "And did you ever see a photograph of Miss Latham and Mrs. Delaney together, or did you ever talk to Mrs. Delaney on the telephone?"

Daniel frowned. "No, I didn't, but—"

"So what you're saying is that all you have to go by is what Miss Latham told you, is that correct?" Douglas Armstrong gave Daniel a steely look.

Daniel lowered his eyes and blinked rapidly. "Well, yes, but she—"

"So you have no proof that Miss Latham and Mrs. Delaney were friends or were romantically involved."

Daniel sighed. "No, I have no proof, but Vivian is—"

"And you have no proof that Mrs. Delaney loved Miss Latham or that she even liked her, is that correct?"

Daniel sat back, looking defeated. "No, I don't have any proof."

"Thank you, Mr. Frazier," Mr. Armstrong said firmly. "No further questions, Your Honor."

As Daniel rose from the witness chair and began walking toward the back of the courtroom, I scrutinized his face. He looked utterly demoralized. As he walked by, I caught his eye, smiled, and mouthed, "Thank you." He gave me a small nod, and I watched him leave the courtroom. As the doors swung closed, I was seized by the feeling that I would never see him again.

Fergus called Aunt Dorothy to the stand, and she bustled up to the front of the courtroom. The bailiff swore her in, and she took her seat in the witness chair. She sought out my eyes and gave me an encouraging smile. I smiled back even though inside I felt deflated. Daniel's testimony hadn't gone quite as I'd imagined, and I was in a gloomy mood.

Fergus stood and approached Aunt Dorothy. "Thank you for coming today, Mrs. Perkins."

"Certainly," Aunt Dorothy said.

"So tell us how you're related to Vivian Latham," Fergus said.

She looked at the jury. "Vivian is my brother Roger's daughter, so she's my niece."

"Your niece. So would you say you know her well?"

She nodded and smiled warmly. "Yes, I know her well."

"What kind of person would you say Miss Latham is?" Fergus asked.

She thought for a moment. "Vivian is very honest and kind. She took care of my brother when he was dying, and I never once heard her complain." She paused. "And she's smart. She did real well in school, and she went to college. She was a teacher for many years."

Fergus moved closer to Aunt Dorothy. "Tell us more about how Vivian cared for her father when he was dying."

Aunt Dorothy sat back and drew in a deep breath. "Roger was diagnosed with pancreatic cancer in the fall of 1973, and Vivian moved in with him so she could take care of him. She arranged for nursing care for him during the day, and she took care of him at night. And when he died…" She paused, and I could see the glisten of tears in her eyes. "When he died she took care of his affairs. She was a good daughter."

"I'm so sorry for the loss of your brother," Fergus said gravely. "And how did you respond when you heard that Miss Latham had been charged with murder?"

She harrumphed and waved her hand in the air. "Oh, for heaven's sake, I thought it was ridiculous. Vivian could never kill someone. She's a gentle person. She's not capable of that."

"Thank you, Mrs. Perkins," Fergus said. "No further questions. Your witness."

Douglas Armstrong stood and walked slowly up to Aunt Dorothy. "Mrs. Perkins, you testified that you know Vivian Latham well, is that correct?"

"Yes, I know her well," Aunt Dorothy said.

"But didn't you move from Iowa to Washington State when Vivian was just two years old?"

She nodded. "Yes, I did."

"And after you moved, how many days would you say you've spent with Miss Latham since then?"

She frowned and didn't speak for a long moment. "I'm not sure. We saw each other four or five times for a week at a time until she moved out here."

Mr. Armstrong tapped his fingers against his mouth, as if he was puzzling something out. "So you moved out here when Miss Latham was two, and Miss Latham moved to Washington State when she was thirty-two, so in thirty years you saw her four or five times for a week at a time. Seven days multiplied by five visits is a total of thirty-five days. Is that correct?"

"Yes, that's right," Aunt Dorothy said stiffly.

Mr. Armstrong cocked his head to the side. "And then Miss Latham moved to Olympia eight months ago. How many days in those eight months would you say you were with Miss Latham?"

She shrugged. "I don't know. Maybe twenty-five," she said.

Mr. Armstrong smiled condescendingly. "So over the past thirty years, you've spent sixty days with Miss Latham." He paused to look at the jury. "By contrast, two people who truly do know each other—a married couple, for example—have spent ten thousand nine hundred and fifty days together over the course of thirty years. So, Mrs. Perkins, do you believe you truly know Miss Latham well when you've only spent sixty days with her in thirty years?"

Aunt Dorothy shifted in her seat. "Well, she's my niece. That must count for something."

Mr. Armstrong gave her a thin smile. "Madam, can you honestly say you really know a person you've spent only sixty days with in thirty years?"

She scowled. "No, I guess not."

"Thank you," Mr. Armstrong said. "You also testified that Miss Latham is honest, is that right?"

"Yes, she is," Aunt Dorothy said, glancing at me.

"Prior to her arrest, did you know Miss Latham is a homosexual?" Her cheeks reddened. "No, I didn't."

"So can you really say Miss Latham is honest when she kept something that significant from you?"

"I'm sure she had her reasons," she said briskly.

Mr. Armstrong raised one eyebrow. "A simple yes or no will suffice."

"No," she said, lowering her eyes.

My heart sank. I was beginning to think Fergus's idea of bringing in character witnesses was not such a good one. Daniel and Aunt Dorothy might be doing me more harm than good.

Mr. Armstrong looked at Aunt Dorothy closely. "And did you know Miss Latham was let go from her teaching job in Iowa because of immoral behavior?"

I gasped. How had Douglas Armstrong found out about that? I saw Fergus glance at me, his brow furrowed. I had already told him about losing my job, but he was probably also wondering how the prosecutor had unearthed this information.

Aunt Dorothy gave me an accusatory look, her mouth set in a hard line. "No, I didn't know that," she said in a tight voice.

Mr. Armstrong smiled stiffly. "Thank you, Mrs. Perkins. No further questions, Your Honor."

Aunt Dorothy rose from the chair and began making her way out of the courtroom. I tried to catch her eye, but she stared straight ahead. I watched helplessly as she walked through the double doors without looking back. Fergus gave me a brave smile, but I could see the concern in his eyes.

The judge called for an early lunch recess and said court would resume at one o'clock. I spent the next two hours in shock at the way the morning court session had gone. Not only had I called Daniel here from Iowa to be disparaged by the prosecutor, but I had put Aunt Dorothy in an embarrassing situation and alienated her in the process. To add insult to injury, neither Daniel nor Aunt Dorothy had helped my case. Quite the opposite, it seemed to me. I knew that after lunch Fergus would put me on the stand and it would be my last chance to try to save myself.

The bailiff came at 12:45 p.m. to take me back to the courtroom, and I took my seat next to Fergus.

"You know I'll be calling you to the stand next, right?" Fergus said.

I looked down and nodded. "Yes, I know."

He touched my arm lightly. "Just tell your story. Talk to the jury like you're telling a friend what happened. Make eye contact. These next few minutes are all you've got, so make it count."

Tears were blurring my vision, and I didn't trust myself to speak. I just nodded.

A few moments later the jury filed in, followed by the judge, and court was called into session. To an outsider, I'm sure I looked resolute, but inside, my heart was pounding and my stomach was in knots. I knew my story like the back of my hand, but I was terrified that I'd say the wrong thing and get caught in the prosecutor's snare.

"The defense calls Vivian Marie Latham to the stand," Fergus said in a booming voice.

I took a deep breath and then rose, steadying myself on the edge of the table. I stepped up to the bailiff.

"Raise your right hand," he said. "Do you solemnly swear to tell the truth, the whole truth, and nothing but the truth, so help you God?"

"I do," I said.

"Please state your full name," the bailiff said.

"Vivian Marie Latham."

"Please be seated."

I sat in the chair as Fergus came striding toward me. "Miss Latham," he said, "when did you first meet Tambra Delaney?"

I cleared my throat. "I met her on February nineteenth, 1974. The day I moved into my house at seventeen-oh-three Walnut Street."

"So she was your neighbor?" Fergus asked.

"Yes, she lived right next door to me."

"Would you say you were friendly with Mrs. Delaney?"

I nodded and looked at the jury, making eye contact with each one in turn as I spoke. "Yes, Tambra was very warm and welcoming to me, unlike the other neighbors. She invited me over to her house the day after I met her. We started spending time together."

"So would you say you and Mrs. Delaney were friends?"

"Yes, we became quite close," I said.

"Did Mrs. Delaney confide in you?"

I nodded and looked at the jurors again. "Yes, she did. She told me she was lonely. Later, as we got closer, she told me other, more personal things."

Fergus came closer to me. "What kinds of personal things?"

"She told me her husband, Tom, was very critical of her. She eventually told me he was hurting her."

"Hurting her?" he said, raising his eyebrows. "Hurting her in what way?"

"He grabbed her, slapped her, pushed her, slammed her head against the wall. That kind of thing." I glanced at Tom and noticed that Tambra's mother, who was sitting at his side, was looking at him out of the corner of her eye. I wanted to scream at her, "Your son-in-law is a mean bastard! He was beating on your daughter! He killed her!"

"Did you see any evidence of this?" Fergus asked. "Did she have bruises or broken bones?"

I looked at the jury. "Oh, yes. On a number of occasions, I saw Tambra's injuries. Bruises on her arm and face, a black eye, and a laceration on her cheek that needed stitches."

"Did you offer Mrs. Delaney any advice about her situation?"

"Yes, I did," I said. "I encouraged her to leave him."

"And how did Mrs. Delaney respond to that?" he said.

I shrugged. "She told me she knew she needed to leave him but it wasn't the right time."

He nodded thoughtfully. "And how did your relationship with Mrs. Delaney progress over time?"

I looked down at my hands. "In early May we became lovers." I raised my eyes to look at Tom to see his reaction, but his face was stony, and his eyes were fixed on the floor.

"And how did your relationship progress after that?"

"We spent a lot of time together," I said. "I kept pestering her to leave Tom, but she kept saying the time wasn't right." I paused and took a deep breath. "Then, in late July, Tom beat up Tambra really badly. That's when she had the black eye and a laceration on her cheek. I had to take her to the emergency room. After that Tambra said it was time to leave Tom, and we made a plan to run off together with Claire."

Fergus folded his arms across his chest. "And who's Claire?"

"Claire is Tambra's daughter. She was just a week shy of her first birthday when Tambra, uh, died."

"And when were you planning to leave?" he asked.

"On August eleventh," I said in a quiet voice.

"And August eleventh was the day Mrs. Delaney died, is that correct?" Fergus said softly.

"Yes," I said, my voice cracking.

"Can you tell us what happened in the early morning hours of August eleventh?" he said.

I closed my eyes for a moment and tried to compose myself. I opened them and looked directly at Fergus. "On Saturday morning Tom left for Bellingham to stay with his brother for the weekend, and our plan was to take off while he was gone. The night before we were going to leave, Tambra wanted me to stay with her at her house, so I did. In the middle of the night, we woke up to Tom Delaney standing over us and screaming obscenities. He had come home to ambush us." I paused. I saw that my hands were trembling. "He was enraged and violent. He was hitting Tambra and pushing her around. I ran out to the living room to get the baseball bat to try and protect her, but then he grabbed it from me and started swinging it at me. Tambra jumped between us to try and stop him, and then he swung it at her. She got really angry, and ran at him and scratched his face. He put his arm around her neck, and then she bit his arm. He let go of her then, and we ran out to the living room to try and get out the front door. I tripped and fell, but Tambra made it to the door. Tom came running out of the bedroom and grabbed her before she could get the door open." I stopped to take a deep breath. "Then he started beating her with the bat. He hit her in the ribs and then in the head. He split her skull open. He killed her." I looked at the jury. They were all listening raptly, their mouths hanging open.

"Then what happened?" Fergus asked.

"Then he started yelling at me. He told me if I hadn't gotten the bat, this never would have happened. He blamed me for turning Tambra against him. He said if I'd just left her alone, this wouldn't have happened—he wouldn't have killed her. I told him to stop saying that. Tambra had loved me, and he said nobody would believe that. I guess that gave him the idea to frame me, and he called the police and told them I'd broken into their house and killed Tambra. He lied to them."

"And that's how we ended up here," he said.

I nodded. "Yes."

"So your fingerprints were on the bat because you were trying to use it to stop Mr. Delaney from harming Mrs. Delaney," Fergus said. "Is that correct?"

"Yes, that's correct," I said.

Fergus looked at me. "The investigating officers also said that Mrs. Delaney's blood was on your nightgown. Can you explain how that happened?"

I looked at the jury again. "I was holding Tambra as she died. Blood was pouring from the wounds on her head and face." A sob escaped my lips, and I paused. "That's how I got her blood on me."

"Miss Latham," he said, "did you kill Mrs. Delaney?"

My gaze was unwavering and my voice was firm as I answered. "No, I did not. I loved Tambra. I never would have hurt her. Never."

"Thank you, Miss Latham. No further questions, Your Honor." Fergus turned on his heel and headed back to his seat.

Douglas Armstrong stood and walked toward me. "Miss Latham, prior to moving to Washington State, you were a teacher at Applewood Elementary in Applewood, Iowa. Is that correct?"

"Yes, that's correct," I said. I could feel my body tensing. I knew what was coming.

"You were the physical education teacher there for nine years, is that right?"

"Yes," I said between clenched jaws.

"And you were fired from your job there earlier this year. Is that accurate?"

I looked down. "Yes."

"Now, the school didn't give details, but they said you were fired for immoral behavior. Is that correct?"

"That's what they called it," I said angrily.

"Please answer the question, Miss Latham," he said.

"Yes," I said.

"Was the immoral behavior related to your homosexuality?"

"Objection!" Fergus said loudly. "Relevance, Your Honor."

"It goes to the defendant's character, Your Honor," Mr. Armstrong interjected.

"Overruled," the judge said gruffly. "I'll allow it."

"Was the immoral behavior related to your homosexuality, Miss Latham?" Mr. Armstrong repeated.

"Yes," I said in a tense voice.

"Thank you," he said, a self-satisfied look on his face. He walked over to the prosecution's table, and his assistant handed him several papers. He turned back toward me. "Now, Miss Latham, you testified that you took Mrs. Delaney to the emergency room for a black eye and a cheek laceration that you claim resulted from a beating from Thomas Delaney. However," he said in a dramatic voice as he waved one of the papers in the air, "the hospital records show that she went to the emergency room because she fell down her porch stairs."

"Tambra lied to the doctor. She went there because Tom beat her up. She didn't want to have to explain that to the doctor," I said in a clipped voice.

He gave a mirthless laugh. "That's what you say, but the official hospital record says otherwise."

I said nothing but just stared at him in stony silence.

He flashed me his disingenuous smile. "You also testified that Thomas Delaney was visiting his brother in Bellingham the weekend Mrs. Delaney was murdered and that he came home in the middle of the night to, as you claimed, 'ambush' you and Mrs. Delaney. However, a signed statement from Michael Delaney, Thomas Delaney's brother, proves otherwise." He held another paper in front of my face. "Mr. Michael Delaney stated, and I quote, 'I have not seen my brother, Thomas Delaney, for several months.' So again, your testimony seems to be in direct conflict with the testimony of others in this case."

"His brother is lying," I said through gritted teeth.

Mr. Armstrong tipped his head to the side and regarded me silently for a moment. "And why do you suppose Michael Delaney would commit perjury by lying for his brother?"

I shrugged. "I don't know. Because he's Tom's brother and he's covering for him."

He smirked. "Or perhaps it's because you've fabricated your own version of events to save your own skin."

"Objection!" Fergus roared.

"Withdrawn, Your Honor," Mr. Armstrong said quickly in his oily voice. "Now, Miss Latham, to your knowledge, did Mrs. Delaney tell anyone of what you claim was your plan for the two of you to leave Olympia?"

I drew in a long breath and let it out slowly, trying to keep my cool. "No, she did not."

"And to your knowledge, did Mrs. Delaney tell anyone about your alleged, uh, relationship?" He gave me his tight-lipped smile.

I sighed. "No, she did not."

He looked at me smugly. "So there's absolutely no one who can confirm your version of events, is that correct?"

I sat up straight and pointed at Tom Delaney. "Tom could if he wasn't such a Goddamn coward!" I shouted. Again I noticed Tambra's mother give Tom a sidelong glance. Mary Sorenson was definitely wondering about her son-in-law's character.

"Miss Latham!" the judge said sternly as he banged his gavel. "You're out of order! The jury will disregard that outburst."

Douglas Armstrong sneered. "I'll repeat the question. So is there anyone who can confirm your version of events?"

"No," I said stiffly.

"Thank you," Mr. Armstrong said. "No further questions."

Fergus stood, and bowed his head toward the judge. "Redirect, please, Your Honor."

"Certainly," the judge said.

Fergus came toward me and gave me an encouraging smile. "Miss Latham, you said you lost your job at Applewood Elementary due to immoral behavior. Is that correct?"

I nodded, not sure where he was going with his question. "Yes, that's correct."

"Did this immoral behavior have anything whatsoever to do with the children at your school?"

I shook my head fiercely, suddenly realizing what he was getting at. "No, absolutely not."

"Did this immoral behavior have anything to do with children in any way, shape, or form?"

"No, it did not," I said.

"Thank you, Miss Latham." Fergus glanced at the judge. "No further questions, Your Honor."

"You're excused, Miss Latham," the judge said.

I pushed myself out of the chair and walked uncertainly back to the table, where I sat down. Fergus joined me and gave me a sympathetic smile.

"Mr. Atkinson," the judge said, "please call your next witness."

Fergus stood. "The defense rests, Your Honor."

"What?" I whispered urgently as Fergus sat back down. "There has to be someone else."

Fergus looked at me and shook his head. "Vivian, I don't have anyone else. I'll do my closing argument, but that's all I've got."

I sat back in my chair and sighed. My mind sifted through the events of the trial. Would they find me not guilty? Did the jury have reasonable doubt? Or would they believe Tom's twisted version of that night? I could hear the low rumblings of the prosecutor's voice, but I wasn't listening. Then Fergus stood and began speaking, but I couldn't focus on what he was saying either. I knew he was making a last-ditch effort to convince the jury of my innocence, but his words were gibberish to me. All I could think about was Tambra and my own fate.

"Vivian!" Fergus whispered. "Stand up."

I started and then stood as I watched the judge exiting the courtroom. Then the jurors stood and filed out behind the bailiff. "What's happening?" I asked.

Fergus looked at me for a long moment before speaking. "The judge just gave the jurors their instructions, and they've gone to the jury room to begin deliberating."

I leaned in toward Fergus. "Is this it? Are they deciding the verdict?"

He nodded. "Yes. This is it."

"How long does it take?" I asked.

He shrugged. "It depends. It might take a few hours or a few days. You'll have to go back to your cell, and they'll come and get you when the jury has a decision. It's already two-thirty, so I doubt it'll be today."

The bailiff was hovering behind me. He cuffed me and led me from the courtroom. I didn't have a good feeling. The bailiff pushed me into the cell and locked the door. I stretched out on the cot as tears began streaming down my face, and I just lay there and cried.

I awoke with a start to the sound of the bailiff calling my name. "Miss Latham!" he said loudly.

I struggled to a sitting position and peered at him. "What?"

"The jury's back with a verdict."

"What? Already? What time is it?"

"It's five thirty," he said as he unlocked the cell door.

"Five thirty? Three hours? That's all it took?" I asked incredulously.

"Sometimes it goes quick," he said as he snapped the handcuffs around my wrists. He led me out of the cell and down the long hallway to the courtroom. Once we entered the courtroom, he deposited me next to Fergus.

Fergus raised his eyebrows and gave me a tiny smile. "This is it, Vivian."

I looked at him wordlessly. The bailiff was leading in the jury. I tried to read their faces. Guilty? Not guilty? I caught the eye of one of the female jurors, who immediately looked away. That couldn't be a good sign.

The judge entered the courtroom, and everyone stood. The bailiff called court into session.

"Will the jury foreman please stand?" the judge said.

I saw a portly older man stand and turn toward the judge.

"Has the jury reached a unanimous verdict?" the judge asked.

"Yes, Your Honor, we have," the foreman said.

I noticed that he held a piece of paper in his hand. The bailiff took the paper from the foreman, walked over to the bench, and handed it to the judge. The judge looked at the paper and then handed it back to the bailiff.

The judge turned to the jury. "What say you?"

The foreman cleared his throat. "In the matter of the State of Washington versus Vivian Marie Latham, we find the defendant, Vivian Marie Latham, guilty of murder in the second degree."

"No!" I cried, covering my face with my hands. In the background I heard Tom give a loud whoop.

Fergus looked at me helplessly, his hand on my arm. "An appeal. I'll file an appeal right away," he said. I was in shock, and I nodded without speaking. Even though my head had told my heart this was coming, the reality hit me like a ton of bricks. Falsely convicted of murder. Falsely convicted of murdering the only woman I had ever truly loved. I couldn't understand the judge's words after that. Fergus had to tell me that the sentencing hearing would take place in one week. I felt the handcuffs being fastened around my wrists, and I stumbled from the courtroom and back to my cell.

One week later I was in the courtroom for the sentencing: twenty years in the Women's State Penitentiary in Bakersville, Washington. I put my head down on the table and sobbed. Fergus put his hand on my shoulder and tried to comfort me, but I was inconsolable.

The bailiff was at my side, the handcuffs open, ready to take me to prison for twenty years. As he moved toward me, I heard a voice behind me.

"Can I have a word with her first?"

Tom. I'd know that voice anywhere.

"Certainly," the bailiff said, taking a step back.

Tom leaned down and pressed his vile mouth against my ear. "And that's what you get for fucking my wife, you bitch," he said in a low growl.

I pushed him away from me. "Fuck you, you fucking bastard!" I yelled. "You can live the rest of your life knowing that Tambra didn't love you! That she couldn't stand the sight of you!"

"All right, that's enough," the bailiff said, roughly pulling me to my feet and snapping the handcuffs around my wrists. "Come on." He led me back to my cell, pushed me inside, and locked the door.

33

The next morning I was transported to the Women's State Penitentiary in Bakersville, Washington, a two-hour drive from Olympia. I was questioned, strip-searched, examined by the doctor, issued a prison uniform and bedding, questioned some more, and eventually shown to my cell. The cell was small—six feet by eight feet—with a bunk bed, a small metal desk and chair, a toilet, and a sink. There was a small window, just big enough to let in a sliver of light. On the bottom bunk sat a woman of about seventy with long gray hair, rheumy brown eyes, and a wrinkled face. She looked at me and gave me an almost imperceptible nod.

I threw the blanket and pillow on the top bunk and sat down in the chair. "Hi, I'm Vivian," I said in a timid voice.

"Ruth," the woman said. "Whatcha in for?"

"I was convicted of killing my lover, but I didn't do it," I said.

Ruth cackled. "That's what they all say, honey."

I glared at her. "No, I really didn't do it. I loved her. I never would have killed her."

She eyed me curiously. "Her? You a dyke?"

I hated that word, and I didn't want to dignify it with an affirmative response. "I'm gay," I said.

She cackled again and leaned forward with her elbows on her thighs. "Dyke, gay, lezzie. It's all the same. You play cards?"

I nodded. "Yeah, I love to play cards. Why? Do you have some?"

"Yeah, I got a couple decks," she said. "What do you like to play?"

I shrugged. "Anything, really. Blackjack, crazy eights, pinochle, poker."

Ruth grinned, and I noticed that one of her front teeth was missing. "Well then, Miss Vivian, we'll get along just fine," she said as she pulled a deck of cards from under the bed and began shuffling them.

My prison life fell into a routine of sorts. Meals happened every day. Showers and exercise in the yard were less frequent. Every morning after breakfast and every afternoon before dinner, I played cards with Ruth. The rest of the time I sat on my bed, my back against the cold brick wall, staring at nothing. I'd close my eyes and daydream of Tambra and the life we could have had. I imagined our little house in Santa Barbara with a big back yard where Claire would play, my job at the school there, long walks on the beach every evening, and nights sleeping next to Tambra. I thought of Claire and wondered how she was faring without her mom.

I'd found a pencil stub in the desk drawer. The pencil part was useless, but I used the metal on the eraser end to scratch marks on the brick wall. I kept the pencil in my pillowcase, and each morning I went through the ritual of taking the pencil out of the pillowcase and scratching a mark on the wall to record the passing days. So far there were thirty marks on the wall. I couldn't imagine how many marks there would be twenty years from now. They'd probably fill the entire wall.

On day thirty-five, Fergus came to the prison to meet with me. The prison guard ushered me into a small meeting room and then stood sentry in the corner.

I was overjoyed to see him. "Fergus! It's so great to see a friendly face."

He smiled warmly. "It's great to see you too, Vivian. How are they treating you?"

I grimaced. "Well, it's prison. Not great."

"Yeah, prisons aren't known for their luxury accommodations," he said.

We sat down at the table. Fergus rummaged through his briefcase and pulled out a file. "So, I'm getting ready to file your appeal, and I just wanted to review it with you and get your signature," he said. He opened the file and pushed a paper toward me.

I scanned it and then looked at him. "So you think you can get the conviction overturned?"

He held up his hand. "Let's not get ahead of ourselves, Vivian. The appeal has to do with the evidence presented at trial. I still stand behind what I said when I questioned the detective—the evidence they had was largely circumstantial, and my contention is that shouldn't have led to a conviction. I'm also going to contend that the prosecutor deliberately tried to bias the jury against you because of your homosexuality. It's a long shot, Vivian, but I've got to try."

I nodded. "Okay. I trust you, Fergus."

"If they deny that appeal, then I'll file another appeal that your sentence wasn't appropriate given your past. No prior arrests or convictions. A teacher for many years. A productive member of society. You've never even had a speeding ticket, for God's sake. I'll contend that twenty years is too stiff given all that. I have a better chance with that one. Your sentence could be shortened."

I shook my head. "I don't want a shorter sentence. I want to get out of here."

He ran his hand through his hair. "I know, Vivian, but it's not that easy. I'll file it and see what happens. That's the best I can do right now."

"All right," I said reluctantly. Fergus handed me a pen, and I signed the form.

"It'll be two or three months before we hear anything," he said. "I'll be in touch." He stood and began gathering his papers, stuffing them into his briefcase.

I rose, shook his hand, and followed him with my eyes as he walked out of the room. The guard was at my side immediately, ready to take me back to my cell.

※

The days crawled by as I waited to hear something from Fergus. I ate; I played cards with Ruth; I walked in the yard; I slept a lot. Then I woke up the next morning to do it all again. The boredom was almost enough to drive me mad.

On one of the many afternoons that Ruth and I sat side by side on her bed staring at the wall, she suddenly piped up and told me that after I'd been there a few more months, I might get assigned a job in the prison.

That was news to me, and I wanted to know more. "What kind of job?" I asked.

"You know, working in the laundry or the kitchen. That kind of thing," she answered. "They pay you pennies per hour, but at least it keeps you from going crazy."

I frowned. "Why don't you work?"

"They say I ain't able-bodied anymore," she said, laughing. "Back in the day, I worked in the laundry. Now I got a bad ticker, and I'm too old."

"What's wrong with your ticker?" I asked with concern.

"I don't know," she said with a shrug. "I just know the prison doctor told me I have a bad heart."

"Oh," I said, falling silent. I'd come to like Ruth. She was the one bright spot in an otherwise hellish existence. I didn't know what I'd do if anything happened to her.

"Anything happening with your appeal?" she asked.

I shook my head. "No, I'm waiting to hear from my lawyer. It's been two months since he was here to have me sign the paperwork. I don't know what's taking so long."

She patted my knee. "It takes a while, honey."

I looked at her curiously. "Ruth, you've never told me why you're in here."

She chuckled. "I robbed a bank—me and this fella I was in love with. It was his idea, and I went along with it because I was crazy about him. The shitty thing is that he got away and I didn't. Fucked up, ain't it? A man died in the bank robbery, and I got forty years to life." She paused. "At this rate, it'll be life."

I let out a long sigh. "How awful. How long have you been in here?"

"Thirty-seven years, honey. I was only thirty when that happened. I've been in here longer than I've been out," she said sadly. "I've made a Goddamn mess of my life, all because of one stupid mistake."

"Thirty-seven years?" I said incredulously. "How have you kept from going insane?"

"Good question," she said. "I've had some interesting roommates over the years—like you—and the cards keep me busy. Beyond that, I just try and keep my mind occupied. It ain't easy, I'll tell you that."

"I know," I said. "I feel crazy after only three months."

She looked at me sympathetically. "The first year or two are the hardest. After that you just get used to it, I guess."

I didn't say anything. I couldn't imagine ever getting used to prison. To me it was all just one long, horrendous day without a shred of hope or light.

At that moment the announcement came over the loudspeaker that it was time for the evening meal and that prisoners should line up by their cell doors to be escorted down to the dining hall. Ruth winked broadly at me. "Let's go eat," she said.

34

The next morning the prison bell jarred me awake. "Jeez," I murmured grumpily, swinging my legs over the side of the bed. "Why do they have to wake us up so early?" I jumped down and poked Ruth, who was still sleeping. "Get up, Ruth. It's time for breakfast."

She didn't stir, and I poked her again. "Ruth, wake up. It's breakfast." She still didn't move, and I shook her roughly. "Ruth! Get up!" Her head rolled toward me, and I stumbled backward when I saw her ashen skin. "Ruth!" I yelled.

Some part of my brain knew she was dead, but the other part couldn't accept it. That part kept yelling, "Ruth, wake up!" Finally I couldn't deny the reality of the situation anymore, and I ran to the cell door and shouted, "Help! I need help here!"

The prison doctor came to our cell and pronounced Ruth dead, and then the guards carted her body away. I sat in stunned silence for the rest of the morning and into the afternoon. I skipped breakfast and lunch. At two o'clock the guard was at my cell door.

"Your attorney's here to see you," he said.

Now? Why today of all days? I rose from the metal chair, and the guard unlocked the door and escorted me to the meeting room. I saw Fergus sitting at the table, sipping coffee from a Styrofoam cup.

I moved slowly toward him, anxious about the news he brought. "Hi, Fergus," I said.

"Vivian, hello! How are you?" he boomed.

The false cheer in his voice made me freeze. "Not so good," I said. "My cellmate, Ruth, died this morning."

His face fell. "Oh, Vivian. I'm so sorry. What happened?"

I looked down at the floor. "They think a heart attack."

"I'm sorry," he repeated. "That's rough."

I nodded. "Yeah, I liked her. Anyway, why are you here? Did you hear something about my appeal?"

"Why don't you sit down," he said, motioning to the chair opposite him.

I sat in the chair and met his eyes. "What is it, Fergus?"

He took a deep breath. "I'm not going to sugarcoat this, Vivian," he said. "Your appeal was denied."

I let out a loud cry and threw my head back. Why did I have to learn about this today, when I was still reeling from Ruth's death? I looked at him. "What happened?"

He leaned his elbows on the table. "Vivian, the vast majority of appeals are unsuccessful. This one wasn't any different."

"But you sounded so optimistic," I said.

He gave me a thin smile. "I'm always optimistic when I file an appeal, but I also always know it's a long shot."

"So what happens now?" I asked in a shaky voice. I could feel tears burning behind my eyes, and I was trying to hold them back.

He looked at me sympathetically. "I'll file a different appeal contending that your sentence was too harsh given your past. That could take five years off your sentence. Maybe more."

"Fergus, I can't stay in here for fifteen years," I said in an urgent whisper. "I can't. I'm practically going crazy already, and it's only been a little over three months. And now Ruth's dead." A sob escaped my lips, and I covered my mouth with my hand. My eyes were filled with tears now, and I felt like I was going to vomit. "I didn't kill Tambra. Do you know what it feels like to be serving prison time for something you didn't do?"

He looked away, saying nothing. I leaned toward him, forcing him to look at me. I wanted him to feel my pain. "Fergus, can you imagine what it's like to be convicted of killing the person you loved more than life itself? Do you know what that feels like? Do you?" A tear rolled down my cheek, and I wiped it away angrily.

He shook his head. "No, I have no idea what that feels like. No idea."

"It's hell on earth," I said flatly.

He covered my hand with his. "Vivian, I'll file the second appeal, and we'll go from there. That's the best I can do right now."

I shook his hand off mine and sat back. "Fine. What choice do I have? I'm a prisoner. Do what you think is best."

He stood and grabbed his briefcase. I knew he couldn't wait to get out of there. "I'll be in touch," he said, extending his hand toward me.

I turned away from him and then said loudly, "Guard, I'm ready to go back to my cell!"

I descended rapidly into a deep depression. I stopped eating and drinking and just lay on my bed staring up at the ceiling. I would often fall into a fitful sleep that was almost always filled with dreams of Tambra. The guard came to my cell and warned me that if I didn't start eating and drinking soon, they'd take me to the infirmary and feed me intravenously and I'd have to talk to the prison shrink. I just stared at him and didn't say a word.

On the third day, I began studying the ceiling. My eyes followed the network of steel pipes overhead, carrying water to different parts of the prison. Sometimes at night, when the prison was quiet, I could hear water rushing through the pipes. The pipes looked strong. They looked practically indestructible.

That night I dreamed of Tambra. In the dream I was walking down a hallway in a building that was foreign to me. I passed an alcove and caught movement out of the corner of my eye. I turned to see Tambra standing before me, the most radiant smile on her face. Her blond hair was loose and flowing, and a golden aura glowed around her head and shoulders. She moved toward me and extended her hand. I took her hand, and she pulled me into an embrace. She wrapped her arms around me and held me close against her.

I startled awake, staring into the dark. As I played the dream over again in my mind, tears filled my eyes. I turned onto my side and sobbed quietly into the thin pillow. Tambra had felt so real. I could still feel the press of her body against mine. And she had looked so beautiful—like an angel. Grief and despair coursed through me. I missed Tambra with every fiber of my being. I wanted to be with her more than I had ever wanted anything before.

I thought about my life here, if you could call it a life. Now that Ruth was gone, I had no one. Aunt Dorothy had been deeply insulted by what had been divulged at my trial, and she had not come to visit me. My cousins, Louise and Linda, hadn't come either, probably out of loyalty to their mother. Fergus was my attorney. He wasn't a friend. There was Daniel, but he was two thousand miles away. If he came to visit, it would be once every five years at best. I thought of how many days made up twenty years. I did the math in my head—7,300 days. I realized there would be five leap years over the course of the next twenty years, so that would add five more days to my sentence. My entire sentence was 7,305 days. I'd only been here for 102 days, and it already felt like an eternity. I still had 7,203 days left to go. 7,203 days of nothingness. 7,203 more days of paying for the crime of loving Tambra. I thought of my dream. Right now all I wanted was to be with Tambra.

I turned on my back and stared up at the ceiling. The light from the full moon came in through the tiny window and illuminated the pipes overhead. I stared at the pipes for several minutes, my breathing shallow. I was forming an idea, and I was almost afraid to think it through to its conclusion. But I also knew this was the only thought I'd had in three months that had given me a shred of hope. My mind began to churn through the details of what it would take to execute my idea. I knew in my heart that I'd made my decision.

I suddenly thought about the money my dad had left me. I still had fifty thousand dollars left, and it was safe in the bank. I needed to do something with it. I thought about that for a few minutes. Suddenly the perfect solution came to me, but I needed Fergus's help. I'd call him first thing in the morning and convince him to help me. Satisfied, I wiped my eyes and nose with the edge of the sheet, closed my eyes, and went back to sleep.

The next morning I rose when the prison bell went off. When the guard came around to my cell, he was surprised to see me standing by the door.

"You ready to eat?" he asked.

I shook my head impatiently. "No, I need to make a phone call. Please! It's urgent."

He thought about that for a few moments and then pulled the hefty key ring from his belt and unlocked the door. He held my arm tightly as he led me to the bank of phones. "Five minutes," he said. He stood off to the side as I picked up the phone and dialed Fergus's number.

"Fergus Atkinson."

I'd never been so happy to hear his voice. "Fergus, it's Vivian," I said in a rush. "I have something really important I need your help with, and it's not about the appeal. It's something completely different." I told him what I was planning, and he said yes, he could help me with that. "So can you come and see me today?" I asked.

"Vivian, it's Monday morning, and I have meetings today. Can't we do it later in the week?"

"No, that's too late. It has to be today." He was silent on the other end, and I knew I had to convince him. "Fergus, this is really important. I promise I'll never ask you for another favor, ever."

He hesitated for a moment. "All right. I can be there by two o'clock this afternoon. Will that work?"

"Yes. Thank you, Fergus. Thank you so much," I said.

"Sure. See you this afternoon."

Fergus arrived promptly at two o'clock. He'd brought the appropriate paperwork, and he reviewed it with me, and then I signed.

"Are you sure this is all I need to do?" I asked. Fergus said not to worry. Everything would be taken care of according to my wishes.

"This is a very kind thing you're doing, Vivian," he said. "But I'm left wondering, why now?" He searched my face.

I shrugged and avoided his eyes. "I guess Ruth's death has taught me that you just never know what might happen. I don't want the state to decide what to do with my money. I want to be the one to say where that money goes."

"Fair enough," he said, gathering up the papers.

This time when he left I gave him a hug and said in his ear, "Thank you for everything, Fergus."

"Sure," he said, pulling back to look at me, an odd expression on his face. "I'll see you again soon, though. This isn't over yet."

"Yeah, okay," I said in a neutral voice. "Thanks again. Bye, Fergus." I stood and asked the guard to take me back to my cell.

I whiled away the rest of that day, drawing circles on the wall with the metal on the end of my tiny pencil. I scratched a message on the wall: "Fuck you all." I read the words over and over and felt a perverse satisfaction.

Dinnertime came and went, and I again refused to eat. "Tomorrow's day five," the guard informed me. "If you don't eat and drink by then, we'll be feeding you with a tube. Is that what you want?" I shrugged but said nothing.

Later, when the guard came by to call "lights out," he said, "Tomorrow's the day, Vivian. You'd better eat breakfast in the morning, or you know what'll happen." I kept my eyes on the wall and said nothing.

I lay down on my bed and thought about what I was going to do. Was this the right decision? That number kept marching through my mind: 7,203 days, 7,203 days, 7,203 days. Nothing to look forward to. No one to love. No one to love me. 7,203 days of nothing. 7,203 days of hell. This was the right decision; I was sure of it.

I waited quietly in bed for two hours. I waited until the only sound I could hear was the soft snoring of my neighbor and the periodic passing of the guard. I wondered how often the guard went by. The next time he passed, I began counting silently to myself, and I didn't stop counting until he came by again—1,560 seconds. I calculated quickly in my mind. Twenty-six minutes. Was that enough time? I told myself it was.

I waited until I heard his footsteps fade away, and then I slipped silently from my bed. I pulled the sheet off my bed and then pulled the one off Ruth's old bed. I stood on the floor in the center of my cell, the sheets in my hands. Was this the right thing to do? I thought of my father and, once again, remembered his prophetic words: "You have a hard road ahead of you, Viv. I just want you to be happy, but I'm not sure the world will let you be happy." Could he have known how my life would unfold? Had he known that I would be faced with this terrible choice? Somehow, it seemed he had. I knew he would be disappointed with me, but I also knew his love for me had no boundaries. I would see him where I was going, and I could ask for his forgiveness. He understood love, and that meant he would understand why I had made this decision.

Next, my thoughts turned to Daniel. He was my only living friend; the only person left on earth who truly knew me. What would he think of what I was about to do? I knew he wouldn't understand, and part of me longed to explain to him why I felt I had no other option. But I knew there was no time for that. One day I would see him again, and I could explain then.

Then I thought of Tambra. In my mind's eye, I saw her the way she'd looked in the dream. I felt her arms around me. Tambra was waiting for me. I desperately wanted to be with her, and this was the only way to get there. In my heart, I knew this was the right decision. I knew it as surely as I knew my own name.

I gathered my courage and lifted the sheets. I tied them together with a tight knot and tucked them under my arm. I tiptoed over to the desk and climbed up onto the chair. I raised my arm as far as I could, but I couldn't quite touch the pipes. I climbed onto the desk and reached again. I could just touch the lowest pipe now. The moon was bright again, and I could see the glint of the pipe. I kept the pipe in my sight. I took the sheets out from under my arm and smoothed them lengthwise though my hands. I reached up and threw the sheets toward the pipe. On the first try, they cleared the pipe and appeared on the other side. I grabbed the end and then tied it as tight as I could around the pipe. I pulled down hard on the knot to make sure it would hold. It did. The other end of the sheet was hanging down, and I took the fabric in my hand. I turned and looked at my cell—my hell, more like it—and felt relief wash through me that I would be leaving it.

I took a deep breath, circled the end of the sheet around my neck, and tied it tight. I filled my head with thoughts of Tambra and only Tambra. I knew she was waiting. I could feel her. In seconds, I would be with her.

I took a deep breath, whispered a brief prayer, and then stepped off the desk. And then there was darkness.

35

Josie
July 2015

I spent the next three hours combing over the police report and trial transcript, trying to find a crack in the investigation or trial. I couldn't find anything. I could identify the places where I thought Tom Delaney had lied, but I didn't know where to go with that information. He'd thought of everything. I envisioned Tambra's house and imagined the number of families that had lived there over the past forty-one years. No evidence would remain there. I didn't know where else to turn.

I called my mom and then Celeste and updated them on what had happened. They were both sympathetic, but neither one had anything helpful to offer.

At one o'clock I decided I needed a break, and I strolled down to the deli near my hotel. I ordered a veggie-and-cheese sandwich and a Diet Coke from the woman behind the counter and then carried my lunch outside to one of the tables on the sidewalk.

As I ate I tried to clear my mind. I was making myself crazy with my constant thoughts about Tambra, Vivian, and Tom. I now knew without a doubt that Tom had killed Tambra, but I didn't know how to prove it. I knew DNA was the key, but Sean O'Neil had made it very clear that until I found something concrete, the police would not perform a DNA analysis. I feared I had hit a brick wall, and there was nothing left to do but give up and go home.

As I finished my sandwich, my phone rang. I didn't recognize the number. "Hello, this is Josie."

"J-J-Josie, I n-need to t-talk to you."

It sounded like Claire, but she was sobbing so hard I could barely understand her. "Claire, is that you?" I said.

"Y-yes. Josie, p-please come over n-now."

"Claire, what's the matter?" I asked, alarmed.

"J-just come. Now."

The phone went dead. I took off at a sprint and was back in the hotel parking lot a few minutes later. I found my car, jumped in, and tore out of the parking lot.

I drove like a mad woman through the streets of Olympia. I was testing my memory, but I thought I knew how to get back to Claire's. Fifteen minutes later I was turning onto her street, immensely relieved that I'd found it.

I parked and ran up the sidewalk to the door. I knocked urgently. She must have been standing just inside the door, because she opened it immediately. Lola was standing beside her, her eyes sad.

"Come in," Claire said, ushering me inside.

I looked at her. Mascara was running down her cheeks, and her eyes were red. "What's the matter? What happened?" I said frantically.

She just shook her head and led me silently back to the kitchen, Lola padding quietly behind us. She motioned for me to take a seat at the table, and then she sat beside me. "Claire..." I began.

A sob escaped her lips, and a fresh wave of tears began pouring down her cheeks. She covered her face with her hands and cried. Lola pressed herself against Claire's leg and whined.

I didn't know what to do, so I leaned over to rub her shoulder. "Do you want some water?" I asked.

She nodded, and I went over to the cabinet and pulled out a glass. I filled it with tap water and brought it back to her. She drank thirstily, pausing to take several deep breaths.

"Okay," she said in a weak voice. "I think I can talk now."

"What happened, Claire?" I asked softly.

She threw her head back and sighed. "Where do I start?"

"How about at the beginning?" I said. "Start there."

"Okay," she said, settling into her chair. "So you left on Monday. I was so angry at you I could barely think." She took another sip of water. "I spent the rest of that day just fuming. But on Tuesday I woke up and got it in my head that I was going to read the court transcript. So I did." She paused. "I read all of it three times. I paid attention to the thing you mentioned—that my dad was supposed to be staying with my uncle in Bellingham. So I called my uncle Mike and asked him."

My eyebrows shot up. "You did? What did you find out?"

She was quiet for a moment. "It took me a long time to get it out of him, but he finally admitted it to me," she said. "Josie, he lied. The cops called him and asked him point-blank if my dad had been there, and he told them no. He covered for him." She paused and let out a long breath. "My dad *was* there that weekend. Uncle Mike told me my dad woke him up at one in the morning to tell him my mom had called and the baby—I—was really sick and he needed to come home."

I couldn't speak. I just shook my head.

"My dad called my uncle later and begged him to lie if the cops asked if he'd been there. And he did. He lied for my dad."

I saw that her eyes were brimming with tears, and I reached over to cover her hand with mine. "Oh, Claire," I said. "Why would he do that?"

A sob caught in her throat. "I was stunned, and I asked him that. He said he owed my dad a huge favor and that was his way of paying him back. He said he couldn't tell me any more than that. He said not a day goes by that he doesn't think about it. He apologized to me over and over, but I don't think I can ever get over this. It's a huge betrayal."

"I'm so sorry," I said somberly.

She sniffed and angrily wiped the tears from under her eyes with the heel of her hand. "Yeah, so you were right."

"Vivian was right," I said.

She gave me a sad smile. "Which reminds me of the other thing I did—I bought this e-book about reincarnation, *Many Lives, Many Masters* by Brian Weiss. Do you know it?"

"Yes, I know it. I read that one several years ago. It's good."

Claire nodded. "Yes, it is. I stayed up half the night reading it to the end. It was fascinating. I'd never really thought about this stuff before, but it made a lot of sense to me." She paused and shook her head. "I still don't know exactly what's going on here, but at least I know something about reincarnation now." She took a sip of water. "I read some other reincarnation stories on the Internet—lots of stories, really—and there are other people who've had experiences like yours. I didn't see anything about murders, thankfully," she added quickly. "But lots of stories about dreams and remembering things from past lives." She looked at me sheepishly. "I'm sorry I called you a psycho, Josie."

I touched her shoulder. "Don't worry about it, Claire. I know this has all been very shocking for you."

"The other thing is…" she began, and then her voice trailed off.

"What?" I asked.

She closed her eyes for a moment before continuing. "I called my dad and asked him to come over. I asked him about what Vivian had said at the trial and what my uncle told me, and…" Her voice broke, and her eyes welled with tears.

"What happened, Claire?" I was impressed that she'd asked her dad about this, but based on what I knew about him and her response now, I guessed it hadn't gone well.

She looked at me helplessly. "He got so angry. I've never seen him so angry." She hesitated. "Josie, he slapped me."

My mouth fell open. "Oh my God."

She nodded. "Yeah, he slapped me and said, 'You're just like your fucking mother. You can't leave well enough alone.' Then he stormed out, and I haven't talked to him since."

"Oh, Claire. I'm so sorry," I said. I felt bad for Claire, but I wasn't surprised.

"And there's something else I should have told you…" She looked down at her hands.

"What?" I asked.

She chewed her lips nervously, not looking at me. "Vivian Latham left me fifty thousand dollars."

"What?" I said, my voice a little too loud.

She nodded and looked at me. "Yes, she did. I got it when I turned twenty-five."

"Claire, why didn't you tell me?" I asked, my eyes searching her face.

She shrugged and shook her head. "I don't know. There was never a good time, and then we had our argument, and…" She looked at me, her hands open in a gesture of contrition.

I sighed. "That would have been really helpful information for me to have."

"I know. I'm sorry." She paused. "Vivian left me a letter—a note, really. It said, 'I loved your mother, Claire. I never would have hurt her. And I love you. I can't change what happened, but I can give you this money. I hope it helps you in some small way. Love, Vivian.' I read that note hundreds of times. I memorized it."

"Wow." It was all I could say. I wondered why that hadn't tipped Claire off all those years ago, but I didn't want to question her about it now. What good would it do?

"There's more," she said. "And this one's big."

I raised my eyebrows. What more could there be? "Okay, what?"

"After my dad stormed out, I was crazy to figure out what had really happened. I had the idea to go through every single thing I had of my mom's to see if I could find a clue, any clue."

"And you found something," I said.

She nodded. "Yeah, I found something major."

"What?" I asked, about to go mad with anticipation.

"It was in her desk—the one I have in the attic," she said. "I'd already gone through it years ago, but this time I pulled out all the drawers and felt every crack and crevice. And that's when I found it."

"Found what?" I said impatiently.

She took a deep breath. "Inside the bottom drawer, there was a secret compartment. If you didn't know it was there, you'd never guess. Clearly my dad didn't know about it."

I was about to burst. "What was in it?" I asked.

She walked over to the counter, picked up some papers, and handed them to me. There were two letters. One was in an envelope with "Tambra" written on the front in a looping script. The other was a single loose page. I unfolded the loose page and read the first three words: "My Dearest Vivian." I gasped.

"This was also hidden in the desk," she said, picking up what looked like a bookmark from the counter. She handed it to me. It was one of those photo-booth strips, with four black-and-white photos. The photos showed four different poses of a brunette woman, a blond woman, and a baby. Vivian, Tambra, and Claire.

"Claire, I can't believe this," I breathed. I stared at the four photos, tears filling my eyes. The photos had faded some over the past forty-one years, but I could still see their happy expressions. In the first photo, Vivian had her arm around Tambra's shoulders, and Tambra was leaning in to her. Tambra held Claire on her lap between them. I studied Vivian, realizing that I was looking at myself. Her brown hair was chin length, and it looked thick. Her bangs just brushed the tops of her eyebrows and were swept to the side. Her eyes were large and dark, and they were lit up with happiness. Her smile was wide. I wouldn't have called her pretty, exactly, but she had a pleasing appearance. Tambra looked just as she had in the photo Claire had shown me a few days ago—the same radiant smile, the same lovely eyes, and the same long blond hair parted down the middle.

In the second photo, Vivian was kissing Tambra's cheek, and Tambra was grinning and looking at the camera straight on. In the third photo, Tambra kissed Vivian's cheek. And in the last photo, they kissed each other on the lips as Claire gazed up at them. I looked at the back of the strip. Tambra had written, "Me, Vivian, and Claire, June 20, 1974."

Claire sat down beside me again. "Read the letters," she said, her voice almost a whisper.

I looked at her and then picked up the envelope addressed to Tambra. The seal had been broken, so I knew Tambra had read it—a thought that made the hair on the back of my neck stand on end. I withdrew the single page and unfolded the letter.

July 2, 1974
My Darling Tambra,

I had given up on love. I thought I would never meet a woman I'd want to spend the rest of my life with. And then I met you. How can I explain what I feel for you? The love I feel for you knows no bounds. It fills me up and makes me feel complete. You are my heart, my soul, my life. I want to be with you always.

That's why I want you to leave your husband. He doesn't love you the way you deserve to be loved. He hurts you. He disrespects you. Seeing the way he treats you is like a knife in my heart.

I want you to be happy, safe, and loved. You can have that with me. I want you and Claire to come away with me. We'll go anywhere you want to go—just as long as it's away from here. I know how much you love Claire, and I promise to love her as much as you do. I already love her as if she's my own daughter. We can be a family.

Tambra, I love you more than life itself. Please be with me forever.
Yours,
Vivian

I finished reading and looked up at Claire, my eyes wide. "Claire, this is just incredible."

She nodded. "Read the other one."

I unfolded the loose page and began to read.

> *August 9, 1974*
> *My Dearest Vivian,*
>
> *I can't believe that in two days we'll be away from here and on our way to our new life together. As we begin our journey, I want you to know how much I love you. I have never known a love like this—I never knew a love like this was even possible. You are my best friend, my lover, my soul mate. You're the first thing I think of in the morning and my last thought when I fall asleep at night. You've made my dreams come true.*
>
> *On Sunday we'll be gone from here forever. Thank you for giving me the courage to leave Tom. Thank you for loving me and Claire. I know the life we'll live together will be full of happiness and love every day.*
> *I love you, Vivian,*
> *Tambra*

I looked up at Claire. "Do you think this means she never gave the letter to Vivian?"

She shrugged. "That would be my guess, but I don't know. It seems like if she'd given it to Vivian, it wouldn't have been in the desk."

I nodded. "Yeah, that's what I was thinking too. I wonder why she never gave it to her."

She shook her head. "I don't know," she said. "Maybe she was going to give it to Vivian on the day they left, and..." She fell silent for a long moment. "Well, you know what happened."

I nodded somberly. As I read the letters again, it dawned on me that I now had the evidence I needed to show Sean O'Neil. After seeing these letters and the photo strip, there was no way he could deny that there was probable cause to analyze the DNA from the crime scene. But that also meant Claire's father would most likely be sent to prison.

I carefully folded the two letters and handed them and the photo strip back to her, as I considered how to tell her my news. I cleared my throat. "Claire, I've been busy too," I began. I told her about my conversation with Vivian's friend, Daniel; my meeting with Fergus Atkinson; and my talk with Sean O'Neil. "Sean O'Neil told me I needed to find actual evidence before he'd test the DNA from the crime scene." I paused, looking at her closely. "Claire, the letters and photos are what I need."

"Oh." That was all she said.

"I can't imagine how hard this is for you," I said. "If the DNA proves that it was really your dad who killed your mom, then…" My voice trailed off. I couldn't complete my thought.

"Then my dad is going to prison, and I'll have no one," she said in a wooden voice.

"Yes," I said.

"Well, Josie, in this situation no one wins," she said. "Either I do nothing and live with the knowledge that my dad got away with killing my mom, or we show the letters to the detective and my dad most likely goes to prison. Either way, my mom is still dead, and either way I now know what really happened."

I nodded. "Yes."

She took a deep breath. "And right now I'm so furious and so hurt to think that my dad lied to me about this all these years. That he was the one who killed my mom. That he denied her the chance to be with the person she loved. That he sent an innocent woman to prison out of vengeance and jealousy and hatefulness and what all I don't know."

I looked at her and saw tears in her eyes again.

"Would I even want to have a relationship with him now, after all this?" she asked, looking at me for an answer.

"Probably not," I said.

She looked away, her eyes distant. "And if that's true, then I think I want him to pay for what he did. He killed my mom. He shouldn't get away with that, should he?"

I shook my head. "No, I don't think so."

She closed her eyes for a long moment. Then she looked at me and slowly slid the letters and photo strip across the table toward me. "Please take them, Josie. Show the detective."

"Are you sure, Claire?" I asked, touching her hand.

She gave a firm nod. "Yes, I'm sure."

36

I called Sean O'Neil immediately and told him I'd made a major find. "I think this is what you need," I said. I arranged to meet him at Pie in the Sky at four o'clock. As I stood at Claire's front door ready to go, I said again, "You're sure about this, right? Once I show him, there's no going back."

She nodded. "Josie, I'm sure. Go."

I told her good-bye and then went out to my car. I drove to Pie in the Sky, my anxiety building by the second. By the time I walked through the door of the pie shop, I was about ready to burst. I saw him right away, and he motioned me over.

"What did you find?" he asked as I slid into the booth.

I pulled the letters and the photo strip out of my purse and set them down in front of him. He studied the photos first, his eyebrows raised. Then he picked up the letters and read them carefully—first Vivian's and then Tambra's. When he finished, he raised his eyes to look at me.

"This is good work, Miss Pace."

"So can we test the DNA now?" I asked.

He nodded. "Yep. I'm a man of my word," he said. "I'll call down there and get the ball rolling."

I let out a long sigh. "Thank you, sir."

"In the meantime, I'm going to ask Detective Ramirez to work the case."

My heart leapt at the prospect of seeing Laura again. I didn't want to dissuade him from involving Laura, but I was curious about his strategy. "May I ask why you think Detective Ramirez should get involved?" I said. "Isn't the DNA enough?"

"Here's what I'm thinking," he said. "Weren't there neighbors who gave statements and testified at the trial?"

"Yes, there were," I answered.

"Do you know if they're still alive?"

"Agnes Reed is," I answered quickly. "Why?"

"They implicated Miss Latham in this crime. If what we think happened really did happen, then they would have seen or heard something. And that means they lied under oath."

"True," I said.

"I want Ramirez to go out and talk to that neighbor again. See what she can find out. You can go along, but I want her to take the lead. The DNA will be solid, but I'd like at least one witness statement to go along with it."

"Great idea," I said.

"I'll call Ramirez and fill her in. I think you should go out there tomorrow," he said.

"Will do," I said, immensely relieved that he was taking this seriously.

"We'll get him," Sean O'Neil said firmly.

The next morning I met Laura Ramirez at her office at ten o'clock. When I saw her, my heart skipped a beat. If anything, she looked more beautiful today than she had when I'd first met her.

She gave me her crooked smile. "Hey, Josie."

I looked at her shyly. "Hi, Detective Ramirez."

She rolled her eyes. "Call me Laura," she said. "Shall we go?"

"Ready when you are."

We drove in silence to Mrs. Reed's house. I kept stealing glances at Laura. I knew I was attracted to her, but the powerful draw I felt toward her went beyond attraction. There was something more—something inexplicable. I'd never felt anything like it, even with Erica. Laura was one of those people I felt as if I'd known for eons.

At ten thirty we pulled up in front of Mrs. Reed's house. I saw a man out walking his dog and a woman working in her yard, and they both eyed the police car curiously. I got out and waited on the sidewalk for Laura. As she joined me, I noticed she had an odd look on her face.

"Is something wrong?" I asked.

She looked up and down the street, her brows knit in confusion. "I don't know. This neighborhood seems really familiar to me. I don't think I've ever been out here on a call, but it feels like I've been here before."

"Maybe you had a friend who lived here when you were a kid," I offered.

She shook her head. "No, I grew up in Lacey. The only time we came over this way was to go to Big Tom's, and that's at least a mile from here." She looked around for a few more seconds and then shrugged. "Weird." She looked at Mrs. Reed's house. "C'mon," she said, motioning to me to follow her.

She knocked on Mrs. Reed's door, and we waited. A few seconds later, Mrs. Reed opened the door and peered out at us. She noticed Laura's uniform right away, and her eyes widened.

"Yes, can I help you?" She looked at Laura and then me, and I could tell she recognized me. "Oh, you again," she said.

Laura glanced at me with a puzzled expression and then looked back at Mrs. Reed. "Ma'am, we were hoping you had a few minutes to answer some questions," she said. She showed Mrs. Reed her badge.

Mrs. Reed opened the door wider. "Sure. Come in."

Laura and I entered the house, and Mrs. Reed ushered us into the living room. It looked exactly the same as it had when I'd been there before.

"Is everything all right?" Mrs. Reed asked, sitting down in the overstuffed armchair. "Is it those drug addicts on the corner?"

Laura shook her head. "No, nothing like that. We wanted to ask you some questions about your former neighbor, Tambra Delaney. Do you remember her?"

Mrs. Reed nodded toward me. "She was here a few weeks ago asking about the same thing. Why are you people getting that all stirred up again? That happened ages ago."

"Can we sit?" Laura asked.

Mrs. Reed motioned to the couch across from her. "Be my guest."

We sat side by side on the couch, and Laura pulled a small notepad from her breast pocket. "We have reason to believe that the wrong person was convicted of Tambra Delaney's murder." She paused to let that sink in. "We wanted to ask what you remember."

"That woman—Vivian Latham—was convicted of her murder," Mrs. Reed said, her tone combative.

Laura gave her a thin smile and nodded. "Yes, I know, but some new evidence has come to light, and we're beginning to suspect that Ms. Latham was not the perpetrator."

Mrs. Reed snorted. "What are you talking about? The cops did an investigation, and they arrested her. Then the jury convicted her. Pretty clear, don't you think?"

Laura ignored her comment. "Mrs. Reed, you testified that you had no knowledge that Mrs. Delaney and Ms. Latham were friends. Was that a true statement?"

"That's what I said, isn't it?" she said loudly.

Laura smiled indulgently. "That's what you said, but is that what was true?"

Mrs. Reed didn't say anything. She pressed her lips together and began picking at a loose thread on the arm of the chair.

"Ma'am, was your testimony truthful on this matter?" Laura pressed.

Mrs. Reed looked at Laura, but she did not speak.

Laura cocked her head to the side. "Mrs. Reed, are you aware that lying under oath is a crime?"

The older woman was silent for several moments. Then she sighed deeply and said sharply, "All right! Yeah, I knew they were friends. I saw them at each other's houses and out walking that baby. Sometimes they'd go out together in the car. Yeah, they were chummy."

"Thank you," Laura said, making a note on her pad. "You also testified that you had never seen or heard any violence between Mr. and Mrs. Delaney. Was that a truthful statement?"

Mrs. Reed folded her arms across her chest. "I don't see what that has to do with anything."

"Actually, it has a lot to do with it," Laura said mildly.

Mrs. Reed shrugged. "Yeah, I heard them fighting sometimes, but every couple fights."

"I'm not talking about garden-variety arguments," Laura said. "I mean screaming and yelling. Screams that might indicate that someone is being hurt."

Mrs. Reed rubbed her mouth and looked down at the floor. "I don't know," she finally said, not looking up.

"Ma'am?" Laura said.

Mrs. Reed raised her eyes to meet Laura's. "I heard them screaming and yelling, yes," she said reluctantly. "I heard them lots of times, with their carrying-on. They lived right next door—how could I not hear them? And I saw Tambra with a black eye a couple times, and bruises on her arms. I got it in my head that that man—Tom—was beating on her. But it wasn't my business. That was their business."

"It became your business when you lied about it at the trial!" I yelled. Laura gave me a warning look, and I sat back and glowered at Mrs. Reed, who glared right back at me.

Laura looked at Mrs. Reed, her pen poised over her notepad. "So, Mrs. Reed, are you saying you believe Thomas Delaney was physically abusing his wife, Tambra Delaney?"

Mrs. Reed stared at her for a long moment. "Yes, that's what I'm saying."

"And what about the time of the murder?" Laura continued in a smooth voice. "At the trial you said you didn't hear a disturbance at the Delaney house. Was that a true statement?"

Mrs. Reed narrowed her eyes and stared at Laura silently for several seconds. Finally she nodded. "Yeah, I heard them. They woke me up. They were screaming and yelling. I heard Tom and Tambra and that woman—Vivian."

Laura wrote more notes on her pad and then looked at Mrs. Reed. "Anything else you can add?"

Mrs. Reed took a deep breath. "I went outside to see what the ruckus was about, and I heard that man yell something like, 'You want to go with this bitch and leave me? I don't think so!' Then a minute or two later I heard a woman scream, 'Tambra!' I think that was Vivian."

Laura and I exchanged glances. What Laura didn't know was that chills were racing up my spine as I heard Mrs. Reed repeat that terrifying scream from my dream.

"'That man'? Whom do you mean?" Laura asked. I figured she needed an actual name for her report to make sure there was no mistake.

"Tom Delaney!" Mrs. Reed almost shouted.

"Why did you lie at the trial, ma'am?" Laura asked. "You realize it's very likely that an innocent woman went to prison."

Mrs. Reed scowled. "I'd rather not say."

"Ma'am, it's becoming more likely that another individual committed this murder," Laura said calmly. "For that reason it's imperative that you're completely truthful now."

She stared at Laura for several more seconds, an antagonistic look on her face. Finally she burst out, "Because we didn't want that woman—Vivian Latham—in our neighborhood, that's why!"

Laura looked at her coldly. "So rather than trying to coexist peacefully with someone who was different from you, you lied under oath to do your part to send her to prison."

Mrs. Reed didn't speak.

"All right, then," Laura said as she made a note on her pad. She stood, and I followed her lead. "Thank you for your honesty today, ma'am," she said. "We'll need you to come down to police headquarters and make a formal statement. I'll be in touch." She gave Mrs. Reed her business card and then asked for her phone number. Laura wrote it carefully on her pad.

Mrs. Reed showed us to the door and opened it. "Thank you again," Laura said.

As we turned to leave, Mrs. Reed grabbed Laura's sleeve. I saw the fear in her eyes. "Am I going to jail?" she asked in a quiet voice.

Laura shook her head. "I highly doubt that, ma'am. I think at this point the best thing you can do is tell the truth."

Mrs. Reed nodded curtly, and Laura and I walked out.

Laura and I climbed into the police car and looked at each other. She gave me a wan smile.

"Well, I guess we got what we needed," she said.

I sighed deeply. "Yeah, I guess we did." I could hear how shaky my voice sounded. I was feeling emotional after our talk with Mrs. Reed. Her confession that she had lied under oath with the express purpose of sending Vivian Latham to prison had angered and horrified me, but it had also saddened me.

Vivian and Tambra had done nothing more than love each other, and they had paid a very high price for that love. I gazed out the window at Tambra's house. I recalled the strange feelings that had overcome me the first time I'd explored there—the feelings of happiness, joy, and hopefulness that I'd felt in Tambra's bedroom. At the time, I'd guessed I was experiencing the happy feelings Tambra had felt for her husband, but now I knew these were the imprints of the feelings Tambra and Vivian had felt for each other. The fear imprinted in the room had been caused by Tom. I'd had it all wrong. Thank goodness I'd finally figured it out.

I imagined Vivian and Tambra the night before they were to escape—their excitement and anticipation as they were about to begin their new life together; their relief at finally being free of Tom Delaney. And then in the blink of an eye, he had brought it all to a terrible halt. I felt a tear slide down my cheek, and I hurriedly wiped it away.

Laura touched my shoulder. "Are you okay, Josie?"

I turned toward her. "Yeah, I'm fine. I just wish these people would have left Vivian and Tambra alone and let them love each other."

Laura nodded. "Yeah, I know. I wish they would have done that too. It's very sad."

"Yes, it is."

I could tell she wanted to ask me why I was so interested in this case, but I knew she wouldn't. I wasn't sure at that moment if Laura would be part of my future, but if she was, I would tell her the whole story one day. But not today. I met her eyes and smiled. "Let's go, Detective. We've got a murderer to catch."

37

The next morning the Olympia Police Department secured a warrant to bring Tom Delaney in to provide a reference DNA sample. Laura called me that afternoon to let me know they had the sample.

"How did he respond?" I asked.

"I wasn't there, but I heard he was furious," she said. "Detective Willard handled it, and he said he was yelling and cursing. He told Tom not to leave the area, so he knows something's up."

I was intensely curious if Tom suspected that I was the one behind this. I thought about the way he'd looked at me that day at Claire's. Maybe he did suspect. For a moment I considered asking Laura, but I knew I couldn't. That would have to remain a mystery for the time being. "So what happens now?"

"They'll test the evidence from the crime scene and compare it to the reference sample and see what they find. It'll take a couple weeks to get the results, though."

I sighed. "So now we wait."

I could think of no good reason to stay in Olympia, so I went back home and back to work. Every time my phone rang, I answered it quickly, eager to get the call that the tests were complete.

I called Laura every couple of days to ask if there'd been any news.

"Not yet," she always said.

"Why is it taking so long?" I asked every time.

"It takes a while, Josie," she'd say patiently. "And they do have other cases they're working."

Truthfully, I enjoyed my phone calls with Laura because, once we got the DNA talk out of the way, we'd have a nice conversation. I learned a lot about her during those calls. When we talked the first time, Laura came out to me, which was no surprise. I came out to her too, and I don't think she was surprised either. She was single, having ended a four-year relationship the year before. She wanted kids, and that was a huge relief to me. I knew I was getting ahead of myself, but still it was nice to have that big question out of the way early on. I found out that she was thirty-four, the oldest of six kids, and a lapsed Catholic. She played on an all-female softball team, and she liked to write poetry in her spare time.

I told her about myself, too, although I never said anything about my dream. I wasn't ready to tell her the truth, so I stuck to my story that I was a writer who had just stumbled upon the story of Vivian Latham and become curious. She never questioned me, although I knew she had begun to wonder.

Three weeks after I'd left Olympia, my phone rang on a Thursday morning when I was at work. I glanced at the caller ID and saw that it was Laura. "Hi, Laura," I said.

"The results are in," she said excitedly.

"And?" I said anxiously.

"We got him," she said.

I sighed with relief. "Tell me."

"Hang on. Let me grab the report." I heard papers shuffling, and a few seconds later she was back on the line. "Okay, here goes. The epithelials from the bat were tested. There were some from Vivian Latham, but the majority were from Tom Delaney. They were deep in the cracks of the bat, which they said indicated significant pressure and gripping on the bat."

"Good. Go on," I said eagerly.

"There was blood on the collar of Vivian's nightgown that matched Tom Delaney's DNA and spots of blood on Tambra's nightgown—also from Tom Delaney." She paused, and I could tell she was scanning the report. "And the saliva in the bite on Tom's arm was a match to Tambra's DNA."

"Great. Anything else?" I asked.

"One more big thing," Laura said. "The scrapings they took from under Tambra's fingernails matched Tom Delaney's DNA. There was none of Vivian's DNA. The scrapings under Vivian's fingernails also matched Tom Delaney's DNA. There was none of Tambra's DNA. And the scrapings they took from under Tom Delaney's fingernails had DNA from both Tambra and Vivian."

This was even better than I'd imagined. "Thank God," I said. "So what happens now?"

"They sent a police cruiser out to Yelm, where he lives," she said. "He was home, and they brought him in for questioning."

"So he's there now, being questioned?"

"Yep," she answered. "He's here."

"Did you see him, Laura?"

She was quiet for a long moment. "Yeah, I saw him," she finally said. "Josie, I can't explain it, but I had the most visceral response to that man—I recoiled in horror when I saw him." She paused. "I was trembling and practically hyperventilating. It was the weirdest thing. I've seen a lot of suspects over the years, and I've never had a response like that to anyone. In fact, I had to ask one of my colleagues to question him because I didn't think I could do it."

I knew exactly what she meant. "I responded that way when I saw him the first time too, so I understand," I said.

"What's that about?" she asked. "Why do we respond to him that way?"

I wasn't sure what to say. I knew why I'd had that response to Tom, but why had she? Suddenly I remembered her saying that Tambra's neighborhood had seemed familiar to her. I considered how we were intensely drawn to each other. And now her response to Tom. Suddenly, awareness dawned. I inhaled sharply. Could it be?

"Josie, what's wrong?" she said.

"Nothing," I said quickly. "I don't know why you had that response to him, but it could just be because he's an evil, ugly man."

"Yeah, maybe," she said. She was clearly not convinced. "Anyway, I'm pretty sure they'll be arresting him today. I'll let you know what happens. The best outcome would be if he just confesses. No trial and straight to prison."

"Amen to that," I said.

"So, you want to tell me now why you're so obsessed with this case, Josie?" she said. "Is Vivian Latham a relative or..." Her voice trailed off.

"No, nothing like that," I said lightly. "I'll tell you someday, but not now."

"Fair enough," she said, and I could hear the smile in her voice.

"Call me back when you know something more," I said.

We ended our conversation, and I sat back in my chair, dumbfounded. There was no way for me to confirm the epiphany I'd just had, but as I thought it through a second time and then a third, I knew it in my gut: Laura had been Tambra in her past life.

Tom Delaney confessed after nearly four hours of questioning. Although Claire was devastated by her father's confession, she told me she felt some small measure of relief because that meant she wouldn't have to tell the cops about her uncle Mike's lie. I didn't feel as charitable about letting him get away with such a monumental untruth, but given all that Claire had lost, I elected to let it pass.

Tom was arrested and booked into the Olympia jail. Because he'd confessed, there was no need for a trial, and he went straight to the sentencing phase. The judge sentenced him to forty years in prison, but because he was sixty-nine years old, it was, in effect, a life sentence.

I was in the courtroom for Tom's sentencing, Claire on one side and Laura on the other. After the judge read the sentence, I found myself seized by a sudden impulse to confront Tom before they took him away. I knew I should stay and comfort Claire, but I couldn't help myself. I pushed my way to the front of the courtroom, where the bailiff was moving to handcuff him. Tom caught sight of me, and his face reddened with rage.

"You!" he shouted. "You did this!"

I felt a perverse satisfaction that he knew this had happened because of me. I leaned close to him, not breaking eye contact. "Ain't karma a bitch, Tom?"

"You fucking bitch!" he yelled, swinging his fist in my direction.

The bailiff caught his hand in midair and then jerked him to his feet. "That's enough," he said. "Come on." He pulled Tom's arms behind his back and snapped the handcuffs around his wrists.

As the bailiff led him from the courtroom, Tom looked back at me, screaming, "You bitch!" over and over. I stood stock-still, fixing him with my most evil stare, until he had disappeared from sight.

I returned to Claire and Laura. Claire was crying, and Laura was comforting her. I sat next to Claire and enclosed her in a tight hug, whispering, "I'm so sorry," over and over. I felt terrible for her. Her mother was dead, and now she had to live with the knowledge that her dad had been the one who had killed her.

I knew Tambra and Vivian had endured a punishment much worse than Tom's, but still it was gratifying to know that he hadn't gotten away with murdering his wife and framing Vivian and he'd spend the rest of his life in prison.

I stayed with Claire for two days after the sentencing and then headed home. It felt strange to have this behind me, but at the same time it was hugely freeing.

The day after I got home, my phone rang. I looked at the caller ID and saw that it was Laura. I answered eagerly. "Hi, Laura," I said.

"Hey, Josie."

"What's up?"

"Well, now that this is over, do you want to go out with me?" she asked in a shy voice.

I laughed. "Absolutely. I thought you'd never ask."

EPILOGUE

July 2019

Laura and I stood at Claire's front door, Laura's hand poised to knock. She looked at me. "Are you ready for this?"

I nodded. "As ready as I'll ever be."

She smiled and then rapped on the door. Seconds later it swung open, and Claire stood there looking beautiful, as always.

"Hello, you two," she said, her face lighting up with a wide grin.

"Hi," I said, stepping into the foyer and then reaching forward to give her a hug. Over her shoulder I saw the big banner she had hung for the party: "Welcome, Baby Liam!" Instinctively, I reached down to touch my belly and was almost immediately rewarded with the bump of a tiny foot against my hand. He'd been active today, turning around in there like a little dolphin.

Claire turned to hug Laura and then led us to the kitchen. Jake was at the counter, readying a platter of hamburgers for the grill.

"Don't worry, Josie," he said with a wink. "I made you a veggie burger."

I smiled. "That was considerate of you."

Claire had met Jake early last year, and they'd hit it off immediately. He was a seventh-grade math teacher and was divorced, like Claire. They had begun dating, and before long they were spending all their free time together. He'd moved in with her six months ago, and they seemed blissfully happy. Jake wanted to get married, but Claire was reluctant. I thought she'd come around eventually, but either way she was happy. I was thrilled she'd found someone who loved her the way she deserved to be loved.

Claire hadn't fared well in the weeks following her father's arrest and sentencing. She'd gone into a deep depression and, at my urging, had begun intense therapy to try to work through her complex issues. For the first year after her dad had gone to prison, she'd seen her therapist twice a week. Now she was seeing her therapist every other week, and she was thriving. I couldn't have been happier for her.

I looked at Claire. "Where's Celeste? I saw her car outside."

She smiled. "She's out on the deck."

I walked out to the deck, and Celeste hurried over to envelop me in a hug. "Josie, it's so great to see you," she said. "It's been a while."

"It's great to see you too. I've missed you." I pulled back to appraise her belly. "Wow, you're almost as big as I am."

Matthew Devine sidled up to Celeste and put his arm around her. "Yeah, you two are only a month apart. Pretty amazing."

Celeste and Matthew had gotten married three years ago, and they were expecting their first baby too—a girl. Laura and I had waited a little longer to get married. We'd done the long-distance-relationship thing—one weekend at my place, another weekend at hers—for nearly a year, but we'd grown weary of all the back and forth. I made the difficult decision to sell my house, leave my job at Harmony, and move to Olympia. I sold my house in record time—four days on the market—and made a tidy profit. Laura and I found an apartment together, and a few weeks later I landed a terrific job at a growing nonprofit. The hardest thing had been leaving Celeste, but we talked on the phone two or three times a week and saw each other once or twice a month.

Then, two years ago, as Laura and I had walked through Burfoot Park—our favorite place to go with our dogs, Indigo and Luna—she had fallen to one knee and pulled a ring box out of her jacket pocket.

"Josie, I fell in love with you the moment I first saw you," she said with tears in her eyes. "I want to spend the rest of my life with you. Will you marry me?"

I said yes, of course. We were married six months later in a small ceremony with close family and friends, and we had a hell of a party afterward.

We bought a house together not long after. I'd recently been promoted to assistant director at my job, and Laura was making good money at her job, so we figured it was the right time. We started trying to get pregnant four months after we moved into our three-bedroom rambler. It took us five tries, and when the plus sign had finally appeared on the pregnancy-test stick, we had hugged and cried with joy. Our son, whom we would name Liam Miguel Ramirez-Pace, would be with us in a little over a month.

Claire had insisted she throw me a baby shower even though it wasn't really my thing. She'd invited several of my friends from work and a couple of old high-school friends, who'd be here later to celebrate.

Claire stepped out onto the deck and looked at me, a radiant smile on her face. "I have a surprise for you," she said. "A special guest."

I glanced at Laura, my eyes questioning. Had she known about this? She shook her head and shrugged. "Okay," I said.

I saw movement behind Claire, and a moment later my mom appeared. For a second I couldn't move, and then I rushed to her and wrapped my arms around her. "Mom, oh my God! I can't believe you're here!" I said in her ear.

She pulled back to look at me, tears in her eyes. "I couldn't miss your baby shower, sweetheart."

I gazed at her face, realizing how desperately I had missed her. "I'm so happy to see you."

"Me too," she said. "You look beautiful, Josephine. Pregnancy becomes you." She kissed my cheek and took my hand in hers. "And I have news. I'm selling my condo and moving back to Seattle. I'm going to be a grandma. I can't miss that. Life is too short."

I hugged her again, and a sob caught in my throat. "Oh, Mom. That's fantastic news. I'm so happy!" I caught Claire's eye and mouthed, "Thank you." She beamed, and I saw tears glistening in her eyes too.

"And you know Gwendolyn and Scott are trying to get pregnant too," my mom continued. "So I need to be here with my girls."

"That's wonderful, Mom. I'm really happy."

I settled into a chair, my mom on one side and Laura on the other, and considered how much my life had changed over the past four years—all because of a dream. I had finally told Laura about my dream after I'd moved to Olympia. She was quiet as I told her, but afterward she said that she'd thought about reincarnation quite a bit, and it made sense to her. I was just happy she didn't think I was a nut. A month later, I told her my theory that she had been Tambra in her past life. She tipped her head to the side, smiled, and said, "I'll have to give that some thought." We hadn't talked about it again, but at some point I wanted to take her to see Susan Krause and convince her. I didn't need convincing—as soon as I'd first had the thought, I had known in my gut that it was true.

That knowingness was affirmed for me the first time I introduced Claire and Laura. I saw the initial spark pass between them, and observed the almost instantaneous affection they had for each other, which had only intensified over the past few years. Even if their conscious minds weren't aware of it, their souls knew that they had once been mother and daughter—a bond that could never be broken.

I myself had been back to see Susan Krause several times over the past four years. Through the painstaking process of past-life regression, I had been able to piece together many of the details of Vivian's life, including what had happened in the early morning hours of August 11, 1974.

Vivian had been officially exonerated for Tambra's murder, and the governor had sent a letter of apology to her cousins, Louise Maguire and Linda Davidson, Vivian's only living family. There had been a small article in the Olympia paper, which I had carefully cut out and mailed to Daniel Frazier. He'd called me several days later to express his thanks.

"I can't tell you how much this means to me, Josie," he had said, his voice choked with tears.

I'd also talked to Fergus Atkinson, who had been equally thankful. He had been astonished by my perseverance and also curious about my motivation to clear the name of a woman I hadn't even known. I couldn't begin to explain that to him.

"Let's just say that I believe in justice and redemption and leave it at that," I'd said.

"Fair enough," he'd replied.

I never had the dream again. From time to time, I still had dreams that I thought were about Vivian and Tambra, but they were happy. I looked forward to those dreams now. For one long year, I had felt as if I was living dual lives—one in the past and another in the present. Once the trauma of that awful August night had been healed—by Tom Delaney paying for his crime and, more importantly, by finding Tambra and Claire again in this life—I could put Vivian's life behind me and live in the present. Now I was free to just be Josie.

ACKNOWLEDGMENTS

Writing is largely a solitary activity, but once the writing is done, one must emerge from the solitude and seek input from family and friends. That's both exciting and unnerving. I was blessed to have the help of some wonderful readers, all of whom provided me with excellent feedback. Thank you to Cynthia Hernandez, Kathy McInnis-Chavez, Nancy McInnis, Donna Gates, Rhea Hernandez, and Courtney Hernandez. You all gave me wonderful—and different—feedback that made my novel even better. In addition, I want to thank fellow author Kristel Wills Gibson, who gave me some great advice about the self-publishing process.

Also I must thank my dear aunt and uncle, Betty and Gene Nye, whose love and generosity made it possible for me to publish this book the way I wanted to. I miss you both every day. And a special thank you to my dad, Bill McInnis. He's no longer with us on the earth plane, but while he was here, he encouraged my writing in ways he probably didn't even realize. I love you, Dad.

Above all, I want to thank my wife and fellow writer, Cynthia Hernandez, who encourages, loves, and supports me no matter what, and my son, Gabriel, who reminds me every day that being a mom is the best job in the world.

Made in the USA
San Bernardino, CA
04 November 2016